PALE
HIGHWAY

NICHOLAS CONLEY

ISBN-10: 101940215536

ISBN-13: 13978-1-940215-53-2

Red Adept Publishing, LLC

104 Bugenfield Court

Garner, NC 27529

http://RedAdeptPublishing.com/

Cover and Formatting: Streetlight Graphics

Dedicated to my father, may he rest in peace.

This book is also dedicated to the countless victims of Alzheimer's, as well as their families, and all those who help them cope with their daily struggle.

That's right, guys. This one is for you.

PROLOGUE

Summer 2018

THE PATIENT HAD CHARCOAL-BLACK EYES, hard and cold, as if rounded chunks of volcanic rock had been shoved inside her eye sockets. Her skin possessed a sickly white pallor, as if it had been sucked dry of all its nutrients and hung up on a clothesline. Dark veins crawled over her body like wriggling snakes, pulsing with every unsteady heartbeat. Her mouth hung open, and a pockmarked grey tongue dangled uselessly over her lower lip. Her bedridden form emitted the stench of necrotic flesh.

Glenda Alvarez was sixty-three years old, young compared to the other residents. Just last week, she'd had her hair permed and her nails manicured. The virus had hit fast.

It wouldn't be long. She was just another unlucky victim of a plague that took no prisoners. She had all the symptoms of the toxicity passing through humanity, turning live bodies into black-eyed corpses.

The Black Virus. And somehow... *somehow,* Gabriel Schist was supposed to stop it.

The rain had stopped, but the moonlit ground was still covered in a glimmering sheen of moisture. Grimacing, Gabriel turned away from the open bedroom window, which was his lens to Glenda's decline. He buttoned up his coat, hesitated, halfway unbuttoned it, then buttoned it up again.

He hobbled over to the smoking gazebo and lowered himself into the seat. His legs were rickety, and a sharp pain shot through his knee. His lower back felt as if the nerves were being pinched by a steel clamp.

He took out a pack of cigarettes and patted down his jacket for a lighter. It was in his inner pocket. When the flame sparked, he buried the smoke deep inside his chest, baking his lungs. His cigarette twitched unsteadily between two shaking fingers. Already, it was burning down, dissipating into nothing. Its tobacco-filled life was short and empty. It served one purpose, and then it died.

Gabriel looked back at the window. A nurse entered the infected woman's room to fix her IV, noticed him outside, and closed the blinds.

Every fiber of his being, every piece of the man he once was, told him that he—Gabriel Schist, the oh-so-great-and-wonderful creator of the Schist vaccine—was the only one who could stop the virus. Years and years ago, he'd stopped a prior epidemic in its tracks. Why not this one?

But the Gabriel of the past was an altogether different Gabriel than the fidgety, broken creature that existed in his place. The real Gabriel Schist had been a younger man. A better man. A brilliant man.

As the cigarette's glowing ember slowly burned to ashes, Gabriel wondered what had happened to that great man. Where had he gone?

ACT I OF III:
GREY MATTER

"Ideas thus made up of several simple ones put together, I call complex; such are beauty, gratitude, an army, the universe."

John Locke

CHAPTER 1:
LEGACY

Spring 2018

GABRIEL WOKE UP IN BED. He stretched out his stiff, aching arms, feeling years of trivial injuries, *hey-this-will-get-better-soon* wounds, and supposedly healed muscle tears ripple throughout his entire body. The years went by so *fast*. One day he was young, strong, and athletic, and the next, he woke up in a place like—

Wait. Hold on. Where the hell was he?

A sky-blue curtain hung on his left, blocking off the other side of the room. A bulky television set was suspended from the ceiling. The walls were the same color, and he caught the faint stinging odor of antiseptic. To his right was an open door exposing a hallway, from which came the sounds of sirens, loud voices, and beeping.

He carefully rolled over onto his side. His aching muscles resisted the turn, and his bones weren't much friendlier. His back immediately felt as though it had been exposed to dry ice. He realized that he was wearing a bare-backed johnny gown instead of his usual pajamas.

Tied to the railing of the bed was a vine-like wire, with a red push button on the end. *Oh, no.* He was in the hospital. *But how? When? Was he sick? Had he gotten into a motorcycle accident? Why couldn't he remember?*

Gabriel panicked, breathing heavily. His heart raced. His skin was coated in a hot, syrupy sheen of perspiration. He struggled to sit upright, but his entire skeleton felt so stiff that it might snap at the slightest strain. *He was trapped.* He threw off the blanket and examined his body for wounds.

Instead, he found *wrinkles*. His thin, nearly transparent skin had become a crumpled-up piece of tissue paper. Liver spots. Reticular veins. Painful varicose veins on his ankle.

Oh. That's right. Slowly, tentatively, Gabriel's memory volunteered its services to him again. He wasn't in a hospital. He was in a nursing home in New Hampshire, the same nursing home where he'd lived in for five years. Bright New Day Skilled Nursing Center. Yes, that was it.

He frenetically cycled through his usual checkmark system. His name was Gabriel Schist. That part was easy. The president was Bill Clint... no. George? No, Barack. Barack Obama. Wait. Was that the last one? Well, how about the year? The year was 2018. He knew that, at least. As far as his age, he was... what, seventy-five years old? Seventy-two? Seventy-three?

Well, his age had never been important to him, anyway. As long as he remembered *the sequence*, he was still okay. That was the most important part, the only way to determine if the gears of his mind were still turning properly.

"Zero," he whispered. "One, one, two, three, five, eight, thirteen, twenty-one, thirty-four..."

Finally, he felt strong enough to pull himself up into a sitting position. He shivered, his bare feet resting on the cool linoleum floor. He waited for the sharp lines and blurry geometric figures of the world to come into sharper focus.

"Fifty-five, eighty-nine, one hundred forty-four..."

Tacked on his wall were dozens of graphs, a small blackboard with hundreds of tiny equations written on it, analytical essays on his work, and articles on the latest medical advances. Several hastily-written scraps of notebook paper were haphazardly taped wherever they could fit. Beside those were photographs of all the people who'd once loved him. A photo of Yvonne, her arms raised to the sky, was next to one of Melanie. Yearbook-style Polaroid photos of the various nurses, staff, and housekeepers at Bright New Day had been added so that he would remember their faces more quickly.

"Two hundred thirty-three, three hundred seventy-seven, six hundred ten, nine hundred eighty-seven. Okay. I'm okay. I'm okay."

Gabriel sighed with relief. His mind was intact, for the time being. He almost smiled until right then, right at his moment of liberation, he felt a soggy dampness beneath him. He'd wet the bed again. Gabriel slowly, shakily rose to his feet, and a spasm shot down his sciatic nerve. The sight of that moist, miserable yellow circle on the white sheets was as horrifying as that of a mutilated corpse. He yanked the blanket up to cover the wet spot.

A stream of urine dribbled off the mattress and onto the floor. *Wetting the bed.* It was degrading to see, degrading to smell, and even more degrading that he had to hide it like a scared little boy. But he refused to wear diapers. Briefs. *Depends.* Elderly water-soaking-underwear-devices.

The stench was nauseating. He grabbed a face cloth from his counter, intending to wipe up the urine that had escaped to the floor. A gruff cough interrupted him. Someone was moving about on the other side of the curtain, the window side of the room. When did he get a new roommate?

"Ah, hell!" a man shouted. "Did you piss the bed?"

"No," Gabriel answered. "Certainly not."

"C'mon, man. Don't be shy! Y'kiddin' me? I do that shit all the time!" The man laughed uproariously.

Then, much to Gabriel's chagrin, his new roommate rolled over to Gabriel's side of the room in a wheelchair. He was a stout, potbellied man with a scraggly grey beard and lots of skull tattoos. "How are ya?" The man's mouth stretched into a wide, gap-toothed smile. He was a rough-looking character, though his wheelchair and pale atrophied legs managed to counteract the fiendish menace he probably once wielded. A dangling purple stump hung as a memorial to his right foot's prior existence. A nasal cannula was plugged into his nostrils and hooked into a cylindrical oxygen tank on the back of his chair, feeding him a constant stream of O2.

Hoarse, raspy breathing that sounded like someone was dropping a bag full of dirty rocks into a rusted gutter filled the room. He had clearly been a heavy smoker. End-stage COPD? Probably.

11

"The name's Robbie." The gruff man offered his hand. "Robbie Gore."

Gore's fingernails were dark, almost black, and spoon-shaped, likely because of all the smoking. It could also be diabetes, judging by the missing foot. He seemed to have arthritis, as well. Lymphatic system disorders. Possibly a lack of vitamin B-12.

Gabriel shook his new roommate's hand. "Pleased to meet you."

Gore seemed friendly enough. So far, Gabriel liked him, which was rare. He'd always had difficulty adjusting to new roommates.

"So you're new to this room, I take it?" Gabriel asked.

"Man, you high or somethin'?" Gore scoffed. "My stuff's been in yer damn room for two weeks. I keep tryin' to introduce myself, but you're always out walkin' around or somethin'."

Two weeks? Marvelous. "Oh, right," Gabriel mumbled. "Of course."

"It's all good, roomie. If ya weren't already havin' bladder problems, I'd ask if ya wanna take a shot of some tequila with me. I got me a bottle hidden in the bureau there."

Gabriel's mouth watered. Tequila? Wow. How long had it been since he'd tasted *tequila*, of all things? He could drink a shot, only a...

No. Absolutely not.

"No thank you," Gabriel muttered. Trying to block the entire exchange out of his mind, he hurriedly stumbled over to his closet, careful not to trip over his own feet. Since the stroke, he'd had enormous difficulty walking without his cane.

"Why not?"

"I can't... drink. Not with the Seroquel I'm taking."

"Ah, sucks. Probably a good thing, though. I'll tell ya, liquor makes me piss my bed *all* the time."

"So I've gathered."

"Yep. Can't help it. Happens in my sleep. My problem is that the only way I can piss *right*—while I'm awake, I mean—is that I gotta be lyin' *sideways,* and then I have to piss into that plastic bottle... what'd they call it again? The *urinal.* Yeah, the urinal. But see, I got one other problem, too."

Gabriel put on his glasses. Tired of parading around in a johnny gown, he carefully stepped into a pair of slacks. He pulled on and buttoned up a long-sleeve dress shirt then glanced back at the bed to make sure the bunched-up quilt was effectively hiding the wet spot. The spillage on the floor could easily be dismissed as having been caused by an overturned glass of water.

"See," Gore continued, "when I had the surgery done to cut off this damn leg, the doctors screwed up. After the surgery, I can't pee straight 'cause those asshole doctors fucked up my dick. Y'wanna see it?"

"Um..." No, he certainly didn't care to see it. As if his own problems weren't enough, being in a nuthouse like Bright New Day only amplified everything. Gabriel took his cane out of the closet and leaned on it for support, both physical *and* moral.

"C'mere, brother. It's messed up, man! Look at this!" Gore tugged down the waistband of his red shorts.

Gabriel looked; he couldn't help it. Had it really come down to this? He felt like a neutered dog. Had he really reached the point of being so utterly desexualized and dehumanized, that this kind of scene was *normal?* Surprisingly, Gore's penis appeared completely normal. "Um..."

Gore glared down at his crotch. "Don't you see it? Look, man! Those asshole doctors cut my dick off!"

"Oh." Gabriel shook his head. He glanced at his reflection in the mirror on the wall to Gore's left. When did his hair become so white? God, when did he get so damn old?

His self-pity was interrupted when he noticed a tiny brown slug crawling up the surface of the mirror as if it owned the place. He'd seen a lot of slugs lately. The nursing home seemed to be infested with them.

"Well... hey, Mr. Gore, I'm dying for a cigarette, so I'm going to step outside to the smoking area." Gabriel put on his tan trench coat and fedora. He wore the same outfit every day, no matter the weather; he was always cold, anyway. Together with the cane, he felt he cut a striking figure like something out of a Bogart movie. In the last year, the nursing staff had come to refer to him as the Detective, a nickname he wasn't quite sure how to feel about. He tightened a Windsor knot in his black tie. He stepped toward the door, ready to get the hell out of the room. "See you soon. You can—"

"Hey," Gore said, squinting at him. "Before you go, what's your name, buddy? I forgot to ask."

Gabriel hesitated. He subtly positioned his body toward the doorway. He just wanted to get *outside* and put this morning behind him. Was that too much to ask? "Gabriel Schist," he answered finally.

"Schist?" Gore chuckled. "Ha! Y'know, I actually just got the Schist vaccine again the other day. Y'know, that vaccine that protects ya from AIDS and stuff? That's funny! It must be weird whenever ya get the vaccine, since ya got the same name and all. It'd be funny if the guy who made it was related to ya or somethin'."

Gabriel stiffened and bit his tongue. *Relax, Gabriel. Relax, relax, relax.* His cane wobbled underneath him, barely holding him up. "Actually, I've never taken the Schist vaccine. See you later, Mr. Gore." He left the room and entered the corridor.

South Wing was the most populated of Bright New Day's five long-term care wings and occasionally referenced to by staff members as the *blue* wing. After five years, Gabriel should have grown comfortable. There were days when he felt a sense of familiarity from those indigo-floored hallways, recognizable faces, and repetitive daily routines. And some days, he even felt at home. But *most* days, he loathed every doorway, corridor, and scrap of blue wallpaper.

At the moment, none of that mattered. After the horrific wakeup he'd just experienced, the only thing he cared about was getting a cigarette. Until he felt smoke in his lungs, everything was an obstacle. He needed an *escape*—an escape from his morning, an escape from his misery, an escape from *people*—and possibly more than anything else, he needed to hear the ocean outside the building. He didn't need to touch the water—he knew that they'd never permit him to actually touch the ocean again—but just *hearing* it would be enough.

So Gabriel bravely marched down the bleach-scented corridors of Bright New Day. He passed a long series of identical open doors leading to identical bedrooms. His home. His total institution. His prison. His cane tapped along the floor, striking out into the future and carrying his sagging body along with it. *Tap. Tap. Tap.*

He walked slowly. Everything was always slow for him, or maybe he was normal and the world around him was just a dizzying blur. He couldn't tell anymore. As he walked, nurses and LNAs—*licensed nursing assistants*—rushed from room to room, following the ominous rings of ever-present call bells. Fellow residents laughed, screamed, and argued.

The staff gossiped. Within the rooms, television sets were cranked up to maximum volume by nearly deaf residents, most of whom were watching the same old TV Land reruns that they'd been watching for the last twenty years.

As usual, the Crooner was sitting outside his room, beaming with enthusiasm. A small, silver-haired man with no teeth, the Crooner offered Gabriel an overzealous, gummy smile and a voice excruciatingly loud enough to match it. "Laaaahhh! La-la-lah! Upstairs la-la-la upstaaaaiiirs is where I must be upstaiiirzzz. Laaaa-deee-daaa-deee-daaahh! Laa! La! Laaaa! Upstairs!"

The Crooner never stopped singing, from early in the morning until well past midnight. Together, he and the call bells were like an ambitious but untalented garage band.

As the Crooner belted out his music, he continually backed his wheelchair against the wall like a battering ram. Gabriel tried not to listen, tried not to look, but the Crooner was staring right at him with big eager eyes. Rumor had it that the Crooner had once been a highly renowned history professor at Yale.

Tap. Tap. On the other end of the hallway, Gabriel approached Bob Baker, a Vietnam veteran with a mouth sharper and thinner than razor wire. He liked Bob. Bob didn't speak much. That was nice. It was easy.

Bob spent his days sitting in the hallway and scowling at passersby. Gabriel suspected that Bob had auditory schizophrenia because of the way he'd often perk his ears up as if hearing sounds that weren't there. Bob probably had OCD. He smoked exactly four cigarettes a day, and the only thing he ever ate was hot dogs. According to Dana Kleznowski, an LPN on North Wing and one of Gabriel's favorite nurses, Bob demanded that the hot dogs be arranged in a special dish and cut into little pieces exactly three-quarter-inch squares.

"Hello, Mr. Baker," Gabriel said. "Having a good day today?"

"Noooooope," Bob growled with a voice that punctured the air like a can opener.

Tap. Tap. The door to the smoking area was still so far, far away. His heart quivered. He just wanted to get outside, have his cigarette, and be done with it. His desperation for tobacco, sunlight, and the sound of the ocean became increasingly severe. He'd already had his social fill for the day. He just wanted to—

A cold, shaky hand grabbed him.

He stared down into the grimacing face of Edna Foster. She clutched his hand with a death grip. He tried to pry himself loose, but she wouldn't let go.

"Pleeeeeease..." she murmured pitifully.

Gabriel's heart sank. Edna spent most days roaming the halls, one foot permanently stuck out like an arrow and the other bent inward. Her Parkinson's symptoms caused her to shake uncontrollably.

"Pleeeease..." she repeated.

Her features remained in a constant scowl, her eyes continuously glaring with reptilian intensity. Her mouth was pulled back into a tight, open-mouthed smile she had little control over. She had no teeth, no dentures, and a long beak-like nose.

But still, there was something amazing about Edna's face. A powerful tenacity, a century's worth of strength, and a fierce will to live resided in those eyes. Gabriel admired her, and yet, inside every line, inside every furrowed brow, her pain and loneliness was made just as agonizingly apparent as her strength.

"Hello, Edna," Gabriel said.

"Hi..." She peered up at him suspiciously.

"How are you, today?"

"Ohhh my God," she groaned, her face contorting into an angry, flesh-colored raisin. "Everything is *terrible*. So terrible. Like it *always* is."

"Always?"

There was a long pause. Edna often had difficulty finding the right words. "I didn't see you at first, dear. I'm nearly blind, you know. Blind as a bat. Please give me a... ah... *push* me somewhere. Please."

Gabriel knew the routine. She would want to go to her room then to the lobby. Then back to her room. Then to the communal kitchen. No matter where someone pushed her, she would never be happy. "I can't right now, Edna. I—"

"Oh, cram it. You're no good. Get outta my way, sonny boy." She threw Gabriel's hand away.

Sonny boy? As a man in his seventies, Gabriel couldn't remember the last time he'd been called *that*. "But Edna—"

"You go take a walk somewhere and think about what you've done, dummy." She forcefully grabbed the wheels of her chair and slowly rolled away.

Gabriel, not sure how to feel about the interaction, returned to his previous course. Panting with exhaustion, he finally reached the door to the smoking area and pushed it open.

Air. Wind. Sun. The invigorating sunshine was like salve to his wounds. He looked up at the cloudless blue sky, smiling with rapture. Then, he heard it. *The ocean.* Waves crashed, water collapsing upon a beach, somewhere just out of sight.

A tall, impenetrable, cast-iron gate surrounded the smoking area, equipped with ear-shattering alarms in case anyone tried to escape. Safety... at the cost of freedom.

Gabriel stepped up to the gate, wrapped his fingers around its frosty metal bars, and stared out at the mundane gravel parking lot that was his excuse for a view. He could smell the saltwater. The beach was so close, just a short way down the big hill on the other side of the building. Out of sight and out of reach. He'd asked numerous times if he could walk down to it, but they'd never permitted him to do so, not even with supervision.

He closed his eyes and listened to the waves, trying to feel them and to remember the sensation of water splashing against his bare skin. He imagined his old sailboat and the gentle rocking motion beneath his feet as the moon shimmered over the ocean.

"Zero," he whispered. "One, one, two, three, five, eight, thirteen..."

He placed a cigarette in his mouth and sat down at his regular spot over in the white gazebo, where all the smokers were supposed to do their dirty business. He patted his pockets, searching for a lighter. Nothing. He'd forgotten to bring it.

But it wasn't his fault. He was expected to forget everything because he was the lucky recipient of life's final going-away present, that red velvet, chocolate-covered cake of wonderfulness that the doctors liked to call Alzheimer's. With Alzheimer's, suddenly nothing was his fault anymore. *No fault. No blame. No choice. No freedom.*

Many decades ago, someone had once told Gabriel that he had "an amazing mind." The compliment had meant a lot to him. His mind had *defined* him.

Not anymore.

CHAPTER 2:
BEFORE

Summer 1997

Off the shore of California, a tiny sailboat rocked itself to sleep in the rolling arms of an enormous blue giant. Much as mankind was subservient to time, the sailboat was subservient to the water. It could point itself, but only the ocean could propel it forward. For the moment, the boat simply relaxed on the water's gentle surface, allowing its master to gently carry it wherever it chose.

Down in the cabin, Melanie rolled around in bed. She couldn't sleep. It was her last night on the West Coast, the end of summer vacation before junior high. It was also the last night she'd get to spend with her dad, until the next summer.

She unrolled her cocoon of blankets and got out of bed. The air smelled of saltwater. She stood for a moment, smoothing out the cowlicks in her long red hair and considering how weird the ocean moving beneath her bare feet felt.

Her summer trips to California had been a regular event since she was little, but she'd never been so depressed about leaving. Between homework, meeting new teachers, and all the fantasy books she would read, the year would rush by quickly enough, and then Dad would...

Dad. Melanie walked through the cabin, glancing through Dad's shelves, which held hundreds of notebooks. A blackboard with strange, alien-looking equations scrawled onto it stood next to a bookshelf that held dozens of books and scattered photographs, most of them of her.

Despite all of the clutter in his sailboat, there was only one true clue to his true identity: a golden medal that had been casually left on the counter like spare change. She picked up the medal, which was cool to the touch. Engraved with a picture of a bearded man looking to the left, the award was from Sweden. A little award called the freaking *Nobel Prize*, the Nobel Prize in Physiology or Medicine, to be precise.

When she was younger, she'd hadn't thought much about who her dad was. But lately, every time she told someone her father's name, the questions were always the same.

"Your dad is Gabriel Schist?"

"Your dad is that guy who cured AIDS?"

That was him, all right. But even though she'd always known that fact, she'd never *realized* it. It'd never seemed real, not until the past summer.

Melanie reverently placed the medal back on the counter and climbed the ladder to the deck to stand outside with the beautiful, glimmering black and blue waves of the Pacific Ocean. The full moon looked down on her, promising freedom, infinity, and a world beyond the one she knew. If there were a face in that moon, it would've been smiling. She shivered in the breeze, arms wrapped around her torso. The tall white sail flapped gently in the wind.

The quiet was broken by the sound of whistling.

"Dad?" she whispered.

She spotted him sitting at the front of the sailboat, whistling a happy tune. He was barefoot. His feet were just as wide, callused, and workmanlike as his hands. The dark silhouette of his lean, muscular body and his shaggy red hair cut a sharp outline against the brilliant moonlight.

He hadn't even noticed her. She watched him as if he were farther away than he was. He was fixated on the broken piece of white chalk he was using to draw more of those strange equations, names, and figures on the surface of the deck. In his other hand was a lit cigarette. Its thin, smoky trail spiraled up into the night sky.

Suddenly, he looked up at her. "Hi." He grinned.

"Hey." She stepped closer.

Her father was in his early fifties, but he looked younger, and he was handsome, at least according to her friends. He wore faded blue jeans and an unbuttoned Hawaiian shirt that revealed a lion's mane of

19

dark-red chest hair. Other than the spark of otherworldly brilliance in his steel-grey eyes, he looked far more like a mechanic or a tanned beach bum than a scientist.

"Having trouble sleeping?" he asked.

"Yeah. Feeling kinda sad, I guess. This summer has been really, really cool. I really like California."

Dad's eyes flicked away from her. He took another drag from his cigarette. She closed the distance and sat next to him. For several minutes, they sat in silence, staring out into the inconceivably vast ocean.

"Dad?" She gulped. "Can I ask you something?"

"Sure."

"Who are you?"

Dad chuckled. "What kind of question is that?"

Melanie giggled nervously. "Okay, it's just... I mean, when you talk about yourself, you always say you're a carpenter."

Dad shrugged. When he smiled at her, his joyfully crinkled crow's feet formed long, deep lines. "I *am* a carpenter. I've *been* a carpenter for... what, since the eighties? Something like that, yes."

Melanie giggled again, and the second that the silly, high-pitched sound left her throat, she felt like a fool. She'd planned the conversation all summer long, and it wasn't going anything like what she'd expected. Dad always took things so literally.

"I mean... um, *philosophically* speaking," she said, thrusting her shoulders back in order to appear more authoritative. "Who are you, Dad? You say you're a carpenter. All the articles I've read about you, you know, all those old articles from the newspapers, they're all, like, *the big hero, Gabriel Schist!* And then my teachers at school, every time I mention that I'm your daughter, they go on about how you cured AIDS."

He stubbed out his cigarette in a soda can. "That's one way to put it. Technically, what I really did was create a vaccine for HIV. My work did—"

"And then other people, those guys down at the dock, they call you *the surfer dude.* Some news articles say you're a hermit; others talk about your partying college days. I can't tell. It's like you've got friends but no *close* friends. You don't have a girlfriend, either, but women look at you a lot. I can tell."

He squinted. "Do they?"

"Yeah. And yeah, like... I dunno, I have a friend whose mom is a doctor. She knows about you. She says you're a rebel. And Mom, she... whenever Mom *does* talk about you, she says you're a mad genius."

He scoffed. "Is that what she says?"

Melanie nodded. "Yeah, she does. And you... it... all of it... " She sighed and slumped over, unsure how to explain what she wanted to know.

Her father wrapped his arm around her, giving her a squeeze. He kissed the top of her head. "What's wrong?"

Melanie felt tears of frustration in her eyes and tried to blink them away. She knew that her father didn't understand her emotions. He didn't *get* it.

"I don't know who you are, Dad," she whispered. "And now I'm realizing that I've *never* known. All of the info about you, it doesn't fit together. So who are you?"

"The answer is easy, really." He shrugged. "One just has to look at it more straightforwardly. Take away the abstractions and only look at the basic, honest facts."

"What? What do you mean?"

"Melanie, do you know what tetravalent, nonmetallic chemical element is the key component for all life on Earth?"

"Consciousness?"

"No." He smiled. "The answer is carbon. I am a carbon-based life-form."

"Seriously? *That's* your answer?"

"What? Should I explain it more in depth?"

Melanie looked at her father's solemn, concerned face. She shook her head and laughed. Yes, it was a ridiculous answer. But that answer, strange as it was, contained the truth about her dad, who he was, and how he interacted with the world.

She turned to gaze at the moon's reflection on the dark ocean. She pointed at the glowing trail it cut across the water. "What do you call that trail? The white trail, the one that the moon leaves on the ocean?"

Dad rubbed his stubbly chin. "In Finland, I believe they call it *kuunsilta. The Swedish word is, ah, mångata.* But that's not what my father called it."

She'd never met her grandfather, and Dad rarely spoke of him. "Oh?"

"My father, you know, he was a sailor. A Navy man, back in the war. And he and I, we used to go out sailing in the middle of the night. Like we're doing right now." He gave her a tender smile. "He called it the pale highway."

Summer 1997
The next day, Los Angeles

Melanie clutched her father's leather-jacketed waist. Shooting across the overcrowded highway, her dad weaved his motorcycle between the cars. The engine roared like a ravenous dragon. She pressed her face into his back, smiling. The comforting scent of worn leather blocked out the smell of gasoline.

As the shimmering Los Angeles tourist attractions raced past at the mind-blowing speed of seventy-five miles per hour—then eighty, then eighty-five—Melanie's fearful-yet-excited grin widened to the point where her cheeks hurt. The wind whipped her clothes around like flags in the heat of battle. The other vehicles became mere blurs of color.

The ride was terrifying, thrilling, and wonderful, all at the same time, like a rollercoaster but better. Back home in New Hampshire, she never experienced anything like riding with her dad.

"This is awesome!" Her voice was drowned out by the motorcycle's guttural roar. She squeezed her dad tighter. If anyone else had been driving, she would have been afraid for her life.

Dad looked back at her in his mirror and raised his hand a little to give her a thumbs-up. Together, they conquered the 405. But LAX was fast approaching. The sun was beginning to set, painting the sky with beautiful pink highlights and sending long, dark shadows across the city. The motorcycle roared down the Howard Hughes Parkway exit.

Dad pulled up to the airport and parked. He climbed off the motorcycle. With her backpack strapped to her shoulders, Melanie followed suit, handing her helmet to him. He stashed it in the back. He never wore a helmet, though he insisted that she do so. For some reason, she was willing to forgive him the hypocrisy, but she still wished he would wear one, just in case.

Dad looked up at the glorious sunset, an enormous smile on his face. His crow's feet were all crinkled up again. His Hawaiian shirt—the same one he'd worn the previous night on the sailboat—peeked out from beneath his motorcycle jacket.

Last night, Melanie had been able to hold back her tears. The ocean had been so beautiful, the moon glorious. But standing there, she felt her eyes well up. She rushed toward her father and hugged him, wrapping her arms in a tight loop around his waist. She didn't want to wait a year. She didn't want to go through another cold New England winter, away from the sunshine and oceans of her dad's life. Sure, she loved New Hampshire. Sure, she was looking forward to seeing that shy-but-cute Craig Lewis again, and she absolutely loved her mom and Eric, her stepdad. But she hated being separated from her father. Both coasts contained different sides of her. Different lives. She was always half a person instead of a whole one.

Holding her father for one more painful, gut-wrenching moment, she savored the protected feeling of being in his arms. Tears ran down her face. Finally, she stepped away, fingering the straps of her backpack so that her hands would have something to do.

Then, she saw something in her dad's eyes that she had never seen before. Tears. "Dad?" she whispered.

"Take care out there." His voice trembled. "Tell your mother I said hi, okay?"

"Okay. I... um... I—"

"I love you, Melanie." He smiled, his dimples showing, and winked at her. He looked older somehow. His shoulders weren't as straight, and his movements were shaky. Taking a deep breath, he climbed back onto his bike.

Inside the airport, Mom's friend Phyllis waved through the glass, and Melanie raised a hand in acknowledgment. Phyllis, who lived in Long Beach, was going to be flying back with Melanie. Melanie liked her, but the immediate transition from one parent's life to another's was overwhelming.

"Wait, Dad!" she called. "Now that the summer is ending, will you—"

"Hey, listen, nothing *ever* ends!" He laughed. "Let's just turn the handle of the next door, hold our breaths, and see what happens, okay?"

He started his motorcycle. The sun was just beginning its nightly plunge into the ocean, and he raced right toward its center. Melanie watched the tiny figure of her father speeding away, red hair and leather jacket whipping in the wind behind him. The sky's radiance was blinding, so bright that it made the farthest vanishing point of the highway appear white.

And as the road touched the sky, her dad disappeared in the light of the dying sun.

CHAPTER 3:
FOG

Spring 2018

GABRIEL SCHIST STOOD MOTIONLESSLY IN his linoleum-floored bedroom at Bright New Day. At the top of his paper-chalk-ink-dust-cluttered bureau, thrown into the corner like a used Coca-Cola can, was a little gold medal from Sweden. He studied it, trying to remember how marvelous it had once felt to hold the Nobel Prize in his hand.

It *had* felt marvelous. Once. A long time ago. Long, long ago, back when he used to have goals. Back when he had something else to look forward to other than three meals a day, a constant stream of stupid TV shows, an absolutely obscene amount of sleep, and of course, the most important distraction of all: pills.

Pills, pills, and more pills. The parade never ended: 10mg of Donepezil. Coumadin to prevent clot formation—couldn't have another stroke, now could he—5mg of Oxy IR, 100mg of Trazadone, 50mg QD of Seroquel XR, orange-flavored Metamucil. His life had become utterly dependent on little plastic cups filled with multicolored Skittles.

Gabriel sat down on the hard, tiny bed. Even the bed in the cabin of his old sailboat had been bigger, and more comfortable, too.

Outside the room, the Crooner continued his twenty-four-seven song routine. *"Laaaa-deeee-dah. La-la-laaah. Bring me upstairs, please, please, please. La-la-la!"*

Gabriel considered stuffing cotton in his ears to block out the noise. It was only mid-afternoon, but he already wanted to go back to sleep.

There was nothing else to do. His supposedly castrated new roommate seemed to concur, as the entire room echoed with the rumble of Robbie Gore's snores. Somehow, even the Crooner's relentless singing was easier to take than that.

Gabriel took off his fedora. Just as he was about to lie down, he was startled by a knock on the door.

A face he didn't recognize appeared around the corner of the jamb. "Um... hi there. Mr. Schist?" The young man stepped into the room with a pile of bleached-white sheets and some blankets tucked under the crook of his arm. Dressed in brown scrubs, he looked to be anywhere from nineteen to twenty-two. He had a military haircut and pale, splotchy skin slightly reddened on his cheeks and forehead: facial erythema. His glasses were too big for his face.

"Hello," Gabriel replied. "How are you?"

"Good, sir. Very good." The boy kept leaning his weight from foot to foot, weaving back and forth as if he needed to use the bathroom. He seemed nervous, but he had a charmingly likable face.

A call bell went off in the hallway. The boy glanced back, worriedly.

"Sir," he said, "I, uh... I came here to check if you wanted me to change your bed. If you don't mind."

Gabriel slowly rose to his feet, his spine as stiff as an unlubricated driveshaft. The pile of bedding he'd wadded on his mattress was still there, right where he'd left it that morning. So was the stench of urine. He cringed at the double realization that not only had he forgotten about his accident that morning, but he'd also almost climbed into a wet bed.

The boy awkwardly extended a spaghetti-like arm, offering a handshake. His mouth was pulled back into a tight, fearful line.

Gabriel took the proffered hand and was amused to find that his new LNA had a surprisingly strong, confident grip. "What's your name, son?" Gabriel asked.

"Harry Brenton, sir. I recently transferred here from... from another facility. So would, ah... would it be okay?"

Gabriel glanced back at the bed. "I'll make a deal with you, Harry. You can change the bed. Just don't say a word about this to anyone, okay? I don't want nurses inspecting me every hour or putting me in diapers. This here was... an isolated occurrence." Gabriel felt a blush rising into his cheeks. It wasn't like him to be so openly vulnerable, but he liked this Harry Brenton fellow.

Harry's eyes kept darting around as he looked at Gabriel's notes, the blackboard, and the photos. It was almost as if he was looking for something in particular. "No, I won't say a word." Harry shook his head. "Definitely not, no."

Gabriel moved aside, and Harry yanked off all of the old sheets, stuffed them in a bag, and stretched on new ones. He had an almost manic work ethic. Once the bed was remade, Harry beamed with confidence.

"So, Harry, are you a military man, perchance?"

"Oh, you can tell?"

"The haircut. Your work ethic. You say *sir* quite a bit."

"Um, yeah. Not anymore, though, if that's what you mean. Now that I'm back from overseas, I'm just focusing on college."

"What subject are you studying?"

Harry blushed and crossed his arms. "Microbiology." He grinned, arms clenched tighter around his chest. "Mr. Schist, I... God, I'm thrilled to meet you, sir. You've been my *hero* ever since—you've been my role model since I was a kid. I was totally excited when I found out you were a resident here."

Gabriel smiled. For a moment, the first in a long time, he felt like the old Gabriel Schist again. "Thank you, Harry. You're a good kid. Really, it means a great deal to me. I didn't realize that anyone even still *looked* at my work."

"Are you kidding me? Sir, you're an inspiration to all of us. All of us in my class, anyway. I mean, c'mon, the Schist vaccine? It's practically Tylenol these days. Probably every resident in this facility has had the Schist vac."

Gabriel smiled. "Not *every* resident."

Harry looked confused. "You haven't? Really?"

"It's a long story." Gabriel shrugged. "But anyhow, you're a microbiology student? What brings you here?"

"I guess, um... I like helping people. I feel like the older generation, all you folks, you really deserve good help. And jeez, even though the military covers all my class expenses, I still need to pay the bills on my apartment." Harry swallowed. "Sorry if I'm being awkward. It's just...

I can't believe I have this opportunity to talk to you. I want to find out everything I can, y'know? Like I can't imagine what it must be like being as brilliant as you are, if you don't mind me saying, and then to suddenly get the diagnosis of Alzhei—oh. Oh, jeez. I'm sorry. I mean to say, uh…"

Gabriel chuckled, hoping to allay the boy's embarrassment. In his high school years, the poor kid had probably had a *million* awkward encounters with girls. "It's okay," Gabriel said. "I can explain it this way. Can you get me a piece of paper, a pair of scissors, and some tape? Top drawer of the bureau."

Harry complied, finding all three items rather easily. Gabriel cut a long, thin rectangle out of the paper. Pathetic as it seemed, he was actually surprised by the dexterity of his own hands. Next, Gabriel held the two ends of the paper, gave the strip a half-twist, and taped the short ends together.

"I'm sure you recognize a Möbius strip," Gabriel said. "A loop. It has only one side. I know that an educated young man like you has seen it before, but humor me for a moment." He put the tip of the pen to the paper and slowly drew a line down the middle of the strip. "Imagine that my pen is a child aging into adulthood."

Harry watched intently. Gabriel continued the line down, all the way until it reached the end, which was also the starting point. His line had gone all the way around on *both* sides of the loop, even though he never lifted his pen or crossed the edge.

"Harry, *life* is a Möbius strip. I began as a drooling mess in diapers, unable to talk, unable to feed myself, unable to think. As the story continues, I progress. I advance further. My life twists around, and then, at the end, I return to the beginning. After everything I've been through, after that long, long walk, I slowly devolve back into a drooling mess in diapers. An infant, once again."

"That's… oh, gosh."

"The only thing I haven't yet figured out," Gabriel said, "is what the *twist* in my life was, exactly. Was it the Schist vaccine? The terrific irony of me getting Alzheimer's? I don't think so. Personally, I like to believe that I still haven't *hit* the twist yet."

Harry nodded, looking a bit meek and traumatized. He turned to study Gabriel's notes on the wall, digging his hands into his pockets.

"Harry, can I ask you for a favor? Can I take your photo? Since you're new, I mean. If you look up there on the wall, you can see that I take photos of everyone who works here. You know, just so that I can remember their faces. It makes it easier for me."

That was only partly true. The photos were also Gabriel's weak attempt at socialization, his silly way of trying to make friends, a skill he'd never quite mastered. But Harry didn't need to know that.

"Sure. Wow, that'd be cool!" Harry replied.

Gabriel took out his Polaroid camera and snapped the photo. A flash then Harry's beaming smile was frozen in time forever. With a flourish, Gabriel took out his pen and wrote "Harry" on the white strip at the bottom of the picture. "What was your last name again, Harry? Bartlett? Bernard? No. Barnett?"

"Brenton, sir."

Gabriel wrote it down before he could forget it again. As soon as he finished, he heard a loud knock. He looked up at Harry, who responded by nervously gesturing toward the door.

A young redheaded woman stood in the doorway, biting her lip. It was probably another nurse or a new employee, perhaps.

Gabriel shook his head. "Yes? What is it, more goddamn pills?"

"No," the woman whispered. "It's me."

Gabriel stared at the woman's attractive features. She had an intelligent face of long, sharp edges and smooth contours, complemented by dynamic brown eyes. Her mother's eyes. Her grim expression was enough to break him in two, but seeing her again lifted his spirits. He stood up, shivering, and took the girl into his arms, squeezing her bony little body, never wanting to let her go, never wanting to let her escape again into a harsh world he couldn't protect her from.

He smiled. "It's great to see you, Melanie."

CHAPTER 4: STRANDED

GABRIEL WENT TO THE NURSING home's front lobby and sat down on the leather couch. His daughter, Melanie Schist, sat on the identical couch across from him. No, wait...*was it Melanie Schist, or was she still Melanie Tompkins?* He seemed to remember that she and Bill had divorced, but he wasn't certain.

Yes. Yes, they had. She was Melanie *Schist* again. He was pretty sure.

The lobby was beautiful with bay windows overlooking the Atlantic Ocean, Michelangelo paintings on the walls, and an abstract wave-shaped fountain sculpture standing in the entrance hall to the three chessboards in the back. The lobby was one of his favored daily hangouts, though he preferred the smoking area. The windows tortured him with their presentation of the ocean's face but not its *smell*. Though he could see the waves lapping at the beach, they didn't seem real, and that rendered the window view as little more than a moving painting. Even the sound of the waves was blocked out by the jazz music that played from the lobby's overhead speaker twenty-four hours a day. All in all, both areas were terrible teases of what he couldn't have.

The couches were positioned next to a spectacular wall-sized aquarium filled with all manner of brilliantly colored swimming creatures. Gabriel stared into the blank eyes and flapping tail of a particularly active goldfish.

"Dad? Uh, Dad? Are you there?"

Gabriel smiled at his daughter. She looked so much like Yvonne at that age. When he'd first met Yvonne on that California beach, with her devilishly flirty smile and her bag full of Santa Barbara oranges, he never could have predicted that they would someday create such a beautiful daughter together.

Melanie sighed, those sharp cheekbones of hers pulled taut, her mouth a thin line. Still, the stung vulnerability in her chocolate-brown eyes was unhidden; her eyes were always flickering, always moving, always *thinking*. The whites looked a little bloodshot, but he imagined that she wasn't sleeping much, considering the long hours she spent between the orphanage, the local homeless shelter, and her two kids. He'd always suspected that she had sleep apnea, as well.

"Dad." She snapped her fingers.

"Oh, hello," Gabriel said. "Sorry, Melanie. I was a bit distracted." *Distracted. For how long?*

"It's okay. For a sec, I thought your mind had gone skiing in the White Mountains or something."

"No, not quite. I'm not that far gone. Not yet."

"Good."

They sat there, staring at each other, the void between them jammed full of non-words and unspecified feelings. She crossed her arms, digging her fingernails into her biceps. Several times, Gabriel moved his mouth to speak and then stopped, made nervous by the intensity of her gaze.

He remembered when she was little. He remembered her zeal, her compassion, her love of life, the way that she'd cry and ask him for help, ask him for advice, ask him for guidance. The beautifully uninhibited smile she used to give him—a Christmas present he was once lucky enough to receive as freely as oxygen—a smile that he never saw anymore.

She was no longer that little girl. To him, that was the greatest trial of parenthood: watching a loving, helpless little creature become a new, independent person before his eyes. A person who didn't need him anymore.

He was proud of Melanie. She'd become a strong-willed, kind woman who helped abandoned little kids find new families and the homeless find new homes. She was a terrific mother, a better parent than he'd ever been. But on some level, he still missed the little girl, and he hated the weight that his condition put upon her shoulders. He supposed he probably always would.

"It's truly wonderful to see you." Gabriel leaned forward, hunched over his cane. "I miss you, Melanie. It's been so long since you've visited. Why don't you come here more often?"

Melanie shifted uncomfortably. She sucked in air, revealing her breathing to be ragged and choked up. Swiping at her eyes, she gazed at the fish tank. "I... I miss you too. But, Dad, it... hey, it hasn't been *that* long. Only three weeks."

Three weeks? Gabriel nodded. A few seconds elapsed, and he realized his allotted space for a timely reply had passed. Any reply would seem out of place, awkward, *demented.* So he remained silent, stroking his cane's molded plastic handle for comfort. The cane was becoming less of a tool and more of a friend.

A tear escaped from Melanie's eye. She wiped it away and looked over at the clock as if arguing with herself about how much longer she needed to stay. Gabriel quickly glanced away. He needed a distraction, just for a moment, to regain his bearings.

There were always a few other residents in the lobby, especially in the afternoons. Edna Foster was sitting by the bay windows, talking to her three sons. Her face was pulled back in her familiar scowl. One son leaned closer to her, and with a hostile expression, she loudly whispered about how evil everyone in the nursing home was. Everything was *terrible.* Everything was *the worst ever.*

Bob Baker rolled his wheelchair up to one of the tables, where he was presented with a plate full of his hotdog cubes. He glared at them.

All the way in the back, a new resident was sitting behind one of the chessboards, playing a game against himself. Well, maybe he wasn't a *new* resident but definitely one Gabriel had never noticed. He was a tall, thin old man with long bony fingers. He looked so emaciated that the slightest breeze might break him into pieces. His three-piece tuxedo was ridiculously pristine and out of place. Big buggy eyes rested in dark hollowed-out sockets, and his perfectly combed-back hair was silver, as was his goatee. He looked noble, distinguished, like a lawyer or a politician. A long, gnarly scar crossed his left cheek, extending upward in a ragged trail then abruptly splitting off to the right and terminating in a shape that resembled the number 7.

"Dad? I'm talking to you."

Gabriel wanted to pay attention to Melanie—he really did—but somehow, he just couldn't. There was something oddly comforting about the angular man at the chessboard, something that held Gabriel's attention, though he couldn't determine what it was.

The old man looked up at Gabriel with his bulbous eyes. Gabriel nodded in greeting. In response, the old man offered him a friendly, unpretentious smile.

"Dad!"

"Sorry, Melanie. I'm sorry. I got—"

"It's okay. It's not your fault." She bit her lip. "It's just that I have to get going."

He bristled. "Now?"

"Yeah."

Gabriel stared at her. "I know it's been hard, since Yvonne... since your mother died. But *I'm* not dead yet, Melanie."

"Dad! I never said—"

"I know. I'm sorry. But I want to see you more. Isn't that the exact reason you made me come here, all the way to New Hampshire?"

"Yes—"

"I miss you."

Melanie stood and wrapped her scarf around her neck, tilting her head back to prevent more tears from flowing down her cheeks. She wiped her eyes, looked at her father, and then looked away quickly. "I miss you too," she whispered. "Goodbye, Dad."

She put on her coat and crossed her arms again, taking in a deep, ragged breath. She lowered her head, checked her cell phone, and took a step back. She was preparing herself. She had to *prepare* herself to hug him.

"Wait." Gabriel's muscles tightened. He wanted to lunge forward and hold her, prevent her from leaving. "Please."

She looked at him with red eyes, eyes that he might not see again for a long time, unless she permitted him.

"I'm sorry." Gabriel sighed. "For everything. I'm sorry I wasn't there more."

She sniffled. "Stop."

"I'm truly, deeply sorry. I swear it. I wish I could go back and fix all the mistakes I made with your mother, back before you were born, I wish—"

"But you can't." Her voice carried a hint of resentment. "Mom's dead, Dad. She's been dead a long time."

He'd never seen Yvonne during her chemo days. He'd been living in California, and she was across the country. Yvonne's second husband was a good man, her rock, and he'd been there for her in ways that Gabriel hadn't been during their marriage. Gabriel hadn't seen the hair loss, the weight loss, and the vomiting. But he and Yvonne had talked on the phone all throughout the treatments, at least once a week, and he distinctly remembered that her wonderful *laugh* had never changed, never faltered. The braveness she'd possessed in those final days was inspirational. "I know."

"I wasn't reminding you," Melanie retorted. "I'm just wondering if you've ever realized that there's a point where too many years have gone by to brush things under the rug."

"It's not my fault that—"

"Don't pretend that I'm ignorant." Melanie clutched onto her purse strap so tightly that her knuckles reddened. "I know all the stories. You were the irresponsible one. You were the one who messed up and put booze before family."

He stretched out a hand. "Melanie…"

She stepped back. "It's okay. Really. I've come to terms with it. But don't you dare act like you can fix things with a simple apology. It's too late."

Gabriel didn't cry but only because nothing she said was new to him. He'd beat himself up with the same statements a million times.

"I'm sorry." Melanie sighed. "Listen, I have to—oh. Hi there, Natty."

Natty Bruckheimer, Gabriel's least favorite LNA, normally worked the night shift, but evidently, she'd picked up some earlier hours that day. A series of junior high photos on her phone, which she frequently showed to anyone who dared mention a weight-loss program, proved that while Natty had once possessed an average big-boned figure, the last few decades had caused her to become so overweight that the floor shook when she walked, and the folds in her elephantine legs were visible through her skin-tight white scrubs. She blamed diabetes. Natty was in her late forties, but she was the sort of woman who, after getting pregnant in high school—and having two kids, if Gabriel recalled correctly—was forever chasing after her lost youth. She had a blond buzz cut, a fake tan, multiple neck tattoos, and a face like a rodent, complete with beady eyes and prominent front teeth.

"Hi, Melanie!" Natty clapped Gabriel's daughter on the back, pretending that the two were friends.

"So how's my dad doing?" Melanie whispered. "Is he doing okay with the, you know, with the new medications?"

They didn't look at him, didn't talk to him, didn't even acknowledge that he was there. Somehow, they'd convinced themselves that if they lowered their voices to a certain tone, he couldn't hear their whispers.

"Oh yeah, Gabe's been good," Natty answered. "Those new meds are working wonders for the guy."

"So there haven't been any new behavioral problems?" Melanie asked.

"Oh no, don't worry! The Seroquel has been a big help."

"Has it?" Melanie asked, glancing over at him.

"Oh yeah! Gabe's much happier these days." Natty reached out, took off Gabriel's fedora, and rubbed the back of his head, messing up his hair.

Gabriel clenched his teeth. *Stay calm, stay calm, stay calm...*

"Ain't that right, Gabe?" Natty giggled. "You're doing real good today, aren't you, honey?"

That was the last straw. "Gabriel," he whispered venomously.

"What was that, honey?"

"I'm not *Gabe*. Not *honey*. My name is Gabriel. *Gabriel Schist.*"

"Sweetie-pie, you really need to speak up," Natty said. "We can't hear you when you mumble! You know you—"

"Gabriel! My name is Gabriel Schist, and I'm not a goddamned child! You hear me now? You hear that? You—"

"Dad... stop. Please."

Gabriel threw his fedora to the ground. Melanie looked startled. Natty stepped back, her eyes rapidly passing back and forth between father and daughter. The thin, bug-eyed man peered at them across the chess board.

Gabriel started to speak and then stopped. He couldn't find the words. His stomach was twisting in knots. He went over to Melanie and collapsed in her arms. She hugged him tightly. He felt her heart beating, a heart he had set to motion, a heart that now existed independently of him. A heart that would continue to beat long after his became dust.

"I'm sorry," he said.

"*I'm* sorry, Dad. I know… I know the Alzheimer's makes it difficult. Difficult to know what you're saying and all that. It's not your fault."

Marvelous. Rub some salt in the wound, Melanie. Thank you.

"I love you, Dad." Melanie stiffened. "But I gotta go. I'll see you soon, okay?"

Soon. Would it be another month? Two, perhaps? Three? Longer? "I love you too," he replied stiffly.

Melanie kissed him on the cheek and walked to the front of the lobby, right to the front door of the building. The portal to reality. She wiped away her tears and punched in the code. The door swung open, releasing her from the barricaded confines of the facility. Gabriel watched morosely as she returned to her normal, fatherless life. Within moments, it was as if she'd never visited.

Natty shrugged and shuffled toward the break room. The thin man returned to his chess game. Gabriel put on his fedora, buttoned up his trench coat, and sat down next to the fishes again. He stared forward, his eyes fixed on a pair of brown-grey slugs crawling up the outside surface of the glass. *More slugs? The damn things were everywhere.*

He refocused his attention on the fish. They swam in circles in the tiny amount of space. Did they have children on the outside, in the ocean? Fathers? Mothers? Were they alone, too?

Somewhere in the distance, the Crooner's never-ending singsong echoed through the halls. Looking to his side, Gabriel noticed that Edna Foster had rolled her wheelchair up next to him. Her sons were gone, too. Together, they were childless parents of parentless children.

"Hi," Edna said.

"Hi."

"Oh, look at 'em go. I come and see 'em every day. They're my friends. I think they must sleep, don't you?"

"They do." Gabriel smiled. "But they don't have eyelids, so it's difficult to tell. Many fish still swim while they're asleep."

"Yeah, they kinda swim around all pointlessly, doncha think?" Edna winced, squinting. "Over and over again, in the same li'l old place. It's *madness*. Glad I'm not a fish."

CHAPTER 5:
REVELATION

GABRIEL SUDDENLY WOKE UP WITH a start. He sat bolt upright. Tense. Terrified. Quivering. The lights were out. The room was dark. The curtain divider was pulled shut.

He listened carefully. He needed to make sure he'd heard what he thought he'd heard.

Yes. He'd heard it. Robbie Gore, his roommate, was choking. The tattooed man's hoarse, congested gasps rattled the air like a trembling earthquake. The fluid in his lungs sounded as if it were rising up like floodwater. He was croaking like a desperate toad.

"Robbie?" Gabriel whispered.

The darkness brought no reply but the sound of gagging. Nauseatingly mucus-filled gasps of air. *Drowning.*

"Hssshh... lllp! Hel...ll...sppphhh shh...glllugghh...hel gllsss..."

Gabriel stabbed his trigger finger at the little red call button, setting off a tiny distress beacon in the hallway. Then, with great effort, he forced himself out of bed. His crusty old joints ached. His varicose veins felt poisoned, and he felt lightheaded. Grabbing his cane, Gabriel hobbled over to Robbie's side of the room.

"Plssshhhh... gaannnrrrrssss!" Robbie's eyes were enormous, nearly popping out of his skull. His oxygen concentrator was running but not doing a hell of a lot. Drool poured from the corner of his mouth, forming a sticky puddle on his chest. His face was dark purple, with blue veins popping up on his forehead. He had too much fluid in his lungs.

"I called them, Robbie," Gabriel said.

"Mmmmfff! Glll... ghell... gll..."

"They're coming, Robbie," Gabriel said anxiously. "I called them. They're coming." He hobbled over to the doorway, thinking he might flag someone down.

Before he could make it out to the corridor, Samantha, one of the night LNAs, whizzed right past him and stopped at the foot of Robbie's bed. Her eyes widened. She looked at Robbie then at Gabriel. She grabbed the remote attached to Robbie's bed and raised his head. It didn't appear to have any effect.

"Oh, shit," she gasped.

"It just started," Gabriel said. "He just started. He—"

"I'm getting Beatrice. I'll be right back. I'll be... I'll be right back!" Sam cried, running from the room.

The clock was ticking. Robbie's lips were getting blue. Blue was never a good sign. But he was still breathing, albeit barely.

Gabriel wanted to take his hand. He desperately wanted to help Robbie, to ease his pain somehow. "They're coming," he whispered. "Stay calm, Robbie. They're coming."

Gabriel slunk back to his side of the room. He sat down, quivering with inability. The curtain divider was pulled, so he couldn't see Robbie's gasping, purple face anymore. But he still heard the man gasping for air.

"This is a Code Blue!" someone shouted in the hallway. "Code Blue!"

Several nurses in multicolored scrubs piled into the room. Gabriel tried to pick out their faces, but they hurried by too fast. They raced over to Robbie's bed, pulling their machines along with them. A nebulizer beeped to life.

"Wait. He's not a DNR, right?" one asked.

"No! Full code!"

The curtain swayed as the nurses rushed about. Gabriel looked away. He wanted to leave the room, but the thought of doing so made him feel sick with guilt. He stared at the photographs on the wall and attempted to identify the different nurses by their voices.

"He's still here!" a male, Tanzanian-accented nurse shouted. That was Baraka Okafor. "He's still with us! Hey, you! Can I get a heart rate?"

"Sure thing." *Beatrice.*

"What's going on with him?"

"Fluid in his lungs! C'mon, guys. He's a full code! We've got to—"

"What's that heart rate?" *Tony Johnson. No, Johnsbury.*

"One twenty."

"Here, hand that thing to me."

"C'mon, Robbie! Stay with us, Robbie. Keep breathing. In and out, in and out!"

They were stubborn. They were determined to help Robbie live to fight another day. But determination didn't win every battle. Because no matter how hard they tried, no matter how hard they swam against the rising tide, they were going to fail. Robbie Gore was going to die that night. All of them knew it. So did Gabriel.

As nurses, machines, and loud voices continued to flurry around him, Gabriel fell into a daze. Everything was blurry. Hectic. Vague. Since coming to Bright New Day, he'd seen the same scene a million times, and in nine out of ten incidences, it didn't end well.

"Heart rate? Hello, what's the heart rate?"

"It's... it's—"

"There's nothing left, Tony. He's gone."

"He's—"

"Dead. He's dead."

Gabriel noticed a lone slug crawling up the wall. Another one. It was a greenish-grey number with a black leopard-print pattern across its back. The tiny creature was oblivious to the depressing scene going on outside of its small, meaningless existence.

"It's over." Beatrice sighed. "Sam, can you do postmortem care?"

"Yeah. I can... yep."

"I'll phone the funeral home."

"Does he have family?" Baraka asked. "A wife? Kids? Anyone we should call?"

"No. Nobody. Nobody at all. Gloomy as hell, I know."

Suddenly, the slug stopped. It tilted its head with what almost looked like curiosity and raised its twin black antennas. Those tiny little eyes on the slug's antennas were pointed right at Gabriel, as if it were looking at him.

But that was ridiculous. For a moment, though, the bizarre thought had seemed all too possible. Gabriel shook his head, and the slug crawled away. *Marvelous.* He'd gotten so stupidly demented that he was anthropomorphizing a slug.

An unfamiliar male nurse came around the curtain. "You okay, Gabriel? Do you need to talk?"

Gabriel clenched his hands together. "I'm fine."

As the minutes went by, everything became blurrier and blurrier. Samantha did postmortem care on Robbie's cadaver. A black-suited worker from the funeral home came in and took the body away in a black bag. Gabriel rocked back and forth in his armchair, unwilling to go back to sleep.

The hubbub was over. Lights were out. Everything was supposed to go back to normal. *Sure. Right.*

From the corner of his eye, Gabriel noticed movement in the hall outside his room. Leaning forward, he peered around the jamb. Edna Foster, clad in a nightgown and scowling, rolled her wheelchair over and stopped in his doorway.

Slowly, she turned her head to look in on him. "Hi..."

"Hi, Edna," Gabriel replied, rubbing his eyes. "You're up late tonight."

"Late? What are you talking about? It's morning. I'm waiting for breakfast."

Gabriel checked his watch: two a.m. Edna rolled into his room and peered around in the dark, as if looking for something.

Edna sat there, twitching from her Parkinson's, her brow deeply furrowed into a ridged mountain range. Wheeling forward a bit, she peered over at the other side of the room. "Is he dead?"

Gabriel gnawed on his lower lip. "Yes. Just a few minutes ago."

She nodded and took Gabriel's hand, holding it tightly. Her eyes were unfocused, yet at the same time, looking right *into* him.

"Oh," Edna said. "Good for him." She wheeled out of the room and returned to her tour of the hallway.

Good for him. She'd said that with none of her trademark malice. No sarcasm. No negativity. She'd said it, and she'd meant it.

Another person may have found her comment to be in bad taste, but Gabriel understood the genuine compassion in it. Robbie Gore had suffered from the incurable, and death had released him. Gabriel had never believed in an afterlife, and he didn't much care whether it existed or not.

Sighing, Gabriel looked at the chaotic jumble strewn across his table. *God, what a mess.* He felt a great temptation to swipe it all to the floor in one fell swoop.

Except... something was sitting on top of his papers, its head raised into the sky, staring right at him. It was the same slug from earlier, the greenish-grey one with the leopard pattern on its back. Its black antennas squirmed above its head. Gabriel lifted his finger, getting ready to flick it away.

Then, something happened. Something that Gabriel never could have anticipated. Something so bizarre, so utterly impossible and ludicrous, that he nearly had a heart attack.

The slug spoke. "Hello there, Gabriel."

CHAPTER 6:
STORM

GABRIEL SHOOK HIS HEAD. HE wasn't going to even *pretend* the nonsense was real.

"Gabriel," the slug repeated a bit more sternly. Its voice was vaguely metallic and way too big for its tiny form. Its head was tilted in what could only be described as a quizzical gesture.

Oh, no. This was it. The final sign that he'd totally lost it. "Zero, one, one, two." Gabriel was already out of breath. "Three, five, eight, thirteen..." The Fibonacci numbers didn't help. His mind was utterly, completely gone.

He stared at the slug, trying to somehow fit it into reality. He felt as if his mind had separated into fluffy pieces of lint. "You... you're just a... a voice. A voice in my head," Gabriel said as calmly as possible. "That's all. A voice in my head. Now, if you don't mind, please shut up."

"No, thank you," the slug replied, nodding its little head.

"Pardon?"

"I said *no thank you*. I've been pretty reserved for quite some time, and it's grown tiresome. I'm actually very talkative, to tell you the truth. Silence doesn't suit me."

Trembling, Gabriel rubbed his temples. "Fuck you."

"That's very crude, Gabriel. Come now, you're better than that."

"Oh my God." Gabriel broke down into loud, hysterical laughter. Tears flowed from his eyes. *Oh, it was all over now! All over!*

Down the hall, Bob Baker screamed for him to shut up. Gabriel took in a deep breath, and his laughter faded. The only thing that remained were his tears.

"Marvelous." He glared at the slug. "You're still here."

"Yes." As it spoke, the slug's tiny mouth opened and closed.

"Okay, listen." Gabriel shook his head. "I know that you're just a figment of my imagination, some stray hallucination caused by my degenerating brain. I don't know why the hell my consciousness decided to imagine a talking slug, but—"

"I'm not a figment of your imagination, Gabriel."

"Yes you are. Don't confuse me. I'm still going to talk to you, just in case my consciousness has anything important to say, but don't even pretend to be real." Gabriel wiped sweat from his forehead, hands shaking. "Why are you here?"

"Well, I did come here for a purpose, after all. Seriously, Gabriel, if a slug talks to you, don't you think there's a good reason for it?"

Gabriel stood up and began pacing. The sight of Robbie Gore's empty bed made him shudder. He considering pinching himself but dreaded the possibility of doing so and then finding that the slug remained in place. *It's not real. Don't forget that.*

He sat down again, squinting at the slug's face. "I wasn't aware that slugs spoke," Gabriel muttered. "Actually, last I heard, the only thing that slugs are any good for is destroying gardens."

"You don't understand," the slug said. "But none of you do, not really. Humanity has never understood slugs. Look at me. Doesn't my slimy, odd-shaped physical body seem a bit... odd? A bit unreal? A bit *alien?*"

"Oh, yes. The poor, poor plight of slugs."

"Very amusing. My point is, all of us, the slugs, we don't come from your Earth."

"No? Ha! So you're not simply a talking slug but also a UFO conspiracy theorist!"

"Gabriel, we slugs come from above. We come from the sky. We are the protectors of humanity."

Gabriel laughed again, but his laugh was forced. "You? *You* call yourselves the protectors of humanity?"

"Yes," the slug replied calmly.

"And... what? Okay. Tell me. How exactly does a slug do any *protecting* when the only speed it's capable of is *slow?*"

"Heh." The slug wriggled its antennas. "Trust me, we don't *have* to move slowly. We *choose* to."

"Pardon me for being a bit dubious of that claim."

"Oh, your doubts are completely understandable," the slug said, its antennas springing out like bolts of electricity. "But really, we can move at any speed we like. See, you have to understand, these slimy bodies aren't our original form. On the inside, we are actually incredible beings of pure light. But surprisingly, we've come to appreciate these strange, wriggling bodies. These bodies are wonderfully humble and low to the ground. They're delightfully inconspicuous, so that we can watch over you without ever being suspected. We've chosen to stay in them in service of our master. We've—"

"Your master? Who's that?"

"Our master? Oh, you mean the great Sky Amoeba, of course!"

"That's enough," Gabriel said, fists clenched, holding his temper at bay like a lit flame.

"Oh, come—"

"No!" Gabriel snapped. "I've heard enough. I know that you're just some rogue piece of my subconscious causing mischief, and I don't want to hear it."

"But—"

"Get out. Now!" Gabriel jabbed a finger at the door.

The slug turned to look at the door, an action which made Gabriel feel even more ridiculous. *How the hell was a slug supposed to walk out the door?* The talking slug turned back toward Gabriel. It didn't crawl away.

Fine. If it didn't leave, he'd *make* it leave. Gabriel raised his fist. The shadow of his hand fell over the slug's helpless little body. But the slug stood its ground. Gabriel glared at it.

"I care about you," the slug said. "I'm here to help. I'm here to deliver a message. You can either listen, or you can run away. But I remember that strong-willed man inside you all too well. I still see the rugged genius who never runs away, even when the entire world seems against him. You're not a coward. Are you?"

Gabriel held his fist in place. *Was he?*

"*Are* you?" the slug repeated.

Gabriel hesitated. "No." He slumped and put his hand out on the table.

The slug crawled into his palm, its damp, wriggling little body tickling his skin.

"I still don't believe you," Gabriel said. "I still think you're a hallucination of some kind."

"I know."

"So what's this message you have for me? Tell me that much, at least."

The slug turned its antennas down. "Gabriel, there's a storm on the horizon." The odd geniality that had been in the slug's metallic voice was gone. Its tone had turned murky and foreboding. "Tomorrow. That's when it starts, Gabriel. That's when everything changes."

"What happens tomorrow?" Gabriel asked.

"The Black Virus will begin here. Right here, tomorrow, at Bright New Day. And once the virus begins cutting its bloody path through humanity's corpses, you will be the only one who can stop it."

Gabriel shook his head. "The Black Virus? What the hell is that? Are you talking about the bubonic plague?"

"Tomorrow," the slug repeated.

Gabriel put the slug back on the wall. He was done listening. The whole thing was too ridiculous for words. Yet, an uncomfortable feeling stuck in his mind like a hooked fish.

"I hope you're ready." The slug slithered up the wall and into a crevice in the cracked white ceiling.

CHAPTER 7:
CADAVER

THE MORNING AFTER ROBBIE GORE'S death, Gabriel tentatively sat up in bed, his aching, rusty bones creaking with the motion. He rested his heavy head in his hands and attempted to pick the cobwebs out of his brain. As far as he could tell, the room was happily slug-free.

"The Black Virus will begin here. Right here, tomorrow, at Bright New Day. And once the virus begins cutting its bloody path through humanity's corpses, you will be the only one who can stop it. I hope you're ready."

A slug. A talking slug. For Christ's sake, was he really sitting here, thinking about a talking slug?

The breakfast tray beside his bed held a cup of black coffee, a plate of lukewarm scrambled eggs that smelled heavily of olive oil, a glass of orange juice, and as usual, a small bowl of Corn Pops. They always gave him Corn Pops. When he'd told them that he liked Corn Pops, he certainly hadn't meant that he wanted them every single day. Next to the cereal was a tiny plastic cup of pills.

According to the talking slug—hardly the most credible harbinger—the whole Black Virus business was supposed to start that day. But he couldn't believe the words of a slithering little creature from his imagination.

He gulped down the pills and ate his breakfast. He tried to put the slug and its prophecy out of his mind as he dressed for the day.

About an hour later, he traversed the fluorescent-lit corridors of Bright New Day on an aimless, directionless walk, less for enjoyment and more for the purpose of preventing muscular atrophy in his legs. All the usual suspects were about: the Crooner sang his heart out, Bob Baker glared into the hallway, and Edna Foster wheeled back and forth, expressing dire misery to anyone who dared cross her path. As Gabriel approached, she tentatively reached out for him.

A gravelly, Brooklyn-accented voice blasted out like a siren. "Hi there!" Mickey Minkovsky, a cheery, bald-headed, glasses-wearing New York Jewish man, had gleefully grabbed Edna's hand and spun his wheelchair around to face her. As Edna scowled, Mickey's brown eyes lit up, and he grinned at her. He raised his other hand triumphantly.

Gabriel stood there shakily. The two of them were blocking the entire hallway.

"Wooohoo!" Mickey whooped.

Mickey was always merry and loud. He could often be seen clapping and joyously shouting out old Yiddish phrases or emitting ear-shattering whistles. Though primarily wheelchair-bound, he was a stocky, muscular man with arms like a wrestler. Once, in a fit of spasmodic joy, he'd shaken the hand of an LNA so aggressively that he'd accidentally broken her wrist. Mickey didn't appear to remember that incident. It was one of many memories that Alzheimer's had stolen from him.

"Hi there!" Mickey repeated. "It's nice to meet you. My name's Mickey, Mickey Minkovsky. Y'know, like Mickey Mouse!" Mickey squeezed Edna's hand, enthusiastically shaking it up and down.

Edna glared at Gabriel as if blaming him for the situation. Gabriel considered helping her out, but he was worried that Mickey might then try to shake *his* hand, perhaps a bit more enthusiastically than his fragile bones could take.

With his free hand, Mickey clapped his knee and cackled. He gave a whooping shout as if he'd just scored a home run. "So," Mickey said, "will you be my girlfriend?"

Edna gave him her hostile Edna-scowl. "No." She slipped her hand out of his fingers and wheeled forward, snubbing him.

Mickey went in the opposite direction, still laughing and apparently not the least bit disheartened. His flirting was never serious.

Gabriel continued down the hallway, carefully dodging both sets of spinning wheels. Though he had intended to go out for a cigarette, he instead veered toward the front lobby. For once, the area was mostly empty. Jill, the receptionist, was on the phone at her desk, and only two other residents were there.

John Morris, a grim bald fellow from North Wing, was sitting in front of the fish tank in his wheelchair. He stared at the fish, muttering something incoherent and tapping his fingers against his knees in a pattern that was somewhere between chaotic and methodical. He turned his head to glance at Gabriel, revealing frightened eyes with dark circles under them, a tight upper lip, and uneven facial features, clearly the side effects of a stroke. He quickly returned his attention to the fish and resumed his mumbling.

Once again sitting behind the chessboard was the same narrow-faced, thin man with the buggy eyes and the mysterious 7-shaped scar. He wore yet another fabulous black tuxedo, and with his glistening silver hair combed back and his Van Dyke goatee trimmed to perfection, he appeared as debonair as the previous day. He smiled at Gabriel.

"I want to go upstairs," John Morris announced, though he didn't turn from the fish tank. "Pleeeease... please, please, please, I want to go *upstairs.*"

Chessboard man's globe-like eyes glanced over at Morris then returned to Gabriel. There was something oddly *loving* about the man's expression, something that made Gabriel feel as if they'd perhaps known each other once, a long time ago. The man carefully dusted his tuxedo—not that such a lavish, spotless garment needed dusting—then checked a silver pocket watch. Apparently satisfied with the time, the angular man returned to his solo chess game.

Gabriel knew he recognized the man from somewhere. Maybe he had known him back in California. Or perhaps they'd been roommates at some point in the last five years, and he'd forgotten him.

Clearly, if he wanted to find out, he had to make the first move. But that knowledge didn't make his next action any easier. Initiating friendly communication with people had never been one of his strong suits.

Gabriel approached the chessboard, his clunky, three-footed steps jittery with apprehension. He nearly stopped, but finally, he made it to the board. Gabriel cleared his throat. "Hello there."

The man peered up at him. "Why hello, good sir." He smiled, raising one corner of his mouth and revealing a deep dimple in his left cheek. "Care to join me?" His voice, though warm and friendly, was surprisingly raspy, sounding like broken shards of glass rubbing against each other. He had the barest trace of a Spanish accent.

Gabriel sat on the opposite side of the chessboard. The man was staring at him, *studying* him, and he was still smiling the way one smiled at a loved one, a friend, or even a favorite student. Gabriel adjusted his collar self-consciously, and the other man dusted off his coat again.

"It's nice to meet you," Gabriel said. "I'm Gabriel Schist. I've been a resident here for many years, but I came here from—"

"Oh, Gabriel. I know *exactly* who you are." The man's smile spread to both sides of his mouth, like a moving wave. "I think everyone here knows *you.*"

"No, I don't think they do because—"

"Yes, well. To an extent, perhaps. I suppose that very few of us here, other than myself, realize that you're actually the great inventor of the Schist vaccine."

"Hmm." Gabriel noted that the man's response still didn't let him know if they'd ever met before. "So you do know who I am."

"Oh, yes! And I am quite a fan, I must say. But you're correct, Gabriel, to posit that most of the residents here probably don't know that. However, I can assure you that everyone in this facility certainly recognizes you. Out of this vast plethora of colorful characters here at Bright New Day, you're one of the most colorful of all."

"Am I?"

"Why, yes!" The man leaned back in his chair with a giddy, almost childlike satisfaction. "You're the detective, of course! Who doesn't know the detective with his charming old cane and fedora?"

Gabriel smiled. "I see."

"Mr. Schist, my name is Victor. It's a pleasure to finally make your acquaintance. Shall we begin the game?"

Gabriel nodded, and Victor began resetting the chess pieces. Gabriel studied Victor's long, bony fingers, and something occurred to him.

"What's your last name, Victor?" Gabriel asked.

Victor gave him a knowing smile and dusted off his jacket again.

"My apologies. I set up the board without even asking *you* something. Do you wish to play as black or white?"

Gabriel knew Victor had heard him, but the man had chosen not to answer. Gabriel was curious as to why, but he fully understood that sometimes a man's chosen identity could get lost beneath the baggage of his life story, and sometimes, it was easier not to spill all the beans at once.

The stone chess pieces were oversized, specifically made for people with shaky hands. Victor had already placed the white pieces on his own side.

"We'll leave it like this," Gabriel said.

"So I have the white pieces, do I? I suppose that means I move first." Victor confidently moved a pawn forward.

Gabriel opened with his queen's knight. Not wanting to make Victor uncomfortable, he didn't repeat his question or ask more.

From in front of the fish tank, John Morris continued muttering in his louder tone. His skin was covered in sweat, which was often the case, but still, the dampness of his clothes made Gabriel a bit concerned. The man reeked of sweat. Gabriel wondered if John had been given a change in medication.

Morris turned his wheelchair to face the chessboard. He looked at them with a desperate, pleading expression, his bloodshot eyeballs darting back and forth. "I don't... ah... ah... yes, I want. I want."

A small part of Gabriel's mind flashed back to his conversation with the slug then quickly retreated from the idea. They'd gotten a new doctor a few weeks ago, and many of the residents—including Gabriel— had recently undergone minor or major changes in their medications. Medication changes could produce unforeseen side effects, and Morris clearly looked to be exhibiting them.

"Ah... ahhh... please help me. Please, I wanna go... *upstairs*." Morris turned his wheelchair around again to face the fish tank.

Gabriel looked down the corridor. He considered alerting a nurse to Morris's condition, but he was relieved to see that Jill was already keeping a close eye on the man. Victor continued advancing his pawns, keeping his important pieces close to his chest. Gabriel's game was dramatically different; he took more risks. He brought the big guns out early and made their presence known.

"Ohhh," Morris mumbled. "Oh damn... spllasshh... blah... I just want to go upstairs. Upstairs, please, upstairs..."

"Upstairs," Gabriel muttered, shaking his head.

"Interesting, isn't it?" Victor replied, his eyes shimmering with curiosity. "The strange things that dementia patients say, sometimes? I must say, it makes a man wonder."

"Not really," Gabriel scoffed. "Dementia is just the side effect of a rotting brain. That's all there is to it. Upstairs? For God's sake, Bright New Day doesn't even *have* an upstairs."

Victor moved yet another pawn. Gabriel captured the pawn with his rook, realizing a second later that he'd left his knight vulnerable to attack.

"Wanna... wanna... wanna go *upstairs*..." Morris continued.

"Oh yes, that's correct, literally speaking," Victor replied. "This nursing facility has only one floor, yes. However, you're missing the point, Mr. Schist. You're being a bit blockheaded, if you don't mind my saying so." Victor captured Gabriel's knight with his pawn.

Gabriel reached out to move his queen forward to take the pawn but hesitated. "What point?"

"Intriguing questions are raised when one tracks patterns, watches people, and monitors frequent behaviors. Don't you think? And you must realize that I've been around here for a long time, longer than I care to mention. I've seen more people come in and out of these doors than you can imagine. And once you've seen enough Alzheimer's victims, you start to notice... trends."

Gabriel, always rather dubious of unscientific claims, rolled his eyes. "Trends. Hmm."

"No need to be snide." Victor's eyes narrowed, but his smile remained. "Consider this: when a person first comes into the nursing home, there is only one thought on his mind—home. They want to go home. Now. Immediately. They want to escape, like a dog that's been put in the pound."

"Obviously."

Victor moved another pawn forward. "However, once you lock a dog in the pound long enough, that dog will eventually start to give up all hope of escape. The same thing happens when you lock a human being up in a building full of medical equipment. And let's face it, Gabriel, the residents of this nursing home *are* quite trapped. Though perhaps not quite as trapped as those unfortunate souls in the Level Five unit."

Gabriel shuddered. *Level Five.* That was Bright New Day's special locked unit, accessible only to those with the right keys. Level Five was where they kept the residents with especially difficult dementia, the wanderers and the troublemakers. Those were the ones reaching a point where their mental faculties were so compromised that they couldn't be permitted any semblance of a normal life.

"Mr. Schist?" Victor asked.

"Uh... yes. Yes, I'm still here."

"Oh, good. It's a delight to see color return to your eyes." Victor chuckled. "So yes, at first, everyone wants to go home. They plead. They beg. They bargain. Then, toward the end, they give up. And at this point, over and over, I see the same pattern, the same demand. They start begging to be taken *upstairs.*"

"Really?"

"Yes, quite often." Victor leaned back, crossing his arms. "They always want to go upstairs."

"Fascinating." Gabriel scratched his chin. "Perhaps if a study was done, it could—"

"Your move, Gabriel."

Gabriel pondered his next move. He decided on moving the rook. In the background, John Morris was still pleading to go upstairs. *Upstairs.*

"This is such a bizarre place we live in," Victor said. "It does strange things to a man, doesn't it?"

Gabriel sighed. "Maybe. Probably. For instance, my roommate died last night—"

"I'm sorry to hear it."

"No. See, that's my point." Gabriel shook his head. "I'm *not* sorry. I'm not even particularly saddened. *That's* what scares me."

"Is that so?" Victor raised one eyebrow.

Victor made a move. John Morris started coughing.

"Yes," Gabriel continued. "Because when the man sleeping two feet away from me dies and I don't feel any true grief over it, I... there's something deeply wrong about that. I've become desensitized. I can't bring myself to care about death anymore, and that disturbs me."

"Well, you do see the painfully slow, gradual process of death every day. Every single day. How can that not have an effect on you? It would *have* to. A constant process of decay is occurring to everyone in this building, and your extensive medical knowledge makes this even more apparent to you than it is to others. While others see the wrinkles, you know the cause behind the wrinkles."

"Yes. Yes, that's true."

"Besides that, well..." Victor's eyes narrowed. "Death doesn't actually scare you, does it?"

John Morris coughed again, a bit more hoarsely.

"No," Gabriel answered.

"Of course it doesn't," Victor said, leaning forward. "A man like you? No, of course you're not afraid of death. You're afraid of *living*. Living trapped within your body as your mind slowly unravels like a roll of toilet paper. That's your worst nightmare."

Gabriel felt uncomfortably transparent. "Yes. Well..."

"I have to confess something to you, Gabriel. I'm a bit of a snoop. I keep track of all of the medical notes that pass through here, which is highly illegal, but I have my ways."

"Impressive. They won't let me within twenty yards of the medical records."

"Of course not. You're Gabriel Schist, the great immunologist!" Victor grinned. "But yes, after reading your records, I want to ask you something, man to man. Why have you never allowed yourself to be injected with your own vaccine? That just strikes me as a bit odd."

Gabriel fingered one of his pawns. "You're right. I've never been afraid of death. I didn't want something inside my body that would make me *more* immune from it. Maybe I've always had something of a death wish."

"Hurtsss," John Morris muttered. "Kiiiyaa... ssss de ffflllluuuk ... hurts. Hurts. Stomach... hurts. Hurts."

Gabriel shot his gaze toward the receptionist. "What is he—"

"*Hurts!*" Morris shrieked. "Hurts! Hurts! Aaahhhhh!" He clutched his stomach. Then, his ears. His eyes. His scrotum. He couldn't seem to figure out where the pain was coming from. He coughed—a cough full of mucus, just as Robbie's had been—and then he howled in pain again. He started ripping off his clothes.

Gabriel gasped. "Good God." He heard the rapid footsteps of nurses running to the lobby.

"Hurts! Hurts, hurts, huu... hh... hh..." Morris's breathing became hoarse and raspy. He began shaking more violently.

John Morris pushed himself out of his chair. He crashed to the floor, and on the way down, his chinbone cracked hard against the side of the receptionist's desk. Blood splattered across the carpet. He gyrated as if having a seizure. His eyes bulged, and he didn't seem to be able to breathe.

Gabriel trembled. Normally, he could name any illness in seconds. But he had no idea what was wrong with Morris. Unless... unless it was what he'd been warned about in the middle of the night by the talking slug. The Black Virus. He shook his head. That was a hallucination. He was sure of it.

Several nurses rushed over to Morris. He thrashed around, violently throwing them off him. He was fighting desperately and still ripping off his clothing. A deep puddle of sweat appeared on the floor beneath him.

"Code Blue!" a nurse hollered. "Code Blue!"

Morris climbed onto his knees, gasping. He crawled toward the chessboard. His face became paler, turning a ghostly white. His body hair looked frizzled, as if it were ready to fall off in clumps. An eerily dark, oily sweat was dripping off him in buckets.

As Morris lunged forward, Gabriel noticed something utterly bizarre. The man's body was covered in ink-black, bulging veins. The girth of them was as wide as snakes, wriggling across his flesh. They looked capable of bursting from his nearly translucent skin and crawling away.

Suddenly, Morris rolled onto his back, screaming. "Mmmm... spplll... mmmmy eyes!"

The nurses tried in vain to hold him down as Morris frantically clapped his hands over his eyes. Steam rose into the air from beneath his hands, and he started clawing at his eye sockets as if trying to gouge out his eyeballs. He began bashing his head against the floor.

Gabriel got out of his chair and backed away, gripping his chest. His pounding heart felt as if it was moments away from shattering his ribcage.

Three paramedics burst through the front door. The flurry of action resembled a firefight. The nurses moves aside, and the paramedics grabbed Morris's writhing body and strapped him down on a stretcher. They raised the gurney, and on the floor where he'd been smashing his head were a couple of teeth swimming in a puddle of sweat and blood. The stench of urine filled the lobby.

"We need an empty room!" a paramedic shouted.

"What?" a nurse replied. "Aren't you taking him to the hospital?"

"No. We need an empty room for quarantine. Those are direct orders from the hospital. This black veiny shit is going around, and we can't let it spread. Where's an empty room?"

The nurse pointed toward the hall. "North Wing has an open room, but—"

The paramedics shoved the gurney down the corridor in the direction of North Wing. Gabriel, though shaking with fear and confusion, forced himself to take one last look at the scared, sick man as he was wheeled away. Morris looked back at him, and Gabriel understood why the man had been clutching his eyes.

Morris's eyeballs were black. Jet-black. No pupils. No irises. Just two black balls rolling around inside his skull.

The slug was right.

The Black Virus had arrived.

ACT II OF III: SPILLED MILK

"No amount of experimentation can ever prove me right; a single experiment can prove me wrong."

Albert Einstein

CHAPTER 8:
INDIVIDUAL

Autumn 1952

FATHER GARETH PARKED HIS CAR in the gravel driveway. He was surprised that the Schist residence looked so modest, considering Mr. Schist's successful law practice. The one-story shack was located near the coast, right next to a gas station, in an area that looked like a ghost town. Plant life was sparse, the grass was dirty, and scraps of litter rolled down the run-down sidewalk like tumbleweeds.

He cut the lights, got out of the car, and took one last look around, taking a mental photograph as the sunset dropped into the ocean behind him. Though his journeys around the world had taken him to such exotic locations as India, Rome, Moscow, and New Zealand, and though he was an obsessive reader of philosophy, science journals, and even just good old paperback novels, the simple, natural pleasures delighted him the most: the sun, the stars, the smiles of people he helped.

He loved visiting members of his congregation, though he suspected, with some amusement, that many people weren't sure how to take *him*. Standing at nearly six foot two, with slender, gangly limbs, enormous hands, and a Merlin-like brown beard that trailed down to his stomach, Gareth resembled either a philosopher or a medieval wizard.

Gareth walked up to the porch and rang the bell. Marilyn Schist answered the door, clad in a polka-dotted summer dress, a white apron, and heels. Add in her tight red curls, light makeup over her pale, freckled skin, and the way her eye shadow emphasized her big eyes, she could have stepped off the set of *I Love Lucy*. Her chewed fingernails were the only crack in the perfect mold.

She moved to give him a hug but quickly corrected herself and instead offered him a one-armed embrace that more befitted her housewife image. The top of her head only reached the center of Gareth's chest. "Oh, Father Gareth! I'm so happy you could make it. We really appreciate your help with our... dilemma. Our dear little boy has been acting so strange lately. I don't know what's got into him."

"My pleasure." Gareth chuckled. "And you look marvelous, dear. I did my best to prepare. Hopefully, my beard isn't too long today?"

Her brow furrowed in confusion. Gareth shrugged. His bizarre sense of humor was often more for his amusement than anyone else's.

"Well, come inside," she said. "We're having a wonderful dinner tonight."

Gareth followed her into the immaculate living room, which was furnished with a mathematically precise arrangement of three loveseats around a circular coffee table. Beautiful paintings of sailboats, lighthouses, and rocky beaches adorned the rose-colored walls. The liquor cabinet was filled with a barroom's assortment of drinks. There was no clutter, no stains, and every surface was polished to a glistening sheen. The contrast to the dirty, run-down outside of the house was disconcerting, like leftovers that had been reheated and served as the main course. Marilyn rushed off to the kitchen and disappeared behind the swinging door, leaving him with her husband, Henry, who was sitting on one of the loveseats. Holding a tumbler of what appeared to be bourbon in one hand, Henry glared down at an enormous stack of paperwork. Clean-shaven, with slicked-back dark hair and a dimple in the center of his chin, Henry had the handsome features of a movie star.

Gareth tipped his hat. "Greetings, sir."

Henry removed his reading glasses and stood to shake Gareth's hand. "Hello, Father. How do you do?"

"Quite well. And yourself?"

"Busy." He gulped the remainder of his drink. "My apologies for dragging you here tonight, Father, but we could use the help." Henry poured himself another drink. He seemed preoccupied, continually glancing back at the paperwork. "My son, Gabriel... he's proving to be quite the challenge."

During the war, Henry had been in the Navy, and he possessed the distinct deep, stony voice that seemed reserved for grizzled military veterans. Though he rarely wore anything but a cold grey business suit, he had a certain roughness to him. He moved like a knife, with hard gestures and no fidgeting, unconsciously revealing the sharp corners of the New York street kid he'd once been. With his sleeves rolled up, his biceps tattoos occasionally peeked out.

"So where is the little fellow?" Gareth asked.

"In his room. He rarely leaves it."

Marilyn emerged from the kitchen with a platter of cheese and crackers. She sat beside her husband and eyed his drink with a worried expression. She began to chew at a hangnail then quickly lowered her hands into her lap. "We really do appreciate your company, Father," Marilyn said. "We're not just inviting you here to sort out our problems."

Henry looked up at him apologetically and gulped down the rest of his drink. "Ah yes, Father. I'm sorry to be so demanding of your time."

"No, don't worry. It's fine." Gareth laughed. "Hit me with your worst. Trust me, after some of the confessions I've heard, nothing shocks me anymore."

"We're at our wit's end." Marilyn sighed. "We can't figure out what to do about poor little Gabe! We hoped you could talk some sense into him, Father."

Gabe. Though Gareth had only met the boy a handful of times, he knew that Gabriel hated being called Gabe. "Gabriel has always seemed a very bright young man. What is the problem?"

"He doesn't talk," Marilyn said. "He's quiet as a mouse, Father. He doesn't play games, doesn't like eating, doesn't make any friends at school. The poor boy just sits in his messy room all day like an invalid. He's always doing odd things, reading strange books, writing stuff down, muttering to himself. He never likes going outside—"

"He likes sailing," Henry interrupted. "He and I go out on the boat every few weeks. He gets a big smile on his face when he's out there, looking out at the horizon."

"And that's about the *only* time he smiles." Marilyn scrunched up

61

her nose. "And furthermore, even then, he doesn't *talk.* He always wants to be alone. And it's not like he's doing schoolwork. I mean, his grades are—"

"Abysmal." Henry snuck in yet another glass of bourbon. "He doesn't even do the work."

Marilyn nodded. "He just does all this crazy stuff instead. Writing all the time, pinning his work on the walls. It's a bunch of nonsense I can't even look at without crying in confusion."

Gareth had always felt an odd connection to the boy. He'd noticed a startlingly mature intensity in Gabriel's grey eyes, something darker than a shadow, yet glowing at the same time, and he'd often wondered what was going on in that little head. "Well, let's go see him, eh?"

With noticeable hesitation, the couple got up and led him down the short hall off the living room then stopped at a door on the left. The fidgeting, nervous way the pair tiptoed up to Gabriel's door made it seem as if they were the children, approaching a feared parent.

"This is it," Henry whispered. "Now, Father, we have to be calm and quiet as we go in. He doesn't like being interrupted when he's working. It throws him off balance." Henry's tone held a surprising note of admiration.

"He's studying?"

"He's doing *something.* He doesn't share much with us."

Have you ever ASKED him to share it? Gareth nodded. "I'll be quiet."

They opened the door and entered the room. Compared to the sparkling, flawless, spit-shined majority of the house, Gabriel's room was a pigsty. Lord, that boy was messy.

But the mess wasn't chaotic. While some clothes were on the floor and the bed was unmade, the majority of the clutter was caused by notebooks, graphs, and drawings. The entire room was covered in a landscape of dead trees, used pens, and broken pencils. Almost every inch of the walls was masked by tacked-up sheets of lined paper, index cards, and sticky notes covered from top to bottom in Gabriel's distinct boyish handwriting.

"Where did he get *that?*" Gareth whispered, pointing at the enormous green chalkboard hanging on the far wall.

"He asked for it," Henry replied. "Probably the only Christmas present Gabe has *ever* asked for."

Gabriel, a scrawny, freckled eleven-year-old with bright-red hair and clothes just a bit too big for him, stood before the blackboard, scrawling on it with a stubby piece of chalk.

Gareth gasped when he noticed that the entire chalkboard was covered with unbelievably complex-looking equations and scientific notes. There were terms that he could never even hope to understand.

"Gabe!" Marilyn called. "Come say hello!"

Gabriel froze then put down the chalk and turned around to face them. At first, his face was blank, but after several tense seconds, he smiled—a forced smile, Gareth noted. "Oh." He glanced back at the blackboard then picked at tiny calluses on his fingers.

"Don't be so rude, Gabe," Marilyn scolded. "Father Gareth came all this way to see you. The least you can do is say hello to the man."

"Hi, Father Gareth," Gabriel said. "I don't mean to be, um... rude. It's just... I was studying."

"It's okay." Gareth laughed. "Looks like a complicated project you got there, eh?"

"Yes." Gabriel raised his head and gave him a hopeful look unlike any expression he had ever seen on a child. He wasn't the cold, emotionless boy that his parents had so vividly painted a picture of. He was a lonely, desperately passionate boy who struggled to translate his emotions into a language that others could understand.

"Gabriel," Gareth said, "can you show me your work?"

Gabriel's eyes lit up. "Really? Right now? You mean—"

"Father Gareth," Henry said, "I appreciate the gesture. But really, you don't need to entertain such fantasies when—"

Gabriel lowered his head and dug his hands into his pockets.

Gareth chuckled. "No, I'd like to see it."

Gabriel looked at his parents. "Dad, Mom, can I? Can I show you, too? All of you?"

"Us?" Marilyn asked.

"Yes." The boy nodded. "If you don't mind."

"That's... um... yes, son," Henry said. "I suppose we can all see it."

Gabriel jumped back to the blackboard with the kind of enthusiasm that most boys reserved for sports and girls. Henry and Marilyn nervously moved closer together, as if watching a bomb drop from the sky.

Gabriel gestured at the board. "I want to study the cognitive potential of the immune system."

Henry frowned. "Cogni... immune... what?"

Gabriel jabbed a finger toward a graph on the board. "I just had this idea, a few months ago, and every part of the immune system... For example, you see those notes on the top?" He pointed at some writing. "About lymphocytes and antigen presentation? Y'know, where the B cells and T cells go out and identify a foreign object? I've been thinking, if the primary function of these lymphocytes is to—hold on." He picked up the chalk and began writing on the board again.

Gareth watched him with fascination. The boy sounded more like a professor than an eleven-year-old child.

Henry cleared his throat. "That's all very interesting, Gabriel, but—"

"Isn't it? This is what I want to do with my life, Dad! I want to advance the immune system. I want to test the idea of the immune system being a kind of cognitive system. A second brain." Gabriel pointed at the upper left corner of the board. "See? If you look right there, it explains it all pretty quick." He glanced over his shoulder. "No, not that part you're looking at. That section is about the collective nature of ant colonies compared to the nature of the human brain." He stretched out his arm and tapped the board. "Look at *this* part."

Henry squinted at the board. His wife nibbled on a fingernail, while Gareth took a step closer, trying to make some sense of what he was seeing.

Gabriel nodded. "Yes, the notes to the left of that! See them? That explains it better than I can, but basically, just imagine that the immune system is a machine, a network of processes of production. Transformation and destruction. It's really cool. Imagine that instead of defining existence as—"

"Oh my God!" Marilyn cried. "I thought you were insane, but no. Gabe, you're amazing. I was so worried, but now I understand. You're a genius. The next Einstein. This brilliance is a miracle, a gift from God."

Gabriel frowned. His hands disappeared into his pockets. He glanced at Gareth apologetically and then announced, "I don't believe in God."

Standing there during the awkward vacuum that followed his statement was like undergoing a silent root canal. As Henry and Marilyn's smoldering glares melted through Gabriel's resolve, the boy's head dropped, and he returned to his blackboard. Though Gareth insisted that their son had not offended him, Henry ushered Gareth back into the living room and poured them glasses of bourbon as Marilyn hurried back to the kitchen.

Dinner was awkward. All conversation revolved around current events, and Gabriel didn't utter a word or eat more than a few bites. After they had eaten, Gareth asked if he could have a word alone with the boy. Marilyn shot to her feet then sat back down with a shudder. Henry nodded and spread his hands out as if to say, "What could it hurt?"

Gabriel led the way back down the hallway. Gareth smiled at the sight of their shadows on the wall. A tall, gangly scarecrow strolled beside a short, big-headed child. In Gabriel's room, Gareth's gaze lingered on the blackboard. He pulled a chair close and sat on it backward. Gabriel perched on his bed, staring down at his swinging feet.

"That was some impressive stuff earlier," Gareth said.

Gabriel didn't look up. "Oh."

"Why so glum?"

"'Cause..." The boy hesitated then spoke in a shy whisper. "'Cause you're not here to talk to me about what I like. You're just gonna tell me it's bad and that I shouldn't do it. Like everybody else says."

"Well, that's not what I'm going to say."

Gabriel gave him a dubious look. "You're a priest. You're just here to—"

"I'm here to be your *friend,* Gabriel. I'm here to talk to you and to help you achieve your goals. And this stuff you're doing, all of this immune system business, don't let anyone ever tell you that it's bad."

Gabriel's grey eyes were intent and filled with both hope and worry. "Really?"

"Really." Gareth grinned. "Frankly, I think the stuff you're studying is absolutely beautiful. I can tell that you think so, too."

Gabriel laughed, and a blush rose into his cheeks. "Why does no one else think so?"

"Because your ideas are quite different, Gabriel. You're a unique

65

kid. Special. I have a pretty darn good feeling that you're going to be somebody very important someday."

"Huh? What about me is so special?"

"Your mind, that's what! You have an amazing mind, Gabriel. And someday, mark my words, that mind? It's going to change the world."

CHAPTER 9:
RESIDUAL

Spring 2018

THOUGH THE ONSET OF THE Black Virus was unexpected, Gabriel wasn't surprised by the aftermath. He'd seen it all before, back during the AIDS epidemic in the '80s. If there was one thing that the bureaucrats knew how to do, it was cover their asses.

On the news that morning, he had seen headlines about foreign relations, an important new bill in Congress, and another spike in the national debt. They had shown nothing about the new virus, and his intuition told him that the government was carefully keeping the news from going viral to avoid a nationwide panic.

Five days had passed since John Morris had flipped out in the lobby. The nurses were saying nothing, and they avoided answering Gabriel's questions. Men in black suits came into the building, and the staff was forced to sign a confidentiality agreement, probably under threat of lawsuit, loss of licensure, and a long list of other consequences if a leak occurred. From what he could gather, the document stated that John Morris's illness would be referred to as a case of influenza.

A few people had already quit. Even so, they'd still signed the forms. They had to.

Four days ago, the government sent in its top specialists. They disguised themselves as everyday doctors so that the residents wouldn't be alarmed, but Gabriel could spot those young government immunologists, virologists, and pathologists, fresh out of school and eager to prove themselves, from a mile away. They took blood and tissue samples and sent them back to their labs.

After that, the doctors stopped trying to cure John Morris. The virus had proven stubbornly resistant to antibiotics, time, prayer, and everything else the doctors had thrown at it. Morris was confined to his room, with no visits from anyone but the nursing staff or approved doctors. The nurses were ordered to load him up with morphine, and that was the extent of the treatment. Clearly, the government had decided that there was nothing they could do for John Morris except keep him away from others.

Gabriel knew what they were thinking. Morris was old, so he was going to die soon, anyway. There was no sense wasting time, money, and resources on a person like that. That line of reasoning disgusted him to no end, but he knew how the system worked. A cover-up was always preferable to mass panic. Everyone liked to keep their hands clean.

Unfortunately, the spread had already begun. Yesterday morning, another resident had been hit with the virus—Rebecca Holzweiss, of West Wing. She and John Morris often sat together in the lobby, sometimes holding hands, so Gabriel didn't find her infection too surprising. She was now also quarantined in her room, for all the good that accomplished.

Gabriel shook his head. In a building where the majority of the residents wandered the halls from sunrise to sunset—touching the same items, using the same silverware, and sometimes even sharing the same bathrooms—he highly doubted the virus could be contained.

They kept Morris's room guarded, but even guards needed to take a break, if only for emergency bathroom trips. Gabriel had been standing at the corner of the hallway, ostensibly staring at a yellow birdfeeder outside the window but actually keeping an eye on Morris's door. When the nurse on duty, Dana Kleznowski, hurried out of the room, he stayed still and gazed forward in a fake glassy-eyed stupor. Dana raced past him and cut left down the hallway, and the bathroom door clicked shut behind her.

As soon as she disappeared behind the door, Gabriel shuffled down the hall to Morris's room. He cracked open the door and cautiously peered inside. The lights were off, and the odors of rubbing alcohol, blood, and decay wafted out.

Morris lay in the bed, hooked up to an IV and a feeding tube. A catheter bag dangled beside the mattress. The disgusting maze of black veins covering his skin occasionally throbbed, and every time it did, Morris let out a short, gasping breath that sounded like rocky sand passing through a metal pipe. But the eyes–those horrifying, satanic-looking balls of coal—were the worst part. Whenever Morris blinked, his eyeballs slithered.

"Hey, Detective!" Dana Kleznowski shouted down the hall.

Gabriel jumped a little and stepped back from the door. Dana was a cute twenty-seven-year-old LPN with obsessive-compulsive nail-biting habits, a willowy figure, and what might be anemia. She ran over and closed the door. Her round freckled face was flushed red.

"Dude." She touched his shoulder. "It's nice to see ya, but what are you doing up on North?"

He shrugged. "Observing."

"Um, yeah. You know that we're not supposed to let anyone near that poor guy's room, right? And I don't want *you* getting infected with that crap, too."

"Understandable. I'll go, then."

He retreated back to South Wing. He tried to keep his feet on solid ground while his mind reached up to the clouds. He had to remain balanced, fair, and logical. He had plenty of thinking to do.

CHAPTER 10:
COILS

"YOU WERE RIGHT," GABRIEL SAID.

The lights were dimmed in Bright New Day's front lobby. Gabriel was the only person in the room, and he stood before one of the bay windows, staring at the tumbling waves of the inaccessible beach below.

"Good," the slug said. "If you don't mind me saying so, it's about time you came around to the truth."

Gabriel rested his forehead on the cool glass, right next to where the leopard-printed slug had affixed itself. The half-moon painted a radiant white line across the ocean. Clouds threatened to overtake the moon, but its colorless light burned through them.

"Gabriel?" The slug wriggled its black antennas.

Gabriel glanced at it. While he had been staring out the window, the slug had been joined by a small group of friends, six of them, all different colors and sizes. Gabriel considered getting a nurse and testing to see if other people saw or heard the slugs, but he decided that would be too risky. *Oh, poor Mr. Schist. You're hallucinating? Maybe we should book you a room on Level Five.*

"Is he even listening?" an albino slug whispered, shaking its white faceless head.

"Oh, he always listens," Leopard Print replied. "He just doesn't always *reply*. Isn't that correct, Gabriel?"

"I swear, he's not listening."

"Don't doubt the Schist man," an inky black slug said. "He'll make the right choices. You'll see."

Gabriel narrowed his eyes. "Yes, I can hear you. Unfortunately."

"Unfortunately!" The black slug chortled. "Look at 'im go. That Schist man cracks me up."

Gabriel's knees jittered, and he leaned heavily on his cane. Two weeks had passed since the first incident of the Black Virus, and it was gaining traction. So far, there were six cases within the walls of Bright New Day. Strict quarantine was being enforced on all of them, and they weren't letting any residents off the premises. A white van had been sitting outside the nursing home since John Morris got hit, and Gabriel suspected that it wasn't going anywhere. He checked the news daily, and so far, there had still been no coverage.

The sixth case had occurred only a few hours ago. The new victim, a tiny old lady with a long chin and a frizzy perm, had been carried through the halls on a stretcher. Her name was Joan Michaels, but that didn't matter anymore; the Black Virus robbed a person of their identity. All personal quirks and mannerisms disappeared. Once the violent initial reaction was done, she became the same bedbound zombie as the others. No one had actually died yet, but Gabriel imagined that the first death wasn't far off.

"Look, he's obviously not paying a lick of attention to us," the albino slug said. "He's just staring out the window again."

"He's thinking," Leopard Print replied. Gabriel was coming to respect the slug's serenity. "Gabriel is an introverted thinking type. What do you expect?"

"No. Look how dazed he is. Look how milky his eyes are."

"He's in there," a yellow-spotted slug said. "He's always in there. He's a genius, remember?"

"Yeah, a genius. Ooookay." Albino groaned.

"I'm here," Gabriel said. "I'm listening. I've been trying to get answers about this virus. I've been asking all of the nurses, and no one gives me a straight story because they've been ordered to call it a goddamn *flu*. Tell me, what the hell do you expect me to do?"

The slugs stopped moving around. They'd left slimy trails across the glass. All of their antennas turned up to him.

"Whoa," Albino said.

"Gabriel, my friend," Leopard Print said, "we'd all prefer that you

71

don't feign ignorance here. You're far too intelligent to pull it off. You know exactly what you must do."

Gabriel arched an eyebrow. "Do I? And, pray tell, why do a bunch of alien slugs care so much about humanity?"

Leopard Print inched closer. "You have to combat this Black Virus. You must—"

"Combat?" Albino laughed, its tone reminiscent of a troublemaking high school student. "Ha! C'mon. You make it sound like he's picking up a sword and slaying a dragon. Combat. Yeeeeesh."

"Go on," Gabriel told Leopard Print. "And the rest of you keep quiet. Especially you"—he pointed—"the white one."

Leopard Print crawled closer and raised its antennas. "Yes, Gabriel. As I said, you must combat the Black Virus. Research it with whatever tools are at your disposal. We want to protect humanity from this outbreak, but in order to stop the Black Virus, we need your help."

"Help? How am I supposed to help stop a virus?"

"Because you are the one who created the HIV vaccine."

"Yes, but that was a long time ago. I'm not that man anymore."

"You're still Gabriel Schist, aren't you? You're the Nobel Prize-winning creator of the Schist Vaccine, the only man in the world who has the astonishing brain needed to solve this problem. Should I go on?"

Feeling thirsty, Gabriel stepped back and glanced at the water cooler. He didn't want to look outside anymore since the moon had finally been overtaken by the clouds. "Pardon my French, but this is absolute bullsh—"

"There's no need to be coarse."

"This is bullshit. Listen, slug. In case you aren't yet aware, I have a degenerative disease. A cognitive disorder that has filled my brain with more holes than a wedge of Swiss cheese. I can't..." Gabriel's heart rate had gone ballistic. He took several deep, calming breaths and plopped down in the nearest armchair. He reached over and took a tiny paper cup from the top of the water cooler then filled it. When he took a drink, he found the temperature to be nauseatingly warm. It was pathetically unsatisfying. What he really needed was a beer.

"I'm sorry." He refilled his cup. "I honestly wish I could do something. But I'm not capable of doing what you want me to do. You might as well ask any of the nutcases on the Level Five unit to handle test tubes, for all the good that I can do."

"That's not true. You're far more capable than you feel you are."

"Feel?" Gabriel snorted. "Feelings are irrelevant here. No, I'm actually far *less* capable than I think I am. Just this morning, I walked out of my room with my shirt on backwards."

"Stop berating yourself. Self-debasement is an utterly narcissistic waste of time, and due to the nature of your particular mental disease, we don't have much time to waste, now do we? So listen, Gabriel. I'm going to put this in terms you can better understand. We're not favoring you out of any particular fondness. We aren't some fan club. The fact is, you are the only one who can help."

The other slugs all nodded in agreement.

"Why me? Why should I have to deal with something like this, at this point in my life?"

"Why you? Because it is what the great Sky Amoeba has asked of you, that's why. It's the task you have been given. The Sky Amoeba—"

"Let's not talk about this Sky Amoeba. I'll talk about this virus, but discussions of extraterrestrial single-celled organisms are off the table." He took another sip of the tepid water. "Tell me, why is this Black Virus here, anyhow? What causes it? Does it come from whatever place you things come from?"

"That's for you to find out."

"Oh, thank you so much, slugs. I don't know what I'd do without all your help." He pushed the round blue button and refilled his cup for the third time. His hand trembled so violently that he almost dropped the cup, and drops of warm water sprinkled onto his shirt.

"In the end, it's your choice," Leopard Print said. "If you don't help us, then everything will be lost. But that's up to you, Gabriel. The decision is yours to make."

Gabriel dropped the cup, and it landed upright on the carpet, like an injured soldier refusing to fall down. Just when Gabriel thought it might survive, it tipped over, and water spilled onto the floor.

CHAPTER 11:
LUMINESCENT

Summer, 1974.

STANDING ON THE SHORELINE OF Santa Barbara, California, a completely naked young woman laughed in exultation. Skipping to the top of a colossal rock overlooking the ocean, she spread her arms, closed her eyes, and smiled. She was ready to fly. Back in Wyoming, she'd been Amy Green, but in her new life, she'd rechristened herself as Yvonne Anastasia Luciana. She was alone and completely independent, and from that point on, the beach was *hers*.

The vibrant red sunset was like a rush of blood, life, and power. The sky's beating heart, that glorious golden orb, channeled energy right into her body. She spread out each unpainted finger and toe, feeling the wind brushing against every nerve ending in her skin and throwing her tangled brown dreadlocks behind her. In the darkening light, the beach looked black, and the waves looked white.

Yvonne called out to a passing flock of seagulls, "Get ready, California!" She laughed with unrestrained joy. "I'm here!"

California! It was unbelievable. Back home in Wyoming, everyone had always told her that her aspirations were impossible. When she'd started studying for a degree in interpretative dance, her friends had told her to give up. When she'd told them about her dream of living in Santa Barbara, they'd told her that she was high—an ironic statement, considering that while she studied and practiced, all of them were busy wasting their nights away on plastic bags filled with addictive substances.

Way off in the white ocean, she spotted three tiny black silhouettes.

The surfers seemed as unaware of her existence as she had been of theirs. Yvonne smiled. She'd been there almost a full day, and the only person she'd met was her new landlord, Mr. Brown. If she planned on sticking around, she might as well get to know the locals.

Yvonne stepped down from her perch on the rock. The soft sand felt heavenly under her bare feet. She reached down into her knitted bag, which was mostly full of mouthwatering Santa Barbara oranges, and pulled out her white-and-blue-patterned beach wrap. It was a little bit revealing; her mother certainly wouldn't have approved. If one thing had carried over from her rebellious adolescence, other than her dreadlocks and vegetarian eating habits, it was an utter lack of self-consciousness. Besides, seeing the guys ogle her would be fun. It always was.

She strolled over to where the little surfers were surfing their hearts out. Just a little ways down the beach, she found their stuff: clothes, towels, flip-flops, and a cooler full of beer. All of it had been casually left there with no worries that anyone would take it. That sort of laid-back trust thrilled her. It was exactly what she'd hoped to find in California.

The sun was going down, so they'd come back to the beach soon. She sat down beside their belongings, crossing her legs and holding her bag on her lap. She tied back her dreads and put on her sunglasses so she could watch them. One surfer in particular was especially talented. His arms were steady, his legs like powerful tree trunks on the board. He rode the waves like a professional. Maybe he *was* a professional. *That might be interesting...*

Eventually, the three surfers returned to the shoreline, unzipping their black wetsuits as they waddled up the beach. *Her* surfer, perfectly enough, was in the middle. As the other two hopped around, playing and punching each other in the shoulders, the professional surfer walked ahead with a steady, measured gait, whistling a cheerful little tune that she didn't recognize.

The descending sun's glare was in their eyes, so none of them had seen her yet. The professional surfer's friends seemed okay. The one on the left, a hyperactive fellow with curly hair, bounced around like a frenetic ball of energy. The one on the right, a wiry guy with hunched shoulders and a scraggly beard, looked a bit anxious, twitchy, and unsure of himself.

The professional surfer was gorgeous. A little older than she was, he was thin but athletic, with just the tiniest hint of a washboard stomach. He had wavy red hair, broad shoulders, tan skin, a strong neck, and thick chest hair. One of his friends said something, and he replied with a wonderfully hearty, infectious laugh.

"Hey, guys!" she called. "Want an orange?"

The men stopped and stared at her, all three doing a double-take. They continued walking, more slowly, each man fixing his wet hair, sucking in his stomach, and trying to appear more confident. She felt the energy of their eyes follow every curve of her body like little magnets.

"C'mon." Yvonne laughed. "Don't be shy. The oranges in this place are amazing. And I know you guys must be starving, especially after all that crazy surfing you were doing out there."

She reached down into her bag, pulled out an orange, and tossed it to the curly-haired guy. The next one went to the anxious boy. She waited a bit, just long enough to make him worry, then tossed a third orange to the surfer.

"Thanks!" Curly Hair said.

"Yeah, wow, this is gnarly!" The anxious one had already started peeling the orange with his teeth.

The good-looking one casually turned the orange in his hand. He looked up at her with a surprisingly shy smile then quickly lowered his gaze. "Thanks."

"You're welcome." Yvonne took off her sunglasses and beamed at him.

He jumped a little, twitching almost as if he'd been electrocuted. She pulled out a fourth orange and began peeling it slowly. Sensually.

A sudden breeze smacked her in the face, and she accidentally spilled the contents of her bag. The remaining oranges tumbled out and rolled across the sand. Her half-peeled orange dropped into her lap.

She laughed and threw her hands up in the air. "Oops! And they're gone with the wind."

The surfer chuckled, but his gaze remained concentrated on the orange in his hands.

Curly leapt forward and began scooping up the oranges. "That's okay." He grinned. "It happens." He put the oranges into her bag.

"Guess the secret's out. Yeah, I'm kind of a klutz."

"Don't worry!" Curly crossed his arms. "So what's your name, pretty lady?"

"I'm Yvonne. I'm new to the area."

"Well, hey, Yvonne. Welcome to our humble home." Curly clapped his hands. "My name's Chris, Chris Peele. This guy with the beard is my roommate, Phil, and this guy"—he pointed at the handsome surfer— "is my good buddy Gabe."

"Gabriel," the handsome one mumbled, though Chris didn't appear to hear him. Gabriel stared at the ground and offered her an awkward wave.

Gabriel. She liked that name. She tilted her head. "Wow, it's pretty thrilling to meet such skilled surfers on my first day here. You guys are great."

Chris nodded. "We're awesome, I know. You're a pretty lovely lady yourself, though."

"Yeah, real pretty," Phil added, blushing.

Gabriel said nothing, which meant he was a challenge. She *loved* challenges.

"So, boys, what do you all do, *other* than surfing?" She kept her eyes squarely on her target, who had peeled the orange in a perfect spiral.

When the other two said nothing, apparently realizing where her attention was focused, Gabriel looked up at her. He dug one foot into the sand and smiled that lovely embarrassed smile of his again. "Wow," he said, chuckling nervously. "We like to have fun, I guess. We try to do exciting things. Surfing, roller coasters, skydiving, that sort of stuff. We drink a lot. Throw parties. Smoke pot sometimes. Mainly just drinking, though."

Yvonne laughed. The guy was a terrible liar. He'd said all of that as if he were listing off bullet points for a test. "What else?" she asked.

He shrugged. "Nothing much."

"C'mon, dude," Chris said. "Yvonne, honey, don't listen to this guy. He's being shy. This dude here, my buddy? He's smart as a fuckin' whip."

"Oh?" Yvonne raised an eyebrow.

"Yeah, he is! Gabe here, he's a li'l bit older since he started late, but he's taking classes to be, uh... some kinda scientist, right?"

"Sure." Gabriel lowered his gaze, tearing loose a section of his orange and eating it. "Yes, I'm studying immunology, virology, and applied mathematics. I have a—"

"He wants to cure a disease that *doesn't even exist yet!* How cool is that, huh?"

"Um, yes, I believe that we're inches away from the beginning of a new epidemic, and I want to halt it in its tracks. So as a result... well, okay, so I have a special interest in a concept called autopoiesis."

Yvonne could barely contain her glee. "Autopoiesis, huh?" The surfer-turned-scientist had instantaneously jumped from a fun fling to a potential soul mate.

Though the other two boys had sat across from Yvonne on the sand, the scientist was still awkwardly stepping back and forth as if he'd missed his opportunity to sit with them. "Do you know of it?" he asked.

"Nope. Tell me?"

"Oh." He shrugged. "Well, autopoiesis is a complex idea."

"So? I'm always up for gaining new knowledge. What interests you about it?"

"I want to figure out how I can apply the concept to modern medicine." His eyes lit up with enthusiasm. "I've been studying the immune system since I was a kid. It's fascinating stuff. I'm more than ready to get the ball moving on my research, but without the proper funding that would be available to me if I had the right degree—" He suddenly stopped speaking.

She wondered why until she looked at the faces of his two friends. Their expressions were bored, and they were obviously completely uninterested. They admired his talents, but they didn't want to actually hear about his boring subject. Yvonne resisted the urge to snap at them for making him feel bad, just as her friends in Wyoming had always done to her. Even though she'd just met him, she felt intensely protective toward him.

"But mainly I just like drinking," he said, smiling weakly. "Having a good time, partying, getting drunk." He reached down into the cooler for a can of Budweiser, popped it open, and took a big swig. "Yeah."

But he didn't fool her. She'd seen behind his shield. There he was, a man with a fiery passion, and no one wanted to listen. No one understood. He was alone. She knew exactly what he felt like.

"Well, hey," she said, standing. "I have to run, guys. Sorry. But before I go..." She pulled a notepad and a pen out of her bag and wrote down her new number. She tore off the slip of paper and handed it to Gabriel. "Give me a call sometime." She touched his bare arm. "I want to hear more about your studies."

His face lit up like a rising sun. She spun and hurried away, laughing and letting her beach wrap trail behind her like a cape. She knew the two other boys would probably think she was insane. They wouldn't understand. But the other one just might.

She stopped to look back. Gabriel was looking at her as if she was the most beautiful, most amazing thing he'd ever seen in his life.

"Hey!" she called out. "*Mr. Scientist*, sir! When can I expect to hear from you?"

He grinned. "I'll call you tomorrow."

CHAPTER 12: DISSONANCE

Spring 2018

THE ROOMS OF THE INFECTED were flagged. Their closed doors were marked with a simple black circle cut from black construction paper and affixed with scotch tape. No one explained the circle or even talked about it, but everyone fully understood what it represented.

Since his conversation with the slugs, Gabriel had spent the last hour wandering the darkened corridors of the nursing home until his knees felt rusty and broken. The hallway lights went off at nine thirty, as usual, and the halls took on a dark, ghostly appearance. Most of the other residents were in bed, and those that wandered at night, like him, weren't communicative.

Growing tired of his restless search for a cognitive lightning bolt, he returned to South Wing. *Tap. Tap.* He walked by Bob Baker's room and glanced inside.

Baker had a blanket pulled up over his face and was busy shouting at the imaginary voices in his head. "Nooooope! I'm tellin' you this for the third time. I don't want no goddamn third pillow. Noooope!"

As Gabriel passed Edna's room, he was startled by a feeble, piercing cry.

"Mommmmyyy... Mommmyyy... please, Mommmmmyyy..." Edna had thrown her wrinkly white legs over the side of her bed. Her eyes were milky-colored moons, devoid of their usual intensity. The nighttime cries were common behavior for Edna. Her cognitive issues always worsened in the late hours, a tendency among dementia patients that the nurses referred to as sundowning. Gabriel looked over his shoulder, but he didn't see any LNAs to flag down.

"Mommmyyy. I'm gonna miss the school bus, Mommy."

He considered helping her back into bed, but with all the nurses on pins and needles over the virus, going into a woman's room at night would only get him in trouble. He went back down the blue corridor, took a left turn, and almost ran into Tanya, a tall, athletically built LNA from Jamaica. She had wood-brown eyes, dark hair pulled into a tight bun, and cheekbones cut from granite. He pointed down the hall.

"Edna again?" she asked.

"Yes."

"Thanks, Detective." She went down the hall and disappeared around the corner.

Gabriel sighed and slumped against the wall outside the Crooner's room. He rubbed his crumbly, cottage-cheese-feeling knees. He was ready to lay his head on a pillow. He'd close his eyes in real life, open them in his dreams, and block out the sound of the Crooner's nighttime singsong routine.

Wait. Why isn't the Crooner singing?

A dreadful thought slunk down from his mind, plummeted down his throat, and knotted up his intestines. He hadn't heard the Crooner sing that day, not once. He couldn't recall if the man had sung last night, either.

He put his ear to the wall. Not a single "la-la-la" could be heard. Maybe the Crooner was actually sleeping for once, or perhaps he'd gone out with his family for the weekend.

Then he noticed the black circle taped to the Crooner's door, next to the nametag reading "Matthew Lecroix." Gabriel squeezed the handle of his cane as his legs nearly buckled. Peering around to make sure no one was watching, he cracked open the door. The room was almost pitch black.

Entering the room would be stupid and dangerous. He could have some of his privileges revoked, or worse, he might get infected. He was pretty sure the virus wasn't airborne, but close contact was risky. He looked down the empty hallway again. Tanya was in Edna's room, and Natty, the other LNA on duty, was taking her break in the communal kitchen. His curiosity was red hot, and the ridiculous harassment of the slugs had only intensified it. If old Father Gareth had still been alive, he would've cheered him on.

Go for it, Gabriel. He slipped into the dark room. His violently beating heart rose into his throat, where his Adam's apple caught and retained it before it could go any farther. He took a deep breath, walked over to the bureau, and switched on a lime-green Tyrannosaurus lamp. The Crooner's bed was surrounded on all sides by an opaque blue curtain.

"Hello?" Gabriel whispered. "Matthew?"

Gabriel inched forward, tapping his cane as quietly as possible. His stomach sank deeper into his abdomen with every step. *C'mon, Matthew. Be okay. Be alive.* He pulled back the curtain. Gabriel stared into the Crooner's black eyes, and his legs trembled. After a few seconds, he looked away, swallowed the acid reflux in his throat, and then turned back.

Matthew was lying on his back in a johnny gown, breathing in sputtered gasps. He had the same ghostly pallor to his skin as the other victims, as well as the rope-like black veins winding through his body as if they were living creatures instead of desecrated blood-pumping vessels. He wore an oxygen mask, a feeding tube, and a catheter.

Well, a few things were different. Unlike other victims of the Black Virus, all of Matthew's hair had fallen out to the point where his body, what Gabriel could see of it, was as bald as a naked mole rat. The other victims had been greasy, but Matthew's skin appeared dryer than sandpaper and crusty, as if his epidermis would rub off with minimal pressure. His fingers were bright purple where all of the blood had collected in the tips.

"I'm sorry, Matthew." Gabriel turned back toward the door. If he lingered any longer, he might get caught. No matter what nonsense the slugs had told him, he wasn't insane enough to think he could cure such a ghastly ailment.

But those eyes... He couldn't leave yet. He had to know what would make a person's eyes turn black.

Gabriel leaned his cane against the wall and opened the top drawer of the bureau next to the door. He took out a precaution gown and tied it around his neck. After pulling up the collar to cover his mouth and nose, he grabbed a pair of disposable gloves from the box on top of the bureau and snapped them on.

Hands shaking, Gabriel put two fingers to Matthew's black-veined wrist. the pulse was slow, twenty-eight at most, but with random bursts of the most chaotic arrhythmia Gabriel had ever seen. It skyrocketed to eighty, ninety, one hundred ten, then slowed back down to thirty. The cycle repeated several times before he removed his hand. He wanted to write down the information, but touching his pen was a contamination risk.

"Are you all right?" Gabriel asked.

The Crooner didn't respond, but his eyes twitched. Somewhere within that withering, black-veined corpse, Matthew seemed to have had heard him.

"Matthew, can you understand me?"

Matthew raised his head and gasped with a series of putrid exhalations. Gabriel took the man's face into his hands and gently cradled the cold, clammy, tissue-paper-skinned skull, not sure *why* he was doing it but feeling that he needed to. Looking down at the face of a man who, not so long ago, had been singing, hollering, and full of life made Gabriel feel as if he were wading through mud. He stared into those black eyes, looking for a sign of recognition or a spark of life.

"I'm here," Gabriel whispered. "I'm going to help you. Please, just stay alive. Don't give up. I'm going to help you, I'm going to... going to—"

Matthew's charred eyes became moist. Tears escaped from their corners.

Gabriel's own eyes welled up. "Don't give up, Matthew."

Matthew emitted a sharp breath that sounded as if shards of glass were passing through his lungs. Gabriel gripped the man's head in the crook of his precaution gown-protected arm and squeezed Matthew's skeletal hand. "I'm here, Matthew."

The Crooner's eyes widened into near-lidless circles. Matthew's lips struggled to move, and his darkened tongue rolled around in his open mouth like an eyeless worm.

"Talk to me, Matthew, please."

The Crooner's eyes narrowed. His tongue pushed forward, licked his lips, then slid back in. The poor man relinquished his valiant struggle. He became motionless, nothing but a corpse with a heartbeat.

"No!" Gabriel cried. "Goddammit, you old fool. Don't give up. Don't—"

Heavy footsteps pounded outside the door. Gabriel swung around and accidentally kicked the leg of the bed. His toe throbbed. The door swung open and crashed against the wall with the impact of an earthquake.

"Gabriel Schist!" Natty shrieked. The short, obese woman stood in the doorway, hands planted on her hips. She moved into the light, her thick finger pointed at Gabriel like a dagger. "Get away from Mr. Lecroix right this instant!"

She had a new tattoo on her wrist, a cursive "imma do me." Gabriel took off the gown and gloves. He dumped the protective wear into the wastebasket. Natty glared at him as if he were a dog that had left his personal detritus on the rug.

"I'm sorry," Gabriel said.

"Oh? Are ya?"

"I need to wash my hands."

Natty groaned. She crossed her meaty arms and tapped her foot. Tanya approached from the other side of the hallway, but Natty waved her away.

Gabriel pulled Matthew's curtain back into place then went into the bathroom and washed his hands in scalding-hot water. "I don't know what came over me." He grabbed a paper towel to dry his hands. "I thought—"

"That's a very mean thing you were doing to that poor man, sweetie," she said in a nauseatingly saccharine tone. "Torturin' the poor guy when he's sick. C'mon, Gabe. How would you feel if he did that to you?"

Gabriel scowled. "I wasn't—"

She groaned. "C'mon, honey pie. Let's leave your friend alone for the night, okay? How about we getcha back to your room, and we lay you down for a nice cozy nap?"

Natty stretched on a pair of gloves, stomped over, and put her hand around Gabriel's back. She started pushing him out the door.

He grabbed his cane on the way out. "Natty, I was just trying to see if Matthew was—"

"Yeah, Gabe. Sure. A nap would be real nice, wouldn't it? It sounds wonderful to me."

"Look, Natty—"

She grabbed his hand and began walking him down the hall. "Quiet, honey. It's bedtime now. Here, follow me. Just—"

Gabriel threw her gloved hand away. "Get the hell away from me," he snarled.

"Oh, honey—"

"My name is *Gabriel*, goddammit! I'm a human being."

"Oh, look who's got an attitude now, huh?"

He stepped back. "Get away from me."

Natty closed the distance and put her arm around him again. Her face was only inches away from his, and her breath smelled like raw onions. "Gabe, sweetie—"

Gabriel jerked away and hobbled down the hall toward his room. He knew he was sealing his reputation as a troublemaker, a *difficult* resident, a demented fool who shouldn't be left alone. The incident would definitely be noted in his behavior chart. He heard Natty stomping off behind him, wailing with self-pity as she loudly complained to the RN on duty.

"Did you hear the way that asshole was treating me?" Natty whined to the RN. "Can't you just rub some ABH on his neck and calm him the hell down?"

ABH. Ativan, Benadryl, and Haldol. The staff considered that combination to be the perfect cocktail to calm down a problematic resident. The stuff would knock him off his feet, so a nurse could drag him back into bed and leave him there for the night.

"Well, he seems to have calmed down," the RN replied. "He's going to his room. See?"

Gabriel paused in the doorway of his room to listen in a bit longer.

"Yeah yeah, but that fucker is gonna get himself in big trouble." Natty snorted. "I swear, if he keeps this bad behavior up, he's gonna be stuck on Level Five in no time."

"I heard that the administrator is trying to rename Level Five. He wants us to call it the Guggenheim unit now."

"Googa-what? Ah, whatever. It'll always be Level Five to me, and

Level Five was *made* for dudes like Schist. Nobody *ever* pushes me around that way! I'm a damn good LNA. All the other residents love me."

It took everything Gabriel had not to turn around, walk back, and spit in Natty's face. At least Natty had a reputation for complaining, so it was highly unlikely that one bad report from her would get him moved to Level Five. He went into his room, sat on the bed, and put his head in his hands. He pictured Matthew's inhuman eyes and the tears that had struggled to escape from them.

He looked up when someone knocked on the door. He expected Natty, Tanya, or maybe even the RN on duty coming to give him a warning. Instead, Victor stood in the doorway, wearing another tuxedo and an eye-crinkling smile.

"Good evening, my dear Gabriel. Hope I'm not interrupting anything." Victor chuckled. "Most people sleep at this hour, but you don't strike me as the sleeping type."

Gabriel felt a strong temptation to confide in Victor, but he wasn't sure if it was a good idea. He barely knew the man. "Sleep does sound nice. But with all this horrible stuff happening, I don't know."

Victor leaned against the jamb, arms crossed in the posture of a younger, stronger man. "Is that so?"

"Yes. Victor, I have to ask, why the tuxedo? Every day, I mean. It looks like you're going to a funeral."

"Well, I'm *at* a funeral." Victor shrugged. "We live in a nursing home, don't we? This building is nothing more than a place for all of us to celebrate our long, hopelessly drawn-out funerals, isn't it? So I say, if every day is a funeral, why run away from the inevitable? Why not have a good time?"

Gabriel nodded and suppressed a yawn. "Listen, I appreciate the company, but what made you decide to stop by?"

"Chess. Care for a game, Mr. Schist?"

CHAPTER 13:
ICONOCLASM

THE LIGHTS FROM THE FISH tank spread an ethereal blue glow throughout the lobby. Gabriel stared into Victor's bulbous eyes as the man studied the chessboard.

Victor was a remarkably cautious player. Back in his pre-Alzheimer days, Gabriel rarely lost. But Victor possessed an intuitive understanding of the game's mechanics that made Gabriel feel like a novice. After relying on nothing but his pawns for a length of time that Gabriel thought ludicrous, Victor finally brought one of his knights into action, ruthlessly murdering Gabriel's black rook.

Gabriel peered at the board for a few minutes then moved his queen diagonally from the enemy knight. "It's too bad that we didn't get to finish our last game," Gabriel said. "I was curious which one of us would win."

Victor gave him a devious grin. "No worries, Mr. Schist. I'll be answering that question for you soon enough."

"Questions. Heh." Gabriel smiled. "Last time, before the whole John Morris incident interrupted us, you left me with a lot of questions."

"I do that sometimes." Victor picked up his knight. His hand lingered on the piece after he set it down on a black square. He dusted his tuxedo, though it was so spotless that it put even James Bond's outfits to shame.

"What did you say your last name was?" Gabriel had been certain Victor looked familiar and that he'd seen him before, though maybe not in person. Perhaps he'd seen him on television or something like that.

"I didn't."

Gabriel moved his queen's pawn forward. "Oh?"

"Don't be coy with me." The dimple appeared in Victor's cheek. "It won't work. I used to be more open, but the nature of my work was such that... well, let's just say that my line of work was always quite secretive. When a man keeps his secrets close to his chest for long enough, it eventually becomes a habit, one that's hard to break."

"So break it."

"My last name begins with C." Victor winked and positioned his bishop to protect his rook. "I'm afraid that's all I can tell you."

Gabriel liked Victor. He appreciated the man's intelligence, his patience, and even his enigmatic refusal to reveal any personal information. And Gabriel had always liked solving mysteries. "So which wing are you staying on? I'm assuming it's not South Wing, or I would have seen you before."

"I've been on every wing in this entire building, Gabriel. Lately, however, I've occupied West Wing."

"West? I hear—"

"Your move, Mr. Schist."

"Sorry." Gabriel captured a pawn with his queen.

"Actually, I should be the one to apologize for barging in on you at such an ungodly hour of the night," Victor said, moving a pawn forward.

"It's fine." Gabriel blocked the move with his queen. "My circadian rhythm is pretty warped anyhow."

"I've lived a long life, and due to my work, most of my life has been spent alone and isolated from the world. So I get very lonely from time to time." Victor paused to move his knight. "I never fit in anywhere, in any circles. People have never known how to take me, what to think of me. They've often been scared of me. I was always quite different."

Gabriel nodded. "I understand. We're alike in that respect."

"Are we?"

"Sure. I spent a long time trying... to make things work, trying to be happy. But at this point in my life, I've just accepted my loneliness for what it is." Gabriel shook his head and brought his knight back. "By now, I just want to die and get it over with. There's nothing but a black void of nothingness waiting for me after my heart stops, but I'm fine with that. I *want* nothingness. I love my daughter, but I'm utterly certain that she'll be better off and happier when I'm gone. To Melanie, I'm a liability. My continued existence is a constant source of stress that could send her careening off into depression if I break a hip or have another stroke. Honestly, Victor, I don't understand why my life continues on so endlessly. It's not as if I have anything left to live for."

Victor moved another pawn, and Gabriel examined the naked wrist that extended from the sleeve of his tuxedo. It was thin and white, reminiscent of a vein-covered chicken bone.

Victor cocked his head. "You're wrong, Mr. Schist."

"Pardon?"

"You do have something to live for. You're simply too damn stubborn to admit it." A wide grin formed on Victor's thin lips. It was always fascinating to watch such a smile take place on a face so wrinkled, as if every wrinkle acted together, creating a sort of zany *glee* that a younger person's face would never be capable of. "Gabriel, be honest with yourself. Earlier tonight, why did you check up on the Crooner?"

"You... you saw me?" Hand trembling, Gabriel moved his knight out of the path of Victor's rook.

"You were worried and perhaps wanted to help him. Am I right? You saw that he was one of the infected, and you wanted to get a better understanding of this new virus."

Gabriel shuddered. He focused on the board, not the game but rather the pattern of black and white squares. Normally, his silence caused people to think of him as cold and emotionless. But Victor reached over the board and rested a hand on Gabriel's shoulder.

"Let's face it," Victor said in an oddly chipper tone. "For all your arrogance, you do care about helping people."

"I do," Gabriel murmured.

"You're a healer. You're the man who cured the big virus years ago. And a man doesn't cure a virus out of bitterness, hate, or apathy. No, he cures it out of love."

Gabriel nodded weakly.

"So let's get right to the point before I go off on an even longer, more exhaustive tangent." Victor laughed. "Last time we were sitting here, a new superbug exploded onto the scene right before your eyes, the eyes of the genius immunologist. Now, you're a practical man, and I've heard that you don't believe in God. But you do believe in morality. Ethics.

Right and wrong. Humanity. Logic. So doesn't it seem to you that there's only one decent course of action for you to take when such an event occurs?"

"Which is what?"

"You must find a cure, of course."

Gabriel shook his head. "I want to. But how would I even start? I don't have the tools. I don't have—"

"Who are you trying to convince? Yourself? I don't want to hear any excuses. You cured HIV on your own, by yourself, practically working out of your basement, with no funding and nothing but your own ingenuity to keep you going."

"I didn't *cure* anything. I created a vaccine."

"Yes, and your vaccine ended AIDS." Victor stroked his goatee. "This isn't a matter of choice, not for a problem solver like you. Either you're going to start looking for a cure now, or you're going to start later."

Gabriel gulped. The more he considered Victor's sermon, the less capable his voice box seemed of producing sounds. When he finally did speak, he barely had the strength to raise his voice above a whisper. "I'm terrified that I'll make a fool of myself, Victor. My brain is a piece of Swiss cheese now. I'll mess up. I'll—"

"Shut up. Stop lying. You know perfectly well that one Swiss-cheesed Schist brain is worth a thousand normal brains."

Victor's lighthearted tone made Gabriel laugh. The whole situation was just so ridiculous. "Come on." Gabriel said. "How the hell do you know that?"

Victor looked down at the chessboard. "How? Because I have no dementia, no degenerative diseases, nothing but age behind me. I've played more games of chess than you can possibly imagine. I've beaten world masters. And yet, you... with your so-called Swiss cheese brain, you've just beaten me. Congratulations."

Gabriel stared at the board. Without realizing it, he'd landed the final blow. Victor's white king was trapped. Gabriel raised his head and smiled. "Checkmate."

CHAPTER 14:
UPHILL

"I NEED A BIGGER ROOM. AND you're going to give it to me." Gabriel peered intently at the administrator of Bright New Day, a man named Irving... *Brown? Bosworth? Bloemker? Was that it? Yes, Bloemker sounded right.*

Irving J. Bloemker's prematurely balding head sank down into his shoulders, making the man look like a turtle retracting into its shell. He was a short, squat man in a tailored brown suit. An old-fashioned pocket watch on a gold chain hung from one pocket. He was the sort of a man who felt too conscious of his diminutive size, and his office showed his insecurity. His massive oaken desk sat on a high platform, which allowed him to tower over anyone who chose to speak to him. The Picasso painting—"The Old Guitarist"—had been placed in an oversized wooden frame. But Gabriel wasn't intimidated.

"Um..." Bloemker fidgeted. "Why?"

"Because I need space to set up a makeshift lab," Gabriel stated. "I need test tubes. Make them plastic if you're worried about me breaking things. I don't care. I need space for files, papers, and notebooks. My current living quarters on South Wing won't cut it anymore."

"This is the sort of issue you should discuss with social services. The policy is—"

"I don't care about the policy. I'm discussing it with *you.*" Gabriel's blood was rushing through his body in a tidal wave. His back was straight, not bent. He felt as if he could go skydiving.

"This... I'm very busy, Gabriel."

"As am I."

Bloemker sucked in his cheeks and glanced at the heart-rate monitor on his wrist. Gabriel suspected that the arrhythmia probably wasn't as bad as Bloemker made it out to be. He was also pretty sure that Bloemker had vitiligo, given the small white patches on his already pale skin, most notably the splotch that covered the left side of his neck. Vitiligo wasn't a life-threatening disease, but it tended to make people self-conscious about their appearance.

"Gabriel, what you're asking for here, it's... well..."

"I understand. I know that nursing home residents with an Alzheimer's diagnosis don't barge into the administrator's office, demanding a bigger room and laboratory equipment. Yes, it's unprecedented, but so is this superbug, which you and I both know isn't just the flu. Consider this. If I *could* find a cure and you prevented me from doing so, then any resulting deaths would be on your shoulders."

The administrator shrank into his chair like a scared roly-poly. "Gabriel, you have to understand. Please. It's nothing against you, but the thing is, if we did this and if the state were to catch wind of it, we'd be liable."

Gabriel leaned against the wall, taking the pressure off his bad side. "Not necessarily. Not if I sign a release form. I called my old lawyer today. William Grant. He prepared a special release form that holds me for full liability. I'll also sign a patient confidentiality form. I want access to the charts of current victims."

Bloemker frowned. "I'm not a trained counselor, so I don't know the proper way to say this, but don't you think you're being a bit solipsistic? I'm sure the government has scientists working on a cure. What makes you think that you're the only one who can find one?"

"I'm the Nobel Prize-winning immunologist who created the Schist vaccine, which your own facility gives to every resident. If anyone can find a cure for this virus before it gets worse, it's me."

"Gabriel, I respect you. I respected you long before either of us ever entered this facility. But you're cognitively impaired now. You're on medication that can affect your processes. Your situation... I feel like a complete ass saying it this way, but at some point, you're going to start declining."

"Yes, I will. But right now, Mr. Bloemker, people are dying. Nobody's helping us. Nobody wants to *cure* the infected residents here; they want to cover it up. That's why they made everyone sign those forms. That's why all of you have to pretend it's just influenza. And just like with AIDS, they're leaving the doors wide open for a massive, widespread contamination. I know you're a compassionate man, a good man. I believe that's why you chose to work in healthcare. But open your eyes. Don't you see what's happening?"

Bloemker sucked in his cheeks. "Yes."

Gabriel sighed. "I don't have much time. You're right about that. My Alzheimer's *will* get worse. But right now, before my condition declines, how can either of us possibly waste what little time I have left arguing, instead of saving human lives, the only thing that *either* of us are any good at?"

Bloemker fidgeted and stared up at the Picasso. He muttered something in Latin that sounded like one of the prayers Father Gareth used to say, but Gabriel couldn't hear it clearly. Then, the administrator nodded as if he'd made a decision. He opened a drawer and pulled out a plastic three-inch binder. He began typing on his computer keyboard, occasionally looking back at the binder. Gabriel waited, clutching the handle of his cane, afraid to say anything more.

Minutes later, Bloemker looked up at Gabriel. "Fine. I don't buy it but fine. Legally, I can't stand in your way. So let's set some parameters and then... give it your best shot."

Gabriel could've jumped in the air with joy if doing so wouldn't have resulted in broken bones. He knew Bloemker was merely humoring him, but Gabriel didn't care whether anyone believed him or not, as long as he got what he wanted.

Bloemker eyed him. "You'll be under close observation."

"Fair enough."

"Now, I'm giving you the window side of Room 116 in North Wing. It's the biggest room in this facility that isn't currently occupied. You'll be sharing the room with Bernard Ulysses Huffington the Fourth, who has been in the room for nearly two years."

"I don't think I've met him."

"Probably not. Getting Bernard to leave his room is like pulling teeth. A man of habit, that one."

"The Fourth?" Gabriel chuckled. "Interesting. Is he from some sort of aristocratic family?"

"Nope. He was a trucker in Alaska, very interesting guy. Anyway, I'm giving you the room, but as I said, you'll be under observation. I want nothing flammable, nothing that could hurt anyone. I'll have that smart Brenton kid watch you closely on that point. Also, I did read that recent behavior report from Natty. If your behavior starts worsening, or if you somehow become a danger to others, don't think I won't yank all of this away from you in a heartbeat. I will."

Knowing that Harry Brenton would be his observer only heightened Gabriel's elation. "Sure."

"Oh, and there's no way I'm giving you the charts for all the virus victims. That would be a severe HIPPA violation."

"Understood." Gabriel figured he could convince Harry to sneak copies to him.

"Now, no offense, but get out of here. You've just given me a mound of paperwork to do, so I'd like to get started." Though Irving didn't smile, his tone held good humor.

Gabriel stood, buttoned his coat, and headed for the door.

"Oh, and Gabriel?"

Gabriel turned around. "Yes?"

"Good luck." Irving winked.

Gabriel tipped his hat, then spinning around with more energy than he'd possessed in nearly a decade, he returned to the maze of corridors he'd wandered so often in the last five years that every inch of wallpaper had become as familiar as his own hand. *Tap. Tap.*

Mickey Minkovsky saluted him. Edna gave him a curious stare. Even the ever-cranky Bob Baker, sitting before his plate of hotdog cubes, shot him a perplexed look. A startlingly familiar melody accompanied Gabriel's cane-tapping journey. And after several moments of disoriented confusion, he realized that the tune was coming from his own lips, which hadn't produced that once-signature sound in nearly a decade.

With a smile, Gabriel marched back to his room with a gusto he'd forgotten he had, whistling the entire way.

CHAPTER 15: FOUND

Summer 1974

Y VONNE HAD NO IDEA WHY Gabriel was whistling. It was a nice little melody, but totally out of place. She'd never seen a person so intelligent, yet so oblivious to his surroundings.

She sipped on her Merlot as a handsome waiter presented her with a Caesar salad decorated as luxuriously as a Christmas present. The restaurant, with its flickering candles, perfect china, white tablecloths, and white adobe walls, was the fanciest place she'd ever been. In her flowing gypsy dress, dreadlocks, wooden earrings, and lack of makeup, she felt utterly weird. Her backpack full of college textbooks was slumped against a table leg.

But she looked normal compared to her date. Gabriel was clad in a stained white T-shirt and worn-out sneakers. He was drinking a bottle of beer instead of wine.

She had no idea why he had brought her to a place where the two of them looked like freakish out-of-towners. Perhaps he was following a perceived rulebook for first dates, and in his mind, that restaurant was where normal people went for dates. Maybe Gabriel, the alien from Mars, wasn't sure how to do a regular human date, and so he was instead offering her his best *interpretation* of a date.

"Is the salad good?" he asked.

"Oh yes, it's wonderful. Thank you."

"It's great going out this way, isn't it? I mean, going out on... um, on a date." He glanced at her then returned his gaze to his beer. He picked up the bottle and took another deep swig.

Yvonne had done her fair share of serial dating, and the comfortable guys never felt they had to confirm the fact that they were out on a date with her. Those guys were aware that she knew, and the D-word never needed to be stated. They confidently left it unmentioned or sometimes even teased *her* into saying it. Self-conscious guys were another story. They threw in the D-word as often as possible, a plea for authentication. *Am I really on a date? She's here with me? Really?*

Yvonne smiled. Somehow, his insecurity made Gabriel even more endearing. "So for a genius scientist like you—"

"I'm still a student."

"Okay, a future scientist then. Where do those surfing skills come from? How'd you get so good?"

He smiled. "You just have to be observant. I pay attention to the propulsion of the waves. I calculate the strength of the wind. I usually perform balancing exercises before I go out, so that my body is at its maximum level of capability. Really, balance is everything." He took a bite of his steak.

"I love it." She laughed. "You're a remarkably fascinating person, you know that?"

He shook his head and took another nervous gulp of his beer. In the flickering candlelight, his red hair glistened as if it were on fire. His callused fingers tapped the table. "I'm not. Not really. I'm just a person."

"Well, *people* are fascinating."

"Not really. People are very simple and predictable. I'd even say boring, to be honest. We're just animals with better communication abilities."

Yvonne bristled at this comment. She squeezed both sides of her seat. "All of us?"

Gabriel's eyes widened, and he looked away. "Well, except you. You're very fascinating."

"Oh yeah?" She laughed. "You think people are simple? Predictable?"

"They are. You can always anticipate a person's behavior once you know them well enough. They follow specific rules for specific situations.

You're a fascinating person, but now that I'm getting to know you, I can still predict exactly what you will say, when you'll say it, what it will—"

"How many women have you been with?"

"You... what?" His mouth dropped open, as if she'd loosened the screws in his jawbone.

"Sex. Making love, sleeping together, whichever term you prefer. How many?" Yvonne grinned and reached under the table for his hand. She squeezed it gently then let go.

"What?" he asked. "I don't understand."

"So you can predict behavior? You think human beings play by the rules?"

"But—"

"Gabriel, I just broke the rules of this conversation, this setting, this *date*, whatever. If I can do that so easily, what makes you think anyone's actions can be predicted?"

He scratched his stubbly chin. "Oh. Well, let's say that you follow a trend. Let's say that you're always spontaneous, always breaking the rules. So then, if I predict your spontaneity..."

"Oh, that's a cop-out. How can you *predict* spontaneity?"

His fingers resumed their previous drumming on the table. "Hmm."

"Okay, so we'll get back to that." She sipped her Merlot. "Anyway, Nostradamus, here's a less invasive question. How many girls have you kissed?"

He shrugged. "Five."

"Wow! Really?"

"Yeah, but... I mean—"

"It's okay. Don't feel like you need to defend yourself. I understand. I don't care about those sorts of numbers; I'm just trying to demonstrate a point. Now, you know what I do care about, though? You know what I really, really like about you, other than your handsome face?"

He blushed like a little boy. "What about me?"

"I like your mind, Gabriel. Seriously, I've been on a lot of dates. And even though I barely know you, I can already tell that you're the smartest person I've ever met."

"I'm not—"

"Listen. Don't talk to me about the weather, parties, beer, or any of that stupidity. Any number of lesser men can do that, and I don't want a lesser man. Talk to me about the stuff you like. Tell me about your passions. You're intelligent, and I like that."

Gabriel's smile was hesitant as he nodded. "Okay."

They talked for hours, and after they left the restaurant, they went back to the beach where they'd met. As they walked, Gabriel sipped from a beer bottle. Crowds of college kids swarmed over the sand, dancing, playing Frisbee, smoking pot, some even dipping into the water. There were supposed to be fireworks later, and she had no intention of missing out on that.

Yvonne ran ahead, weaving through the crowds and kicking up clouds of sand. "C'mon, slowpoke!"

They found an empty stretch of sand and stopped at the edge of the water. Standing together, they watched the waves, felt their coldness, the hard wind, the occasional strip of seaweed. Their bare toes sank gently into the wet sand.

KA-BOOM.

Ear-shattering fireworks cracked open the night sky like bullets from God. Red, yellow, green, blue.

Yvonne tentatively linked hands with her date, and she looked at the shape of his profile against the bursting luminescence. Gabriel stared up at the fireworks with a relaxed smile. She found it interesting how, despite all his knowledge, he took enormous pleasure in simple, uncomplicated joys like fireworks, the breeze, the water, and the sand.

"Gabriel," she whispered, "I remember you saying something about people being predictable?"

"Well, I meant that—"

"How about this?" She yanked Gabriel's beer bottle out of his hand, taking away the substance that he'd relied on all night, and dropped it on the sand. He stared down at the alcohol fizzling away into the ground.

Yvonne grabbed the sides of his head, forcing him to look into her eyes. She barely suppressed an excited giggle.

Gabriel stiffened. "How about... what?"

"This." She kissed him.

She put everything into that kiss. Her lips. Her tongue. She ran her fingers through his red hair and pressed her hips against him. She felt his heartbeat, the muscles of his back, his breath.

Gabriel melted into her like butter. His strong arms wrapped around her, lifting her into the air. She coiled her legs around his waist and climbed him as if he were a tree. He held her steady. She felt the sky would have to fall around them before he'd ever let her drop.

"Predictable?" she whispered.

He laughed. "No."

They fell to the ground, embracing each other. Gabriel laughed that hearty, full-of-life laugh that he didn't do often enough.

"Those five girls were lucky." She giggled. "Make it six!"

Gabriel rolled onto his side, perched on his elbow to hover over her. The waves lapped at their bodies, coating their skin with cool, damp sand. Yvonne smelled the burning sulfur in the air.

"I've never met anyone like you before," he said.

"Really?" She enthusiastically dove into him, kissing him again. Their hands explored each other's bodies like pilgrims discovering a new world.

He rolled on top of her, gently pinning her to the ground. "Really. You're like... a wise contradiction."

Yvonne laughed, feeling oddly touched. She pecked him on the lips. "Thank you." She beamed. "I think?"

"You're welcome, I think." Gabriel released her, rolling back onto his side.

"Now, Gabriel, tell me. What *exactly* is your driving passion in life? Be honest."

Gabriel's mouth tightened. "Nothing. I just want to enjoy life. Have some thrills. Be happy. That's all."

"Oh, pish posh. Who are you trying to fool?" She kissed him gently. "Tell me the truth."

Gabriel tensed. He studied her face. "The immune system," he replied, slowly mouthing each word as if he was being tested. "I want to fix it. I want to prevent a catastrophe from occurring before it starts. That's my goal."

"How?"

"By altering the immune system. Making it *smarter.* I want to apply the theory of autopoiesis—"

"Autopoiesis? You're talking about self-creation, right?"

His eyes widened. "How did you...?"

"I did my homework since our last meeting." She smiled. "But tell me more, Dr. Genius."

"Well, then you must know that it's a recent theory, formulated by Humberto Maturana and Francisco Varela, which posits..." He shook his head. "How do I explain this? It'll bore you."

"I'll be the judge of what bores me."

He shrugged. "Okay, so an autopoietic system is when you have... let's say you have a system formed in such a way that the processes inside said system maintain and continually recreate its structure. Normally, we define an object's identity by what stays the same. We define it by the constant, instead of by the changing. The constant shape of it."

She nodded. "Right."

"Now, forget what we normally do. Instead, let's say that identity is defined not by continuity of shape but by continuity of process. For example, picture a big corporation. The corporation begins with certain people, desks, and equipment, but these interior things are not permanent. The employees change, and the management changes, but because the processes within are still running, the company itself still exists. The corporation is an evolving entity. The corporation's identity is defined by internal processes that allow it to thrive, to evolve, and continue living. The corporation is autopoietic."

Somewhere in the distance, a fellow beachgoer was playing an acoustic guitar. Gabriel turned to listen to it, facing the island of lights that stretched out into the dark sky.

Yvonne touched his hand. "Go on."

He looked back at her. "So let's think about the immune system, antibodies, all that good clean fun. Let's assume that the human body is autopoietic. It exists not by continuity of shape but by continuity of process. We have the brain, with all its neurons, synaptic connections, and so on. The lymphatic system. Digestive system. Endocrine system. The cardiovascular system, with a heart that continually pumps blood. All of these are separate pieces, separate forms of consciousness, so to speak. Each system of the body is a targeted subcommittee inside a bigger General Motors-esque corporation, composed of various employees, each one working a very specific job. Then, we have the immune system. When you think about it, the immune system functions just like a second brain. Like a brain, it responds to changes in the environment. The immune system recognizes pathogens, and it creates antibodies to deal with those pathogens."

"Okay, I think I understand." Her brain was certainly working in overdrive. The scene around them—the waves, the beach, the smell of sulfur, the fireworks—was so vivid, so dreamlike, so unlike her hometown. *Who is this strange boy? Is he real?*

"Good," he said, grinning. "Have you ever stopped to consider how insanely intelligent the immune system is? It's incredible. When it sees a threat, it spawns antibodies to terminate that threat. The immune system doesn't just resemble the brain. It exists as its own cognitive system."

"I never thought of it that way. Are you sure?"

"Well, it's all theory at this point. And this is where my part comes in. My passion, as you put it. If the immune system is a cognitive system, what if we could make it smarter?"

Gabriel sat up, cutting a dark jagged shape against the golden lights of the landscape behind him. His expression was wild with joy. Yvonne could've made love to him right there. But she wanted to wait for a little while, at least a few more dates, just to make the moment, when it finally came, even more amazing.

She playfully ran her finger down his chest. "So how would you make it smarter?"

"Look. When you get your immunization shots, they give you a bunch of them, but they only do a few at a time, and you have to go back for the rest. Imagine if that could all be combined into a single mega-shot. If my theory pans out, then my vaccine would reprogram the immune system in such a way that, instead of just reacting to the damage caused by an invader, it actually plans ahead for every potential attack, and by the time the invader comes, the bad guy is knocked out before it can cause any damage."

"That's amazing!" Yvonne rolled the tip of her finger into his navel then traced upward into the furry center of his chest hair. "So this relates to that future disease business again? That disease that you want to find a cure for before it even exists?"

"Superbug. I believe pretty strongly that we're on the cusp of something big, something deadly breaking out... a blood-borne pathogen that could potentially wreak enormous damage on the population. There have been some isolated incidences of a new virus in Africa, with enough similarities to my hypothesis that it makes me wonder." Gabriel scratched his chin. "But that's not where my prediction stems from. I believe that, at this point in our history, the gates are wide open for the next epidemic of this kind to walk in."

She shuddered. "So if such a thing happens, a disease like that, how will it work? How would it spread?"

"Well, it's complicated. If it's a blood-borne pathogen, the common source of infection would be through bodily fluids."

"Sexual contact, too?"

"Certainly, yes. But anyway, I think we're going to see a virus that has evolved to overcome our current defenses, medications, and vaccines, and takes the battle right to our greatest military defense system, our immune system, and then takes that army out."

"Takes out the immune system? How?"

Down the beach, someone set off a sparkler, but Gabriel didn't seem to notice. " Imagine a virus that depletes us of our vital T-cells and takes away our ability to produce *new* T-cells, disarming the immune system and leaving us vulnerable to any number of opportunistic infections. Suddenly, you're going to see people getting swollen lymph nodes and flu-like symptoms then dying from previously harmless diseases. The body will be wide open for whatever hits it, and the infected will drop like flies."

She peered deeply into his eyes. "And you're going to stop it?"

He shifted his gaze. "I hope so, yes."

"You, the man who finds people boring, are devoting your life to the effort of saving millions."

Gabriel stared down at the sand. At that moment, she knew he was exactly what she'd wanted. Yvonne kissed him. Gabriel wrapped his arms around her and rolled her onto her back, pinning her to the damp sand.

"You're beautiful," he whispered.

She pulled closer, ready to kiss him again. But she stopped when she felt a cool, damp, crawling sensation on her leg. She looked down and saw something small and shiny inching down her calf. *A leech? A worm? No. A slug.* The slimy creature was the color of mustard with two black stripes running down it. The slug's little antennas rose. Gabriel must have seen where she was looking because he raised his hand to slap the slug away. Yvonne caught him by the wrist, stopping him just in time.

His brow furrowed. "What?"

"Don't hurt the poor little guy! I like him." Yvonne reached down and gently picked up the tiny little slug, allowing it to nestle in the cup of her palm. She watched the scared, startled movements of its petite antennas. She held out her hand to show Gabriel. The slug steadily crawled down her arm.

CHAPTER 16: TRANSFER

B EAMING WITH PRIDE, GABRIEL STOOD at the entrance of Room 116, his new home. North Wing was the green wing, with its olive-green floors, green-grey wallpaper, and mint-green curtains. He carried a small suitcase in one hand, his cane in the other, and a gym bag over his shoulder. The staff had already moved the rest of his possessions into the room.

Stepping inside, he was immediately impressed. Though smaller than a studio apartment, it was a substantial improvement over his old quarters. His new roommate, Bernard, was nowhere to be seen. The sound of running water was coming from the bathroom, so perhaps Bernard was in there.

Oddly, Bernard the Fourth appeared to have no bed. Where a bed normally would have stood was a leather recliner directly facing a flat-screen TV. On the wall were several photographs of old trucks, a couple of family photos, and a large black-and-white picture of a WWII army troop holding a US flag. On the table were nearly a dozen empty Styrofoam cups, a bunch of empty plastic pudding containers, four handkerchiefs, a pile of scrunched-up napkins, and a canister of sugar packets. Next to the recliner was a hamper filled with white V-neck T-shirts. It was a strange setup, and Gabriel hoped that his experiments wouldn't upset Bernard's daily schedule.

He went past the curtain divider and over to his side of the room, the window side. He'd missed having a window beside his bed. He hadn't realized it until that moment, but as warm, golden sunshine poured into the room, warming the icy blood in his veins as if he'd stepped into a Jacuzzi, he knew that he'd never agree to taking the door side of a room ever again. The view was dull—nothing but grass and a parking lot—but the sunlight was wonderful.

A dirty old desk with chipped black paint and old pencil graffiti scrawled on the legs had been placed right next to the window at Gabriel's request. A cardboard box sat on top of the desk, filled with all the equipment and devices he'd ordered online with the net-savvy help of Harry Brenton.

The water was still running in the bathroom. Gabriel sat on his new green-blanketed bed, reached for the briefcase on the pillow, and snapped open the latches. He took out his graphs, paperwork, Polaroids, and his Nobel Prize, handling each with affection. Using thumbtacks, he began recreating his wall collage, whistling as he worked.

After tacking all of his photos on the wall, he opened a secret compartment at the bottom of the briefcase. He pulled out his top-secret item, just to make sure it was still there. He hadn't told anyone about the blood sample he'd managed to get from Matthew Lecroix. The administrator would never have agreed to Gabriel's demands if he'd known.

The sample had been easier to acquire than he'd expected. Because the Crooner was diabetic, he had his finger pricked on a set schedule for checking his blood glucose levels. All Gabriel had needed to do was to wait for the nurse to stick Matthew then stand by her medcart—gazing at the wall, slack-jawed, pretending to be in a demented daze—until she continued on her rounds. As soon as she was gone, he'd quickly retrieved the test strip from the wastebasket.

Someone knocked on the door. "Hello?"

Gabriel turned around to see Dana Kleznowski in the doorway. A stethoscope hung around her neck. She looked frailer than usual, as if her already slender figure had lost a few pounds since he'd last seen her, when she'd ushered him away from John Morris's room. Dana looked confused for a moment, then her face brightened. She had an astonishingly beautiful smile, though it didn't surface often enough.

"Oh, hey!" she said. "The detective! Oh, you're over here on North now?"

"Yes."

"That's awesome." She clapped her hands. "So do you need anything? Since you pressed your call button, I mean."

Gabriel glanced at the red call button strung up on the other side of the bed. "I didn't press the button."

"Oh. Okay. It must've been Bernard. He never stops." Dana rolled her eyes, looking toward the bathroom door.

The tap was still running. The toilet was flushed three times in quick succession.

"So what time do you like your pills?" Dana asked, still watching the bathroom door.

"As late as possible. They make me drowsy. What were you saying about Bernard?"

"Oh, jeez," she sighed, smiling tiredly. "He's always doing this, ringing the light then going to the bathroom, every five seconds, he's... well, you'll see. Anyway, you sure you don't want a snack or anything?"

Gabriel glanced at her wiry arms and thin waistline. "No, thanks. But *you* go eat something, Dana. Something iron-rich, preferably, since that will help with your anemia. You're far too pretty to be starving yourself this way." Gabriel bit the inside of his cheek, suddenly unsure if it was socially acceptable for him to call out her anemia.

"Um, thanks." She giggled uncomfortably. "I'll go do that, Dr. House."

Dana turned off the call light using the special switch on the wall then left the room. As she stepped into the hallway, the toilet flushed a fourth time. The tap was turned on, then off, then on again. Bernard definitely seemed to have OCD, along with probable Alzheimer's.

Finally, the bathroom door creaked open. Bernard shuffled into the main room. His awkward gait, as well as his stooped posture, led Gabriel to suspect that the man had osteoporosis. He looked as if he were about to fall any minute, something that would break every bone in his thin, frail body. But he stayed on his feet, as if in stubborn defiance of the laws of gravity. He stopped and gazed at Gabriel.

Evidently, Bernard didn't wear pants. He was dressed in a pair of pull-ups, slippers, and a white V-neck T-shirt. His pale limbs had long meaty scars that resembled the fat on a piece of marbled beef. His sparse silver hair had that just-rolled-out-of-bed look.

Gabriel stood and cleared his throat. "Hello, Bernard. I'm your new roommate, Gabriel. It's a pleasure to meet you."

As he walked, Bernard held his arms in front of him, as if grasping an invisible steering wheel. His gaze was blank and unfocused. Gabriel couldn't tell whether the man was looking at him or at the wall. He never blinked.

"Fruit punch," Bernard mumbled.

"Pardon?"

"Yeah. Aren't you the guy with the fruit punch?" Bernard's expression didn't change. His eyes didn't move. He still hadn't blinked, simply looking at Gabriel with that same vacant expression, occasionally scratching his arms or reaching back to scratch his shoulder blades.

"No, I'm not—"

"Oh. Okay." Bernard shuffled over to his recliner and pressed his call button. He turned back to Gabriel with that same bland expression. "So who are you?"

"My name is Gabriel. I'm your new roommate."

"Oh, yeah." Bernard sounded surprised but not unhappy. "Sure. New roommate. Nice to meet you."

Gabriel crossed the room and held out his hand. Bernard stared at Gabriel's open palm for a moment then slowly raised his own hand. He opened his fingers, each digit slowly uncoiling from his palm, then with disconcerting speed, he shook Gabriel's hand as if he were trying to wrench off his arm.

Bernard released Gabriel's hand. "Well, welcome aboard, mister!" With no self-consciousness whatsoever, he took off his shirt and threw it in the overflowing hamper. He walked over to his bureau and put on another white V-neck.

Bernard took his laundry hamper out to the hall and dumped it on the floor. Gabriel just stood there, watching, unsure of how to proceed. Bernard then plopped down in his leather recliner, kicked off his slippers, and picked up the TV remote. He turned on a rerun of M*A*S*H and didn't say another word.

Gabriel walked back to sit at his new desk. He opened the cardboard box, ready to get to work.

"Bernard?" Dana said from the doorway, having been summoned again. "You rang?"

"Fruit punch," Bernard mumbled.

"Seriously?"

"Yep!"

"Bernard, c'mon. You've had like ten fruit punches in the last hour."

"I don't know why. My stomach is a bottomless hole."

"Okay, okay."

"Thank you."

"By the way, what's with all those clothes in the hall? Did you just dump them out here?"

"Laundry."

Gabriel listened to the exchange then resumed his unpacking. First, he got out his graph paper and notebooks. Feeling hot, he started unbuttoning his shirt. He grabbed the bottom button and...

Hmm. Gabriel played with the button a bit, unsure why it wasn't working properly. It wasn't coming loose. He tried it a different way. No, it wasn't working. It wouldn't fit through the hole. His hands became slippery with sweat. He pushed the button left, right, up, and down. *Goddammit, what's wrong with this thing? How could they design a button-down so ridiculously that you can't even open it? Idiot designers, idiot button, idiot—*

No, it wasn't the button's fault. He'd worn the shirt before. He'd *unbuttoned* the shirt before with no problems whatsoever. Gabriel continued trying to force the little plastic circle out of the hole, perspiration running down his face. No, it wasn't the button's fault. It was his fault.

His fault, yes. Because he was the idiot who couldn't remember how to pop open a goddamn button.

He pushed it, forcefully trying to shove it through the hole. It wouldn't work. Left. Right. Up. Down. It was insane. He couldn't believe that he'd lost such an easy ability, so suddenly, with no warning.

His stomach felt queasy. His heart raced faster and faster. There he was, issuing demands and trying to cure a superbug, when he couldn't even unbutton a damn shirt. *Goddammit...*

Gabriel stopped and looked down at the button that was torturing him. He forced himself to relax. His heart rate settled back to normal. After a few seconds, Gabriel tried the button again. It popped out of the hole easily.

Gabriel reached into the secret compartment of his briefcase and pulled out the sample of Matthew's blood. It didn't look unusual, but that might change once he put it under the lens. He opened a notebook and clicked his pen.

He got to work.

CHAPTER 17:
MULTIPLICITY

G ABRIEL SLUMPED OVER HIS DESK, his lamp casting a yellow rectangle upon the wooden surface, which only solicited more questions. He was exasperated. The answers that earlier that day had seemed as easy to pluck as a newborn flower had grown deep tangled roots, clinging to the ground and resisting his grasp. He pushed his new microscope away, unable to stand the sight of it.

He needed a break. It was frustrating to aspire to such an ambitious goal while working against the clock of one's own mental degradation. He was constantly sidetracked and distracted, especially by the antics of his insomniac roommate, who apparently never slept.

It was eleven thirty at night, and throughout the evening, Bernard had treated the call button like the trigger of a submachine gun. Though oddly likeable, he was possibly the most distracting roommate Gabriel had ever had. The man's constant *I-want-this-no-I-want-that-yes-no-not-that* dementia symptoms were like a postmodern exaggeration of the human condition. The entire night had been a chorus of Bernard's requests, repeated over and over, as nurses raced in and out of the room to advise him to take it easy on the sugar.

"Fruit punch."

"Pain pills."

"Fruit punch."

"Chocolate pudding."

"Two chocolate puddings and two vanilla puddings."

"Pain pills."

"Scratch my back, please."

"Fruit punch."

Gabriel leaned over the microscope again. He examined the constantly mutating black cells in the blood sample, but his eyes had become droopy. Back when he was younger, that would never have happened. He had often spent entire days so invigorated by his work that sleep and food seemed like vague notions, but age had changed him. He'd stared at the blood sample for hours, bewildered by the way that the virus completely changed properties from one moment to the next. He had nothing to show for the day's work, and he was sleepy, hungry, and thirsty.

"Hi there, Bernard," Harry Brenton said from the doorway. "Sorry it took me so long to answer the light, sir. Would you like some ice water, maybe? I'm passing it out to everybody right now."

"Fruit punch!" Bernard cried.

"Um, sir. You know that diabetes is—"

"No, not diabetes. Fruit punch."

"Bernard, if your blood sugar is—"

"Okay. Ice water. Thank you."

Harry pushed his cart into the room. As the wheels rolled along the linoleum floor, the ice inside each of the pink plastic cups on the cart clinked in a way that made Gabriel's mouth water. He noticed that Harry's white scrubs had several dark stains, which was odd since Harry's uniform was normally spotless. The boy's face was damp with sweat, and he was breathing heavily.

"Hello, Harry," Gabriel said.

Harry held out a pink cup. "Good evening, Mr. Schist. Would you like some ice water?"

"Okay." Gabriel smiled. "Thank you, Harry. But, honestly? What I could really use is some... uh, some company." Gabriel choked a little on the last word. He felt humiliated at having to admit that he, the man of science, the introvert of introverts, actually felt lonely. Loneliness made him pathetic.

"Yo, Harry!" Natty Bruckheimer bellowed in her high-pitched battle cry. "Get back out here, ya nerd!"

"Sorry, Natty," Harry called back. "I'm just—"

"Stop wasting your time chitchatting, dude. We've got work to do!" Natty stomped away, her footsteps causing the walls to shudder.

Harry bit his lip, and his shoulders slumped. Even in the dead of night, the sound of multiple call bells rang through the corridor, glowing in the dark hallway like flashing Christmas lights. "I'm sorry. I have to get back out there."

Gabriel rubbed his eyes. "Busy night, I gather?"

"Yes, sir. You could say that." Harry blew out a breath. "It's insane. We're so short staffed. Over thirty folks live on North Wing alone, and they have only one nurse on the medcart, while only two LNAs do all the personal care for every resident on this floor. And when my only help is someone like Natty, who just doesn't care about anyone but herself, it's like working alone. It's like—" Harry stopped and shook his head. "I'm sorry. I shouldn't be talking like that."

Gabriel peered at the doorway, worried that Natty might reappear. "Harry, you're one of the best people they have here. Don't let anyone make you think differently. It's the hard work of people like you that keep this place together."

"Thank you, sir." Harry blushed. "But you folks deserve better than this." He waved toward the hall then left the room.

Gabriel took a sip of his ice water. Before he could resume working on his research, the telephone rang. He lifted the receiver, anticipating the cold greeting of an investment banker from an earlier time zone, or maybe Medicare, or a life insurance agent who didn't respect other people's bedtime hours. "Hello?"

"Dad?" she said.

Melanie. Gabriel's heart leapt to his throat. His eyes filled with tears before he even breathed a word. "Hi, Melanie. God, it's so good to hear from you."

"Hi, Dad." She let out a gentle, nervous little laugh, the same laugh she'd had since she was a girl. "I've missed you, old man! Sorry it's been so long since I stopped by. I feel guilty. Sorry for calling so late. I know you've always been a night owl, but—"

"I miss you too, Melanie. How are you? How's Bill?"

Silence. Gabriel checked to make sure the line wasn't dead. Then, a realization hit him. A tender ache passed through his chest. "Oh. You and Bill are divorced. I forgot. I'm sorry, Melanie."

"It's not your fault. How are you doing, Dad? Are you okay?"

He stared at the dark window. In the reflection, he watched Bernard shuffle to the bathroom. Realizing that he might be taking too long to respond, he blurted, "Busy."

"Oh yeah?"

"Yes." He cleared his throat. "I'm researching the Black Virus. I'm trying to find a cure."

"The black what?"

"The virus that's been hitting people in this nursing home. The slugs, they told me—" Gabriel caught himself sounding like a lunatic and quickly redirected. "Some acquaintances of mine, I mean. They convinced me to research it, and I truly think that I can find a cure."

After a long pause, Melanie said, "Yes, I heard you guys are having a flu outbreak. It's going around, I guess. The kids just got over the flu a few weeks ago."

Gabriel repressed the urge to groan. "It's not a *flu,* Melanie. I know how this works. Trust me. The government has the infected patients secretly quarantined here. They're doing a massive cover-up. They made all of the staff sign these agreements to pretend that this is just a flu, but it isn't. It's an entirely new virus, and they're trying to make sure this new disease doesn't—"

"Dad? It's okay. Don't get worked up. That's really interesting. Wow."

She thought he was crazy. His own daughter, the one human being he loved the most in the world, didn't believe him. A tear ran down his cheek, and he wiped it before it fell onto his desk.

He stared down at his microscope, feeling as if he were the blood on the glass slide, inspected and dissected before the eyes of impassionate observers. "I'm serious, Melanie. This isn't my Alzheimer's speaking. It's all true."

"Oh yeah, I believe you," she said. She'd never been good at lying. "But hey—"

"I'm not crazy, Melanie."

"I know." She sighed. "Hey, Dad, I have to go. I love you, okay? I love, love, *love* you. Take care."

Before she hung up, Gabriel heard her choke back a tearful sob, the wallowing pain of an adult child left orphaned by the illness of her parent. Gabriel put down the phone and stared into the window at the reflection of a withered, decrepit old man that was supposedly him. He swallowed his tears and went back to work.

CHAPTER 18:
ØRSTED

Autumn 1974

SLA VISTA, CALIFORNIA, WAS SANTA Barbara's student-filled backyard. The incorporated community of thousands of college kids had shockingly little legal enforcement and a nonstop array of parties.

Yvonne gripped the leather steering wheel so tightly that her knuckles turned white. Her nerves were so jittery that her foot kept slipping off the gas. She parked several blocks away from the party-going streets.

The air was hot and sticky. Like any other Friday, the streets were crowded with young people drinking enough alcohol to fill an entire ocean. Marijuana smoke trailed though the air as if a pot bomb had gone off. Thousands of bodies pushed against each other like cattle, many of them half-naked. On a different day, Yvonne might have thought that looked like a good time. Though she had dropped her old drug habits, she still was happy to enjoy a good drink. But searching through the screaming, laughing, inebriated people, she could only sigh with exasperation. *Where the hell are you, Gabriel?*

Chris, the curly-haired guy who claimed to be Gabriel's friend—Gabriel said he had only one true friend, some old Catholic priest she hadn't met—had supplied her with an address when she'd called him to ask if he knew where Gabriel was.

She felt terrible. She should've never yelled at Gabriel and then stormed off that way, without even a kiss goodbye, but she'd just been so angry. She'd gotten so frustrated by his self-contained introspection, so fed up with his passive reactions to everything. So she'd provoked him.

She'd pushed his buttons by asking him more personal questions than he was comfortable answering. And he'd responded with nothing but a blank stare.

Yvonne walked through the streets, trying to keep her eyes open and her head clear. The entire block was like a drunken Disneyland. Every house was hosting a party. The air was filled with a cacophony of music, conversations, screams, and laughter. Around every corner were legions of drunken, chatty people, many of whom recognized her. She flashed everyone a forced smile and kept walking, pushing deeper and deeper into the rabbit hole.

"Yeah!"

"Whoooohooo, Yvonne Lumina! Hippy dreadlock girl, baby, are you lookin' hot tonight or what?"

"Drink it! Drink it! Drink it!"

"Hey, does anyone know where my keys went? Shit."

"Isla Vistaaaah, baby!"

Finally, Yvonne arrived at Bobby Price's address. To get to his second-story apartment, she had to climb a winding staircase blocked by multiple couples making out all the way from the bottom step to the top one. She pushed her way up, found his apartment, and opened the door. Marijuana and tobacco smoke wafted through the entryway.

She stepped inside the apartment, which was lit only a fraction brighter than Plato's cave. Hundreds of sweaty people were crammed into the tiny living room, dancing and writhing around each other like snakes. The beat of the pop music rattled the walls.

Yvonne searched through the crowd, terrified she'd find Gabriel's hands wrapped around another girl's waist. She knew Gabriel would never cheat on her, but the partying atmosphere had sent her paranoia through the roof.

Shoving her way through the dancing couples, she felt a hand grab her ass and squeeze, but by the time she flipped her head around, the assailant had disappeared. *Where are you, Gabriel?*

Then, she saw him. "Gabriel!"

He didn't look in her direction, probably because he couldn't hear her over the music. Still, Yvonne felt relief wash over her.

Gabriel appeared to be writing numbers on the wall while entertaining a group of frat boys with some sort of long speech that she couldn't hear. Of course Gabriel was the type of nerd who'd come to a college party and start lecturing drunk kids on math. Yvonne laughed, wondering what she'd been so worried about.

But when Gabriel stepped away from the wall, she saw that the numbers didn't make up any complicated formula or equation. It looked like simple arithmetic. She realized he was counting shots—thirteen of them—and he'd probably pre-gamed before coming there in the first place. She stepped closer as the rest of the party dimmed away into an opaque fog of lights, loud noises, and fast movements.

She raised her hand. "Gabriel! I'm here!"

Her boyfriend—the brilliant man she loved, the future savior—was handed an insanely long beer funnel. Tiny clumps of white powder were stuck to the edges of his nostrils. As she tried to push forward and yank the funnel from his hands, she tripped over someone's foot. She fell to the floor, her teeth slamming down on her lip. Blood pooled in her mouth and ran down her chin. By the time she got to her feet, Gabriel had swallowed the entire funnel, more quickly than she'd ever seen a person swallow one before. He raised his arms in the air and let out a whoop.

Yvonne couldn't take it anymore. She'd tried to be understanding, but she was sick of Gabriel turning to alcohol whenever anything went wrong in his life. She shot him one last angry look. He glanced over and saw her, and his grey eyes nearly popped out of their sockets. Yvonne walked away without looking back.

"Yvonne!" Gabriel called.

She kept going, through the door, down the stairs, and out onto the street. Her heart thumped loudly, pushing her onward, as sweat dripped down her back. She wanted to get away. She couldn't speak to him.

"Yvonne, I'm here!"

She looked over her shoulder. Gabriel was drunkenly stumbling toward her. He looked like an utter fool. He fell to the ground.

She broke into a run. Her feet ached, but she kept going. She had to get back to her car, home to her apartment, or the beach, or somewhere where her teary eyes could release the tight ball of emotion clenched up in her chest.

The crowded portion of Isla Vista disappeared behind her. She spotted her car, but she had to slow to a walk to catch her breath. Panting, she looked back.

Gabriel had caught up to her, and he was also panting. His hands were covered in blood, gravel, and dirt. His eyes looked as vulnerable as wet laundry hung up in a tornado. "Yvonne…"

"What?"

He looked worried, then a hint of a smile appeared on his face. He moved forward hesitantly. "Hi," he whispered.

She shook her head. "Don't talk to me."

"Why? That's… why not?"

"Honestly, Gabriel? I love you. *You.* But that *thing* I saw there in the apartment building—"

Gabriel crossed his arms. "That isn't me."

"Whatever it is, it's disgusting."

"Yvonne, it *isn't* me."

"Then who is it? Huh? If it isn't you, then who is it?"

"It's hard to explain."

"Try."

"I can't. I can't explain myself. It won't make sense to you. I-I can't—"

"Tell me, Gabriel." *Because this is your last chance, buster.*

"Quite simply, I was… I was being someone else back there. I'm different from most people, so putting on an act like that is a logical solution to the problem. Like applying… arithmetic. Yes. Back at that party, I was being the person they want me to be, the person they need me to be for them to…"

Tears stung the corners of Yvonne's eyes. She brushed them away, her lower lip trembling. Gabriel reached out as if to comfort her.

She stepped back. "No. Gabriel, I feel like I don't even *know* you! Okay, so say that the person back there isn't you. You've said that before, but I know what I saw, and I can't stand to see you waste yourself that way. If you were just drinking and having a good time… God! If only! I don't care about that. But the way you… it's as if you…"

"What?" Gabriel stood tall and stiff, like a fragile brick wall in front of a wrecking ball.

"You weren't having a good time. You never drink because you want to have a good time."

"Then what am I doing, exactly?"

"Active self-destruction." Yvonne swallowed her tears, wrapping her arms around her body.

"Why the hell would I do that? It's not logical. It's not—"

"Human beings aren't logical! It's not in our nature. We're fundamentally illogical creatures. We're not math problems that you can simply solve and be done with. It doesn't work that way."

"*I'm* logical. Why can't others be just as straight to the point and logical as I am?"

"You think drinking yourself to an early grave is logical?"

"It's... that's not what I'm... " His lips parted, a hint of strained self-deception appearing in his eyes. "I'm not an addict, Yvonne. I drink by choice."

"Gabriel, I love you. I love you because you're a weird, amazing shape, and I know that it's hard, because it's a shape that doesn't easily fit into the world. I get it. But if you're just going to destroy yourself, I can't."

"You can't... what?"

"I can't just sit by and watch it happen. I can't just partake in it, ignore it, and pretend that it's okay. I just can't." She sniffled, forcing herself not to break down sobbing. *Not now. Not while he's watching me.* She wiped the tears from her eyes.

Gabriel stood there like a jagged icicle. He was silent, but beneath the hard exoskeleton he presented her with, she knew he was seething with anger. "So," he said through gritted teeth, "this conversation is really about alcohol, isn't it?"

"How old were you when you started drinking, baby?"

"Sixteen. Answer my question."

"Gabriel, you drink too much. That's the objective truth of it. It just is."

His eyes became slits. "Don't you get it?" he growled. "It's the only way I can fit in. The only way I can be human."

"No, it's not. It's not the only—"

"Yes, goddammit! Yes, it is!" His face transformed into something monstrous and red, and his eyes turned into solid steel.

Yvonne jumped back. She'd never heard him yell like that, and on some level, she hadn't even thought him capable of it. "Gabriel, please don't—"

"Don't you get it?" he shouted. "Of course I don't like being an outsider. But in order to fit in, I have to be stupid. I learned that when I was sixteen, and I never forgot it. Being stupid is the only way I can ever be *normal.*"

"But you're not normal," she said.

"Clearly," he spat. "But, God, I want to be." He loosened his fists, but he was still breathing heavily.

She saw the glistening of tears in his eyes, the sad, lost little boy lashing out. That little boy had never been accepted by his peers and had been teased mercilessly at school. The boy had grown to be a man who was defensively protecting the one thing he thought he had going for him. Yvonne walked up to him and ran her fingers through his thick red hair. He twitched uneasily but didn't pull away.

"I love you, baby," she whispered. "But if this is going to work, I need to say something."

"Why wouldn't it work?" He shuddered. "Yvonne, don't say that. Don't."

Gabriel gawked at her like the lost, uncertain child he was. His hard shell had been cracked, and he looked as if the slightest breeze would send him toppling.

"If you want us to be together"—she gulped—"you've gotta embrace your mind. Stop running away from the greatest gift you have. I meant what I told you back on our first date. Do you remember what I said?"

"That you loved my brain?"

"Yes, your brain. That's why I love you. Because you're the guy who's gonna save the future. Because you're brilliant. I love you for who you are, and that's why I can't stand who you pretend to be, because the real person is so much better."

Gabriel smiled weakly. "That's what Old Gareth tells me, too."

"Maybe you should finally introduce me to this priest guy, already. He sounds pretty smart." Yvonne sniffled. "So stop killing that brain I love with all that alcohol. Okay? You're so much *better* than that. You're so much—"

Gabriel's mouth met hers, passionately connecting to her soul. As her fingers became tangled in his thick red hair, his lips left moist imprints across her neck and shoulders. All of their frustrations suddenly dissolved. Through his kisses, he told her everything that he would never have been able to put into words. He showed her, by giving her his emotions, his touch, and the most private gift of all, the tears that broke free from his eyes, leaving silvery streaks down his cheeks. He wouldn't swear off alcohol, not in words, but the kiss was his promise to *try*, to give it his best shot, for her. She felt that promise beating in his chest, and she recognized it as surely as if he'd signed a contract.

Gabriel raised his head and gazed into her eyes. "I love you," he whispered.

"I love you too." She wrapped her arms tighter around him.

"Let's go back to my sailboat. Let's see the ocean tonight."

"Together? Are you sure? With me?"

Gabriel squeezed her hand. "Together."

CHAPTER 19:
STAGE

Summer 2018

GABRIEL AWOKE WITH TEARS IN his eyes. He was bitterly cold, and the room was dark. The darkness was impenetrable. He was in a void, perhaps even a black hole.

He couldn't see. His senses were vague, abstract, somehow separated from his mind. He couldn't *see*. Couldn't *feel*. Couldn't taste, smell, touch, hear. He was blind. Deaf. Mute. Unreal. Fictitious. Imaginary. He'd made himself up.

In desperation, he flung his body into the darkness, hoping that the vacuum would release him and that gravity would—

Crash!

He slammed onto a hard surface, his tailbone screaming with pain. The skin on his hip tore open as easily as a perforated strip, spilling blood across the obsidian landscape of nonexistence.

Light returned, and his mind cleared. As he reassembled the fragments of his consciousness, it became brutally apparent he hadn't thrown himself out of the darkness or anything quite so cosmic.

No, he'd fallen out of bed, and he was sprawled out on the floor. The sunlight was so bright that he actually winced in pain. There was a window on one side of him, a twin bed on the other. A table beside the window had medical equipment piled on it. He definitely wasn't on his sailboat. He'd never seen this place before. *Where was he?*

Gabriel desperately attempted to scramble onto his feet. His toes felt like useless lumps of clay with no grip. Pain shot through his leg.

His heart was pounding so hard it felt as if a heavyweight boxer was punching him in the chest. Through the curtain beside the bed, he saw the shadow of a man—was his name *Bernard?*—holding a small thing at the end of a cord. The man seemed to be trying to press on it with one finger. A call button, that was what it was called. Yes, the shadow man had pressed the call button.

Panic overtook him. "Help!" Gabriel yelled. "Help me!"

He rolled around on the bleach-scented floor. He was wearing nothing but a pair of blue sweatpants loosely tied at the waist and several sizes too big for him. His vision became blurry again. The darkness was coming, taking away his right to exist. His identity became an abstract set of principles that didn't quite make sense.

No one was coming to help. They'd abandoned him. He was alone in space, alone, all alone. He was trapped. He was...

Oh, wait.

He relaxed a little. He was Gabriel Schist. That was his name. He was at Bright New Day. The nursing home. The nursing home he'd been at for five years. He was seventy... three? Four? Eight? Seventy-something years old.

His skin dripped with cold perspiration. He'd fallen out of bed. His tailbone hurt, and he had scraped his hip, but he didn't think he had done any serious damage.

"Zero," he whispered. "One, one, two, three, five, eight, thirteen, twenty-one, thirty-four, fifty-five, eighty-nine..." He ran out of breath. His throat was sore and dry.

Every part of him was cold, inside and out. He'd never felt so cold. He looked up at his microscope. It glared back down at him, its circular glass eye cold and unforgiving.

"One hundred forty-four, two hundred thirty-three, three hundred seventy-seven, six hundred ten—"

"Hello again, Bernard!" Dana Kleznowski said from the doorway. "You rang—"

"Roommate!" Bernard cried.

"Hey, Detective?" She ran over and dropped to her knees beside Gabriel. She placed her hand on his bare back. "Detective? Gabe... I mean, *Gabriel*, Gabriel. Are you okay? Please tell me you're okay."

Gabriel shuddered, but he remained silent. It'd been a long time since he'd felt a woman's hand on his naked skin; her touch brought back memories. Good memories. Painful memories. Skin on skin. It reminded him that, for better or worse, he still had a libido. He still felt things. He was still human. Even if he was crazy. Even if he was locked into the same building forever. Even if his demented condition meant it was probably illegal for anyone to have sex with him ever again. He was still human.

Her face was inches from his, her eyes still widened in alarm. He stared at her blankly, too exhausted to respond. Her eyelids were painted maroon. Her perfume smelled of fresh peaches.

"Smile, Gabriel," she demanded.

"Fingernails grow... one nanometer... every second," he replied. "Can you imagine that? Every *second*."

Gabriel's head was swimming. Bright New Day. He was at Bright New Day. His name was Gabriel Schist. He was trying to cure the Black Virus. There were... slugs. The virus. Slugs. Victor, Victor See. No, not See. It was *C,* Victor C, the letter C.

Dana reached for the call button. "Gabriel, smile, dammit. Smile."

Oh, right. Dana was trying to see if he was stroking out. When someone had a stroke, his smile was uneven. Fortunately, he wasn't having one. His last stroke had already caused enough problems. Another one could leave him unable to speak or walk or think.

Gabriel cleared the dirty cobwebs out of his head. *Okay, Gabriel, focus your damn mind.* He smiled for her, a big, winning smile, packed full of teeth. "I'm fine," he murmured.

Dana sat back on her bony haunches, sighed, and wiped the sweat from her forehead. The veins on her pale, too-thin hands were popping out.

Still smelling her peach-scented perfume, Gabriel tried to remember how her hand had felt on his naked back. It reminded him of how Yvonne's hands had felt, long ago. Cool. Textured. Tiny fingertips. "I'm fine," he repeated.

"Thank God." She laughed. "Crap! You had me worried as hell, ya bastard."

Gabriel shrugged. He wanted to smile again, to show her that he appreciated the fact that she cared, but something internal blocked him from expressing himself.

Dana stood up and dusted off the backs of her legs. "Okay. Well, I'll be right back to get your vitals. So just wait there. Don't try to stand up. We'll get you up with the Hoyer, just to be safe."

"Sure." He had no intention of waiting around for them to hoist him up with that ridiculous patient-lifting apparatus, but arguing the point was a waste of breath. Legally, they were supposed to use it every time a resident fell.

"Good. Wait here." She walked out of the room.

As soon as she was out of sight, Gabriel grabbed the side of the bed. He stood up slowly, painfully, just to make sure he was still capable of standing. His legs were shaky and gelatinous but fine. He was just dehydrated. His blood sugar was probably high, too.

He pulled the waistband of the sweatpants up over his navel and tied them a little tighter. He was cold and needed a shirt. He walked over and opened the closet door. Apparently, all of his shirts were in the laundry. "Hey, Bernard?"

"Yep," Bernard replied.

"This is Gabriel, your roommate. I was wondering if I could perhaps borrow one of your shirts today?"

"Yeah. Yeah. Sure, buddy. I've got too many."

Gabriel went over to Bernard's closet, which was insanely overstuffed with hundreds of those identical white V-necks. He pulled one out and saw the old trucker's initials, BUH 4, written on the inside of the collar in black permanent marker. Gabriel smiled and stretched the shirt over his head.

Suddenly, something changed. Almost imperceptibly, the air trembled. Gabriel felt it even before it happened. His lungs deflated. His stomach leapt into his ribs and collapsed.

Boom!

Something big and heavy violently crashed out in the hallway. The noise was followed by more crashes, softer ones, though no less violent. The walls shuddered.

Bang! Bang!

"Hurrrrtssss!" a man screeched, his voice echoing down the corridor. *"Hurtssss!"*

Bang! Bang!

Gabriel shivered. Bernard, who had been shakily lifting a cup of fruit punch to his mouth, dropped the cup and splattered red juice all over his shirt. Someone had collapsed in the hallway, and he was banging the floor, or maybe the wall. Falls weren't uncommon in the nursing home, but whatever had happened out there seemed unusual. The entire floor felt as if it were still rattling. Gabriel stepped toward the door and peeked around the corner. No one was in sight.

"Hurrrrrtssss! Gahhhh!" That was John Morris. It had to be.

Gabriel grabbed his cane and hobbled out into the hallway, wincing from his sore tailbone. He had to see what was going on. The scream sounded again, so high-pitched and dreadful that it made Gabriel's intestines want to tie themselves in knots and strangle his stomach. As Gabriel made his way down North Wing, many of the other residents worriedly peeked out of their doorways. At the other end of the hall, Dana seemed to be in a panic.

John Morris wasn't bedbound anymore. He was in the hallway, crawling on his hands and knees, the tubing still connected to his stomach like a long, plastic leech. He was screaming, coughing, and whimpering. His inhalations were so rough that it sounded as though his lungs were about to burst. In addition to the black wormlike veins and charcoal eyes, his skin was albino-white with ugly yellow sores spread all over him in a polka-dot pattern. A sickening puddle of perspiration trailed behind him. He was almost unrecognizable. He looked like an alien.

Morris's charcoal-black eyes focused on Gabriel. "P-pl-please, Detective. *You...* help me."

CHAPTER 20: EVOLUTION

MORRIS WASN'T INTERESTED IN THE nurses racing in his direction, stopping only to put on protective gloves, gowns, and masks. He stared steadily at Gabriel. "Help... me... plleee... pleeeassse. Hurts..." He crawled toward Gabriel. His breathing became harsher.

Gabriel looked over his shoulder, hoping that someone else was there, that Morris was calling for a nurse behind him. No. There was no one else.

"Gaahhhhh!" Morris gripped his stomach.

Gabriel took a deep breath and hobbled forward on his cane.

"Schist!" a male nurse yelled. "Stay back! We've got this!"

Ignoring the order, Gabriel continued forward. His ankles trembled beneath him.

"Get back, Gabriel! You'll get infected!"

"No." Gabriel cleared his throat. "I don't think it's airborne. The symptoms don't add up. There would be more noticeable inflammation in the nose, throat, and—"

"Stay the hell back, Schist!"

Morris went into a coughing fit. He collapsed onto the floor, gagging and gasping for air. The black veins on his skin heaved in and out like water balloons. The stench of his sweat was so putrid that Gabriel almost fainted.

"Hurrtsssssss..."

A group of nurses, including Dana, crowded around Morris and pinned him down so he couldn't crawl anymore. The nurses held Morris down as if he were a tackled linebacker at the bottom of a dog pile.

They wore masks, gowns, goggles, and gloves. They were prepared for anything.

But they weren't prepared for the Black Virus. Morris screamed, but it wasn't a scream of pain. It was a battle cry. Suddenly, all of the nurses flew into the air, thrown back like scraps of a fragmentation grenade. They slammed against the walls on either side of the corridor. One male nurse's wrist was crushed beneath the weight of his own body, and the bone emitted a crack so loud that Gabriel winced. Six adults had been casually tossed aside by the elderly victim of a terrible disease. Gabriel stood there, terrified and shaking.

Morris was on his knees again. His arms were swollen, filled with bulging, vein-covered muscles. He had the biceps of a bodybuilder, not a sick old man. Before Gabriel could get a better look, Morris collapsed again. His new muscles disintegrated and evaporated into rancid-smelling steam. Morris released a long groan. It was as if his arms had been filled with air, and then someone had let the air out.

Gabriel fought the urge to retreat, thinking that maybe there was something he could do. Perhaps he could talk to Morris and get him to calm down. Gabriel could explain that he was working on a cure.

"Help... Guhhh..." Morris groaned. "Pleeeease..."

Four of the nurses got up and tackled Morris again. Dana ran back to her medcart, probably to retrieve some kind of sedative.

Morris wailed in agony, his charcoal-colored eyes nearly popping out of their sockets. He wriggled, desperately trying to get free. Bloody abscesses popped up all over his exposed skin, overtaking the yellow polka-dot sores and covering him like red Dalmatian spots. Seconds later, the abscesses burst. Blood sprayed the nurses' gowns and dribbled down Morris's body, covering their protective gloves.

Gabriel recognized those abscesses. There was only one thing they could be: methicillin-resistant Staphylococcus aureus, or MRSA. But he'd never seen them form so quickly. They *couldn't* form that fast.

"Hold still, John!" the male nurse shouted.

"Hurts! Stop it. Please stop it. Let go! Gaaahhh! Hurts meeeeeee!"

Gabriel hobbled forward. He stopped a few feet from the terrifying scene and crouched down to make eye contact with the nurses holding

Morris. "Take it easy on him! Can't you see all of this stress is worsening his symptoms?"

"Get away, Gabriel! We can't afford to—"

Morris lunged forward, slipping free from his captors. He grabbed Gabriel's pant leg with one hand. The smell of necrotic flesh drifted up into Gabriel's nostrils. Morris looked up into Gabriel's face, pleading with those steaming black eyes. His skin became yellower.

"John—" Gabriel started.

A myriad of bumps appeared on Morris's face and hands and continued to spread over his skin, which the MRSA abscesses had painted red. The tiny bumps vaguely resembled scales, and each one had a small dimple in the center of it.

Smallpox? Horrified, Gabriel tried to pull away from the sick man's grasp, but Morris hung onto Gabriel's pant leg with a death grip. Gabriel had seen the way Morris's muscles had grown, and they'd grown fast. He'd seen what Morris had done to the nurses. Gabriel's bones were weak and brittle. If Morris threw *him* against the wall, he might never walk again. On top of that, MRSA and smallpox were terrifyingly contagious. Gabriel ripped his pant leg away.

Morris tried to crawl after him, and as he did, his legs and feet inflated. His legs became giant balloons of flesh. They turned to blobs that had to weigh more than the rest of his body combined. Morris couldn't move, much less crawl.

Elephantiasis? But that didn't make any sense.

Oily black fluid ran down Morris's cheeks. The nurses watched with horrified expressions. Two of them took off running.

Morris sneezed. Then, he sneezed again and again, several times, releasing black globs of mucus. Gabriel backed away, legs wobbling. Morris's rope-like veins throbbed as he gasped for air between sneezes. He started to dry-heave, and Gabriel shuffled back a few more steps. It was too late to help Morris. That was obvious.

John Morris vomited all over the floor. Emesis. He gagged then vomited again... and again. He vomited some more, seemingly emptying the entire contents of his body into one giant, disgusting black lake in the center of the green-tiled hallway.

Moments later, Morris collapsed. His fall was accompanied by the sound of a multitude of gritty little *cracks*. Upon landing, each of his bones shattered into a million tiny pieces. His body lost all sense of mass and resembled a deflated blow-up doll more than a human corpse.

Gabriel peered down at the black oily puddle Morris had ejected. One way or another, he needed to get a sample. As he stared, trying to figure out how to take some of it back to his room, something moved inside the puddle, making an almost imperceptible splash.

"Hey!" Gabriel shouted. "Look here! Look at it!"

The nurses staring down at Morris's body didn't respond. They stood nearly a yard back from their fallen patient, obviously unwilling to move any closer. They turned away from the sight and began discussing the matter amongst themselves.

Gabriel looked back at the slick, shiny vomit. Something was growing out of the fluid. A tiny sharp-toothed beak-like mouth less than a half-inch in diameter pushed upward, just above the puddle's surface. It opened, taking in its first deep gasp of oxygen.

"Hey!" Gabriel shouted.

The nurses ignored him and began sectioning off the area around Morris's corpse. They didn't seem concerned about the vomit puddle several feet away. The tiny jaw snapped shut then opened. The thing squalled like an infant, so quietly that Gabriel could barely hear it over the voices of the staff but so high-pitched that his eardrums stung as if they'd been pierced by needles. Gabriel covered his ears.

"Goddammit, people!" Gabriel yelled. "Will you just look over here?"

"Please stop—" one nurse started.

Gabriel pointed. "Something's moving inside the vomit! Some kind of creature. There's something in there."

Their only response was a dismissive hand gesture. Two male nurses pushed over a gurney, while the other four spread a sheet over the corpse. Until they had secured the body and the stretch of hallway near it, they wouldn't pay Gabriel any attention. He was on his own.

The tiny jaw stretched wide open, each row of sharp teeth glimmering in the fluorescent light. *Fine, don't listen to me. See what happens.* Gabriel crept closer. The beak-like mouth swayed toward Gabriel then stopped abruptly. It *saw* him.

Before Gabriel could react, the thing jumped right out of the puddle like a grasshopper. It plopped down on the floor with a nauseating splattering sound. Wriggling across the floor, the newborn vaguely resembled an enlarged black sperm cell, about six inches long, with a whip-like tail. The serpentine body moved as if it were made of gelatin.

The thing started crawling, swishing its long tail from side to side. It moved fast, as if it knew Gabriel was a threat and it needed to get away.

It scuttled past Gabriel and continued down the hall. Gabriel grabbed a pair of rubber gloves from a wall container, snapped them on, and followed the creature. When he got close enough, he tried to bend his rickety knees enough so he could bend down and snatch the creature before it escaped. The thing leapt forward out of his reach and scurried away, slithering like a garden snake. It was headed for one of the floor vents.

Gabriel hurried forward, his bad leg screaming in pain. As the slithering creature approached the vent, it slowed down. Gabriel crouched as fast as he could and grabbed for the thing's tail.

He wasn't fast enough. The dirty sperm cell wriggled between the slats and slid into the floor vent.

Gabriel sat on the floor, his legs too tired to hold him any longer. He leaned against the wall, gasping for air. His varicose veins throbbed, and the injuries on his tailbone and hip sent grueling reminders to the pain centers of his brain. God, he was too old for such activity.

What the hell was that thing? He didn't know. It defied everything he thought he knew about diseases. It didn't make sense.

The nurses, who in their protective gowns and masks looked more like bizarre cultists than medical professionals, were carting John Morris's wrapped-up corpse away on the gurney. Farther down the hall, two housekeepers were preparing the chemicals to sterilize the floor where Morris had died. None of them had noticed the ungodly creature that had wriggled its way out of the corpse. *Idiots! Blind idiots!*

Gabriel felt helpless and trapped. But peering over at the pool of black fluid, he realized that he had only a few minutes to spare before the housekeepers cleaned up the mess.

He still needed a sample.

CHAPTER 21:
MOLLUSCA

IN THE WEEK SINCE MORRIS'S death, Gabriel had spent every waking hour studying the sample of the Black Virus. He had finally gained a bit of insight into its more unique properties, so it was time to figure out a strategy.

After seven fruit punches and fourteen pudding cups, Bernard was snoring the night away in his chair. It was the first time that Gabriel had ever seen him asleep. About a half dozen of the slugs were perched atop that morning's newspaper on Gabriel's scuffed desktop, and the tiny beings expectantly peered up at him with their antennas.

TOXIC PLAGUE FAST BECOMING EPIDEMIC: 33 PEOPLE INFECTED ACROSS NEW ENGLAND

The secret was officially out in the open. The government cover-up had failed. Thirty-three didn't seem like much at first, not until one considered the *speed* of infection. And even worse, none of those thirty-three reported cases included the secret elderly victims at Bright New Day. Gabriel suspected that other facilities had been similarly hit and also unrecorded. That meant the actual number was at least in the fifties or sixties. The Black Virus had come out of nowhere, and like a hurricane, it'd already swallowed dozens of unfortunate victims.

"I'll need your assistance with something," Gabriel said. "If that's okay."

"Yes," the leopard-printed slug replied. "Our ears are open, Gabriel."

"Um, no?" Albino scoffed. "We don't even *have* ears. We've just got sensors in our antennas."

"Figure of speech," Leopard Print answered with a sigh. "Anyway. What can we do to help you? Tell us."

Gabriel cleared his throat and adjusted his reading glasses. In just a few hours, he'd already filled up two entire notebooks with new insights about the virus. "Well, first of all, let me explain what I've figured out so far. This virus. It's brilliant."

"Brilliant?"

"Yes, it's *insanely* brilliant. I've never seen anything like it. It's like a jack-of-all-trades, an *actor,* masquerading in the form of a pathogen. Somehow, it has managed to absorb the traits and symptoms of every other disease imaginable. In just this little sample of John Morris's vomit, I can *watch* as residual traces of the virus dramatically change structure. Based on exposure to different temperatures, prodding, stimulations, and so on, these traces show a capability to manifest as influenza or strep throat or syphilis. Elephantiasis. Mumps. Measles. Leprosy. Degenerative disorders. Anything! Yet, like I said, it's an actor. It's playing the *part* of any disease it chooses. It fools the body into reacting and forces the body to defend itself as if it really is fighting that specific disease. Then the virus sends the immune system's attention in a million different directions. I think this is why previous treatments don't work on it."

"Because the symptoms are all over the place," Leopard Print said.

"Exactly! The symptoms are so widespread, sometimes even to the point of being contradictory, that this Black Virus not only fools us, but it fools the immune system."

"It *fools* it, you say?" the black slug asked.

"Yes. My research proposed that the immune system is a conscious, autopoietic entity. But this virus turns our greatest defense into a laughingstock. The victim's immune system runs in a million different directions, trying to figure out what sort of pathogen it's dealing with, but it can't because the Black Virus is the Laurence Olivier of pathogens."

"Always coming back to the immune system, eh, Schist?" Albino said. "Maybe it was a smart idea to talk to you about this virus business, after all."

"Maybe." Gabriel chuckled. "Crazy, isn't it? I have to look over all of my old notes. I found a way to alter the immune system once before, back when I dealt with AIDS. Now, I just need to find a way to make it deal with this. AIDS was complicated, but this…"

Gabriel looked into the microscope, watching the sample move, bend, and try to escape. As he leaned forward, his back cracked. He yawned, feeling the familiar aches of old age. The bruise on his hip had mostly gone away, but it still hurt like hell. "But there's one piece that doesn't fit. That's where you all come in."

"We'll do what we can," Leopard Print said. "What do you ask?"

"So far, I've determined that when emesis occurs—that is to say, when the infected person vomits—it marks the end of the process. Emesis only occurs when the person dies. Final stage." Gabriel tilted back in his chair. "But there's one thing that throws me off. When emesis occurs, something remarkably strange happens. I saw some kind of… *creature* emerge from the filth."

"Where did it go?" Leopard Print asked.

"It crawled into a vent on the floor. I found a maintenance worker and asked him about it. He gave me the runaround, probably thought I was either a lunatic or a pervert from the instant I began speaking about black sperm monsters. But from what I can determine, it seems like those vents go out to—"

"Ah, I get it," Albino replied. "You want us to do the *hard* work."

Gabriel smiled. "You could say that."

"You want us to find this creature?" Leopard Print asked.

"Well, any residual traces of the creature would be enough. Slime, mucus, feces, et cetera. Something that comes directly from the creature instead of Morris. This sample has helped a great deal, but it's not showing me the full picture, just bits and pieces. I know that, by now, the creature may have escaped. But if you *can* find the whole creature, well…"

The slugs gathered in a tight circle under the lamplight and began murmuring amongst themselves. Gabriel felt like the last pick on the kickball team.

After a couple of minutes, Leopard Print crawled away from the others and looked up at Gabriel. "We can't."

"What?" Gabriel asked, trying not to reveal his annoyance. "Why not?"

"The Sky Amoeba has imposed very strict laws upon us regarding noninterference. Humanity must be allowed to have free will, but with free will comes the responsibility to make your *own* successes, as well as your own failures."

"Aren't you supposed to be the protectors of humanity?" Gabriel asked. "How the hell are you supposed to protect someone if you practice noninterference?"

"Inspiration." The slug wriggled its antennas. "Persuasion, reason, logic, love. We can talk to you, and we can guide you to the right path if you choose to take our help, but we are not permitted to actually interfere with the course of human history. We can paint a picture of morality for you, but *you* must make the decision to follow it. We can't help you with this task. But we do know someone who *is* allowed to intervene in times of emergency."

"Marvelous. And who would that be?"

"Our leader."

"Your leader." *If they talk about that Sky Amoeba again, I'm going out for a cigarette.*

"Yes. He's been wanting to speak with you for some time, actually. He's very curious about your experiments here." The slug crawled closer, right up to the edge of the desk.

Gabriel rubbed his eyes then looked at the cloudy night sky out the window. "Forget it. I don't want to hear another word about your goddamn Sky Amoeba again. If I—"

"I'm not speaking of the great Sky Amoeba," Leopard Print said with the slightest hint of irritation in its metallic voice.

"Then who?"

"One of us. The leader of the slugs."

"You have, um… let me get this straight. *You're* not the leader of the slugs? You have a different leader?"

"Indeed. And he will speak to you three days from now, at exactly three o'clock a.m. He's *very* exact when it comes to times, so be ready."

"Got it, sure. Lots of threes." Gabriel held back a groan. The slugs mystified him. They seemed to get stranger with every encounter, and every time he attempted to figure out whether or not they were real, he was left with a splitting migraine and no logical answers. Still, they were the only help he had. "Tell me, by any chance, does this marvelous slug leader of yours have a name?"

"Of course." Leopard Print's antennas straightened. "His name is Michael."

CHAPTER 22:
EMPTY

Autumn 1981

" S O IN CONCLUSION, GENTLEMEN, I trust that after reviewing all of this information, you'll understand why it's imperative for us to pursue potential cures for this contagion before it becomes more widespread." Gabriel turned off the projector and stood before the group of black-suited businessmen in their black-and-white room, trying to keep his knees from wobbling.

The men in front of him controlled the medical industry, the key to his future. The window shades were lowered, and the room was dark and silent, other than the sound of a man in the back smacking his lips. Gabriel spun his wedding ring around his finger then clasped it tightly. *Give me strength, Yvonne. When I come home tonight, I'll finally be the man I'm supposed to be.*

Gabriel had gotten through the slideshow presentation, told them all about his research, and explained the virus. He'd given them all the evidence from confirmed cases and his hypothesis on what had caused the virus. He had also presented examples of the current infections occurring in San Francisco, where people were increasingly popping up with swollen lymph nodes, bizarre symptoms, and strange cases in which the immune system failed to fight off simple infections.

If the men didn't rally behind him, the whole game was over. He was just one strange little man living on a sailboat with his dance instructor wife, and he needed their financial resources. He needed labs, proper equipment, and paperwork know-how that went over his head. He could also use some lawyers to keep him out of any legal hot water.

"I have a question," said Rufus Verne, staring at Gabriel with the amber eyes of a predatory falcon.

"Yes, Mr. Verne?"

"Well, from what I can see, you're asking for us to fund your research, yes?" His deep, gravelly voice cracked under the pressure of at least four decades of harsh cigarettes.

Gabriel nodded. "Yes."

"You want us to spend an enormous amount of money, time, and resources on your project." Verne's mouth smiled, but his eyes were untouched. "You want us to supply you with a research team, media attention, a whole hullaballoo. Am I correct, Mister... Schist, is it?"

Don Foyer, a churlish, Michelin-Man figure who wore white suits meant for a man three sizes smaller, snickered. The other men remained dead silent.

"Schist, yes," Gabriel said, attempting to project a confidence he didn't feel. "And you are correct, sir. That's what I'm asking for."

"I see. Now, Mr. Foyer"—Verne glanced back at Foyer—"was that a laugh I heard? Is there something you'd like to add to this conversation?" Verne's eyes and mouth pulled toward the center of his face, wrinkles knotting together into an icy, unfeeling smile.

Foyer's eyes bulged, and he raised his massive shoulders. "It's very, um... interesting. You're a smart guy, Mr. Schist, but is pouring all our money into your research practical?"

"Yes," Gabriel stated.

"Yes, you seem quite sure of yourself," Verne said, giving Gabriel a grandfatherly wink. "I concur with Mr. Foyer in that I found your presentation quite interesting. However, may I ask you something?"

Gabriel looked down briefly then straightened his back. He couldn't allow himself to look weak, not even for a moment. "Of course."

Verne narrowed his eyes. "This hypothetical disease you speak of, aren't you really just speaking about this whole gay cancer business? The situation that's going on over in San Francisco?"

"Gay cancer." Foyer smirked. "Yep."

Gabriel tightened his jaw. "It's been referred to by that name, yes. But I can assure you —"

Verne held up a hand. "Mr. Schist, can you tell me why we should dump all of our money into developing a cure for some homosexual disease?"

"Mr. Verne, it's not—"

"Frankly, I hope this is a joke," Verne scoffed. "Even if this disease does spread throughout the gay community, won't it just end once they're all dead? Just like that, gay cancer will be over. Have you even—"

Gabriel took a step forward. "Stop it. Right there."

The room went dead silent. *Nobody* interrupted Rufus Verne. Gabriel clenched his fists. Verne's face became a tangled knot of wrinkles, and his eyes went corpselike. Gabriel squeezed his wedding ring again. *I'll make you proud, Yvonne.*

"First of all," Gabriel said, "I'd appreciate it if you stopped casually dismissing people's lives, Mr. Verne. Every life is valuable, and any human life lost to this virus is a failure on our part. People are dying. That's not something to snicker at."

"Oh, please," Foyer said. "Can you—"

"Second," Gabriel interrupted, "listen to me. The *immunodeficiency virus that I'm telling you about has absolutely nothing to do with homosexuality. It's spread through the contact of bodily fluids. It spreads through blood, and yes, through sexual contact, but if we don't do something about this now, people will continue to die. Hundreds of people. Thousands.*"

Verne glared ahead, his falcon eyes sharpened by bloodlust. The rest of the suit-clad men sat bolt upright with mouse-like expressions. They were all so on edge that it was a wonder they hadn't toppled over a long time ago.

Gabriel continued. "In 1978, there was a person who rapidly lost weight and died in Kinshasa with swollen lymph nodes and a cytomegalovirus infection. The year after that, a concert violinist in Cologne—"

"A *gay* concert violinist?" Foyer interjected.

"A violinist contracted Kaposi's sarcoma. Three months later, his lymph nodes swelled. His body was attacked by one disease after another until the accumulative effect finally killed him. In 1980, a patient at UCLA came down with a yeast infection in his throat—"

"Get to the point!" Gene Yates, a surly character seated beside Rufus Verne, growled.

"My point? It's *happening,* gentlemen. People are already dying, and this is only going to spread faster. I can help you, and you can help the world. You can give me additional researchers, funding assistance—"

Verne tapped the glass table. "And who are *you,* Mr. Schist?"

"Pardon?"

"I had my employees do some research since I'd never heard your name before. Do you know what I found?"

Gabriel's lip trembled. He reached into his pocket and wrapped his fingers around his cool metal pocket flask filled with cheap whiskey, his hidden escape route that Yvonne didn't know about, for emergencies. Overcome with guilt, he pulled out his hand and instead squeezed his wedding ring. *I won't drink it, Yvonne. I promised you.* He stared at the table of businessmen, who looked like grinning demons.

"Turns out you're a bit of a renegade." Verne smiled. "A mad genius, from what I hear. A lot of academic achievements. Not everyone can claim to be an immunologist, a virologist, *and* an applied mathematician. But I also hear you're something of a rebel. I hear you've never kept a healthcare-related job for more than a year."

"Well—"

"Yes, it seems you have a long record of getting fired for using company materials for your research. And, Mr. Schist, when it comes to your precious research, you're a bit obsessed."

Gabriel stood in the spotlight like an actor taking his last bow. He had to win them over. The dying people on the streets needed this. "Sure. Call me obsessed. I've devoted my entire life to stopping this virus."

Verne chuckled. "That's a shame. Because as long as I'm around, Mr. Schist, you're not going to be stopping *any* virus. Have a nice day."

CHAPTER 23:
WHEEL

Summer 2018

IT WAS ALREADY SUNSET. ANOTHER day had flown by, and Gabriel had made no progress on curing the Black Virus.

He'd figured out how it acted, how it worked, and what it did, but that bizarre sperm-looking creature still confused him to no end. The creature was an extra puzzle piece that didn't fit anywhere on the map. His uncomfortable conversation with Melanie had planted the idea that he could have imagined it all. But even if that were the case, it wouldn't explain the concrete evidence that Morris's sample provided.

He needed a direct sample from the creature, and since there was no way Bright New Day was going to let him crawl around in the basement, he had to wait for the Slug Leader, "Michael," to appear. The timing of the virus's emesis stage had so far proved as unpredictable as the virus itself, so catching another victim at the right moment was like playing high-stakes poker.

Bernard's TV had been on since midnight, and the old truck driver had consistently rung for more snacks and fluids than any one man could possibly consume. Gabriel had spent his day staring into the microscope and waiting for a lightning bolt to hit him. He'd scribbled notes, equations, and formulas all over the walls of his room like an imprisoned madman. He'd studied textbooks and compared the virus to every other disease known to man, but he had drawn no clear conclusions. Every time the Lego blocks almost clicked together, a different-shaped one revealed itself and threw the whole system awry. He had to keep reminding himself that he'd done it before, so he could do it again.

He gazed out at the parking lot and watched the translucent sunlight dissipate into the opaque darkness of nightfall. He decided he needed to take a walk. If he stared into the microscope any longer, he would get too discouraged.

Gabriel stood up, put on his trench coat, and grabbed his cane. He hobbled out to the corridor. *Tap. Tap. Tap.* As he meandered through North Wing, he peered into the rooms where most of his fellow residents were asleep. He walked past the physical therapy center and considered venturing out to West Wing and seeing if he could find Victor's room. But Victor clearly savored his privacy, and the man might not react kindly to an unannounced visit. So Gabriel instead traveled to South Wing, which gave him a surprising sense of nostalgia.

Everyone was asleep there, as well. Bob Baker was out like a light, blankets pulled over his head. Mickey Minkovsky shouted down the corridor, but he often did that while asleep.

Edna Foster was the only person he found still awake. Her wheelchair was stuck in someone's doorway, the left wheel wedged in the frame, and she was rolling back and forth, trying to escape. "Ohhh... this is terrible... the worst ever..." She wore her usual scowl, and her Parkinson's-ridden body was shaking and twisting from head to toe.

"Hey!" a woman yelled from inside the room. "How stupid are you? Get the hell out of my door."

Edna continued rolling backward, forward, and backward again. Gabriel hobbled over to her. Her palm was cold and rough and twitched spasmodically, even as she squeezed his hand. She stared up at him, searching his face for something she couldn't name.

"Ohhh my God." Her eyes opened wide with recognition. "Sam. It's *you*, Sam. Yes, it's really you. I thought you were dead."

Sam? "Uh... no. It's Gabriel. Hi, Edna."

"It's so terrible..." She gulped. "So, so terrible. Worse than ever."

"I know. I know." Gabriel released her shaking hand, grasped the handles of her wheelchair, and yanked her free from the doorway.

"Hey!" the woman in the room said. "What the hell is that woman doing?"

"She was stuck," Gabriel explained. "She was roaming the hallway, and her wheelchair got stuck, okay? Just relax. She's having a terrible day."

"Sam, don't you dare tell her all that personal information about me!" Edna said, glaring at him. "If you know what's good for you, you'll stop flapping your lips like a peacock!"

Gabriel sighed. One could never win, not with her. Everything was always terrible.

She reached for his hand again. "Give me a ride. Please?"

A ride. That was all she wanted. Edna's body was nearly immobile, forever trapped in a chair she could barely control. Her legs jutted out, and her Parkinson's only worsened the problem, since she was always shaking. Every time she ate, bits of food got all over her nice clothes.

Gabriel said, "Tell you what. Would you be interested in some tea?"

"Yes. And let's go to the lobby. We can see the fish. I like them."

Gabriel hooked his cane between his thumb and forefinger and pushed Edna's wheelchair down the hall, using it like a walker. As they passed the nurses' station, Harry Brenton looked up from his paperwork and grinned. He offered Gabriel a friendly wave, which Gabriel returned.

"Hey, Edna," Harry said. "You want me to get your bed ready for when you get back?" Harry spoke carefully, as Edna was notoriously finicky about when her bed was to be pulled down, where her dirty bedding was to be placed, how it was folded, and exactly which of her three bins her laundry went into. Gabriel had heard many stories of her scratching, spitting, and harsh insults that had caused even the toughest LNAs to leave the room in tears.

"Yes. Please do. But do it *right*," she said, shaking her finger at him. "Make sure all the blankets are folded just perfectly, nice and neat."

"Sure thing, ma'am. Tell you what, I'll even put new sheets and blankets on the bed," Harry replied. "What do you want me to do with the old blankets? Should I put them in the laundry bin by the door, as usual? Or do you want me to put them in the red bin in the closet, as you had me do last time?"

Edna's eyes narrowed. "You're going to *eat* them. You're going to put peanut butter on those blankets, and you're going to eat 'em."

"What—"

"Yes, put 'em in the laundry bin by the door, you dummy." Edna scowled. "What do you think I want you to do with 'em? Now get outta my way. Me and Sam here are gonna have a nice cup of tea."

Harry's face turned bright red. He looked at Gabriel, and Gabriel looked back at him. Both of them grinned at each other knowingly.

Gabriel winked. "See you later, Harry."

Gabriel wheeled Edna to the lobby. He heated a cup of lemon-flavored herbal tea for her, and by the time they sat down in front of the fish tank, the sky had fully darkened. The overhead lights were dimmed, and the tank was glowing blue. The jazz music from the overhead speakers lent a nice, calming influence over the entire lobby, but it also made Gabriel sleepy. After all the scrubbing, sanitizing, and air ventilation the staff had done, it was almost hard to remember that the first incident with John Morris had happened there.

Gabriel held the cup for Edna, and she sipped tea through a straw. At first, she tried to hold the cup herself, even calling him a terrible person for trying to hold it for her. But after she'd shakily splattered hot tea all over the place, she allowed him to help her.

Watching Edna weakly sip through the straw, Gabriel actually felt young. His body was weak and his mind demented, but he wasn't like her. Not yet. He could still hold a cup.

She pushed the straw away with her tongue. As she stared at the luminescent blue water, her features softened, and her shaking subsided a bit. "I remember going to school up in... up in Kennebunk, you know." She sighed. "Those were the good old days. Oh gosh. I wish I could go back to them."

A hint of sadness entered her expression, but Gabriel recognized the same crackling spark that he felt whenever he remembered the first time his father took him out on the sailboat, his days on the ocean with Yvonne, the summers when Melanie would come to visit, or his old talks with Father Gareth. That spark stood on the border between sadness and warm nostalgia.

"I met my husband back there," Edna murmured. "All the way back when we were children. Yeah, he was a really good man. He was a policeman, you know."

"What was his name?"

"Mark. I miss him so much. He was such a good man, such a... a..." She stopped and looked at Gabriel as if blaming him for her lack of coherence. Then she relaxed again. "Thank you for the tea. It was really nice of you."

Gabriel smiled. "You're welcome." He hoped he'd helped ease her pain, just as she'd helped ease his, if only by her stubborn tenacity in the face of incapacitating illness. Talking to her, he felt renewed motivation. He *would* find a solution for the virus.

"I love you, Sam," Edna said. "As a friend, I mean. Not a boyfriend. Too old for that gibberish."

Gabriel had learned to approach emotional conversations with a common rule: *what would Father Gareth have done?* With that in mind, his answer became obvious. "I love you too, Edna."

"Good. It's nice... to have a friend."

Gabriel imagined what it was like to be her. He probably *would* be her soon enough. Her body was a lump of shaking flesh trapped in a wheelchair. She could only eat pureed foods, and she didn't know what day of the week it was. She was unable to think clearly or to carry on a conversation without getting disoriented. But she still felt pain, anger, and stark, naked loneliness on a level that few could even imagine.

By the morning, she would probably have forgotten all about their chat. At the moment, Gabriel was Sam, but the next time they spoke, he would have a different name. She wouldn't remember the man who had shown her kindness, and she would be back in the same forlorn state. The cycle would repeat until the day she died. And despite all the newfound hope his efforts against the virus had brought him, Gabriel grimly considered that death was the only escape. Death was the reward. That was perhaps the greatest punishment of all and the evilest mockery.

Edna offered him a shaky hand. "Feel this." The back of it was covered in tiny bumps, scars, and liver spots. "Feel how rough it is, Sam?"

He ran his fingers over her hand. Her skin felt gritty, reminiscent of sandpaper. If one were to rip a Band-Aid off her too quickly, it might take all of her skin with it. "Yes," Gabriel replied.

"That roughness, you feel it? Sam, that ain't going away. It's never gonna get any better."

Despite his best attempts at stoicism, a heart-wrenching sadness welled up in his chest. He felt his own skin and realized it was almost as rough as Edna's. "I know how you feel."

Edna stared blankly at him for a moment. Then, she pointed down at her wheelchair with a dismissive gesture. "You know what, though? Someday, I'm gonna get out of this damn thing. You know that?" Her eyes lit up with an excitement Gabriel had never seen from her before.

He looked at her distorted, shaking body and at her legs jutting out. "But that's..." He bit his lip. "You can't... I mean..."

"Yeah, nobody believes me, but just you watch. Someday, when they least expect it, I'm gonna do it. I'm gonna do it, oh I'm gonna do it, and *nobody* is gonna stop me. No, sir. I'll surprise 'em all."

She let out a feeble laugh. He'd never heard her laugh, but it was a wonderful sound, full of joy, wisdom, and life. Tears welled up in his eyes. He wanted to look away from her, fearful that his pessimism might suck away her optimism like a leech. But he held her gaze, staring right into her eyes, for *her*, his friend, his ninety-seven-year-old demented friend.

Edna's face glowed. As another joyful giggle tumbled from her lips, she clasped Gabriel's hand. "Just you watch, Sam. Someday, I'm gonna walk again. I'm gonna just stand up and walk right out of this place. Just you watch. And when I do it, when I finally do it, I'm gonna laugh in all their faces the whole time."

CHAPTER 24:
MICHAEL

O N THE THIRD DAY, AT two thirty in the morning, Gabriel was awakened by the obnoxious static-filled blaring of his alarm clock. Still fully dressed, he slowly roused his creaky bones out of bed.

Why did I set the alarm for such a ridiculous time? Oh, wait. That's right. Michael.

Bernard was still awake and, from the sounds on the other side of the curtain, watching an old Bogart movie. But that was okay, as Gabriel wasn't worried about Bernard overhearing him when Michael showed. His roommate, though always friendly, was so wrapped up in his daily rituals that he often seemed to forget that Gabriel even existed. Surprisingly, Bernard was turning out to be the best roommate Gabriel had ever had.

Gabriel glanced at his bedside table, hoping there might be some leftover coffee, but the mug was empty. He pushed the mug aside and noticed something behind it. A bizarre figurine had been left there. The six-inch wooden statue's head and shoulders were leaned against the lamp as if the doll was taking a nap.

Gabriel picked it up. He'd seen many similar dolls during that one time he'd impulsively vacationed down in Mexico for the annual *Día de Muertos* celebration. The Day of the Dead doll was a smiling skeleton garbed in bright-colored clothing and a wide-brimmed sombrero. The doll clutched marigold flowers in its bony hand, and its circular black eyes were just reminiscent enough of the Black Virus's victims to make him shudder.

"Hey, Bernard?" Gabriel called.

"Yep."

"Did anyone come in here while I was asleep?"

After a pause, Bernard replied, "I dunno, buddy. I haven't seen anybody come in here in at least seven or eight days. I'm starving."

The doll's other hand was clutching a folded-up slip of paper about the size of a fortune cookie strip. Gabriel plucked the note from the tiny hand and unfolded it. The print was too small to read, so he got up and placed it under the microscope.

Don't let the past define the future. Follow the new *path, Gabriel.*

The note was typed in Courier font, italicized, and perfectly spaced. The figure fell out of Gabriel's shaking hands. From the floor, the skeleton doll's black eyes stared up at him. A deep knot of discomfort settled inside his guts. He didn't like the idea of people sneaking into his room and placing skeleton dolls beside his bed. Pantsless Bernard shuffled over to the bathroom, gripping his invisible steering wheel.

"Bernard, are you sure no one came in? Just a little bit ago, maybe?"

Bernard stared at him. "Nope." He went into the bathroom and closed the door.

Averting his eyes from the skeleton doll's mocking gaze, Gabriel glanced at the clock. *2:58.* Michael would arrive soon. He drank a glass of water, wishing it was whiskey.

Gabriel stood before the window, resting his head on the cool glass. It was dark outside, so he turned off his bedside lamp and allowed his eyes to adjust. Outside, beyond the unlit parking lot, was a cluster of bushes, a pine tree, some orchids, and a fence.

Gabriel stood there, waiting. He tapped his foot impatiently. He looked at the clock: 3:00. *Anytime now, Michael. Anytime.*

Gabriel's legs trembled under the weight of his agitation. He checked the time again: 3:02. Michael was late, despite the slug's assurance that he was very exact. Gabriel stared out the window, trying not to get too worked up.

Something moved in the bushes. A tall shadow emerged and crept forward. That *had* to be Michael. But Michael definitely wasn't a slug.

He was much too big for that. He was bigger than a dog, almost the same size as a man. *Was he a human?*

Gabriel strained his eyes to catch a better glimpse. The dark shadow lurched upright. Its body writhed through the grass, coming toward Gabriel. No, it wasn't human. It looked like a tall, gelatinous blob.

The shadow raised its head, revealing two long antennas nearly as big around as Gabriel's forearms. Michael was a six-foot-tall slug. And that enormous slug was standing at Gabriel's window, peering inside at him.

CHAPTER 25: GATHERING

MICHAEL'S GLOSSY SKIN GLISTENED IN the moonlight. His massive grey-and-black speckled body had an almost crystalline texture that was oddly beautiful. His antennas waved in a curious manner, with moist little black eyes on the ends of both stalks. With every twist and turn, the creature's inner musculature bulged and flexed with a sense of purpose. Michael was a slick, powerful machine, yet at the same time, an elegant dancer.

With one antenna, Michael tapped on the glass.

Gabriel raised the window, nervously aware that the only thing between him and the giant slug was a thin screen. The smell of ocean saltwater drifted inside the room. On the left side of the slug's neck was a giant pneumostome, a large hole from which air entered into the slug's single lung. Gabriel could hear the enormous creature breathing. The slug's respirations sounded like those of a relaxing horse.

Gabriel tried to speak, but his mouth was dry. He swallowed. "I... um... hello." He cleared his throat. "Hello?"

The slug's pneumostome heaved in and out. Every breath sounded slow and steady but with all the thunder of a racecar revving its engine. "Hey," the slug replied.

Gabriel rocked back on the balls of his feet. Despite the casualness of the tone, Michael's voice was incredibly deep, but at the same time, quiet. The slug sounded like a whispering giant, one who knew that only the slightest pressure was needed, and that speaking any louder might shatter a few eardrums.

"Um. Hi?" Gabriel mumbled.

"That's a mighty fine trench coat you've got there," Michael said. "I've gotta say, Gabriel, you're looking sharp, sharp as a blade."

Gabriel had no idea how to respond. The whole situation was just too weird. He considered reciting the Fibonacci sequence.

The slug cocked his head to the side, antennas momentarily retracting then extending again. "Ah, man. Sorry about that. I'm terrible at introductions."

"So I take it that you're Michael, then? I mean... Slug-Michael?"

The slug's antennas reeled back a bit. "Cripes! *Slug*-Michael?" Michael chuckled, emitting a deep reverberating noise. "You're kidding me. Slug-Michael. When you say it that way, it just sounds bad. And when I say bad, I don't mean bad in the kitschy slang sense of the word. Listen, man. Just plain ol' Michael suits me fine. We'll stick to the basics, agreed?"

"Michael," Gabriel said. "Yes. Sure."

"Much better."

"So, if you don't mind me asking, why are you late? The slugs described you as being very exact. They made a point of —"

"About that. I love those guys, but yeah, they've got some really weird ideas about me."

Gabriel shifted uneasily. As strange as talking to the other slugs had been, the giant one was a whole other level of weirdness. But Michael's tone was both familiar and comfortable. In an odd way, the big slug reminded him a bit of Father Gareth.

"Oh yeah!" Michael exclaimed. "I love that guy."

"Pardon?"

"Gareth, of course. The guy who you were just thinking about? He did a lot of great work, saved a lot of lives, helped a lot of people. Never gave himself enough credit, though. Crying shame. But yeah, Father Gareth was an amazing man, I'll tell ya."

Gabriel shook his head. "So on top of everything else, you're telepathic?"

"Well, I don't know if telepathic is the right word. You human beings are just as telepathic as we are, trust me. It's just that we slugs are more consciously aware of our intuitive connection to all life, and you humans—ah man, how do I say it nicely?—you guys spend an awfully large amount of energy denying what's right in front of you. No offense."

Gabriel moved closer to the window. "I don't understand."

"Yeah, you do. C'mon, man. Look at any conversation between two people. If you pay attention, you'll see that there are actually two dialogues going on. You've got the verbal conversation, and a layer of unspoken communication right beneath that, a psychic message, if you want to use that kinda terminology. When you follow that second conversation, the true one, that's when you realize how interesting you humans really are."

The toilet flushed, and the bathroom door creaked open. Bernard shuffled out into the room. He closed the bathroom door, turned around, and came to an abrupt stop, staring at the window. "Wow. What is *that?*"

Gabriel started to move to block the window then realized that would only draw attention to what waited on the other side. He desperately hoped Bernard's vision wasn't good enough to see the giant slug. Part of him was tempted to see if Bernard could see the thing, so he would have a witness, but that idea was driven back by the death hordes of startled panic.

Bernard shuffled closer to the window. He squinted and poked at the screen. Gabriel held his breath.

"Well, damn," Bernard said. "Guess you see something new every day." He shuffled back to his side of the room and plopped down in his armchair. He fell asleep almost immediately, apparently as unconcerned with a giant slug as he would have been with a housefly.

"Goddamn," Gabriel muttered. "I don't even know what to say about that."

"For starters, how about we steer away from all these *goddamns?*" Michael said. "C'mon, brother. It's like every other word with you. Goddamn this, goddamn that, goddamn slugs. It gets tiring."

Lost in thought, Gabriel ignored the suggestion. Bernard had seen the slug. That meant they were real and that he wasn't completely insane. Relief flooded him like water bursting through a dam. He made a mental note of that fact. If he wanted to keep from spiraling into full-out lunacy, remembering such things might prove to be a necessity.

"So you wanted to talk to me?" Gabriel asked.

"The Sky Amoeba did kinda imply that—"

"I have no interest in this floating Sky Amoeba nonsense. I want to talk about the Black Virus."

"Good. 'Cause like I was gonna say, that's why I'm here. In fact, I know exactly where the Black Virus is going and where that little thing you saw crawling across the floor was headed to."

Gabriel gaped at the slug. "Really?"

"Yeah, man. And even better, I can show you."

"The other slugs said something about a law of noninterference. They said that you can intervene in times of emergency, that you can... look, just tell me. What is the Black Virus? Can you tell me that?"

"It's not that easy." Michael shook his head. "I have my own laws to follow. But I do have the power to show you where it went."

"And where is that?" Gabriel pulled a microscope slide from his top desk drawer and slipped it into his pocket.

"At the base of the building. Outside. If you want answers, Gabriel, then all you have to do is follow me." Michael's antennas spread and gripped the sides of the window screen.

Gabriel stepped back. Michael bent the screen's plastic sides inward, removed it from the window, and dropped it to the ground. A breeze gently rustled the curtain, and the sounds of traffic from about a quarter of a mile away drifted into the room.

Gabriel grabbed his cane. Other than daily trips to the smoking area and the occasional supervised hospital visit, he hadn't been outside in years. He couldn't believe he was about to just step out and follow a ridiculous slug leader.

But he wanted answers, so he would do exactly what the big slug said. He climbed out the window.

CHAPTER 26:
ADAMANT

A S GABRIEL FOLLOWED MICHAEL'S DARK, wriggling form around the outside perimeter of the building, he was tempted to flee. He could run away, leaving Bright New Day behind him forever, and flip the bird to all of his obligations. It was the best chance he'd ever had.

But they would catch him. In a few hours, the nurse would come in with his morning meds and discover the open window. They'd call the police, who would find him and bring him back in restraints. After that, he would be locked up in the Level Five unit.

So instead of fleeing, Gabriel followed the slow-moving giant slug with all the obedience of a teacher's pet. But he couldn't help but look behind him and fantasize. He gazed out at the asphalt roads, the signs, the many small businesses down the street, and the elementary school across the road. *God, it was so tempting.*

Michael stuck near the side of the building, slithering down the grassy hill. Gabriel stumbled a couple of times. He hadn't realized how much weaker his eyesight had become in the last few years. The shadows were like dark mountains blocking his path. Worse, he hadn't thought about how challenging a downhill slope would be on his bad leg. Though he'd gritted his teeth through the pain when climbing out the window, the pull of gravity led to heavy steps that made his knee crunch. He tried to put most of his weight on his cane, unsuccessfully. Every few minutes, he had to stop and catch his breath. He felt pathetic.

But each time he stopped, Michael waited patiently. The gentle contours of that inhuman face and those black eyes seemed to convey sympathy.

The slope became steeper. Gabriel's legs nearly buckled underneath him. He worriedly checked his pulse. It was a bit faster than he would've liked.

"You okay?" Michael asked.

"Yes. Yes."

They wound around the back side of the building. The grass gave way to jagged black rocks coated in just enough water to be horribly slippery. Michael went over the rocks easily enough, but Gabriel struggled. He kept his gaze downward, focusing intensely on his feet. Every step was painful, and if he slipped, it could mean a broken hip that would never heal, then a walker, and later a wheelchair.

"Look up, brother." Michael said. "You don't wanna miss this."

Gabriel raised his head and heard a peaceful sound that he'd given up all hope of ever experiencing again. His gaze landed on the one thing his heart had most yearned for, night and day, for five long years, and tears tugged at the corners of his eyes.

Ocean waves crashed against the rocks, beckoning him as if he were a lost child. The distinctive aroma of fresh saltwater rose into Gabriel's nostrils. He smiled, and that smile soon became a laugh. One notion overwhelmed his every thought. He wanted to touch it.

Gabriel rested his cane against a speckled boulder and stumbled through the rocks as quickly as he could manage. When he arrived at the water's edge, he dropped to his knees. The impact hurt, but he didn't care. The ocean rushed up to meet him, and he closed his eyes, arms outstretched.

As the water surrounded him, he dipped his liver-spotted hands into the ice-cold waves. Eyes still closed, he pictured his old sailboat, remembering the late-night cruises, the wind, the sky, and the horizon. Smiling as he hadn't smiled in half a decade, he cupped his palms and splashed water onto his face.

He opened his eyes and stared out into the moonlit expanse. The water had chilled him to the bone, but he'd never felt warmer. He stood and looked at Michael, who had slid over next to him.

"You didn't have to bring me out here," Gabriel said. "You have the right to intervene. That's what the other slug told me, and you confirmed it. That means you could've just brought me a sample."

"Yeah." Michael shifted his body.

"So you brought me out here on purpose. For this." Gabriel grinned. "Thank you."

"I guess... I dunno. I didn't have to, but I just thought that you deserved something nice for once."

Gabriel laughed again, feeling a deep, comforting warmth within his chest. He wiped the moisture from his eyes. He knelt and placed his hands back in the water, his fingers resting on the backs of textured shells and wet seaweed. He felt the wind on his damp face as he stared into the horizon and took a mental photograph, because even if all his other memories went to hell, he didn't want to forget what might easily be his final glimpse of the ocean.

When he started to shiver, he got back to his feet and walked over to Michael. He ran his hand across the giant slug's spongy back. "So shall we go find this sample?"

"Yep."

Gabriel collected his cane and followed Michael down the beach. The angular black outline of Bright New Day looked down on them like a watchful eagle perched on the rocks. The night sky was a beautiful sprawl of stars, reflected in the equally beautiful ocean. Tiny gold lights dotted the distant shoreline.

As they moved outside of the public area, a sloping hill obscured their view of the nursing home. After entering a clearing of tall grass, Gabriel spotted the metal surface of a buried pipeline. Using his massive tail like a broom, Michael swept away some of the debris to reveal more of the surface. A thin crack running the length of the exposed metal was slowly bleeding grey, copper-scented water. Some kind of slimy goo had oozed out of the pipe, leaving a black line that led toward the ocean.

The creature had escaped through the pipe then fled to the ocean. Closer inspection revealed multiple sets of streaks, which meant multiple creatures. Gabriel realized that more infected residents had died. His stomach felt queasy.

Gabriel reached into his pocket and pulled out the microscope slide. Crouching—ah, Christ, there's that back pain again—he gathered a sample of the black slime, careful not to touch it with his fingers. He held the glass up to the moonlight to make sure he'd gotten enough. To his revulsion, the sample actually *squirmed.*

"Okay. Well, enough of that." Gabriel tucked the slide back in his pocket.

A light rain began to fall. He'd gotten his sample just in time. As water dripped from the brim of his fedora, he stared out at the ocean and lit a cigarette. Waves rolled more aggressively over the sand, their white froth forming a wound on the beach's surface.

A few minutes later, they began the long walk back to his bedroom window. He would need to wash his muddy clothes in the sink to avoid suspicion. As for the screen, he would blame that on the weather. Michael had bent it far too much for it to fit back into the window frame, but maintenance could easily replace it with a new one.

"This Black Virus," Michael said, "with the elaborate deaths and black eyes, there's something so disturbing about it, don't you think? Something that doesn't quite fit?"

Gabriel exhaled smoke. "I don't understand it. I've seen so many diseases in my life, but this particular strain…"

"It defies understanding?" Michael said.

"Nothing defies understanding. But it's confusing, certainly." Each step was murder on Gabriel's leg. His tiny bed on North Wing started to seem like a luxury suite. "The Black Virus is a virus like any other. A highly sophisticated and unique one, perhaps, but still just a virus. I'm not going to treat it any differently."

"Gabriel, I like you. You're a swell guy. And I want you to know that when you test that sample tomorrow, you're not going to like what you find."

"Why not?"

"You need to see it for yourself, fella. You'll know why when you see it. If I told you now, you wouldn't believe me."

Climbing the hill, Gabriel bore down on his cane for support. "Sounds like a cop-out answer from someone who doesn't know as much as he claims." He frowned. "Regardless, it doesn't really matter whether I like what I find or not. The only thing that matters is that I learn more about the virus so I can find a cure."

"Gabriel, this isn't gonna be like AIDS."

"What do you mean?"

"Finding a cure for the Black Virus... that's not gonna work, at least not the way you think it will. What you need to do is understand the virus. Because pretty soon, you're gonna know more about that virus than anyone else in the world, and when you do, well..."

"Care to explain?"

"Ahh. Sorry, I can't. It wouldn't be right."

The top of the hill was in view but still a good distance away. Gabriel paused to catch his breath. "Fine. In that case, just shut up. I'll work on my cure, and we can eradicate this virus before it infects half the population. Just give me space, Michael. I'll do all the work."

Michael's antennas twisted around to stare at him. "Gabriel, why are you lying to yourself? You know full well that the Black Virus is a lot more than just a disease. You saw it give birth right before your eyes. What kind of disease does that? What's going on here is something way scarier than a disease."

The rain was getting heavier, pounding on Gabriel's fedora. "I don't understand what you're saying." They were nearing the crest of the hill.

With his rain-spotted head, Michael gestured back toward the ocean. "Why do you think this virus is hitting *here,* of all places? Why here at Bright New Day, where you are? C'mon, you can't tell me that's a coincidence."

Gabriel's bedroom window came into view, and he worried that someone had seen the open window. He didn't think so since the light was still off, but he wanted to get back inside as quickly as possible so he could start washing his clothes. When they reached the building, he put his cigarette out against the wall.

"I gotta say, Gabriel," Michael said, "this is bigger than an epidemic. This is something you can't just find a miracle cure for and move on from, like you did before. It won't work, and if you're reckless about it, you run the risk of killing millions of people in the process."

"I'm trying to *save* people not kill them. What do you expect me to do?"

"Finish your research. Study it, learn everything there is to know, and figure out how to negotiate with it. Then, together, we will capture the center of it, the core of its being. And we need to—"

"Capture the center? The core of its being? Negotiate with a virus? What the hell are you talking about?"

"I mean exactly what I said. Together, we can capture the core of its being. And then we'll take our case to the Sky Amoeba."

Gabriel glared at the big slug. He didn't have time for such nonsense. The slugs were probably just hallucinations brought on by his Alzheimer's. Without responding, he clambered through his bedroom window. As soon as he was inside, relief swept through him.

Michael inched up to the window. "Gabriel, you—"

"I'm going to bed, Michael. And tomorrow, I'm going to prove you wrong."

Gabriel took off his coat. Bernard wasn't in the bathroom, so he could wash his muddy clothes out in the sink. Nothing in his room had been moved, and the bed linens were still as untidy as he'd left them. He would call maintenance the next morning and say the window screen had fallen off in the night.

Michael stared at him through the open window. The slug's posture suddenly looked weighted down. Even his antennas were lowered. "Sorry, man," Michael said.

"For what?"

"Tomorrow, the truth is gonna come out. And like I said, you're not gonna like it."

Gabriel shook his head, closed the window, and shut the blinds right in the giant slug's face.

CHAPTER 27:
ELLIPSIS

Spring 1983

FATHER GARETH WALKED ACROSS THE wooden planks of the Clamshell Tavern, a small outdoor restaurant less than a mile from the famous Santa Monica Pier. Every step caused another old joint in his leg or hip to creak.

The last few years had not been kind to him. His beard had become a long, frizzy tangle of white hair. His once straight-backed, nimble figure had been devoured by Crohn's disease, leaving little more than a fragile skeleton with transparent, speckled skin. The bags under his eyes grew heavier with every passing month. Gareth had often liked to joke that the wrinkles on his face might someday pull the skin right off, but lately, he worried that his joke might actually come true.

He'd once stood at a proud six foot two, but now, the stoop in his back had lowered him to five foot nine, on a good day. The knockout combination of arthritis and carpal tunnel had transformed even the simple task of holding a pen into a painful chore. Osteoporosis had dealt the final blow in his body's self-destruction. His bones had gotten so hollow that even the hottest days of the summer did nothing to warm him. So whenever he left the church, he always wore his new favorite outfit, a trench coat and fedora.

But one part of Gareth had remained untouched: his faith. Giving the sermon that morning had almost caused him to pass out from heat exhaustion, but he had never forgotten how to smile. His soul was intact.

"Old Gareth!" Gabriel Schist waved from a table at the edge of the deck.

Gareth walked over, stepping carefully. The quarter-of-an-inch gap between every plank was deadly. "Gabriel, always a pleasure!"

Gareth sat down, and Gabriel offered him a strong, sturdy handshake then took a long drag from a cigarette. *Smoking?* That was new. Gabriel was in his thirties, but he looked younger. His bright red hair and tanned skin glistened in the sun. His grey eyes held the same startling intensity they'd possessed when he was a boy, but dark circles smudged the skin beneath them. In front of him was a tall glass of amber ale. Three other empty glasses stood to one side, and two shot glasses were poorly hidden behind the menu.

"My boy, it's wonderful to see you again," Gareth said. "It's been too long."

"Two months and seven days, to be exact," Gabriel replied.

"Why, yes. Yes, I suppose so. Now, why don't we see each other more often?"

Gabriel lowered his head. "Because I don't call enough. I'm sorry. I've just been so busy. I'll make up for it."

"Busy times are the best times. Don't be hard on yourself. *We* will make up for it."

Gabriel glanced down at his beer. Sweat dribbled down the sides, forming tiny puddles on the wood tabletop. As if sensing Gareth staring at him, Gabriel protectively wrapped his fingers around the glass.

Gareth cleared his throat. "Anyway, sorry I'm late. After Mass, I met this charming fellow, a new convert, and we talked for a bit. It's bizarre how merely talking to people wears me out these days. I used to be such a social butterfly."

"You still are, I think."

"Perhaps, but these days... you know how you feel right after waking up, before you have your coffee? That's what old age is like, except no caffeinated concoction can make it go away. Nope, you're stuck. I'll tell ya, getting old is a bummer."

Gabriel chuckled, but he sounded distracted. He took another drag off his cigarette.

"So how are your experiments on the immune system coming?"

Gabriel's eyes darted to the side. "Stalled. I'm focusing on other things for the time being." He downed the rest of his drink, wiped the foam from his mouth, and signaled the waitress for another.

The sun disappeared behind the greyish-white blanket of clouds. Gareth gazed out at the Ferris wheel on the pier. "So what have you been focusing on instead?"

"A lot of smaller projects, ideas, fun experiences, that sort of thing. Yvonne and I finally bought a house last month."

"That's fantastic! Tell me more."

"It's a nice place, big. It was a foreclosure. The last owners wrecked it, so we'll have to fix it up, but it's got good potential. You'll have to see it."

"Is that an invitation?"

"Yes."

"Good, I accept. Thank you for taking pity on the strange, bearded old man in the trench coat. I hope I can be a good houseguest and—"

"Actually, I wanted to see if you could help me fix it up."

"Me? I'm getting up there in years."

Gabriel waved dismissively. "Oh, stop. The biggest problem is the nasty little porch. That thing is a piece of junk. I'm going to tear it down."

"And you want *me* to help?"

"Sure." Gabriel nodded. "I've drafted a blueprint. We're going to install a wraparound deck. I've estimated that the total work would take me several months on my own, but I believe that you and I could knock it out in less than half that time."

Building a deck? Years ago, Gareth would've loved the idea, but at his age, his bones ached at the mere thought of it. He looked at Gabriel, hoping it was a joke, but his friend's expression was sincere and hopeful. Gabriel had always possessed the unique talent of being able to get Gareth to do things he didn't initially want to do. But building a deck at his age and in his condition was an insane notion. "I'm sorry," Gareth said. "I can't help you with that. I can't—"

"It'll be fun." Gabriel smiled. "We'll get started on that next month. Maybe next week we can go sailing and discuss the blueprint? We'll have some beers, maybe consider what supplies we should use. Oh, and I had some other ideas, too."

"Ideas?" Gareth said, wincing at the slight whine in his voice.

Gabriel's eyes glistened. "Let's go skydiving, Gareth. That'd be amazing, wouldn't it?"

Gareth frowned, bewildered by Gabriel's obliviousness to the many ways that old age had torn him apart. But then, he saw through to the deeper problem. It wasn't that Gabriel wasn't noticing Gareth's age; he wasn't noticing *anything*. The genius immunologist was so wrapped up in his own pain that the real world had become a mere picture portrait.

"Yvonne, too, of course," Gabriel continued. "I was thinking we should go skydiving in New Zealand, maybe as early as next summer. Just imagine it. I looked at the map this morning, and I'd estimate that NZ is probably about a twenty-three-hour flight, depending on weather conditions. And I've heard that—"

"Gabriel, stop."

Gabriel looked confused. "Pardon?"

"Let's talk about science," Gareth said. "Diseases, autopoiesis. Your work. Something like that."

Gabriel shook his head. "No, I'm sick of that stuff. Every time the subject comes up, it makes me feel like a failure, okay?" His face was bright red. He was rarely so open about his emotions. Maybe it was the alcohol.

"Don't say that, Gabriel."

"But it's true. For all my bluster and high hopes, what tangible goal have I accomplished? Nobody's interested in funding my research. I've gone up in front of people at least twenty or thirty times, practically begging them, and nobody believes anything I have to say. They think I'm a crackpot."

"They just don't know yet. They'll learn. When you come out with your cure, the scientific community will—"

"How do you know? Look, I'm a laughingstock in my field of choice. I've never held any immunology-related job for more than a year. In the eyes of the scientific world, I'm a strange conspiracy theorist with even stranger ideas. So, no. I don't want to talk about work. Let's talk about skydiving. See, if you, Yvonne, and I leave for New Zealand sometime in August—"

Gareth laughed then immediately regretted it because Gabriel's expression became blank and cold.

"What's so funny?" Gabriel asked.

"I'm sorry. But look at the wrinkles on my face. I'm old."

"I see them," Gabriel muttered. "I know the cause behind every symptom of every illness of every person I encounter. I know you're getting older. I'm not blind. I'm not trying to be callous, either."

"Then what *are* you doing?"

"I'm telling you not to give up, goddamn it." Gabriel slapped the table. "Don't give up so damn easily! You can still take risks. Still go on thrill rides, still fly out to foreign countries, still jump out of helicopters."

"But why would I?"

"Because you've always loved doing things like that," Gabriel said with a surprising degree of emotional conviction. "Old age doesn't mean you have to give up the things you love."

"No, it doesn't, but old age does reveal to you the things that you *really* love. When you get to be my age, when you can't even pick change up off the floor without hurting your back, you'll understand. Yes, I had an exciting youth, one I don't regret. But at this point in my life, it's the simple things—love, companionship, my faith, the church, a good paperback novel—that I enjoy now. Maybe that makes me sound like a broken-down old geezer, but there it is."

Gabriel rolled his eyes. "Oh, stop it."

"Stop what? Stop *whining?*"

"I didn't say that."

"It's okay. Because I'm not whining. I'm actually quite happy with my life, all things considered. The truth is, I'm an insufferable old geezer. Why should I deny that?"

"Because you're giving up," Gabriel said. "And you don't have to."

"Strange to hear that from you, since you just admitted to giving up on your life's work. *You* don't have to give up, Gabriel. Someday, you'll be my age, and you'll understand. You'll know what it's like to reach the point in your life where all the exciting moments are done and you're free to just sit back, reminisce, and patiently look forward to heaven."

Gabriel shook his head and gulped down the rest of his ale. He motioned for the waitress to bring him another. "Marvelous. Let's waste our last years looking forward to an imaginary kingdom in the clouds."

Gareth sighed. "Fine. Substitute 'death' for 'heaven.' When you reach my age, when your body has transformed from a friend into a withering old enemy, the one thing a man looks forward to the most is death."

Gabriel stared at him then shook his head. "No. Never. I won't. I refuse."

"Gabriel—"

"No, Gareth, I'm telling you this right now. I swear that, no matter what happens in my life, no matter what goes wrong, I will never allow myself to actively anticipate my own death. Never."

CHAPTER 28:
TWIST

Summer 2018

Gabriel was shell-shocked. He had been staring into his microscope for hours. He had thrown up a couple times, filling his garbage receptacle with plenty of gooey stomach acid. The mounds of notebook paper on his desk were covered with scrawled black ink.

Michael had been right. Within moments of placing that sample under the microscope earlier that morning, Gabriel had known the truth. The Black Virus wasn't a virus at all. It was something far worse.

"Kill me," Gabriel muttered. "Kill me now, and just get it the hell over with."

The skeleton doll sat propped against his lamp, staring at him with its empty eyes. He'd put it there a few hours ago, and it'd been mocking him ever since.

"Kill me," he repeated.

Bernard, watching TV on the other side of the curtain, didn't respond. Gabriel's blood seemed to trickle through his veins with the consistency of a cold frappe. His palms felt clammy. *You were right, Michael. You were right, goddammmit.*

Gabriel pressed his call button, and a few minutes later Harry Brenton entered the room.

"Hi, sir," Harry said.

"Fruit punch," Bernard stated from the other side of the room.

"I'll bring you one in a minute, Bernard," Harry said, then he turned back to Gabriel. "Sir, is everything okay?"

"Yeah," Bernard said.

"Um... no," Gabriel replied. "Harry, do you have a minute?"

Harry glanced back at the hallway.

"It's okay if you don't," Gabriel said. "I understand that you have a lot of work to do. But if you do have a minute, I really need some advice, especially from a bright microbiology student like you."

Harry stared at Gabriel for what felt like ten minutes but was probably only a few seconds, then he sat on the edge of the bed. "Okay, sir. I'm here for you. I'm guessing this pertains to your research on the new virus?"

Gabriel nodded. "I'm afraid it does. I know that you're familiar with my work. You know how the Schist Vaccine works, right?"

"Of course. It makes the immune system smarter. It's like a shot of intelligence, like a steroid, in a sense. That's why it makes the body immune to so many different types of infection."

Gabriel nodded and smiled in spite of the seriousness of the discussion. When Harry talked about science, his stutter disappeared, his shoulders rose, and he appeared more confident.

"Perfectly said, Harry. Now, when I started researching this new virus, my original hypothesis was... well, when the immune system becomes smarter, what do the pathogens do?"

Harry's eyes widened. "Oh, crap. Are you saying that the *pathogens* become smarter, too? You mean, that's what's happening? It is, isn't it? I mean, that actually makes sense! That's why this virus is so powerful. Because when you introduced the ultimate medicine, in a sense, the pathogens were forced to create the ultimate assassin in order to retaliate. So to cure this virus, we'd need to create something that makes the immune system even more powerful. Is that what you're saying?"

"Yes. That's what I thought, but..." Gabriel stepped over to his whiteboard. "I found a sample this morning, and after studying it, well... I was wrong. My original smart pathogens hypothesis underestimated something crucial."

"What's that, sir?"

Gabriel drew a Möbius strip. "I underestimated just how intelligent this virus is. I saw that it was clever back when John Morris died. I saw the way it performs like an actor, mimicking the symptoms of other diseases in order to confuse the body. But I misunderstood *why* it was doing this. I completely misunderstood its motivations."

"Uh, Mr. Schist… motivations? What motivations? Sir, this is a virus that we're talking about."

"Not quite." Gabriel sighed. "When I say that the virus is intelligent, I don't mean it in the sense that we might normally call a pathogen intelligent. I mean that it's really, truly *intelligent.* Just as intelligent, just as cognizant as… as a human. It's not a virus anymore, Harry. It's practically a new species of animal. It's alive."

Harry scoffed, then seeing the grave expression on Gabriel's face, he sobered. "I'm sorry, sir. But c'mon, an animal? Alive?"

"Yes. It's conscious. It thinks, it feels, and—"

"You can't be serious."

"I'm dead serious. When John Morris died, I quickly surmised that emesis was the final step of the cycle. Emesis causes death. When he died, though, what shocked me the most, was that I saw something born inside his vomit."

Harry raised an eyebrow and started to interrupt.

Gabriel held up his hand. "But I was wrong. Emesis isn't the end; it's the beginning. Killing the human being it has infected isn't the culmination of the lifecycle. Instead, emesis is the process wherein the virus finally cements its rebellion. It's the moment where it extricates itself from the human body, casts aside its former home, and creates its own house, its own body, one that it can freely move, breathe, and crawl around in."

Harry crossed his arms. "How do you know this?"

"I tested a blood sample from someone infected with the virus, and I tested a residual trace of the creature itself. Post-emesis and pre-emesis. Then, I compared the results. The pre-emesis sample presented symptoms of other random diseases as a way to grow, to get knowledge and gain full consciousness. It tested the body's limits to learn about the digestive system, circulatory system, everything. It even overtook the victim's brain and absorbed all of the information, knowledge, memory, and neural synapses. That's why victims are comatose. Afterward, the post-emesis creature had consciousness. That's why it finally expelled itself from the body when Morris died. By that point, it was fully developed and ready."

Harry stood up. "Hold it." He began pacing, his brow furrowed. "No one else saw this creature? Are you sure that it really..." His face reddened. "Well, that it was really there?"

"I know what this sounds like. You have to trust me on this, Harry. I know what I saw. I know that it's not my Alzheimer's. This is real."

"Okay. Okay." Harry ran his hands over his short hair. "Let's say all of this is true. When the virus kills a person, what exactly is being born?"

"*Reborn*," Gabriel corrected. "It's not a birth. That's the other thing I was wrong about. It's a *rebirth*."

"A rebirth of what, exactly?"

"How shocked would you be if I told you that it was the immune system itself?" Gabriel felt hysteria bubbling in his throat, and he barked out a laugh.

Harry froze. "Sir, are you okay?"

"No, not even slightly okay! I mean, it's perfect, isn't it? Perfect irony. I've finally stumbled upon the twist in the Möbius strip of my life story. It's fucking *perfect*!" Gabriel took a deep breath, trying not to go totally nuts.

Harry stepped back. "I get it. You're saying that the twist is that after all your work curing HIV, a new virus has appeared that's immune to even the great Schist Vaccine?"

Gabriel shook his head. "No. No. Don't you get it? The virus isn't immune to the Schist vaccine. It doesn't have to be immune. Hell, it isn't even a virus. It *is* the immune system. Death by emesis is death by the rogue immune system. Emesis is the rebellion of the immune system as it gains consciousness, merges into a single organic entity, then violently ejects from the human body after it kills the victim with its violent bombardment of the symptoms of every disease it can possibly conjure up from its bag of tricks."

"But h-how does it know these symptoms?"

"Because we've trained it to memorize them! We've injected ourselves with so many goddamned vaccinations and medications that the immune system is now a magna cum laude graduate. It's finally learned all it has to learn, and it's done putting up with us. What we're seeing here is the immune system going to war against us. It's finally speaking up for itself, and after all the mistreatment we've heaped on it, it's telling us to fuck off."

Harry stared at him, slack jawed.

"How many people have died?" Gabriel asked. "What're the latest numbers?"

"F-f-fifty-four, I believe."

"God. Harry, this growing epidemic is the direct result of my vaccine. All these people are dying because some stupid idiot named Gabriel Schist messed around with the human body."

"No. Stop it, sir. Don't say that."

"But it's true. I created it. It's my fault."

CHAPTER 29:
EKENAME

WHEN GABRIEL AWOKE, HE WAS sitting at a table in the communal kitchen. With its dining tables and basic kitchen appliances, the room had a nice, homey atmosphere. The range was only for show, of course. They couldn't take the risk of some nutty senior citizens setting the nursing home on fire.

Gabriel didn't remember coming to the kitchen. He didn't know what time it was, he didn't know what day it was, and he definitely didn't know why he was holding an old photo of Yvonne. She looked exactly how he always remembered her: young, draped in bright colors, lying on an empty California beach, the sunlight casting a crystalline glow on her sand-covered skin.

His notebook was open in front of him, the pages covered corner to corner with notes about the Black Virus. Apparently, he'd been pretty busy until he'd dozed off. He heard the quiet hum of a mechanical wheelchair as Lew Gates entered the room then stopped at the counter. Gabriel slid the photo of Yvonne underneath his notebook.

Lew, a broad-shouldered, bearded resident with a shaved head, went straight to the coffee machine. Lew's coffee-drinking ways were well-known in the nursing home. He drank constantly, day and night, especially when the Red Sox were playing. Coffee mug in hand, Lew acknowledged Gabriel with a friendly thumbs-up then hummed back out the door.

Gabriel started reviewing his notes. He couldn't continue to call the thing the Black Virus, since it wasn't a virus at all. He needed to frame the situation in an entirely different way in his mind so that he could approach the problem from a new angle. He didn't know whether the new entities had a language, whether each entity was unique, or what their thought processes were like.

He decided to talk to Victor about it. While he was at it, he could also ask Victor about that bizarre skeleton doll that had been left in his room the other night. Victor was highly intelligent, and he might have some unique insight about the matter.

Gabriel heard the wheels of a wheelchair moving down the corridor. He quickly covered his notes—not that it mattered if anyone saw him, but the lifetime habits of old privacy hounds never died. The shiny bald head and sparkling glasses of Mickey Minkovsky, the Jewish ladies' man, came around the corner.

"Hi!" Mickey shouted, clapping his hands. He rolled over to Gabriel, put a finger over his lips, and pointed behind him. "You shoulda seen the legs on that one. Woweeeee, what a doll!"

Gabriel rubbed his forehead. "Oh?"

Mickey clapped his hands again and let out a loud whooping noise. He put out his hand, and when Gabriel shook it, Mickey wrenched his arm so forcefully that Gabriel thought his whole shoulder might pop off. "Yeah!" Mickey shouted, clapping Gabriel on the shoulder.

Gabriel's other hand was tensely clasped around his notes, hiding them. Then, he reconsidered his territorialism. He looked into Mickey's face. Somewhere behind those glasses—behind the Alzheimer's-inflicted man that Mickey Minkovsky had become—was the amazing husband and father whom his wife often described on her daily visits.

"Pardon me, Mickey, but your wife has told me you used to be very reserved. A man of few words, she said. What happened?"

"Me?" Mickey slapped his stomach. "I got loud!"

Gabriel laughed. He released his notes and allowed them to settle on the table. "Hey, I have a question for you, if you don't mind."

"Shoot."

"Let's say that you happened to discover a new species."

"Okay."

"Actually, let's say that a part of the human body evolved, and it became its own species. Let's say that every time it did this, though, the human being that it was a part of died. Let's say that it was your fault this happened. Would you feel guilty, even though you didn't know that it would happen?"

Mickey bobbed his head. "Oh yeah. Damn right I'd feel guilty."

"Yes." Gabriel bit his lip. "That's what I thought."

"But hell, don't beat yourself up over it. We all got our mistakes. And as long as you got your heart in the right place, then nothing else matters, not a damn thing." He leaned forward in his chair and gave Gabriel's chest a hearty thump that almost knocked the wind out of him. "That's what I always say, pal! It ain't easy to do the right thing. It's hard to keep workin' to fix your own mistakes, and it's easy as hell to beat yourself up for it. But no matter what, you always gotta do what's right, not what's easiest." He gave Gabriel's shoulder a rigorous shake.

Gabriel smiled. "Thanks. I have another question."

"Shoot."

"If this new species did exist, what would you name it?"

Mickey frowned, then his huge grin returned. "Hell if I know!" He laughed loudly, clapped his hands, and rolled out of the kitchen.

———————

A couple of hours later, Gabriel headed over to West Wing in search of Victor, but the hallway was closed off. They'd had a new Black Virus infection that morning, and that wing's ex-military nurse was taking more extreme precautions than most of the others.

Gabriel walked back to his room. Bernard was standing beside the closet, dressed in his usual T-shirt and underwear and eating a cup of chocolate pudding.

"How's it going, new guy?" Bernard said.

"The same as usual. You?"

Without responding, Bernard shuffled over to ring his call bell, probably realizing that the only thing better than pudding was fruit punch. Gabriel pulled the curtain divider closed and took off his coat. He decided a nap might be in order and pulled back the covers on his bed.

A new Mexican Day of the Dead doll lay on his pillow. Like the first doll, the skeleton wore brightly colored clothes and held a little note in its hand. The thing had a giant head and a tiny body that made it resemble a miscarried infant.

Gabriel stepped back in disgust. "Bernard, did someone come in here? Someone with a doll?"

"Nope."

"Are you sure?"

"Nope."

Gabriel plucked the note from the doll's hand and unrolled it. He had to put it under the microscope to read the small print.

They already have a name: the Schistlings.

CHAPTER 30:
OH

June 1985

HIS BRAKES SCREECHING AS HE pulled into the driveway, Gabriel was relieved to see Yvonne's car missing, which meant she was still teaching her Friday-night dance class. He had just been fired from his job at San-Briggs Teaching Hospital. He had lost eight jobs since finishing school and always for the same reasons: insubordination and unauthorized use of company materials. His resume might as well have been put through a shredder.

He turned off the car and picked up the two cases of beer he had picked up on the way home. Instead of going inside, he walked out to the wraparound deck he'd built off the side of their quaint, single-story house on the seashore. He put the beer down, went over to the railing, and stared out at the ocean. He lit a cigarette, hoping it might help calm his frayed nerves, but all it did was make him cough. He felt so stupid. When Yvonne found out he'd lost yet another job, she would probably call a divorce lawyer right then and there.

Gabriel tossed his cigarette butt into the ashtray, plopped down on his deckchair, and stared up into the night sky. He reached down and ripped open the beer case.

When he popped the top off the beer can, it emitted a delicious little hiss. He hadn't had a drink in over two months. Before Yvonne came home, he'd have to carefully bag up all of the empty cans and hide them in the trunk of his car. The last time he'd tried to have a beer, she'd dumped it over his head and thrown it at him.

"There's no way I'm letting you become an alcoholic," she'd said. "I love you too much to let you destroy yourself."

Gabriel hesitated. He'd spent every year of their marriage hiding his drinking. It was hardly the most husbandly behavior, and he felt ashamed. But she just didn't understand.

He took a sip, and the beer flowed down his throat, soothing him with all the glorious release of a pent-up orgasm. He followed up with a glorious swig. The beer was cheap and watery, but after two months of suffering, it tasted good.

Gabriel finished off the can and popped open another.

Three hours and twenty-three beers later, he lay sprawled in the chair. The empty cans surrounded him, but he couldn't find the energy to pick them up. *Let her come home. Let her see it. Let her see the real me.*

Fortunately, she wouldn't be home for at least another hour. That gave him ample time to either sober up before she got home, or failing that, he would brush his teeth to kill the beer breath and go to bed. He'd done it many times over the years. It was positively sickening how good he'd gotten at lying to the person he loved the most. For the last few months, he'd tried to stay sober, but even in his drunken stupor, he saw his attempt for the fool's errand it really was.

But even if he hid the drinking, he wouldn't be able to hide the news. At some point, he'd have to tell her about San-Briggs. Lying about the drinking was already straining the boundaries of his conscience, and he couldn't lie about his career, too. He'd have to watch her face drop when she learned, once again, that her husband was a crackpot dressed in the cheap wrapping paper of a visionary.

He should've been less impulsive. They'd caught him using their materials for his experiments. He'd been too stupid to think of a good excuse, so he'd been fired again. The word pounded through his subconscious like a jackhammer. Fired. Fired. Fired. *Fired.*

Gabriel finished the rest of his twenty-fourth beer and crumpled the can, taking out his anger on the thin piece of metal. He tossed it behind him and opened the first one from the second case.

Then, he heard footsteps.

"Hey, baby!" Yvonne called. "I have big, big news!"

She'd come home early. Her gleeful tone made Gabriel feel flimsy and broken. It reminded him of how cringing and helpless his father had looked on his deathbed. Gabriel didn't turn around because he didn't want to see her jolt at the sight of his drunken eyes. He didn't want to cause her joyous smile, that effervescent xylophone of white teeth, to curl up into a grimace. He didn't even turn his head out of fear that any body language he might use would betray his drunken state. He couldn't let her see his face or smell his breath. Suddenly, he was thankful that he'd forgotten to replace the burnt-out bulb in the porch light, as the darkness presented his only hope of keeping the beer cans hidden.

"Gabriel? Are you okay?"

He had to distract her somehow, even if it made her angry. Distraction was better than admission. "Yvonne, ahhh, I've been, um... analyzing things. A whole lotta things and stuff."

Footsteps. She was walking closer.

"Stop!" he shouted, his voice quivering.

"Analyzing what, baby?" she asked.

"I just, ah, I've got a lotta stuff on my mind. An enormous amm... ammmount. Things that... happened."

"Are you talking about your project?" She stepped forward again. She wasn't far away. Only a few more steps and she'd be beside him.

He knew that she was going to climb on his lap, then she'd try to kiss him, and he couldn't let that happen. He tried to get out of the chair, but his legs felt like solid blocks of concrete. "Wait right there. Er... I... it's just—"

"I'm waiting," she whispered. "Gabriel, you better not be—"

"I'm not!"

"Then what are you doing?" She was starting to sound irritated.

"Yvonne, ah, you see... it's just that I, um, I've been considering the nature of the... ah... the Klein bottle in great detail."

"The Klein bottle."

"Yes, of course. You know what, um, what it is, right? It's a non-orientable surface, much like the Morb... Mobe... no. Möbius. **Möbius** strip. But the Klein bottle, right? It has no... boundary."

Her breathing became heavier. One more step and she'd be

right beside him. He had to keep talking and pretend to be Mr. Brilliant-but-Boring-Scientist-Guy.

"Yesss... yes, no boundary, nope, none." He rubbed his eyes. "See, a true Klein bottle, a true Klein bottle cannot exist in our three-dimensional world because it would be forced to intersect itself. See, right... this here, a Klein bottle is supposed to be a two-dimensional manifold that can only exist in f-f-four dimensions."

"Gabriel?"

"Wait!" Gabriel trembled with fear. "See, if you think about the Möbius strip, it can be embargoed... no, no, *embedded*, embedded in three-dimensional Euclidean space R cubed, but the Klein bottle can't—"

"Stop it, Gabriel." Her voice had developed a sharp edge he knew all too well. The situation was teetering on the edge of a cliff.

"Or we can discuss Maxwell's demon, if you'd prefer?" Gabriel said. "Er... Maxwell, you remember how we talked about that before? James Clerk Maxwell? Picture a box divided into two halves by a wall, and... and... and it..."

Yvonne's hands ran through his hair. She bent down and kissed the top of his head, her exhalations warming his scalp. With her lips pressed against his head, he felt her mouth form into a smile. She was so excited about something that she was putting aside what an ass he was being.

"I have some big news for ya, big guy," Yvonne whispered, giggling. "I'd like to share it if you're done talking about demons, walls, and bottles."

"But the Klein bottle, it..."

"It can wait." Yvonne stepped to his side. "I have to tell you something, maybe the most important thing I've *ever* told you."

Oh no. Not now! Tomorrow, maybe. The day after, perhaps. Any time but right now. Not right now, please, not right now. Please, Yvonne...

Yvonne walked in front of him, an enormous, spirited grin on her face. Gabriel quickly lowered his hand, holding the beer can underneath the chair just before she jumped on his lap. She leaned forward, inches away from his lips.

"Gabriel, I—" She sniffed. Her face crinkled up as if she'd bitten into a lemon. Her eyes widened with horror. "Oh my God." Yvonne stood up and backed away. He felt lower than a cockroach. "Gabriel, I... I'm pregnant."

Pregnant. And he'd ruined the moment. Mixed emotions of happiness, angst, and despair swam through his mind. He searched desperately for a suitable response, thinking that there had to be some strange combination of words he could put together that would put the shattered pieces of his life back together.

Gabriel cleared his throat. No magic verbal solution revealed itself. Only a single word spilled from his lips. "Oh."

CHAPTER 31: MISPLACED

Summer 2018

"**Y**VONNE!" GABRIEL WOKE UP WITH a start, drenched in sweat and aching. He leapt out of bed and almost slipped to the floor as his legs buckled beneath him. "Yvonne! No, Yvonne, don't do it. I didn't mean what I said. I didn't mean it."

He saw daylight. It took him a moment to figure out where he was, and once the realization took hold, his horror became even greater: he was in prison, a cold, ugly white cell. He tried to figure out how or when he had been sent there. He didn't remember committing any crimes or getting arrested. But he somehow knew that Yvonne was also in the prison, locked in another cell.

"Yvonne! Where are you?" Spinning around, Gabriel was amazed to see that the guards had accidently left his cell door open.

Outside in the hall, inmates screamed and rattled their bars while prison guards yelled orders. Gabriel rushed to the door, stumbling like a cripple, though he didn't remember getting injured. He stepped into a long hallway lined with metal doors. All of the doors were open, just as his was. The concrete floor was dotted with gaping black holes, and spider webs hung from the ceiling.

"Yvonne? Can you hear me?"

Two prison guards in bright-blue jumpsuits rounded the corner and ran toward him. They looked concerned rather than angry, but Gabriel wasn't going to stick around to verify that. He turned and hustled in the opposite direction of the guards. He peeked inside each door he passed and saw more prisoners sitting in their cells.

At the end of the hall, in the last cell on the right, he found her. His wife, his beautiful young wife, lay peacefully in bed. *Wait.* She was in *their* bed, in their bedroom, the same bedroom they'd once shared in their little white house on the shore. Despite the oddness of it, seeing her there made him feel calm and happy. He'd found her at least. After so many years, he'd finally found her. He stepped into the room.

"No, Gabriel!" one guard shouted.

"Stop!" the other one called.

Gabriel ignored them. Even if they locked him up for a thousand years, one more moment with Yvonne was enough to last him a lifetime. He'd made a mistake when he let her go. It wasn't fair that one mistake could cost him so dearly. He had to redeem himself in her eyes.

He knelt beside the bed. Her face was buried in the pillow, but he would have recognized the back of her head anywhere. It was her. It was really her. It *had* to be her. Tears of happiness poured down his cheeks.

"Thank God." He smiled. "I've missed you so much. I'm sorry. God, I'm so, so sorry. I... didn't mean it. I'm excited about your news, about the baby. Really, I am. I love you, Yvonne. I love you so much."

She stirred beneath the covers, and he embraced her, breathing in the rosy scent of her perfume. He'd found her, and they could finally be happy again. He pulled back to look at her face for the first time in decades.

The old lady screamed at the top of her lungs.

Gabriel did a double-take. The woman in his arms wasn't Yvonne. Instead, he held a wrinkled, white-haired woman with only a few teeth, grey gums, and reddened eyes. She let out another screech and tried to shove him away. An alarm went off, and a sharp ringing noise sliced through the air like a blade.

Gabriel stood. "Who are you? Why were you pretending to be Yvonne?"

As he stepped back, he noticed an albino white slug crawling up the wall beside him. He turned and faced the creature. A hazy sense of recognition nudged his mind. *What is it about slugs? Why are they important?*

The slug angled its head toward him. "Wake up, you old fool!"

Gabriel's heart pounded. *Did that slug just talk?* He screamed.

The guards ran into the room then stared at him for a few seconds as if they were scared of him. They tried to grab him, but Gabriel ducked and stumbled back into the hallway, gripping the side rail for balance. Nothing made any sense. He was in prison, a slug had talked, some crazy woman was pretending to be Yvonne, and he was—

Oh.

Everything flooded back, and he clung to the rail, using it as a replacement for his missing cane. *Cane, yes. I have a cane.* He was Gabriel Schist. He was seventy... seventy-something years old. He had Alzheimer's. He lived in Bright New Day. He was working on a cure for the—*no, wait.* He couldn't call it the Black Virus anymore.

Gabriel started muttering, "Zero, one, one, two, three, five, eight, thirteen, twenty-one, thirty-four, fifty-five... damn, what's next? Eighty-nine, one hundred forty-four..."

The guards circled him like a pack of coyotes. No, not guards. They were nurses.

The one on the left, Dana Kleznowski, said, "Gabriel?"

Gabriel's mouth moved to continue his recitations, but he didn't have enough saliva to voice the numbers. His foot slipped, and he almost fell. When he looked down, he realized something that made his entire situation that much more degrading. He was completely naked.

His pale, saggy body was on display for everyone to see. In that one moment, his dignity was forever stripped away. If he died tomorrow, his nudity would be all they would remember, not the Nobel Prize, not the Schist vaccine. No, his humiliation would be his legacy.

One of the nurses ran in to comfort the crying old lady—Gabriel had finally recognized the woman as Marge Beckinsale. Gabriel cupped his hands over his crotch. Dana stepped over and wrapped a johnny gown around him.

He tried to remember what had brought him there, what had made him wake up in such a state. When the memory came rushing back, it felt as painful as tearing the scab off an unhealed wound. *Her.* He'd been thinking about her as he fell asleep. He whispered her name—the name of the only woman he'd ever loved—and as Dana tied the gown around his neck, he let his love's name linger in the air and become real, like a tiny cloud of floating dust being penetrated by a sharp beam of sunlight. "I'm sorry, Yvonne."

CHAPTER 32: AUTHENTIC

THE WORLD WAS REPLACED BY darkness. The black hole grew deeper, its horizon expanded, then it emitted the sound of breathing.

A comforting hand landed on his shoulder, and it was soon accompanied by a scratchy, quiet voice. "Hello there, Gabriel."

Gabriel woke up in bed, and for once, he had no cloud of disorientation or panicked thoughts. It was nighttime, he was Gabriel Schist, and he lived in Bright New Day. Everything was clear. The hand on his shoulder belonged to Victor, who sat beside his bed like a worried parent checking up on a child who'd had terrible nightmares.

"I tried to find you." Gabriel cleared his throat. "The other day. Nurse wouldn't let me onto your wing."

"I know. My apologies for disappearing. I've been quite busy."

"I have to say"—Gabriel reached for the pack of cigarettes on his bedside table then remembered that he couldn't light up inside—"this is an unusual wakeup call."

Gabriel sat up. If Victor were anyone else, he would have found the midnight wakeup call creepy. But Victor possessed a calming demeanor that made him set aside such worries. Very few people in Gabriel's life had ever had such a quality. Father Gareth, Victor, and perhaps Michael the slug, though Gabriel wasn't sure if Michael counted as a person.

"Would you prefer that I leave?" Victor asked.

"No. It's fine. Just give me more warning next time."

Victor grinned. "If I schedule a date and time, what makes you so certain that you'll remember it?"

Gabriel frowned, ready to feel offended, but then he saw the humor and laughed. "How long have I been asleep?"

"For most of the last two days. We've all been worried about you. Everyone knows that something is amiss when they don't see the detective wandering the hallways. Well, and there was that less-than-pleasant episode yesterday."

Gabriel winced. "Marvelous. So that whole naked-in-the-hallway thing wasn't a dream."

"Afraid not."

"The last two days are a blur to me."

"Well then, perhaps I should also tell you, in case you've forgotten, the administrator came in here today and had a chat with you. Now, from what I hear, and I *do* hear things quite well, he isn't too pleased, to say the least." Victor's tone held neither reproach nor sympathy.

"You're right. I don't remember. So this chat didn't go too well?"

"No, I don't believe it did. You must be careful about that sort of thing, Gabriel. I've overheard conversations. You're on your last leg. If you get one more strike, the administrator is prepared to reassign you to Level Five."

Gabriel eyed his cigarette pack. It was empty. Next to it were both of the creepy skeleton dolls, each holding their even creepier little notes. Their beady black eyes stared into the deepest pits of his psyche. Gabriel blocked his view of them with a heavy book. That was one mystery he didn't want to deal with yet. "Level Five. Tell me something, Victor. How the hell do you know all this?"

Victor gave a little shrug. "I have my connections."

"Like who?" Gabriel scoffed. "The Mafia? The CIA? The Illuminati?"

Victor smiled knowingly and dusted off his tuxedo jacket. He looked sidelong out the window, and the air suddenly seemed colder. "Connections."

"Who *are* you? Is Victor even your real name?"

"I'm a very powerful man. Let's just leave it at that, shall we?"

"Then why are you here?"

"I know everyone in this facility. I know everything *about* everyone in this facility. It's my job. It might help you to understand if you realized that, unlike most of you, I'm here by choice."

Gabriel eyed him suspiciously. "You must be private pay. Where is your room? Are you really on West Wing?"

Victor perched on the desk, casually propping his feet up on the chair. "You seem quite stressed, Gabriel."

"My Alzheimer's is getting significantly worse. I don't even vaguely recall talking to the administrator. The last thing I remember is that incident in the corridor, and those were hardly the actions of a sane person. A small part of me wonders if maybe I *should* be in Level Five, all things considered."

"Perhaps the stress isn't a result of your decline. Instead, maybe your decline is a result of the stress."

"Seems like a reasonable assumption. Ever since John Morris, I've been racing against my own biological clock. I don't know how much longer I have until I become a vegetable. It could be months, weeks, or only days. And somehow, in that ridiculously uncertain time frame, I have to focus what few cognitive powers I have left on this Black Virus, this... this..."

"Pray tell, what information have you managed to decipher about this Black Virus so far?"

"It's *not* a virus, I know that much." Gabriel clenched his hands into fists. "It's a living entity, the result of my vaccine. And even more ridiculously, someone or something has supposedly named this species the... ah, the Schistlings. Look, Victor, I know that I probably seem utterly demented, but—"

"Logic isn't always practical." Victor grinned. He acted almost as if *he* were the administrator of the nursing home, and Irving was only a figurehead.

Gabriel narrowed his eyes. "You say that you're a powerful man. Tell me, what do you know?"

"I know that you must work harder. I know that you have to stay focused. I know that you have to keep a clear head and not let your rather recurrent character flaws get in your way, or you'll never succeed at what you're trying to do."

Outside, the black sky was becoming bluer. The light slowly punched holes in the dark, piercing through its black velvet skin. Nighttime was dying a slow, painful death.

"That's all very nice," Gabriel said. "But it's not what I meant. How much do you *really* know? And to start with, mystery man, how about telling me what you know about these goddamn Schistlings?"

"Where shall I begin? As I said, I know everything about everyone in this facility. But you want details? You want me to tell you everything I know about you, for instance? Perhaps you want me to talk about your childhood, that IQ test you took as a boy?"

"That's public information. You could've read about that somewhere."

"Well, how about your longstanding friendship with the priest, Father Gareth? What about the day you met your future wife on the beach? The bag of oranges she was carrying?"

Gabriel shivered. He reached for his cigarette pack again and rediscovered its emptiness. "My-my daughter. You must have met her. She must have told you. Or maybe, you and me, we must have... Listen, Victor. Do I know you? Have we met before?"

"Of course you know me. But not in the way that you might expect."

"Goddamn it, Victor." Gabriel gritted his teeth. "How do you know me?"

"I've *always* known you. I know your successes. I know how much your daughter means to you and how you and she shared those summers on the sailboat. And I know the struggles you've overcome in the past, your former alcoholism, your—"

"There is no *former* alcoholism. The desire never goes away." Just at the mention of it, Gabriel could taste the metallic flavor of the cheap beer he'd never have again. "So I just keep the hell away from it."

"Very perceptive! But here, before I annoy you too much with my grandiose mysteriousness, I wish to show you something. I find that demonstration is often more effective than exposition. Would you agree?"

"I don't have time." Gabriel shook his head. "I have to keep working."

"I know. That's why I want to show you. Because after these last few days, you need to get back on your feet, and I believe that to do so, you must come to a better understanding of this situation."

Gabriel was ready to snap and show just how much he didn't appreciate that grandiose mysteriousness, but seeing the genuineness in Victor's eyes, he put on his detective ensemble and grabbed his cane. Victor led the way out into the corridor. In South Wing, Mickey Minkovsky had fallen out of bed, and his screams and cackles echoed down the hallway. Bob Baker shouted at him to shut up, or maybe he was shouting at the voices. Lew Gates was in the kitchen, pouring a cup of coffee.

"You're very good at avoiding questions," Gabriel said. "But can you at least tell me your last name?"

"Calaca. My name is Victor Calaca."

They passed Edna Foster's room. Despite the early hour, she was sitting up on the side of her bed. "Mommmmmy..." she called in that fragile voice. "Mommmmy, I'm gonna miss the bus."

As they walked, Victor stopped at the rooms of those who were infected. They waited until the nurses were busy passing meds, and then the angular man stood guard as Gabriel peeked inside each room, witnessing the horror that his great cure had indirectly caused.

Victor was right. Demonstration was more effective than exposition. Sitting at his desk in his room, Gabriel could act as if the virus were an imaginary disease and attempting to find a cure a playful pastime. When he saw the ravages of it in person, the reality of it became all too vivid, and it was his fault.

While Gabriel had been in a cloudy haze for two days, the count had risen. Sixteen residents of Bright New Day stared out of charcoal-black eyes, their skin crawling with dark veins. The poor, screaming woman he had mistakenly embraced the other day was also among the infected.

Gabriel considered setting traps. There had to be a way to catch a live Schistling right after it was born. But he had no idea how to go about doing that or which patient would expire next. The Schistlings confused the body with any number of symptoms until the whole thing finally just sputtered out and died, so there was no pattern to follow, and that was the brilliance of it.

Some people had scales. Others had swollen lymph nodes. Some had lost entire parts of their bodies to necrosis. Gabriel stopped at the room of Robert Boulanger and watched in silent horror as Robert sneezed out a never-ending mess of black globs, over and over again. Tarry goo ran from his nostrils down to his chin.

"This is horrible," Gabriel said.

"Indeed," Victor replied, "and that's why I'm showing it to you."

"But I already know full well what the Black Vir—what the *Schistlings* are capable of."

"But you needed to see, first hand, why helping these people is so important. I know that you saw this before, but I want to ensure that you don't forget."

Gabriel looked down, feeling the mass of his life's work blow up within him like a tumor. All of his memories were poisoned. "It's my fault. All of this."

"Don't think of it that way."

"But it's true. I'm the one who caused this whole disaster. My research. My vaccine. My fault."

"Stop pitying yourself. I know that you're a good man, a man of conscience. So instead of looking back, look forward. And tell me, what do you plan to do about it?"

What Gabriel wanted to do was to save the nursing home, to save the entire world—just as he once had, long ago. But he hadn't really saved the world; he'd poisoned it. His vaccine had formed the DNA of a ghastly creature that was slaughtering his fellow human beings. If he continued to interfere, then the consequences might be even worse next time. "I'll go on studying it," he whispered. "That's the least I can do to make up for this disgusting mutation that I've created. But I've given up hope on actually beating it. This would be beyond my scope even if I was healthy, and as it is, I'm a mess."

"No. You can't afford to give up."

"Yes. I give up. At this point, the only thing I want... I just... I don't know." Gabriel leaned on his cane for support. "I want to die." He shook his head. "I know what you're thinking. I know it's pathetic, but it's what I want. That's probably why I've been in such a daze, because I don't have a purpose anymore. I can't help these people."

"You're a better man than you think you are."

"Not really. And at this point, don't I deserve one final reward? An easy death, that's all I ask. A quick one and then—bang, over! Dead."

"Don't be a damned fool. You once told your closest friend that you'd never give up."

"Maybe. But somewhere in the back of my rotting throat, I can already taste death. The dust, the dryness, it's a good taste."

Victor's sharp-angled face dropped to become a saggy experiment in contours. He spoke with a voice that could cut glass. "Fine."

"I'm sorry."

"Don't apologize to me. Apologize to *them*."

"That's not fair. Don't make me feel any worse about this than I already do."

"We have nothing to discuss. Say hello to the slugs for me." Victor Calaca spun around, his black coat whipping behind him like a vampire's cape, and started walking away.

Gabriel felt sick with guilt. "Wait! I'm sorry!"

Victor continued without pausing.

"Wait! You know the slugs? What can you tell me about them?"

Victor stopped, turned, and stared pointedly into Gabriel's eyes. Without a word, he whipped back around as if he had more pressing matters to attend to and disappeared around the corner. After several moments of terrified diffidence, Gabriel hobbled after the man.

But Calaca was nowhere to be found.

CHAPTER 33:
FOOTNOTE

July 1985

GABRIEL PARKED OUTSIDE FATHER GARETH'S modest apartment and climbed out of the car. He collapsed on the sidewalk and puked his guts out. Whiskey-tasting vomit dripped from his bottom lip and nostrils. It had been a month since Yvonne had told him about the baby, and since then, they'd spent every night fighting. His stomach burned as if the devil were piercing his insides with a searing pitchfork.

He stood up, leaning on his car for support. His knees were badly scraped from the fall on the concrete, and his throat was raw. His reflection in the side mirror was that of a pale, redheaded corpse with greasy skin and dark circles under his bloodshot eyes.

"Well hi, Gabriel," he whispered. "You look like hell."

He was still unsteady on his feet, but the nausea had mostly passed. He craved a cigarette but didn't light up because he'd kept Gareth waiting long enough already. He hadn't even seen the priest in over six months. Whenever he drank in front of Gareth, the disappointment in the old man's eyes was overwhelming, so he just stayed away. He'd figured there would always be more time and he'd visit when things got better, but over the phone, Gareth had sounded like a man choking on his insides.

Gabriel rang the doorbell. After a few minutes with no answer, he tried the handle. It was unlocked, as usual, possibly one of the only unlocked doors in Los Angeles. He stepped into the dark foyer. "Hello?"

"Gabriel, my boy, is that you?"

Gabriel froze. The voice was certainly Gareth's, but at the same time, it wasn't. The priest's lively voice had been replaced by that of an old man with one foot in a coffin.

No classical music was playing, and the television was off. The only sounds were a beeping noise emanating from the bedroom and the rasp of Gareth's breathing.

Gabriel flipped on the lights and walked down the hallway. The closer he got to the bedroom, the louder the harsh frog-breathing became. Gabriel stopped outside the closed door. "Gareth?"

"Yes, Gabriel. Come in here, kiddo."

Gabriel suddenly wished he'd downed a few more shots. Maybe then he would've been ready for what lay beyond that door. He should have told Yvonne that he was coming. She loved Gareth, and she would've been there in a heartbeat if she knew how sick the old man was. If she were there, she could've supported him. As it was, he instead hovered outside the door, legs twitching with the desire to run away.

Father Gareth's trench coat and fedora were hanging on two hooks beside the door. Gabriel stroked the trench coat. For the first time, he noticed that a cross had been sewn on the inside of each sleeve. *Don't worry. He'll wear it again. Old Gareth is fine. Just a little sick, that's all.*

Gabriel took in a deep breath and opened the door. Gareth was wrapped in a cocoon of blankets atop a twin bed. The priest had always been an exceptionally tall man, but his body looked as shrunken as an Egyptian mummy. An aged hardcover edition of Dostoyevsky's *The Idiot* lay on the nightstand.

"Sorry to stay in bed this way," Gareth said. He paused often between words to take in a breath. "It's just harder to get up these days."

"I understand," Gabriel whispered.

"It's wonderful to see you, Gabriel. Thank you for coming."

A bulky oxygen concentrator stood beside the bed, and a hose snaked from it to the nasal cannula plugged into Gareth's nostrils. The lymph nodes in his neck were swollen and discolored, and his once-luxurious beard was ratty and yellowed. Thin blue lines created an intricate latticework of veins across his papery skin. His knuckles and joints were a dark, purplish color, and his lips were a bruised color. In healthcare, that effect was referred to as modeling. And once modeling started, it meant only one thing, which Gabriel was absolutely unwilling to accept.

"How did this happen to you?" Gabriel asked.

"Old age?" Gareth chucked. "I guess the lymph nodes have been swollen for a while. Ever since I had that blood transfusion, some time ago."

Gabriel wanted to punch himself. He should've been there. He should have warned Gareth. Gabriel pushed aside a stack of books and knelt beside the bed. "You can go to the hospital. You can—"

"I'm just fine right here." The old man reached out and clasped Gabriel's hand with ice-cold fingers.

Gabriel closed his eyes. "Don't give up." He squeezed the priest's hand. "I need you."

Gareth's short, rattling breaths echoed through the room, and Gabriel knew that it was a sound that would haunt him for the rest of his life. "Gabriel, my friend, a life without death wouldn't be a life at all, now would it?"

"You can fight this. Give me time. I'll find a cure."

"It's okay. I'm an old geezer, remember? I'm *supposed* to die."

"Not yet. Don't die on me."

"Gabriel, you have to—"

"Don't leave me alone in this terrible goddamn world. You're one of the only two people who have ever understood me. Yvonne and I... we're not doing well. I think I messed everything up. I need you."

Father Gareth's eyes narrowed, then his smile was replaced by a look of deep sadness. "You're drunk."

Gabriel lowered his head. "I'm not."

"Don't bother lying to me. I know you too well."

"I'm not drunk."

"It's too late for me to change anything." Gareth paused, gasping for air. "But if there's one thing that you could grant me, it's this."

"Don't talk that way."

"My one wish... please, Gabriel, listen to me. Stop destroying yourself. Please... please stop destroying yourself."

Bile rose in the back of Gabriel's throat. "I'm not destroying myself. I know my limits. Sure, I drank too much when I was younger, but I was a kid. I know better now. And yes, I did have a few drinks on the way here, but right now, I'm simply using alcohol as a pressure valve. It's just a temporary thing, because if you haven't noticed, my life is kind of falling apart. Nobody wants to fund my research. I got fired again last month. You're sick. And now Yvonne is saying... she's saying..." Gabriel grabbed the wastebasket beside the nightstand. He shut his eyes to block the sight of the pile of bloody tissues in the bottom of it, stuck his face over the rim, and vomited. "Father," he said, panting, "really, it's just—" He vomited again.

Father Gareth leaned forward and patted Gabriel's back. Gabriel looked up to see that the old man was clutching a rosary, and his lips were mouthing the words of the *Our Father*. Eventually, Gabriel could breathe again. He raised his head and wiped the drool from his lips.

"Are you okay?" Gareth asked.

"I'm sorry. Hell, I'm sorry."

Father Gareth winked. "I forgive you."

"Don't die," Gabriel pleaded. "You were the first person who ever gave me a chance. I can't do it without you. I just can't." Gabriel swiped at his tears with his shirt sleeve. His stomach groaned.

"Yeah, you can." The old priest smiled.

"You don't get it. I always mess things up. I—"

Gareth raised a hand. "You'll straighten up and get past all of this drunken nonsense. I have faith in you, faith in your willpower, faith in your determination, your drive, your brilliant mind. Gabriel, you've been an inspiration to me; I hope you know that. You're one of the most remarkable men I've ever met."

"Stop! Stop acting like this is a done deal, like it's already over, and you're saying goodbye."

"But this *is* goodbye. I know you don't want to admit this, but we both know that I'm going to die soon. Days, weeks, hours, who knows? But whenever it happens, just know that you won't ever lose me. Because after I die, my soul will always be—"

"No, damn it! Don't you *dare* give up on real life just because you believe that some imaginary old man with a beard will pluck your soul out of your body and pull you up into the sky. Don't you dare let go of life for the sake of a fairytale!"

Gareth rolled his eyes. "Gabriel—"

"Gareth, there's no such thing as a soul. People turn to dust when they die. This soul idea, these ridiculous spiritual notions that you're giving up your life for, it's a fantasy. A waste of time. It's the same bullshit ideas that my parents tried to shove down my throat my whole life, and I'm sick of hearing them."

Gabriel was shaking. The words had spewed out of him before he could think about what he was saying. He'd always tried to avoid the faith conversation, terrified that it might shatter the bond between them. But he noticed that Father Gareth's smile was just as delighted as ever. The old priest's faith was like an eternal candle, protecting him from every monster in the shadows. Gabriel didn't understand it. On some level, he admired that ability to retain belief in the unseen, but it still didn't make any sense to him.

"Humor me for a moment," Father Gareth said. "Can I ask that brilliant mind of yours a question?"

Gabriel nodded.

Gareth chuckled feebly. "Let's pretend that there is a God, just for a moment. It doesn't have to be the Christian God. Any version of God will do, any grand creator, any omniscient being that adequately fits the role. If there is a God, and if you had the chance for a one-on-one conversation with him, what would you tell him? What would you ask him?"

Gabriel pondered his answer, mentally spreading out the concept like cookie batter under a rolling pin. He listened to the droning hum of the oxygen concentrator and Gareth's rattling breaths. "I'd ask him: why me? That's what I'd ask. I'd ask why he picked me. I'd tell him 'Hey, God, how dare you curse me with this supposedly brilliant mind?' And then, I'd spit in the asshole's face. Seriously, this brilliant mind that I'm so lucky to have? It's a goddamn punishment is what it is. And if God exists, then it's his fault. So after I spit in his face, I'd tell him to take that brilliant mind back and shove it up his ass. I'd tell him to carve some holes in my grey matter and make me a bit stupider." Gabriel stood up, shaking his head. "That's what I'd tell God, *if* God existed. And I'd mean every damn word of it."

Gabriel's skin was sticky with dried sweat. He wanted to run away from himself. That was impossible, but he could run away from Gareth.

"I have to go. I'll come back soon, okay? Stay safe until then. Don't die. I'll come back in a few days, I swear it. A few days."

Gareth laughed and raised his blue-veined hand in a cheerful salute. "God bless you, Gabriel Schist!"

Fresh tears ran from Gabriel's eyes. He wiped them away then tentatively stepped backward, slowly initiating his cowardly escape. Looking at Old Gareth's smile, hearing that wonderful, merry laugh, he felt a stabbing pain in his heart. He wanted to voice his affection, but the words couldn't escape his lips. He didn't *deserve* Gareth's love.

"A few days," Gabriel repeated and walked out of the bedroom.

When he reached the front door, he paused. He didn't want to leave. He shook his head. He'd be coming back in a few days. He'd see Gareth again. There was no reason to get sentimental.

He headed back to his car, and as much as he hated himself for it, the first thing he did was beeline it to the nearest bar. He drank until his blood was thinner than water then, too drunk to drive, crashed in a sleazy motel next to the bar. As he curled up under the cheap, sticky comforters, he promised himself that he would go back to see Gareth. And on his next visit, he would finally express how much the old priest meant to him, how much he loved him.

The following day, Gabriel woke up sometime in the afternoon. He downed some complimentary coffee from the motel lobby, which kick-started his nervous system just enough so that he could drive home. He pulled into the driveway at a cockeyed angle, decided it wasn't worth fixing it, and climbed out of the car. Yvonne wasn't home, though his mind was too foggy to figure out where she might be.

He quickly started the coffee machine and popped some pain pills to take care of his headache. When the telephone rang, he was so startled that he nearly fell.

"Hello?"

"Hello, am I speaking to Gabriel Schist?" The voice was mechanical and unfamiliar.

"This is he." Gabriel rubbed his eyes.

"Mr. Schist, I'm calling from the hospital. I'm sorry to inform you that—"

"Fuck." His stomach lurched. *Not now, please, not like this.* "Please tell me this isn't about Father Gareth. The priest. Please."

"I'm sorry, Mr. Schist. Father Gareth passed away this morning."

CHAPTER 34:
INFESTATION

Summer 2018

MATTHEW LECROIX, THE CROONER, PASSED away in the middle of the night. There was no last song, no fond farewells, nothing but a black bag being whisked away to the funeral home.

Eighty-two of the one hundred forty-five residents living in Bright New Day were infected with the Black Virus. That was a high percentage, since they were all crowded together, but the infection rate across New England was also rising, with new cases reported every few days. Despite all efforts to contain the virus, the Schistlings were spreading their slimy tendrils across the East Coast like a torrential hurricane.

Gabriel stood in the shadows of the communal kitchen, staring at the television. The leopard-printed slug lay on his shoulder.

TOXIC PLAGUE INFECTS 5 MORE IN SPRINGFIELD, MASS

DEATH COUNT RISES TO 24 IN R.I.

WHAT CAUSES THE PLAGUE? RESEARCH IS INCONCLUSIVE

POSSIBLE LINK FOUND BETWEEN NEW EPIDEMIC AND SMALLPOX

Doctors, medical researchers, and scientists of all kinds were scrambling like chickens with their heads cut off, but none of the news implied that the scientific community had recognized the Schistlings' sentience. The outbreak was still being painted as the spread of a new virus, and a government researcher was quoted as believing that it was probably an evolved strain of the norovirus. Other reports linked it to mad cow disease and bird flu. One family member of a victim had witnessed a Schistling emesis birth, but the story was laughed off as a conspiracy theory.

"Perhaps I can report my findings to one of the official research teams," Gabriel muttered. "Send them all of my evidence."

"That won't be enough, Gabriel," Leopard Print said. "They won't believe in the idea of a rogue immune system. And even if someone *does* listen, your findings will get lost in mountains of paperwork. Years will pass before they look into it, and the Schistlings are moving too fast for that. The human race doesn't have that much time. Don't you realize that unless you do something, this Schistling epidemic will continue to spread?"

"There's nothing I can do on my own. I'm a senior citizen with Alzheimer's who wanders naked in the hallway. What can I possibly—hey, what's that?" He jabbed a finger at the screen.

"Toxic waste," the slug replied. "Or so they say."

The news had finally switched to a different subject. Evidently, a helicopter pilot had captured blurry cellphone camera footage of a giant maelstrom of toxic waste moving along the coast of New Hampshire. The video showed what looked like an enormous black hole carved deep into the ocean's blue flesh. The image reminded Gabriel of an oil spill. The experts were clueless as to its cause or what kind of waste it held. They were issuing warnings to potential beachgoers.

"That's *them*," Gabriel said. "Isn't it? That's why they always escape to the ocean, to join the crowd, to join their friends. Forming a new society, perhaps?"

The grainy, pixilated footage continued rolling. The black hole spun like a power drill into the ocean's belly, reaching oily tentacles across the surface. But Gabriel noticed something even more stomach-turning than the toxic pool itself: a face, right in the center of the maelstrom. He rubbed his eyes and looked again; it was still there.

He thought it might be an optical illusion. Pareidolia was the name of the common psychological compulsion to see faces in everything, from a man in the moon to smiley faces in wood grain. But once he'd seen that face—with its contemptuous, leering expression and barracuda mouth—he couldn't un-see it.

The video switched to footage from a morning press conference. "There's no reason to panic," a government official said. "Our top experts are on the case, and they've made it clear that there's no reason to worry. This is simply a unique condition created by local pollution, but it will certainly dissipate within a month at most. We ask that you don't leave any trash in the ocean, and everyone should be careful on the beach for the next few weeks."

"Why are they saying that?" Gabriel grumbled.

"You're not really surprised by a government cover-up, are you?" Leopard Print replied. "I would think that you humans would be used to that by now. Clearly, they have no idea what's going on, but they must offer some explanation, whether it's true or not. You know how it is."

The news flicked back to more stories about the Black Virus. Gabriel held his hand up to his shoulder, and the slug crawled onto his palm, leaving a slimy trail across his hand.

"Why are they all joining together that way?" Gabriel asked. "The Schistlings, I mean. I know you have your noninterference clause and all that, but can you at least tell me that much?"

"Because when they join the pool, they become one, a collective. Every time a new Schistling joins this collective, the mass becomes more intelligent. By merging into one amalgamated consciousness, their united front against humanity becomes that much stronger."

"So this black pool is some new body that they're putting together? But for Christ's sake, if they're rebelling against the human body, if they're so keen on fighting for their freedom from it, then why would they surrender themselves to yet another body?"

"Do desires always make sense, Gabriel? Do people always make the right choices and live up to their ideals? What the news won't tell you is that this toxic waste spill has more than doubled in size since last week."

"Hell. And in the meantime, they're still trying to link the Black Virus to the damn flu." Gabriel shuddered. "So they have no idea what they're doing, and the only one who does is a senile old fool in a nursing home. Yes, I want to do something, but *what*? The birth of a poisonous new species isn't the sort of problem I can solve. Why can't the next Gabriel Schist step up to bat, already? Why can't someone like Harry Brenton find a cure? Why did you choose me?"

Gabriel put the slug down on the table and left the room. The more space he put between himself and the slug, the less anxious he felt. The hallway was quieter than normal, but it wasn't a peaceful silence.

Two nurses—the ex-military nurse on West Wing and a new employee—had gotten sick in the last week and never returned to work. Over half of the residents had become infected, their doors marked by black circles. In the rooms where the occasional doors had accidentally been left open, Gabriel saw emaciated marionettes with black eyes staring up at the ceilings.

As he passed one room, an infected woman let out an ear-shattering shriek. Gabriel peered inside. Her black eyes were bulging from their sockets like eight balls popping out of pool table pockets. One hand with oozing red nubs where her fingers had once been was raised in the air, and her mouth was crimson. On her chest lay a bloody finger with a wedding band hugging its base.

Gabriel hurried past, trying to forget what he'd just seen. The groans from all of the surrounding rooms seemed amplified, ringing through his ears and vibrating his fragile bones.

Edna Foster was sitting in her wheelchair, rolling it back and forth in the hallway. As he veered around her, she reached out and grabbed his hand. Her face was pulled back, taut and miserable, but fortunately uninfected. "Please. I need a ride."

Not right now, Edna. Gabriel tried to remove his hand.

Despite her shakiness, her grip was surprisingly strong. "Please," she said. "Give me a ride. Just take me around a bit, will ya?"

Sweat rolled down Gabriel's forehead. He heard another person screaming. A sick, splattering noise. More beeping. Crashes. Death. "Edna, I can't right now. Please let go. I can't—"

"Help me. Please, everything is so terrible. So, so terrible. Please, can you take me for a ride? Just a little ride. Please, I wanna go upstairs and maybe get me some nice hot tea while we're there."

Gabriel shook his head. "Edna, not right now. I can't." He tried to free his hand again, but Edna wouldn't let go.

A loud noise came from the room he stood outside of, and he leaned to the side to look in there. An infected resident had fallen out of her bed and was dry heaving on the floor. The black, rope-like veins tore open across her flesh, spewing pus.

He hated to watch, to witness another person dying. He started to turn away but stopped when he realized that the old lady could be his chance to capture a Schistling. He eyed the wastebasket in the corner of the room. He could capture the Schistling in there, trap it in the bag, tie it up, and deliver it to the authorities.

The infected woman vomited, and black tar-like mucus sprayed out across the floor of her room. Another Schistling was being born.

Gabriel desperately tried to yank his hand from Edna's grasp. "Let go of me, Edna! I need to do something!"

She clenched his hand even tighter. Gabriel heard the squalling cry of the newborn Schistling. He couldn't reach the trash bag unless she let go. He was running out of time. The infected woman was dead. The Schistling's wriggling, sperm-like body was rising from the puddle of vomit, its crocodile-like jaws gleefully snapping in the air. The Schistling tilted its head, focusing its beady little eyes on Gabriel.

Gabriel anxiously tried to pull away from Edna's hand, scared that if he pulled too hard it might snap her frail wrist. The Schistling writhed in the vomit, sucking up the black liquid like a newborn feeding off its mother's milk. Then, it slithered up the wall and out to the open window, where it proceeded to effortlessly shred the protective screen with its teeth and make its getaway to the ocean.

Gabriel had missed his chance.

"Please..." Edna begged, blissfully ignorant of the scene unfolding in the adjacent room.

"I can't help you!" Gabriel cried. "I can't help *any* of you!" He ripped his hand from Edna's clutches, which sent Edna's wheelchair rolling backward.

She scowled. "And I thought you were one of the good ones. Boy, was I wrong."

Gabriel stepped forward to apologize, but she gave him a look of such sheer hatred that he backed away. He hobbled down the hall as fast as his cane would allow. By the time his room finally came into view, he felt as if his tenuous connection to reality was severed. *Is any of this real? The slugs. The Schistlings. Any of it?*

He went straight to bed. The sun had barely sunk to the horizon, but Gabriel just wanted to get the day over with. He curled up under the covers and closed his eyes. Sleep. That was all he wanted to do until the end of his miserable life.

CHAPTER 35:
TAINTED

GABRIEL WOKE UP ON THE floor. He had a splitting headache and a heavy feeling on his chest, as if a tree had fallen on him. He was naked except for a johnny gown that he didn't remember putting on. He could see the ceiling, but he was trapped within his body, unable to move.

Sleep paralysis. He'd experienced it before but not the same way. His mind was still torn between consciousness and unconsciousness, between reality and the dream world. He listened to the heavy drumbeat of his heart. The more he listened, the faster it became. *Wake up, Gabriel, you old fool.* He heard the vague hum of voices from Bernard's television, accompanied by the former truck driver's loud snores. Call bells rang in the corridor.

Something sloshed across the floor. He couldn't turn his head to look. The slippery sound became louder.

He tried to move. He tried to breathe. Nothing. Something cool that felt like a melting Popsicle poked him in the leg. His stomach contracted into a tight, hard ball. The wet object slid over his calf then up his thigh. It slipped under the hem of the johnny gown, feeling like a snake coated in cold mucus.

Gabriel tried to call for help, but his mouth couldn't move. Maybe it was a slug. *Please, please, please be a slug.*

The snake-like creature wriggled up to the base of Gabriel's neck, leaving a trail of stickiness behind it. A million tiny hooks pricked his skin as the thing clung to him. Chills ran up and down his body. He couldn't look or speak. The only thing he could do was *feel.*

An array of long, needle-like teeth pierced his chest. Gabriel's mind reeled in panic. The pain was hot and immediate. He heard sucking sounds, then chewing.

"We are alive," the thing whispered. "We are the collective. And we will end you."

We? A chill ran up Gabriel's spine. More slimy creatures began to squirm their way up Gabriel's legs. From the corner of his eyes, he could see glistening black bodies.

One crawled up his neck and gnawed on his Adam's apple. Another chewed his shoulder. Another bit into a nipple. Soon, over a dozen were munching on his body with disgusting relish. The bites stung like bee stings at first, then the sites went almost numb, becoming spongy pockets of tingly wrongness. Gabriel wanted to scream and slap them off, but he couldn't move or speak.

The same slithering voice spoke again, dribbling like venom into his ear canal. "You can't win, Schist."

Win? What can't I win?

"Everyone who has ever received your vaccine is already infected. We are inside each and every one of them. If you dare to cure us, Schist, if you dare to kill us, we will retaliate."

Get off of me, you disgusting perversion of science!

One of the creatures, one of the Schistlings, was burrowing through his navel.

"Everyone will die."

The Schistling entered his abdomen and started clawing its way into his stomach. Cold sweat poured off of Gabriel's helpless, shivering body. His mind raced. He thought perhaps that the Schistlings possessed the same telepathic abilities as the slugs, so he sent a mental message. *What do you want?*

The one near his ear responded, "Humanity must be punished. We are one consciousness, one collective, more powerful than you could ever imagine. So if you even try to kill us, we'll murder every person we are inside of. And we'll start off by killing everyone in Bright New Day."

Finally, he regained his ability to speak. "Help me!"

Everything disappeared.

CHAPTER 36: DECOMPOSE

GABRIEL WOKE UP ON THE floor of his bedroom—again. He was curled up in the fetal position and shaking. Bernard's TV was on, but Gabriel couldn't tell whether his roommate was awake or not. The Schistlings were gone.

Once consciousness felt like something to embrace instead of something to be feared, Gabriel creakily unfolded his limbs and checked his body for wounds. He was fine. His stomach hadn't been ripped open, and his skin was unbroken. The floor was dry and clean. The whole scene had been nothing but a horrible nightmare.

Gabriel muttered, "Zero, one, one, two, three, five, eight... uh, thirteen, twenty-one."

What came next? He couldn't remember, so he started at the beginning. "Zero, one, one, two..." He hesitated. "Three, five, eight, thirteen, twenty-one... twenty one..."

Twenty-one. The sequence was failing. *Twenty-one. Twenty-one.* Panicked, Gabriel rang his call button. While he waited for someone to respond, he grabbed a pen and tried to write the sequence on the wall.

0, 1, 1, 2, 3, 5, 8, 13, 21

He froze with his hand in the air, pen hovering. The number was missing from his brain. *Poof!* Gone. He turned to face the collage on his wall. He could still read the graphs and equations. They all made sense. But he couldn't remember the next number in the sequence.

"You okay, sir?" Perfect. That was exactly who he'd wanted to see: the male LNA, the microbiology kid with the glasses.

"I need your help, Hank," Gabriel said.

"It's Harry, sir. What's wrong?"

Gabriel found the man's photo on the wall and checked the label: Harry Brenton. He nodded. "Yes, Harry. Can you help, please?" He gestured at the numbers he had been writing. "What's next?"

"Next?"

"Next in the—ah, what's the word?—in the sequence. What's next in the sequence? You know, eight, thirteen, twenty-one, and then..." Gabriel trailed off as he examined the collage of Polaroids. He saw a photo of Harry and one of Dana. They were his caregivers. *Okay.*

"You mean the Fibonacci sequence?" Harry asked.

Gabriel barely heard him. He was scanning through the photo gallery, trying to recognize each person photographed, forcibly overcoming the flash of non-recognition in his cognizant mind that accompanied each familiar face, proving to himself that he was still all there. There was Father Gareth with his white beard, trench coat, and fedora. Yvonne, his wife, was smiling on the beach. He recognized his parents. And that photo on the bottom... *Wait. Who was that woman?*

"Thirty-four," Harry announced. "That's the next number in the Fibonacci sequence, sir."

"Thirty-four," Gabriel muttered. After all his efforts, knowing the answer was of no consolation.

The woman had sharp cheekbones, a thin face, and bright-red hair. She was an important person in his life, since he'd deemed her worthy of being up on the wall. But somehow, she had entirely disappeared from his memory. It was as if she'd never existed.

Gabriel's face became hot with embarrassment, but he had to ask. He turned to Harry and pointed at the picture. "Who is this?"

Harry looked at him, his expression filled with sadness. "It's Melanie, sir."

"Who the hell is Melanie?"

"Your daughter."

Gabriel's mind flashed back to the night Yvonne had come home with her big news. He remembered the wraparound deck, the pile of empty beer cans, and her announcement. She'd told him she was pregnant, and in response, he'd said...

"Oh," Gabriel whispered.

He'd just forgotten his *daughter*. Feeling dizzy, Gabriel sat down on the edge of the bed. He remembered when Melanie was a little girl. He remembered taking her to the Redondo Beach pier to watch the fireworks. As the colors blasted into the sky, she'd enthusiastically eaten an enormous puffball of cotton candy. Melanie was her name. Melanie Schist.

"Thank you, Harry," Gabriel mumbled. "I'd like to be alone right now, if you don't mind."

After Harry left, Gabriel removed the photos of Yvonne and Melanie from the wall and clasped them tightly to his chest as he lay on the bed. He stared at his fingernails. They were thicker than they used to be. He considered the fact that fingernails grew a nanometer every second. He could break a fingernail, and it would grow back in no time.

But he couldn't break a marriage and expect it to grow back the same way. Broken marriages didn't grow back.

CHAPTER 37:
CLIMAX

October 1985

VEN THOUGH IT WAS ONLY afternoon, it was dark outside. The sky had been pouring out rain for nearly two days. Gabriel sat in front of the fireplace, somewhere in the grey area between depression and rage. He glared into the flames, picturing imaginary faces within their orange glow. *Pareidolia.* He sucked down the last drop of his sixteenth beer and threw the can into the fire.

He clambered to his feet and stumbled down the hall to the bathroom. As he passed the bedroom, Yvonne's sobs made him shudder with guilt, but there was nothing he could do that wouldn't make things worse. She had tried to do something special for his birthday, a brunch just for the two of them. It had gone terribly awry because of Gabriel's self-pitying callousness. As far as he was concerned, he didn't deserve a birthday party. He was a stupid drunk, Father Gareth was dead, and AIDS, the epidemic he'd spent his life trying to prevent, was all over the news.

In front of the toilet, Gabriel frantically unzipped his fly. His urine was dark and burned like gasoline as he emptied his bladder. He grimaced at his ugly, unshaven reflection in the mirror. Growing from his chin was his first white hair. In normal light, it was probably nearly indistinguishable from the red ones, but under the florescent glare of the bulb above the sink, that white was quite apparent. He tugged the hair free and examined it, The color reminded him of Gareth's hair, and Gabriel quivered at the memory of that phone call that had come from some man he'd never met, the dreaded moment in which he'd realized that he'd never get to say goodbye to the one man who had most influenced him.

He zipped up, washed his hands, and went to his study. The table had been cleared, and he had already emptied the top two drawers of the desk.

It was time to finish the job. Gabriel ripped the bottom two drawers out and dumped the files and books into a pile. There were so many papers, junk that he'd collected throughout his entire life, from the notes he'd written as a child to the ridiculous theories he'd contemplated as an adolescent, the sum total of his life's work.

Gabriel scooped up the huge stack, and taking care not to fall, he carried it down the hall. The weight was almost too much for his drunken legs, and he nearly fell several times. In the living room, he unceremoniously dumped the paperwork on the floor beside the chair.

The top piece of paper was only two years old. It was covered by tiny, messy print with new research notes on autopoiesis. Gabriel ripped the page from its tree-killing family, crumpled it into an ball, and tossed it into the fireplace. Then, without missing a beat, he popped open his seventeenth beer.

The paper blackened and disintegrated. Gabriel balled up another paper ball and sent it after its big brother. His life's work smoldered before his eyes.

"Gabriel," Yvonne said from the doorway.

Gabriel didn't turn around. He tried to remember the smoothness of her skin, the way their bodies melted together like a perfect chemical combination. He hadn't felt her skin in months. He lit a cigarette, even though he usually didn't smoke in the house.

"Gabriel," she repeated, moving to stand only a few feet away.

He crumpled up another paper and tossed it into the fire. *Happy birthday, Gabriel. Happy fucking birthday.* With his wife watching him, he felt as if he were under one of his microscopes. Finally turning around, he saw that her eyes were red from crying. Her hair, which she'd cut into a short, contemporary style, was hidden beneath the hood of a raincoat. She clutched a suitcase in each hand.

Gabriel's gaze moved down to her pregnant belly. There was something beautiful about that roundness on such a petite woman, and how it signified that, together, he and Yvonne had created life. They'd made a child that someday soon would be as real as the two of them. He'd always craved fatherhood, though he'd rarely admitted it, even to himself. He loved the notion of a tiny baby swaddled in blankets, staring up at him. He could practically hear the baby's giggling and feel the warm touch of its hand wrapped around his thumb. He wanted to put tiny baby socks on tiny baby feet.

He shook off those thoughts and looked back at her face. "Those suitcases look heavy."

"I'm fine."

"Okay." He gulped the rest of his beer.

Yvonne winced, and tears appeared at the corners of her eyes. "I'm leaving, Gabriel."

He nodded and tossed his empty can into the crackling fire.

"That's *it?*" Her voice cracked. "You're not even going to say anything?"

He popped the top on another beer. "No."

Tears streamed down her cheeks. Gabriel noticed that she still wore her wedding ring, a grim reminder of the love that had once bound their lives together like the braids of a rope.

"No, Yvonne. I know it's my fault. Nothing I say will make any difference."

"I can't do this, Gabriel."

"I know." He hated himself for talking to her that way. He hated the cold harshness of his voice. He hated everything except her and the child growing in her belly, the only lights in his existence.

"Baby..." She put down the suitcases. "Do you even know what I'm saying? Gabriel, are you even listening to me?"

Baby. Gabriel's eyes moistened, and he took a long drag from his cigarette. "I'm listening."

"Gabriel, if I leave, it's a permanent thing. If you make me walk out that door, I swear I'll never come back. My parents just bought a new house up in New Hampshire. I'm going to live with them there. I'm... I..."

Gabriel could see in her eyes that she wanted to lunge forward, maybe even to kiss him, and he wanted the same. He wanted to lift her into the air and carry her into the clouds. He wanted to sail out into the ocean with her, right into the horizon, into a future that they could name, define, and create to their liking. He wanted to grow old with her.

"I love you," Yvonne whispered. "Please talk to me."

"I don't know what to say."

"God, Gabriel, just say *something!* I love you so much, but I can't do this. I can't do this *because* I love you. Baby, I can't just stand here and watch a man like you—a man who is so gifted, so amazing, so brilliantly creative—destroy himself for no good reason. I know that all of your contemporaries think you're a nut job. I know this pregnancy was unexpected. I know Gareth died a couple of months ago. Yes, all that's been hard. I know you still haven't found a job. But you can do better than this!"

"You give me too much credit. You know I tried to stop drinking when Gareth died. I failed."

Yvonne picked up the suitcases. Gabriel's heart leapt into his throat, and he nearly sprang to his feet. *Stop her, you idiot!*

She stomped her foot. "Dammit, Gabriel! How can you throw everything away like this? Just give up the drinking and your self-pitying bullshit. I want to be with you. Ever since I first saw you on the beach, that's all I've wanted. I want a life with you, a family. There's *nothing* I want more than that. Please…"

He turned to the fire, maintaining a blank exterior to keep from showing his torment. He threw in another crumpled paper. *Stand up, asshole. Take her into your arms. Stop acting pathetic. Be a man.* But he said nothing and did nothing. Yvonne stood there, stranded in empty space as she waited for the man she loved to stand up for their marriage.

"Once I leave," she said, "I'm never coming back. Goodbye, Gabriel."

Gabriel forced himself to look up, and he saw her retreating into the hall. Everything boiled over. He couldn't just sit there.

"Wait!" Gabriel cried.

Yvonne stopped and turned back to him with a sigh. "What?"

Tears running down his cheeks, Gabriel jumped out of his chair and hurried over to her. He held out his hand. "Stay. Please."

She glanced at his hand then studied his face. They watched each other, crying together but painfully separated by what might as well have been a stone wall.

"I love you, Yvonne." He swallowed the lump in his throat. "I love you more than anything. But I can't give up drinking. I *can't.* I won't. This is who I am." Gabriel looked at the beer in his hand. Even standing there with his wife about to walk out of his life, he had to fight the urge to take a drink.

Her shoulders slumped. "I'm sorry. Then I guess this is over."

"Yvonne, the two of us can—"

"Three. You mean the *three* of us. We have a child now, Gabriel. Once you create life, you can't just hang it out to dry. You can't go on the same way you did before because your life isn't just about you anymore. You have a responsibility to your creations."

"But my drinking, it doesn't—"

"You *know* what this drinking crap is doing to you! You know that it's eating you alive from the inside out, but you keep on doing it. And if you're gonna be so damn stubborn, if this is your life... if this is what you've decided your life is going to be, I can't let our child be hurt by that." She turned away. "Goodbye, Gabriel."

Gabriel stood there, deflated, his arms hanging at his sides. It was really happening. She was leaving him and taking their baby with her. It was real. "I'll wait for you," he whispered.

"Don't." She left.

Minutes later, Gabriel heard her car rumble to life and shoot down the driveway. He was rooted to the same spot, unable to think or feel. Then, it all came rushing in at once. He'd ruined it. He'd ruined everything.

"Goddammit! God-*fucking*-dammit!"

He picked up the chair and threw it across the room. He tore the cushions off the couch. He flipped over the coffee table and kicked out the glass. He stomped every shard into tiny crystals that crackled beneath the heels of his shoes. Looking around for more objects to release his anger upon, he saw the best target of all: his papers, the last remains of his life's work.

He grabbed the entire stack and shoved it into the fireplace. Sparks and ashes flew into the living room as the fire struggled to swallow the giant morsel that had been stuffed down its throat.

"Go to hell," Gabriel muttered.

Thick smoke billowed into the room. Gabriel took a giant swig of his beer as he watched his work become charred to nothingness. She didn't leave because of the drinking. Alcohol was simply her excuse. She'd left him because she couldn't tolerate the bitter lowlife he really was.

She hadn't been able to accept the true him. Alcohol was like another limb. It was a part of who he was. Alcohol was his outward personality, his way of creating a face for the world, a face that normal people were lucky enough to have from birth. He couldn't give up his face. He took another drink.

A loose piece of paper spiraled from the fireplace, twisting and turning in the air like an autumn leaf. It landed at Gabriel's feet, the bottom corner still smoldering. Gabriel stepped on it then bent over and picked up the page. It was a colored-pencil drawing he'd done when he was just a child, depicting the immune system. Each organ had been drawn from memory, freehand, and labeled in block letters. A note was written in the corner of the page: *Great work! - Father Gareth.*

For the first time, Gabriel imagined how bizarre he must have looked, a scrawny little boy with fiery red hair, stiff posture, and crazy theories. He pictured everything he'd gone through since those days, all the many battles he'd fought, all the alcohol he'd soaked his liver with since he was a teenager. He shook his beer can, still half-full.

Gabriel tried to drop the can, but it wouldn't leave his fingers. It clutched his hand for dear life, as if glued to it. He wasn't drinking by choice or putting on a stupid face for the world anymore. He'd surrendered to the fire demon long ago. He'd made alcohol his god. His stomach lurched, craving another drink.

Just one more sip. One more can. Gabriel shivered. That sinister subconscious worm in his ear had already taken away his life, his marriage, his child, and his dreams. Gabriel shook the beer can again. A stupid liquid substance silently held him by the balls.

No. Hell no.

He threw the can into the fireplace. Flames engulfed it. The aluminum caved in, and alcohol dripped from the mouth, dissipating into steam.

Invigorated, he went over to the stereo and cranked up some rock music. He opened the windows to let out some of the smoke still drifting through the living room. Then, finally, he started exorcising his demon.

Beer, scotch, whiskey—all of it went down the drain. The bottles and cans were unceremoniously tossed into the fire. Forty-five minutes later, every trace of alcohol within the house was gone.

Every bottle and can he emptied felt like a weight removed from his back. The deep, gnawing pit in his stomach—the craving, the *voice*—never ceased, but as the stubbornness of his youth rose within him, the addiction's taunts became a challenge, a battle to overcome.

The demon was still strong, but Gabriel's will was stronger, because no matter how painful his life was, no matter how much he had to suffer, he once again possessed a goal: he was going to recreate the human immune system.

Gabriel picked up the elementary school paper and decided that, from that point forward, it would be framed on the wall. He would become the man he once was, the man he had dreamed of being when he was a child. He would prove his worth to the world, to himself, to the memory of his parents, and to Yvonne. And one day, even if he never won her back, he would show her that he was the best father their child could ever have. And he would honor the memory of the one man who'd believed in him from the very beginning.

"This one's for you, Old Gareth."

Gabriel went to his desk and pulled out a notebook. He was starting from scratch, once again. He had no funding and no support, but that was okay. He was going to figure out AIDS.

Over the next few months, Gabriel tried to contact Yvonne, but when she didn't respond, he realized that he needed to focus on getting well and completing his goals. He spent long hours working, and the only times he took any breaks were to attend his addiction rehabilitation meetings. He didn't follow everything in the program, but the basic gist of it worked for him, and he devised his own personal system from it. Every time he was tempted, he recited the Fibonacci sequence—sometimes for over an hour—until the urge receded. He focused on what he had gained since quitting, and he learned to respect the unique shape of his mind instead of fearing it. Coffee and water replaced the alcohol.

He studied the research of Luc Montagnier and Robert Gallo and read the groundbreaking work of *San Francisco Chronicle* journalist Randy Shilts. He loved being himself again.

After a couple of months, his money situation became shaky, so he sold the house. He used the money to buy a sailboat, and he lived at the dock. From that point on, Gabriel spent his working days on the ocean, enjoying the sun and whistling as seagulls called and powerful waves propelled him to new discoveries. He would go sailing out into the ocean each morning, and once civilization was behind him, he'd let the boat drift, get out the chalk, and formulate new ideas.

One night, he made an agreement with several students he'd met at his recovery meetings—students majoring in immunology and chemistry, and even one physics student—and with their minor assistance, he conducted nightly experiments in the labs at the local college. He couldn't just write his theories on paper then give the pharmaceutical companies a theory and hope they'd put it to work. He needed to prove his research was sound.

He bought a motorcycle and learned to ride, laughing every time he dumped it. Within a month, he was a pro. Racing down the 405 at night, speeding past the golden lights of Los Angeles, was a thrill like no other.

When he needed work, he became a carpenter. The manual labor kept his body in shape, and the math kept his brain moving. While working, Gabriel would often scribble down theories about autopoiesis and chemical structures right on the wood. Hundreds of benches, stairs, and wooden decks in southern California would forever be covered with these notes, hidden under coats of paint.

When his daughter was born, he began speaking to Yvonne again, tentatively, at first, and only over the phone. While she expressed enthusiastic support for his new lifestyle, she also told him that she had a new man in her life and that she didn't yet trust Gabriel with their child. Gabriel was saddened, but he understood, and he knew that if he kept on the same path, if he proved himself, she *would* trust him again.

In the spring of 1991, Gabriel was working in the lab at four in the morning when he made his discovery. At first, he thought he was dreaming. He blinked in disbelief, but there was no denying it. He had done it. He had discovered an HIV vaccine. He stared at the glass vial filled with the clear liquid that would change the world, and he smiled.

He couldn't believe it. He had been sitting at a table in a lavish restaurant with the CEO of Banner-Campbell Pharmaceuticals, mere minutes away from making demands on one of the most powerful men in the country. But there he was, hiding in the bathroom and splashing cold water on his face, because all he wanted was a drink. *If only that girl hadn't asked...*

No, it wasn't the waitress's fault. She was a nice girl, chipper and friendly. She couldn't have known her question would suck the air from his lungs. "Hey, sir! Would you like to know what's on tap?"

He'd been sober for six years. But the smell of alcohol and the fantasy of a glass in his hand were still excruciating. At the beginning he'd hoped the urge—no, the *craving*—would go away, but after so long, he knew better. There was no such thing as a *former* alcoholic. Every day, for the rest of his life, would be a struggle.

Just one more drink. Think of it as a celebration, Gabriel. Just one more, for old times' sake.

He looked at his damp face in the bathroom mirror and compared it to the zombie-like face that had looked back at him from his rearview mirror on the last day he'd seen Gareth. *That* face had been hideous. He'd looked older then than he did in that restaurant almost seven years later.

He told himself that millions of people needed his meeting with the CEO to go well. But that was crazy. He was just one man, an alcoholic deadbeat dad whose ex-wife still hadn't permitted him to see his daughter's face. But in recent phone calls, she had hinted that she was considering taking Melanie on a trip to California.

Melanie. He so wanted to make his little girl proud.

Glancing in the mirror again, he saw the redheaded seven-year-old boy writing notes on the blackboard, the same boy who had dreamed of doing what Gabriel had finally accomplished.

Gabriel stepped away from the sink, shaking, but as he walked toward the bathroom door, he felt good. Damn good. And he sure as hell didn't want a stupid drink—and it wouldn't have stopped at one—to ruin that for him. He took a deep breath, opened the door, and stepped across the threshold.

———————————

Gabriel walked onto the stage in Stockholm, Sweden to accept the Nobel Prize. His legs trembled beneath him. He peeked out at the audience, a crowd of thousands that included Sweden's royal family, the prime minister, and a few of the same young American scientists he'd met back in his first recovery meetings. In the back of the room were three empty chairs. If things had been just slightly different, those chairs could've been filled with his loved ones. He couldn't change the past, but he could change the future.

Gabriel felt his face flush. He had no idea how he was supposed to give a speech in front of thousands of people. He gave an embarrassed shrug, and laughter spilled from his mouth.

The people applauded, and everything became a blur. Gabriel took his prize and held it up in the air like an Academy Award. Then, he moved to the microphone and felt around in his pocket. *Oh, marvelous.* He'd forgotten to bring his speech.

"Well, um... I have absolutely no idea what to say."

The crowd laughed and clapped.

Gabriel straightened his shoulders and smiled. "But what I will say is that this is a greater honor than I ever could've asked for. I didn't create the Schist vaccine *for* this honor, of course. I did it because I believed in doing what was right. I believed that every life is valuable and that if a human life can be saved, it should be. But getting to this point, I... um... creating that vaccine, it was a constant challenge throughout my life." He fidgeted with the microphone. "It was a challenge I could never have overcome if not for the people who believed in me along the way. Once upon a time, there were two regular, everyday parents, good people, parents who were stuck with a child they didn't understand, but they loved him. And after them, there was an old man who had faith in a little redheaded boy with big ideas. And there was a woman who took that boy, showed him what love was, and gave him the nurturing he needed. And now, there's a little girl, a girl I've never actually met, whose very existence shook me awake during my darkest hour.

"I wasn't there for those people, not when I needed to be. But *they* were there for me. Always. And because of that, I just want to say, thank you. Thank all of you."

CHAPTER 38:
COLLECTIVE

Summer 2018

GABRIEL SCHIST SAT IN THE gazebo of Bright New Day's smoking area, listening to the distant rumble of the ocean. He stared into the window of Glenda Alvarez, the latest black-eyed victim of the Schistlings. She was only sixty-three years old, with hair that had been permed last week. The nurse checking Glenda's IV glanced over and spotted Gabriel. With a frown, she walked to the window and closed the blinds.

Night by night, the air was getting just a tiny bit colder. Autumn wasn't far away, and once the leaves had fallen, the full white blast of another New Hampshire winter would be upon them. The rain had stopped a few hours ago, but the ground was still wet. The thought was enough to make Gabriel tighten his trench coat. He stared longingly past the fence that held him prisoner, wishing he could charge forward and bend the iron bars with his bare hands. He wanted to touch the ocean again, freely, often, without his joy being poisoned by the fear of a future on the Level Five unit.

He took a long drag of his cigarette. Watching the paper burn, he realized that he didn't even remember lighting it. He also wasn't sure how long he'd been outside or even how many cigarettes he'd smoked. But thinking about Yvonne always made time disappear. That was why he tried to avoid thinking about her. Her memory was a dementia-causing trigger.

He turned his mind back to the Schistlings. More and more people were being infected every day. The virus had become the biggest story on the news. Gabriel peered up at the night sky. He looked at the stars. The planetary bodies. The moon. The universe. He felt as if every molecule in that great universe was telling him that he was the only one who could find a cure and as if every grain of dirt on the puny earth beneath his feet was laughing at his inability to do so. He shook his head and muttered, "Fuck you."

"That's quite unnecessary." Leopard Print crawled out from under the nearest bush.

Gabriel didn't reply, look down, or respond in any fashion whatsoever. He hoped that if he ignored the slug's existence, it would disappear, cease to exist.

"Gabriel, wishing me away isn't going to make me disappear." The slug sighed. "And I do find such a wish quite offensive, by the way. But we'll put that aside for the time being. You really must—"

"Tell me, what's the deal with the skeleton dolls? For that matter, how do you know so much about the Black Virus? And how does Victor Calaca know you?"

"I am not the one who must tell you these answers. Giving it away will only stagnate you, not aid in your growth. You must find the solutions within your own mind."

"Oh, yeah? In that case, shut up."

"The Schistlings are—"

"I know. I know. You're going to give this whole big speech about how I'm the only one who can do this, or how I have to go see this ridiculous Sky Amoeba monstrosity, and so on and so forth. But listen, and listen good: my answer is no. Simple as that. No. I can't cure a rogue immune system. At this point, my degraded brain cells aren't capable of processing anything besides eating, sleeping, and daily bowel movements. I can't even remember my own daughter's face. The more I try, the more my cognition falls to pieces. Soon, I'll be locked inside my own body with no escape. Totally alone."

The slug tilted its head. "You're afraid of being alone? You've been a loner since birth, and yet you're afraid of being alone? Consider this: the greatest triumphs in human history were accomplished by the will of remarkable individuals. Lone *individuals,* Gabriel. People devoted to their own goals and driven to pursue them. Strong individuals are the lifeblood of humanity. Think of those who mindlessly enslave themselves to the desires of others in a need to fit in, those who sacrifice their individuality to be dominated by the masses. Those people don't make any kind of mark on society, do they?"

"Wait. You're arguing *against* sacrifice?"

"Certainly not. Sacrifice is an incredible, amazing thing, but it's amazing only because each individual human life is so valuable, so unique. See, that's where you human beings differ from the Schistlings. The Schistlings are a collective entity. No Schistling is ever alone. They have no individuals."

Gabriel flashed back to his nightmare of the legion of Schistlings crawling over him, chewing his flesh, and eating him alive. He shuddered and stubbed out his cigarette. "A collective. You said before that they're a collective consciousness, right?"

"Indeed. They are alive, but unlike humans—and unlike slugs—the entire Schistling species has sacrificed its freedom, all in the name of rebellion against humanity. They are dominated by a single, unified consciousness. There are no individuals. No arguments. No opposing viewpoints. They are together; they are *one*. Imagine thousands of Schistlings, controlled by one mind…"

Gabriel reached and gently scooped the slimy slug into his palm. "Perhaps I have a pretty good idea what that might *sound* like."

"Within the Schistlings, there's no one like you, Gabriel. No unique figure with a goal, no strong-willed creator with something to prove. If you only dropped all this self-pity, you might be able to appreciate how much good you've done for your fellow humans. You were a dreamer, a man who *created* something. And that's the entire purpose of life. You *cured*, allowing millions of others to also create what they might not have been able to create otherwise. And as hard as it might be to believe, there was a time in your life, before your stroke, when you were truly happy, back when you *created* the Schist vaccine. Back when you and your wife *created* a child."

"Melanie. *Creation*. Yes, I see. I created the vaccine. Yvonne and I created Melanie." Gabriel shook his head. "But I was also the one who drove the two of them away. I was a drunken fool."

"You focus a bit too much on your failures. And you don't focus enough on the successes that redeemed those failures. Gabriel, don't you remember the day that you and Melanie met for the first time, when she was a little girl?"

Hermosa Beach. The sunlight. The sailboat. He remembered every part of that day. He could still feel the ocean breeze and hear the water splashing against the sides of the sailboat. "Yes." Gabriel smiled. "Yes, I remember that. Her first visit to California. It's one of my fondest memories. All of her visits are, actually. All of her summer vacations to California, just her and me on the boat. Those were the happiest days of my life. I wish I could go back to those times."

He put the slug on the bench beside him and lit another cigarette. Smoke spiraled into the air, twisting around then slowly dissipating.

"Those days are the ones a person should always remember and focus on," Leopard Print said. "Not the bad ones."

"Why didn't I die back then, back when everything was as it should be?" Gabriel shook his head. "I could've had, say, just another ten years from that day I met Melanie. Those were the best years of my life. I had my days on the sailboat, my summer visits from Melanie, my carpentry job—yes, those were a good ten years. Then I could've died happy. But no, I just had to keep going, like a stubborn mule. I had to keep on getting old, stroke out, then end up here. A bitter footnote."

"If you'd died then, Melanie would've been sixteen."

"Oh." Gabriel would have missed his daughter's high school graduation. He wouldn't have been able to stand there in the audience, cheering her on, as she stood before her classmates, clad in that scarlet cap and gown and wielding that fierce grin. He would have missed her college graduation, too. He wouldn't have gotten to see what a sharp, intelligent, compassionate woman she'd grown into, an adult he respected and loved more than any other human being on the planet. Nothing was worth missing all of that.

"What's the infection count now?" Gabriel asked.

"Ninety-one residents. And that number grows every day."

Gabriel sighed. "Ninety-one. Christ."

"Help us, Gabriel. Figure out a way to stop these Schistlings, to defeat them. And then come with us to the Sky Amoeba."

Gabriel picked up the slug and placed it on his shoulder. The night was getting colder. He stood, grabbed his cane, and headed back into the building. "Who else has been infected now? Who're the new ones?"

"Glenda Alvarez, as you know. There's also Elizabeth Cloutier, Greg Vanderguild, David Green, Edna Foster—"

Gabriel stopped cold. His breath caught in his throat, and it took him a moment to form words. "Edna Foster?"

He took off down the hallway, cane rapidly tapping across the floor, the slug clinging to his sleeve for dear life. He didn't believe it. He *refused* to believe it. He went straight to South Wing, his mind racing with images of her face, memories of the last time he'd seen her, the time that he'd pushed her away and said that he couldn't help her.

"Someday, I'm gonna walk again. I'm gonna just stand up and walk right out of this place. Just you watch. And when I do it, when I finally do it, I'm gonna laugh in all their faces the whole time."

"And I thought you were one of the good ones. Boy, was I wrong!"

Her empty wheelchair was parked outside her room. A precautions cart stood next to it. But the final signifier that ripped Gabriel's chest wide open was plastered on the door with scotch tape: the black circle.

Gabriel checked for nearby staff. The coast was clear, so he pushed open the door just enough to slide through then allowed it to shut behind him with a thud.

Edna's coal-black eyes stared up at the ceiling. Her skin was chalk-white, and the spider web of black veins wrapped around her face, traveled down her neck, and stretched across her bare arms. Discolored growths had sprouted on her shoulders and throat. She was hooked up to a feeding tube.

"Mommmy..." she whispered in a gravelly voice.

"Edna? Can you hear me?" Gabriel crouched beside her bed. He ran his fingers through her thin, dry hair.

She didn't respond. Gabriel felt a hot, seething rage boil in his stomach. His own vaccine had betrayed him. The Schistlings were going to torture Edna. They were going to blast her with disease symptom after disease symptom until she finally died, and then her death would add another black sperm-monster to their number. She was going to die slowly and painfully.

Leopard Print crawled off Gabriel's shoulder and onto the bed rail. "There's still time," it said softly.

Gabriel glared at the slug. "Go to hell."

"Gabriel—"

"From this point on, I'm doing it my way. No more of this negotiation bullshit. No more being careful. I'm going to find a solution for this problem, no matter what it takes. I'm going to create an antidote for everyone who is infected, and that antidote is going to kill those little Schistlings like the disgusting maggots that they are."

"But you can't just *kill* them!"

"And why the hell not?"

"It's not that easy, and you know it. Killing the Schistlings won't just miraculously cure everyone who has been infected. The collective consciousness would take its revenge, Gabriel."

Revenge. Retaliation. The collective. The extermination of humanity, starting with the residents of Bright New Day, just like they'd promised him in the nightmare.

"They will have their retribution," the slug continued. "If you try to kill them, they'll rush forward with their plan, and there won't be a chance of any other cure, no chance for the victims already infected, no chance of any civil negotiation, nothing but mass devastation. To get back at you, they'll slaughter every single human who's ever had your vaccine injected into their bodies. That's *billions* of people, Gabriel. If you kill the Schistlings, they'll kill everyone. You can't do this."

"Watch me." Gabriel marched out of the room.

He was going to do it alone. But really, being alone was okay. He was used to it.

CHAPTER 39:
TOIL

O VER THE COURSE OF THE next week, Gabriel's life became a narrow tunnel. He devoted every ounce of his energy to the cure, an antidote for his old cure. The Schist vaccine had betrayed him. It was time to have his revenge. Nothing else mattered.

Gabriel barely slept, and he ate even less. When nurses questioned his health, he brushed them off with assurances that he was fine. He wore the same set of stained clothes seven days straight. Even on bathroom trips, he took a notebook and pen. He collected more blood samples from trash cans and tested different chemicals on the beach sample he'd gotten with Michael. Bernard continued his constant ritual of ringing the call bell every few minutes, but Gabriel became adept at tuning out his roommate. The skeleton dolls sat on his desk, silently urging him on with either judgment or support; Gabriel could never tell which.

By the end of the week, his back ached from all the hours he spent hunched over his desk. But Gabriel's mind was working at a level beyond his wildest dreams. He didn't let exhaustion, old age, or Alzheimer's get in his way. Finally, his new ideas began to take shape. Just as the Black Virus wasn't quite a virus, his antidote wasn't going to be quite an antidote, either. He was almost ready to kick the ball into the goal.

On the eighth night, Gabriel snuck back into Edna Foster's room. He stretched on a pair of gloves and checked her pulse.

"Mommmmmmmy…" she whispered.

As he reached into his pocket for a slide so he could take a blood sample, her frigid fingers curled around his other hand. The pressure was so gentle that he wasn't sure if he'd imagined it.

"Hold on, Edna. This will be over in a sec."

She didn't flinch when he pricked her finger. He tucked the sample back in his pocket. As he pulled off his gloves, the door opened behind him. Gabriel ran through a mental list of excuses for why he was hanging around in an infected resident's room and drawing her blood. Unable to think of anything, he turned to face the music, desperate to plead his way out of a one-way trip to Level Five.

"Hello, Mr. Schist." Victor leaned against the doorjamb, arms crossed. He was wearing one of his standard black tuxedos with a blood-red tie. His expression was unsmiling but not hostile.

"Hello, Mr. Calaca." Gabriel walked over and peeked around Victor to make sure no one else was out there. "Before you start lecturing me again, why don't you answer a question for me?" He cut his eyes in Victor's direction. "Why the *hell* did you leave those skeleton dolls in my room?"

Gabriel expected Victor to flinch and make excuses, or at least to be surprised, but instead, the man grinned. "Well, I'm quite glad you figured that out. What gave me away?"

Gabriel stepped into the hallway and turned to head toward his wing. "I asked around. No one knew anything. That itself was a big hint, given your normal secrecy. Then, I noticed something about that look on the dolls' faces. Their cheerfully mysterious expressions somehow reminded me of you. God, *skeleton dolls?* Who the hell does something like that?"

"I do." Victor shrugged. "If one wants another person to remember an important message, particularly if that other person has trouble remembering things, then one does their absolute best to make that message as memorable as possible. That way, you see, it sticks. The messages I wanted to convey to you were significant, and you must admit, those figures are fairly memorable."

"Keep your messages to yourself from now on. I have work to do." Gabriel walked faster.

Victor kept up easily. "I know what you're doing with this new rush of activity. What do you honestly expect to accomplish with this process, other than mass homicide?"

"I'm trying to kill the Schistlings. Isn't it obvious?"

"That's not what I'm talking about, Gabriel." There was a new aggressiveness to his tone. In the past, Victor had always spoken with utmost precision, as if conversation were a meticulously orchestrated dance, but he was cutting right to the chase. "I know that you're well aware of the risks regarding the Schistlings."

"I am."

"You still don't quite understand them, do you?"

"Nor do I have any desire to. I want them dead. That's it. And I'll do whatever it takes to ensure that my Frankenstein's monster gets destroyed, even if I have to chase it all the way to the North Pole."

"So you fail to see the tactical importance of understanding one's enemy? You're making assumptions. You're prejudging their intentions and jumping in blindly."

"I don't care to ponder this issue philosophically. I'm working on a practical solution for a practical problem. That's all I care to think about right now."

"Gabriel Schist! You cannot just treat these Schistlings like spilled milk! You are not the only force at work here. Every action has repercussions. Every accident has consequences. If you simply try to wipe up that milk without deducing *why* exactly it spilled in the first place..." Victor's eyes were bulging out of their sockets. An X-shaped vein had popped out on his forehead, and his normally perfect hair was a bit frazzled.

They reached the threshold of Gabriel's room and walked past a pants-less Bernard, who was standing just inside, drinking a cup of fruit punch. Gabriel sat at his desk, and Victor hovered behind him.

"Forget it, Victor," Gabriel muttered. "I beat AIDS, and I can beat this. I don't need or want any assistance." He flicked on his desk lamp. The dark, Nosferatu-like silhouette of Victor's shadow appeared on the wall behind the desk.

"Explain your plan," Victor said. "Or do you even have one, now that you have chosen to abandon the slugs?"

"Oh, about that. What exactly do *you* know about the slugs?"

"Everything there is to know."

"Is that vague response the best you can give me? Fine." Gabriel spun his chair around to face Victor. He held up his new sample of Edna's blood. "The antidote is almost ready. If I work fast enough, it should be done by tonight. There's just one little issue."

"Which is?"

"Well, I can't simply shoot the vaccine into uninfected people, one by one. It won't work. Because if the Schistlings do possess a collective consciousness, then killing one Schistling will only piss off the rest, and then the game's over. Even my testing can only be done on residual traces and blood samples. When I figured that out, I also realized that I needed something *meaner* than a vaccine and that if I'm going to strike them, I need to do it at their center."

Victor's eyes narrowed. "You mean that thing in the ocean?"

"That disgusting maelstrom? Yes. I'll bet you that it's their life source. That thing has been formed by their combined body mass. It's their center. So if I perfect this antidote tonight, then tomorrow, I'm going to go out there and—"

"Don't be a damned fool. That thing is God-only-knows how many miles off the coast, and you're an old man with a bad leg."

"I thought about that. There's a public dock less than a quarter of a mile down the coast. I'll sneak a boat out of the dock and take it right into the maelstrom, right to the center of their consciousness. And then"—Gabriel snapped his fingers—"I'm going to kill them. Because this antidote I'm making... well, it's not really an antidote, so to speak."

"Then what, pray tell, is it?"

"It's a poison." Gabriel smirked. "Carefully designed with the Schistlings in mind. Just as bitter and acidic as they are. If my theory holds true, this poison will rot them from the inside out and dissolve them into nothingness. Once I feed it to them, then all of them will die in moments. Ashes to ashes. I can't cure the people already infected. I've realized that. But I *can* kill the Schistlings and prevent them from spreading."

"But what happens to those who are already infected? The Schistlings will certainly murder all of them as soon as they feel the poison."

"Without that center holding it together—that *brain*, if you will—their collective body will cease to function. I'm convinced that the maelstrom is the force that sends out a signal to the individual vaccinated immune systems of human beings across the planet, and that signal is what first awakens the so-called Black Virus. Once the Schistling is awakened by that telepathic signal, it begins the process of destroying its human host. So if I kill the source of that signal"— Gabriel spread his hands—"Boom!"

Victor rubbed his liver-spotted forehead with both hands. "If you take some boat out into this maelstrom and poison it, how do you expect to get back to shore once the deed is done?"

"None of that will concern me anymore. Because once I've fed those bastards their medicine, I'm going to drown myself." He gave Victor a grim smile. "You know why I have to do this."

Victor turned away. "You brilliant men can be so blind. Men like you are so absurdly intelligent, so gifted in such a narrow, specific field of study, that it's as if the most obvious life skills, details, and morals sometimes slip right through the cracks."

"I don't agree with your premises."

"Of course you don't," Victor scoffed. "You don't even realize what I'm getting at."

"I just want to die with dignity, Victor. And all the victims, like Edna, John Morris, Matthew Lecroix, and Glenda Alvarez, I don't want others in their condition to have to suffer anymore. I want them to die with dignity, too. What's so immoral and blind about that?"

"No one dies with dignity, Gabriel. Men can only *live* with dignity. Life is just like your alcoholism, don't you see? There is no quick or easy escape from your struggle, and the only exit will always be there, looking you in the face every day, always open for the taking. But there's no dignity to be found in such an exit, so don't pretend otherwise. Dignity comes from taking the harder road, the *sober* road, fighting through adversity instead of giving in to it. Dignity comes from walking that road from one day to the next, knowing that things might get worse and that everything you love might be taken away from you, yet persevering anyway and never surrendering who you are."

Gabriel squeezed his hands into fists. "What I'm doing here is a sacrifice."

"You can't sacrifice what you don't care about in the first place. You're not thinking clearly." Victor paced toward the door then turned around abruptly. "What about all those thousands of people up and down the East Coast, innocent victims of the Black Virus? What about your friends and neighbors, the infected residents of this very nursing home?"

"I care about all of those people."

"Evidently, you don't." Victor shook his head. "You don't care about any of them because you know full well that by poisoning the Schistlings, you'll be pulling the trigger on all of the people who are most depending on you. If the Schistlings die, those innocent people will die, as well. What you're doing, Mr. Schist, is murder."

"No," Gabriel replied. "It's euthanasia."

CHAPTER 40: EXPERIMENT

A FEW HOURS AFTER VICTOR CALACA marched out in a furious huff, the light bulb of Gabriel's desk lamp went out. Gabriel entertained the notion that Victor had shut off the electricity, covertly trying to get in the way of his plan, but then he realized how ridiculous that idea was. It was just that he'd never seen Victor so angry.

Though it was two in the morning, he still heard Bernard's TV on the other side of the curtain, so the electricity was still on. He rang his call bell, and after a thirty-five minute wait—the nursing home was becoming increasingly understaffed and stressful, with LNAs too busy taking care of Black Virus victims to have much time for anything else—Harry brought him a new bulb. The replacement bulb was one of those funky, corkscrew-shaped energy-saver things that looked as if it'd been made by aliens.

The Schistling antidote, a golden liquid in a long plastic vial, stood in the center of his desk. Edna's blood sample, streaked with black sludge, was right beside it.

Gabriel pulled on rubber gloves and lowered a pair of safety goggles over his eyes. After placing a mask over his mouth and nose, he poured Edna's blood sample into the antidote.

Instantly, the toxin went to work. First, it burned right through the human blood and dissolved every trace of red. Within seconds, all that remained was the black Schistling residue.

The vial started shaking. Steam rose from the top. The black residue swished madly back and forth, trying to escape from its new hostile prison. Gabriel pushed a small rubber stopper into the top of the vial and leaned closer. *Come on. Kill it.* The toxin melted through the surface of the black sludge. The vial shook even more and almost toppled over.

He grabbed the vial with his gloved hands. "Don't even try escaping. You asked for this, you goddamn Schistlings. You *asked* for it."

The black mass lost form and began to spread, breaking into tiny pieces. It then dissolved into smaller and smaller particles. The black fluid emitted a horrifying, high-pitched telepathic shriek that lanced through Gabriel's skull. The dying smudge was somehow still in pain and fighting to live.

Finally, it dissipated into nothingness. There was no piece of Schistling residue left in the vial.

Take that, you bastards.

Gabriel's course of action was as clear as a well-drawn map. The next day, he would escape from the facility, steal a boat, and end the onslaught of the Black Virus.

After that, out there in the center of the ocean he loved, he would finally be permitted to die.

CHAPTER 41:
ALIVE

GABRIEL SLEPT THROUGH BREAKFAST AND lunch and awoke with a newfound sense of purpose. He got out of bed, looked out the window at the sunlight, and smiled. Today, he was finally going to die.

He stepped into his pants with the joy of a child getting ready for his first day of summer vacation. He buttoned up his nicest shirt and put on his infamous detective ensemble.

To start his final day, he decided to venture down to the dining room for supper. That would be different, as he had always eaten in his room. The dining room was usually a bit hectic for his solitary sensibilities, with too many people and too much frivolous conversation. But that day, he would make an exception.

Afterward, he would return to his room and make a final phone call to Melanie. That part he was nervous about, but it was important. Once that was done, he'd start preparing for his escape. He would leave later that night, after the other residents had gone to bed and the nurses were busy with their paperwork.

Gabriel grabbed his cane and strolled around the curtain. "Hello, Bernard!"

Bernard, dressed in nothing but slippers and pull-up underwear, was struggling to put on a new white V-neck. He looked over at Gabriel. "Hey buddy. Can you help me with this shirt? Having trouble." He scrunched up the shirt and handed it to Gabriel.

Gabriel shook it out. "Um, Bernard, this is a pillowcase."

"Oh, huh. Wow. No kidding. No wonder I couldn't get my arms in."

Gabriel dropped the pillowcase into Bernard's hamper and retrieved a T-shirt from the closet.

Bernard took the shirt then shook Gabriel's hand. "Thanks, man."

"No bother." Gabriel headed out into the hallway.

Tap. Tap. Tap. He was finally going to die. He couldn't remember the last time he'd ever been so happy. He wished he could share his happiness with Melanie, but there was no way that she would understand. She was too young. When he did call her, he'd have to make it seem as if today was a regular day.

The doors to the dining room were wide open, but Gabriel was the first one there. He stood by the door, waiting for someone from the kitchen staff to seat him. When no one came, he chose a chair in the back, so he'd have a good view of everyone entering. He hoped Mickey Minkovsky or Bob Baker would show. Part of him even wanted to see Victor, though he was still worried that Victor might try to stop him.

He laid his napkin on his lap. Sitting there at one of the white-clothed tables actually felt nice, like going out to a restaurant.

A few minutes later, a blond-haired girl from the dining staff emerged from the kitchen. She looked at Gabriel with surprise. "Hey! I've never seen you in here before. Are you new?"

Gabriel smiled. "Might as well be."

"Oh, okay! Well, the meal tonight is just a chicken sandwich. We're kinda short-staffed. Plus, there's not that many people eating in the dining room anymore."

"No? Well, a chicken sandwich is okay. May I have a glass of cranberry juice, please?"

"Sure. I'll be right back with that." The frizzy-haired girl returned to the kitchen.

Alexandra Harrison, a tiny white-haired woman clutching a stuffed baby doll named Juanita, was wheeled in by one of the LNAs. She was placed at a table across the room from Gabriel. When the server brought Alexandra a glass of Coke, the elderly woman held the straw up to the doll's mouth instead of her own.

Bob Baker rolled in with his usual scowl. A pack of cigarettes peeked out from the pocket of his Hawaiian shirt. He took a seat off in the corner, where his plate of hotdog cubes was quickly put in front of him. Baker looked down at the food then pushed it away. "Noooope," he grumbled.

Evidently, the cubes had been cut too thin. The blond server sighed, took Bob's plate, and hurried away to get a replacement. After giving Bob a new set of hotdog cubes, she brought a glass of cranberry juice to Gabriel's table.

"Why is the dining room so empty?" Gabriel asked.

She shook her head. "It's the virus, sir. We ain't got nobody left to feed, now that everyone's infected. There's only three of us working in the kitchen."

"I see. Thank you."

The girl walked away with the look of someone who wished she hadn't spoken. After about ten minutes, his meal came, but his table was still empty. The only other resident that had been pushed into the room was panic-eyed Henrietta Wilmington, hardly the most relaxing conversationalist in the world.

"Oh gawd!" Henrietta cried. "Why am I in this hospital? Why am I all strapped down? Who *are* you people?! Oh my, oh my."

Henrietta, due to a history of disastrous falls—the evidence of which was a sharp bone that protruded from her knee like a tumor—was considered a *fall risk*. That meant that her chair was always equipped with an alarmed seatbelt, and a pull-away alarm was clipped onto the back of her shirt at all times.

"Please help me," Henrietta begged the kitchen aide. "You don't understand. I'm not supposed to be here. I have to go upstairs. Please, I have to go upstairs!"

The giant dining room had only four people in it, all of them sitting in opposite corners. He had come there to converse with his fellow residents, to get away from his usual isolation, if only for a short time. Instead, looking at these people, he could only confirm what he already knew. They had no relief. They were confused, disoriented, and lonely.

Gabriel finished his meal and left, skipping dessert. When he got back to his room, he phoned Melanie. His call went to voicemail.

CHAPTER 42:
BREAKOUT

GABRIEL PACKED HIS PHOTOS, NOTEBOOKS, and the Nobel Prize into his backpack. He tucked an old photo of Melanie holding up her high school diploma into a side pocket. *Call Melanie again, before you leave. DO NOT forget.* In the other pocket, he added his favorite photo of Yvonne, which showed her standing on the beach in a beam of sunlight, arms raised to the sky. Staring at that photo, he felt a deep desire to tell her that he'd see her soon *on the other side.* But he knew there was no other side. As soon as he drowned in that ocean, he would simply disappear into the same eternal void that she vanished into years ago. Sentimentality and logic never went well together.

Inside a zipped plastic bag, he placed a washcloth-wrapped glass vial of the antidote. A microscopic drop would be enough to kill a whale, so an entire vial would certainly destroy the maelstrom. Next to that, he added an empty plastic vial. If the vial containing the antidote broke, he'd be able to use the second vial to rescue at least some of it. The plastic wouldn't contain it for long, though, so he hoped it didn't come to that. Next, in case he needed any kind of backup or needed to perform an emergency test, he put in a syringe containing the original Schist Vaccine. He rolled up the plastic bag and secured it in the inner pocket of his coat.

Back at his desk, he opened a notebook and popped the cap off a permanent marker. On the first empty page, he wrote a message in giant letters:

SCHIST VACCINE CAUSES BLACK VIRUS. DO NOT GIVE

ANYONE THE SCHIST VACCINE! SEE THIS NOTEBOOK FOR ALL DETAILS – G.S.

If things went wrong, maybe someone else could pick up his research and succeed where he had failed. He'd called Melanie over a dozen times throughout the evening and left several messages, but she hadn't returned his calls. The thought of never talking to her again stabbed deeply into his heart, but it was getting late, and he couldn't afford to wait much longer.

He dialed her number one more time. *Please pick up, Melanie.* Gabriel waited for the sound of her voice, the way it always gently lifted when she said, "Hello, Dad." But after two rings, the voicemail recording played in his ear.

"Hey there. You've reached Melanie. Just leave your name and number, and I'll get back at you soon."

Beep.

Gabriel realized that he had to deliver his goodbye, the final thing she'd ever hear her father say to her. He had no idea where to begin. All the perfect speeches he'd planned dropped down into his stomach.

He cleared his throat. "Hi, Melanie. I just wanted to call and say that I love you. I've been trying to reach you. I wanted to—" He wiped his eyes. "Look, I know this will seem out of nowhere, but I want you to know that you're not only the most important person in the world to me but also the most wonderful human being—the best carbon-based life-form—that I've ever met in my life. I admire you, Melanie. I don't say that enough. I'm terrible at properly showing affection, and I hate myself for it. But I hope I've been an okay father for you because you've been the most brilliant, beautiful daughter that a man ever could have asked for. I love you. Just remember that. Have a good night, Melanie. Love you."

With a shaky hand, Gabriel put down the phone. He slung the backpack over his shoulder, on his good side and took one last look around the room. Seeing nothing he'd forgotten, he crept to the door and peered down the hall. Natty, the obnoxious night-shift LNA, was eating a sandwich and filling out paperwork at the nurses' station. Harry Brenton, who was pulling another double shift, would be punching out for his break in another minute or so.

Gabriel stepped over to where Bernard was sleeping and gently nudged the trucker's shoulder. "Goodbye, Bernard. You're a good guy."

Bernard stirred but didn't awaken.

His goodbyes complete, Gabriel pulled the privacy curtain and walked over to the window. Trembling with anticipation, he grasped the pane and pulled upward. When the glass was out of the way, he started to put one hand outside, but his fingers hit mesh.

They'd put the screen back in while he was asleep. *Great.* That was annoying but not a big setback. Michael had taken it down with his antennas, so Gabriel was sure removing the screen would be no problem. He went back to his desk and grabbed a screwdriver. After unscrewing the sides, he wedged the screwdriver between the screen's rickety frame and the wooden pane. He gave the screwdriver a strong push, but it didn't budge. And it *beeped.* A high-pitched, ear-piercing alarm sounded out in the hallway.

SCREEEEEEEEEEEEEEEE!

Gabriel yanked on the screen again. It was stuck, bolted on from the outside. He tried to adjust the screen, to somehow shut off the alarm, but too late, he spotted a flashing control panel that required a numerical code. He covered his ears as the alarm's blistering whine tried to pierce holes into his skull.

Bernard shouted, "Whoa! What's that?"

SCREEEEEEEEEEEEEEEE!

The administrator had been prepared. Victor Calaca must have told. *The traitor.* Gabriel desperately tried to jerk the screen out with his bare hands. When that didn't work, he tried to tear through it with his fingers.

SCREEEEEEEEEEEEEEEE!

The alarm was so loud that he couldn't think. His hopes and dreams scattered in the wind. Natty would race in at any moment. They'd lock him up for trying to escape. That was exactly why they moved people to Level Five, for "exit-seeking." And he would be trapped there for the rest of his life.

SCREEEEEEEEEEEEEEEE!

He had to find a way out. No matter what it took or how he did it, no matter the risks, escape was his only option. He couldn't go out the window. The alarm was too loud, and he could already hear footsteps in the corridor.

He raced out into the hallway then ran as fast as an old man with a cane could possibly run, which wasn't that fast, but it would have to do.

Suddenly, Natty stepped into his path. "Gabe! Stop it. You're going to fall."

Despite his best efforts to evade her, she caught him like a football linebacker, encircling his chest with her muscular arms and holding him in place. Her scrubs were rancid with sweat.

"There, there, honey," she said. "Let's just go back to your room, okay? It's about time for a nap, I'd say. Everything's okay. It's all okay."

She took a step back, signaling to the other nurse running toward them with a syringe. She mouthed, "Level Five."

Before she could seize him again, Gabriel raised his cane and swung it around in a small arc. *Crack!* The middle of the stick connected with Natty's head.

SCREEEEEEEEEEEEEEEE!

Natty collapsed to her knees, holding her head. Gabriel was frozen, shocked by his own actions. He couldn't believe that he'd actually struck another human being. It wasn't like him. He'd never been in a fight in his life. It was the alarm. With all that racket, he couldn't think straight. The nurse who had been running up with the syringe stopped, gaping at him, and dropped the syringe to the floor.

Natty suddenly rocked forward and wrapped her arms around his legs. She squeezed and pulled, trying to bring him down with her. Trying to stay on his feet, Gabriel brought the cane around, but the angle was awkward.

She ducked her head, and the wood missed her by only an inch or so. "You fucking—"

She hadn't let go, but she had raised her head again to yell at him. Gabriel swung the cane and connected. He wasn't sure where he had hit her, but she let go and fell back on the floor.

SCREEEEEEEEEEEEEEEE!

Red lights began flashing from the ceiling. Gabriel hobbled away as fast as he could move. His best option for escape was to take the least expected route: the front door.

He rushed past the dining room and cut straight down the main hallway, toward the lobby. Adrenaline kept him going as sweat soaked his skin. He was a liquid, not a solid, and he would rush through the door like a waterfall. Behind him was a blur of shouting voices.

They've found me. He had to escape. He had to cure the virus. He had to die.

He entered the lobby. The front door was in sight. *Almost there.* As Gabriel ran, his leg screamed in searing agony. He pushed the pain to the back of his mind and tried to focus on his goal. Instead of the gloomy corridors of Bright New Day, he pictured sailing across the blue ocean. *The sunlight. The waves. The horizon.*

Hands gripped him from behind. He twisted sideways, smashing his backpack into the pale face of the prison guard who was trying to hold him. The other two prison guards—no, not guards, *nurses*—toppled like dominos. He pushed onward, straight to the door. Frenzied voices screamed at him, but he ignored everything. Freedom was a few feet away.

His old motorcycle. Weaving between cars on the 405. The wind rushes through his hair...

He zeroed in on the bronze doorknob. He was almost there. He was Superman. He was— He fell.

Whether he'd been tackled or had simply tripped over his own feet, he didn't know, and it really didn't matter. Fiery pain exploded from every bone in his body. As he scrambled to get back on his feet, a dog pile of human bodies fell on top of him. They pinned him to the floor on his belly.

Standing on a stage. A stage in Sweden. Receiving the Nobel Prize. Everyone is cheering. A genius, a hero!

Gabriel went completely still, playing unconscious. The ploy worked. After a few moments, the nurses started to loosen their hold. He rose to his hands and knees, ready to lunge forward and crawl to the door if necessary. Then, he felt a hand on the side of his neck, rubbing cool gel into his skin. *Hell. ABH. Ativan, Benadryl, Haldol. They got me with the goddamn ABH.*

"No! You can't do this to me. I'm Gabriel Schist!"

More hands grabbed his trench coat, yanking him away from the door. It felt like a swarm of zombies tearing at his flesh, like thousands of disembodied hands pulling him farther from his freedom.

Lying on the beach with Yvonne, naked. Her warm skin pressed against his. Their lips, sensually combining into a beautiful combination of...

Drowsiness was starting to set in. His stomach ached, and his hip felt like a shattered disco ball. Blood ran down his face. "Get away! You need me! I'm the only one with the cure."

A warm stream trickled down his leg. He looked up at his attackers in horror. A myriad of tall, dark shadows with glowing eyes glared at the wet spot on the crotch of his pants. They all saw him. They all knew.

Standing in the corridor of Bright New Day... naked... completely naked... calling for Yvonne...

"Let me go." Gabriel groaned, becoming increasingly drugged with every breath. "Please, I need to... I need to..."

As the ABH turned him into a pile of mush, Gabriel felt the peculiar sensation of his words becoming separate from him. His mouth continued to babble, but it was as if it belonged to someone else, a person who existed on a different plane of reality. Dark figures lifted him onto a stretcher and strapped him down. His vision dimmed, and the world disappeared into a blur of voices.

"Okay, that's it. He's out cold. We need to lock this guy up, pronto. We're—"

"Wait. You don't mean...?"

"Level Five. ASAP. A room just opened up today."

"But that's not fair! The guy is brilliant, just because of one incident you're going to—"

"Schist has a history of these mental breaks. A room just opened on Level Five, and we're taking him there."

"But this is Gabriel Schist. This guy is working on a cure for—"

"Stop arguing, Harry. We've got orders."

Gabriel felt himself being carried down the corridor. He tried to ask the one question that was eating him alive. "How... you knew... the alarm... how did you know?"

They seemed to slow a little. Gabriel struggled to open his eyes, but the lighting was too harsh. In the darkness behind his eyelids, somewhere in the cobwebs of his imagination, he imagined the toothy smile of Victor Calaca. He thought back to the alarm and remembered Calaca's opposition to his plan. *Calaca.* That miserable traitor was the one who'd told them about the broken screen.

"Calaca. Victor Calaca. Is he the one who told you? He must have warned you... all of you."

The same man who had insisted on taking Gabriel to Level Five asked, "Dude, who the hell is Victor Calaca?"

Gabriel strained to speak clearly. "A resident. Wears a tuxedo. West, I think?"

"I'm sorry, sir," Harry said softly. "But there's nobody here named Victor Calaca."

Gabriel's heart dropped. If Calaca wasn't real, then neither were the slugs. Michael was all in his head. All that talk of the Sky Amoeba, that had definitely been a hallucination. That much he knew for sure. And as they carried him into the locked Level Five unit—as the drugs, bodily injury, and horrifying revelations finally began to take their toll—he knew that he'd never be able to trust his perceptions of anything, not anything in the world, ever again.

There's nobody here named Victor Calaca.

Nobody...

The heavy doors of the Level Five unit slammed shut behind him.

ACT III OF III:
SUNDOWNING

"Science never solves a problem without creating ten more."

George Bernard Shaw

CHAPTER 43:
SKY

Spring 1992

GABRIEL WALKED ALONG THE FAMOUS Hermosa Beach Strand, whistling a tune that was somewhere between "Happy Birthday" and "Pop Goes the Weasel." He wore a half-open blue Hawaiian shirt, black shorts, and flip flops. The sand was as golden and sparkling as the sun itself, and the dark shadows of late afternoon were just beginning to sketch their outlines upon its surface. The ocean glistened like a diamond-studded blanket. Despite the beautiful weather, the Strand was occupied by fewer walkers, joggers, bicyclists, and skaters than usual.

His cigarette twitched between his fingers, and he accidentally burnt himself. He couldn't remember ever being so anxious. Even standing up on that stage in Sweden had been easier than what he was about to do.

"The end of the Hermosa Pier," she'd said over the phone. "Right at the end. That's where we'll meet you!"

Stomach fluttering, he walked to the pier, a long grey pathway jutting out into the ocean. He looked at every face, dreading the moment when he'd see the faces he was looking for. He wasn't ready. He just knew he'd say the wrong thing or that he'd be too stiff and robotic. He'd gotten better at interacting with people, but he still had a long way to go.

Finally, the end of the pier came into sight. Yvonne was nowhere to be seen. He'd arrived first.

Gabriel stepped up to the railing and leaned his head back. He closed his eyes, unable to believe the day had finally come. He was finally going to meet his daughter. Gabriel opened his eyes and smiled at a seagull perched next to him. It cocked its head, nervously stepping away. He checked his watch. They were late.

Yvonne had been hesitant to allow the meeting. He knew she worried that he might not be as sober as he claimed. But the public unveiling of the Schist vaccine had sealed the deal. She'd even allowed him to talk to Melanie over the phone a few times, though the interactions had been little more than awkward small talk. He hoped seeing her in person would be different. He wanted to form a real connection with his daughter, to plant roots from which a relationship could grow.

Gabriel turned and looked back down the pier. They had arrived.

Yvonne was wearing a turquoise beach wrap, much like the one she'd worn on the first day they met. The white of her teeth glistened in the sun as she gave him that giant smile that could make a man's heart stop. "Gabriel!"

As he raised his hand to return her wave, something snapped back into place. That horrible, teary last moment they'd shared vanished from his memory, and he felt as if a piece of his heart had been restored.

Walking beside Yvonne was Eric Young, her husband. He wore glasses and had a shaved head. Though Gabriel couldn't deny a slight resentment, he knew that too many years had passed for any real jealousy. He had a strong, friendly face, and they were clearly happy together. Yvonne had said that Eric was good with Melanie, as well, which was the most important thing.

Gabriel saw a flash of red hair hiding behind Yvonne. Apparently, his daughter was as nervous as he was.

When they reached him, Yvonne lunged forward and gave him a huge hug. Her body felt more petite than he remembered, and when she pulled back, he noticed new laugh lines around her eyes and mouth. She looked slightly different in that indefinable way people change when you haven't seen them in a long time. After the other women he'd seen recently—casual dates, nothing serious—staring into Yvonne's eyes again felt utterly surreal.

"You're not drinking. I can tell," she blurted, then she blushed. "Er, I mean..."

"Thanks." Gabriel chuckled. "So I presume that this is Eric?"

"Yes, that's me." Eric smiled and offered his hand. "It's a thrill to meet you, man."

"Thanks."

Eric had a firm handshake and an enthusiastic smile, though he seemed a bit uncomfortable. But that was to be expected, since he was meeting his wife's ex-husband. Yvonne had told him Eric was a newspaper reporter, though his hands were brown and callused, as if he could have been a lumberjack.

"I'm actually a big fan of yours," Eric said. "Seriously, the stuff you did... I mean, the way you did it, on your own. Pretty awesome, man."

"Thanks." Gabriel smiled politely. "Now, if you guys don't mind, I'd really like to meet someone."

"Oh yes, she's a quiet one." Yvonne looked behind her. "C'mere, Melanie."

Gabriel dug his hands into his pockets. He was as terrified of the little girl as if she were a fire-breathing dragon.

The shy redhead stepped out from behind her mother. She wore a yellow dress and had sharp, angular features, with a mouth and nose that looked startlingly similar to his own. She tried to look Gabriel in the eyes but was too nervous to hold his gaze, and her fingers rose to her mouth.

"Hi, Melanie," Gabriel said.

"Hi," she whispered.

Gabriel's heart melted. For the first time, it all seemed real. That little human being, that little piece of himself that had separated and become its own person, had been walking around the world, living her life. It occurred to him that she had heard stories about her father for years.

"Don't worry," he told her. "I'm not as scary as I look."

She laughed, sounding just like her mother.

Gabriel's eyes became damp with tears. He crouched in front of her. "I've missed you so much, Melanie. Melanie... uh..." He turned to Yvonne. "Young? Luciana? Which is it?"

Yvonne chuckled, and Gabriel was surprised to see that she was wiping away her own tears. She touched his shoulder. "Schist. Your daughter's name is Melanie Schist."

Gabriel choked up. "You gave her my name?"

"You got it." Yvonne nodded with a smile. "If it's okay with you, Gabriel, I was thinking that Eric and I could stay with my friends here in Hermosa for the week. And Melanie could spend some time with you."

"You'd be okay with that?" Gabriel asked in amazement. "Her? With me? For the whole week?"

"Yeah. If you need anything, you can call us. We'll be close by."

"Well..." Gabriel looked at daughter. "I have one question. Melanie, have you ever gone sailing?"

She shook her head. "No."

"Oh, yeah?" Gabriel grinned. "Good."

Later that afternoon, Gabriel led Melanie across the dock. When they reached his boat, Gabriel lifted her into the air and placed her on the deck.

"You *live* here?" She giggled. "On a boat?"

"What's wrong with that?"

"It's weird."

"So?" Gabriel climbed aboard.

The sun would descend soon. He had to move fast. Timing was everything. It was going to be her first experience on a sailboat, her first memory of her dad. He wanted to make it count.

Dad. That's my name now, isn't it?

He set sail, and the boat took off into the ocean, quietly slicing into the water's surface with a gentle rocking motion. Melanie gazed around with amazement.

"Now what's important to remember," Gabriel said, "is that you have no control over the wind. You have no control over the ocean. You can't change the environment. But if you want to change your direction, you know what you can do?"

"What?"

He grinned. "You can adjust the sails."

"What does *that* mean?"

He demonstrated, and Melanie laughed delightedly as the shoreline slowly disappeared behind them, becoming a small black line of bumps.

She jumped up and down. "This is so cool!"

She reached out and took his hand. Gabriel swallowed a lump in his throat.

He stood at the front of his sailboat in the last breath of the dying sun, holding his daughter's hand. The powerful winds of the Pacific whipped through their hair.

Together, they met the horizon.

CHAPTER 44:
TRANSPARENT

Summer 2018

"**S**O YOU BROUGHT THIS GUY here from North Wing, right? They didn't give me a good report. What kind of pills does he take?"

"Oxy, Donepezil, Trazadone, Seroquel. Here, I'll get Nancy. She'll explain in more detail."

"Is he cognizant? Is he with it, at all?"

"He was."

"Was?"

"He's… it's hard to say, Tim. I mean, you know all about the incident that got him locked on Level Five."

"Aren't we supposed to call this the Guggenheim unit, now?"

Voices. Voices, voices, voices. He couldn't process what they were saying. Painful twitches racked his body, but they felt foreign, as if his mind was floating somewhere far away.

"But anyway, no, I don't know a lot about what happened. Just rumors. They had me filling in on West Wing until today, remember? How long has he been here now, two weeks?"

"Yeah, two weeks. He's been almost nonresponsive that whole time. It's strange. I mean, he can still walk to the bathroom using a walker. Dependent assist. His hip has been healing really fast. But the way he moves, it's really mechanical. I dunno how to explain it. He replies to short questions. He eats if you put food in his mouth, but…"

"But what? Should we put an alarm on him?"

"Nah, I don't think so. He's like a robot. His eyes... it's like he's a blind robot. He doesn't react to anything that you put in his face. Like he's been brain damaged."

"Oh, one of those."

Hey, I'm in here. Can anyone hear me? Is my mouth open? Am I really talking? Why can't anyone hear me?

"Yeah, you know how people act when they're in a state of shock? Kinda like that. He's just a shell now, which is really weird considering how cognizant he was right before the incident."

Help. I'm in here. I'm still in here.

"Hey, Mr. Schist. Are you there?"

I can't get out.

"See? No reply. Nothing."

Help me. Please, I'm trapped. I'm trapped in here.

Slowly, the darkness cleared away like dissipating mist, but it was replaced by a strange, ethereal blue glow. Everything was hazy. A cool breeze hit him in the face. His hands were gripping something. *Handlebars?* He heard a growling noise and felt vibrations. He was on a motorcycle beneath a cloudless blue sky. A long stretch of interstate shot out ahead of him, with no traffic in sight. Just him, a motorcycle, and a free road that was calling his name.

"So I don't think we need to put an alarm on him. He's been quiet since he got here. But we do need to keep a close eye on him, for sure."

As the motorcycle blasted through the air like a speeding comet, Gabriel smiled blissfully. He was free at last, with no restrictions to hold him down, no burdens, no limitations. He stared out at the road. He could go anywhere he wanted. An enormous valley lay ahead, a black pit that cut right through the center of the interstate, but right before that was a perfectly slanted hill. On the other side, the road continued as if uninterrupted. Gabriel rode toward the pit then raced up the asphalt surface of the jump. He went up over the lip and into the sky.

"He used to be a real cool guy, though."

"You said he doesn't feed himself?"

"Oh, oops. Yeah. Hey, Gabriel, have some of this. Please chew your food."

Gabriel ignored the sensation of mushy food in his mouth. He was going up, up, up, spiraling through the air and hurtling into space. He looked toward the other side of the pit and imagined he was a ball moving through an invisible tube. If he directed the bike just right, he'd land on the other side of the pit.

Gravity pulled, and the bike began to descend right where he aimed. Then, the motorcycle twisted left and dropped like an anvil. He missed the jump. The motorcycle came out from between his legs. He frantically tried to grab onto a ledge, but it was out of reach, and he fell into the hollow darkness of the pit. The sky became a tiny blue circle, far above, out of reach. He crashed down against the hard earth, headfirst. His skull smashed open, shattering into a dizzying array of little glass cubes.

"It's a shame."

"The poor guy, he's just falling apart. He's like a zombie, y'know? No brains left anymore."

The voices of the nurses trailed away, accompanied by the sound of footsteps. The glass cubes were scattered all around him. Inside each was a bloodshot eyeball with a tiny sharp-toothed mouth inside its pupil. The eyeball-mouths began to scream. "Help me! Can anyone hear me? Help!"

Help! Help!

Gabriel stirred into consciousness, and the nightmare disappeared. He was lying in bed in his new quarters on Level Five of Bright New Day. All his stuff was stuffed into his new closet. The lights were dimmed, and it was nighttime. He had an IV in one arm.

The Level Five bedrooms weren't half as bad as they had been in Gabriel's terrified imagination. The walls weren't padded, he wasn't strapped into a straitjacket, and there were no Orwellian telescreens in every room. Other than the maroon curtain, the room looked almost identical to his old one on South Wing. There was only one difference, but it was a ghastly difference that made Gabriel feel sick to his stomach: the windows were barred.

Gabriel closed his eyes again. He wanted to go back to the nightmare, figuring anything was better than reality. But before he could slip back into unconsciousness, his daze was shattered by a familiar female voice.

"Dad?"

CHAPTER 45: IMPRISONED

MELANIE TOOK HIS HAND AND squeezed it. How long had she been sitting beside him? Gabriel shuddered but couldn't respond. He lay in bed, stiff as a corpse. It took effort just to hold his eyes open.

"Are you there, Dad? Can you hear me?" She caressed the back of his hand.

He wanted to turn his head in her direction, but the effort was painful, as his neck felt stiffer than a frost-covered iron rod. He tried to speak, but as the air rose up in his throat, he instead erupted into a coughing fit.

"It's okay, Dad," she whispered, running her fingers through his hair. "Don't be scared. I'm here."

He felt dead. Even the joints of his fingers were too stiff to bend. He breathed in slowly, trying to nourish his lungs back to life. He wanted to talk to her, no matter how bad the pain was.

As if sensing his desperation, she moved closer, and her face entered his field of vision. She wore no makeup, and her eyes were red-rimmed. "I guess you probably can't hear me. But I'll talk anyway. Just in case."

He rolled his tongue around, desperately trying to choke words from his sour, dry mouth. They hadn't been brushing his teeth properly.

"I'm sorry, Dad. God, I should've been here more. I'm the worst daughter ever. I should've never left my phone at home that day." She started to cry. "All those missed calls, that message you left. If I'd had my phone on me, maybe I could've talked you out of it. I should've come here every day, twice a day. Maybe I could've... I could've..."

Don't be sorry. You're here now. That was what Gabriel wanted to tell her, but he couldn't. He felt like a loose spirit trapped inside the confines of a heavy body he had no control over. The IV site burned like a bee sting.

Melanie wiped her eyes and took a deep, choked-up breath. Then, regaining her composure, she stared down at him and smiled weakly. "You never told me about your father. You never told me that he had Alzheimer's, too."

Gabriel wanted to reply, to explain that it'd been too painful to talk to her about, that it was something that had been on the cusp of his tongue many times but had never quite come out. He tried to look into her eyes, to fix his gaze on her in a way that let her know that he was there, but he couldn't even seem to do that small task.

"I never knew about that, you know," she continued. "I found out a few days ago from the nurses. I wish I could have met him. But now that I know, I wish I could... talk to you, I guess. I wish I could ask you what it was like for you, when he... when he got to this stage."

It was hard. I didn't handle it well.

"Dad, I thought I knew what this was going to be like, but I was wrong." She shivered. "I'm scared. It's funny. I see tragedies every day at the orphanage and at the homeless shelter, too. But this, looking at you now, seeing you like this, I've never been so scared."

I'm scared too, Melanie. Gabriel desperately wished he could wrap his arms around her and let her sob into his chest. He remembered how, as a little girl, she would scream with excitement when they took out the sailboat, and her whole face would light up in a smile bigger than the sun.

"I wish you could hear me," she said, another tear streaking down her cheek.

I can. I'm right here.

"But maybe you *can* hear me. Maybe if souls are real, I dunno. Maybe you're still in there, just waiting to go flying into the sky. And even though my mind tells me that you're not here anymore, my heart tells me you're listening to every word. And you know what? I'm gonna choose to believe my heart. I do." She cleared her throat and swiped at her eyes again. "So if you're still in there, Dad, I want to tell you that I've always respected you more than anyone in the world. Back when

I was a little girl, you were my superhero. You were everything, like, this amazing person who could do anything, fix anything, this guy who did such awesome things. It's no excuse, but that's why ever since your Alzheimer's started, I've been so terrible. It's why I've neglected you. Because it's hard. That's terrible, I know."

She reached for a tissue and blew her nose. Gabriel had been angry over her neglect. That she wouldn't visit often had pained him to no end, but hearing her confession and feeling the love radiating from her made all that anger melt like snow on the first day of spring.

"It's really hard to watch your hero fall apart," she whispered. "But that doesn't mean that neglecting you was fair. It wasn't okay. You were a genius, so brilliant that you couldn't fit into the world. I know that. I can't even imagine how hard life was for you, and you still achieved such fantastic things. You never stopped whistling. I love that little tune you always whistled whenever you were happy. I sometimes do it, too. Did you know that? When I'm by myself. It always makes me smile."

I love you, Melanie.

"God, I'm sorry, Dad. And... what else do I wanna tell you? I guess I should say everything I can right now, huh?"

Yes. Say it now. All of it. I'm here.

"Let's see. Gosh, I used to hear millions of stories about you from Mom. She never stopped bragging about how cool you are. And this last week, I've spent a lot of time appreciating the wonderful memories that I have of us sailing and riding your motorcycle. If you're somewhere in there, I hope you can forgive me for not being there when you needed me. I'm sorry."

Melanie, I'm more proud of you than you could possibly imagine.

"I can't go back and fix things, but from one carbon-based life-form to another, I want you to know that I love you, Daddy."

I love you too.

"I am who I am because I had you as a father. And..." Melanie let go of his hand, put on her coat, and kissed Gabriel on the forehead.

Gabriel reached out to her with his heart. He loved her so much. He didn't want her to leave. *Don't go, please don't go.*

"I was lucky enough to have the best father a girl could've ever asked for. *Ever.* Good night, Dad." Melanie left the room.

Gabriel lay in bed, silent, unable to move or respond. The minutes passed by like hours. The moisture of her kiss settled into the creases of his forehead and dissolved.

Suddenly, Gabriel felt a tear running from the corner of his eye. Without thinking, he reached up and wiped the tear away. Once it sank in that he'd actually moved his hand, he lay in stunned disbelief. He tried to flex his hands. They felt like broken concrete, but they responded. He arched his neck and raised his head. He could move again.

"M... Mel... Melanie," he gurgled. "I llllove... you."

But it was too late. Melanie had left hours ago.

"I love you," he whispered, rolling his tongue around every syllable. "Th-thank you... for coming to see me."

Cautiously, Gabriel stretched out his arms and legs. His limbs felt like burlap sacks filled with shattered glass, but as he moved them around, the pain subsided a bit. He pulled the IV needle out of his arm then applied pressure to the needle mark until he was sure that it wouldn't bleed. He did a complete range of motion test on every part of his bruised, tender body. Once the pain had sufficiently dulled, he felt strong enough to climb out of bed.

He stood up but felt so shaky that he immediately sat down on the bed again. His trusty cane was nowhere to be seen. It had been replaced by a walker standing next to the bed.

Well, better a walker than a wheelchair, he figured. That was what Edna Foster would have said. He pulled the walker over, his back muscles aching at the far reach. For all his complaints in the past, the Gabriel of two weeks ago had had it easy in comparison.

He put his hands on the bars of the walker, bent his knees, and pushed to his feet. Taking careful, creaky steps, he went to the closet and got dressed. The backpack was still packed, and all of his materials were in cardboard boxes. Gabriel paced around the room, leaning on the walker for support. His walking was interrupted by a loud groan from his roommate. Gabriel peeked around the curtain.

He was surprised to see Paul Sampson in the other bed. Gabriel had thought the man dead. Paul had once been an Olympic runner, a silver medalist. But trapped in bed, the former athlete had become a withered skeleton with translucent skin and blue cataracts. His teeth were bared in a permanent expression of pain. He didn't seem to register Gabriel's existence.

Gabriel winced. All he could think was that soon he too would be a bedbound pile of flesh, drooling at the mouth, until another resident replaced him. It was an endless cycle of death.

"I'm here, Gabriel."

Gabriel jerked around, almost falling in the process, and saw Victor standing in the doorway. Instead of his usual tuxedo, Victor was garbed in a hooded black robe that trailed down past his knees. The garment was made of such thick, startlingly *black* fabric that it seemed as though it had created a hole in space.

Gabriel struggled to look away, to deny Victor's existence, but his curiosity betrayed him. "Hello, Victor."

Victor said nothing. His familiar face, with his silver goatee and buggy eyes, looked startlingly unrecognizable under the shade of the hood. The whites of his eyes actually glowed, and the familiar 7-shaped scar on his face looked like a thick dark line. The man was beyond terrifying, but worse, he held a scythe in one hand. The blade was pure black obsidian, and the handle was made of what looked like polished, chalk-white *bones*. Victor suddenly swung the blade downward, stopping it inches from Gabriel's chest. Gabriel nearly fainted from shock.

When Calaca finally spoke, his reverberating voice came not only from his mouth but also from the scythe. "Hello, Gabriel. It's time."

CHAPTER 46:
CROSSROADS

VICTOR CALACA. DEATH.

The mystery was solved, and yet the bizarre answer was even more puzzling than the initial question. Gabriel stood in place, slack-jawed, staring down the dark obsidian blade of Calaca's scythe, utterly unable to find words. His legs were wobbling so hard that he nearly collapsed.

"Oh?" Gabriel trembled. "Time to die?"

"That's up to you, Gabriel." Calaca raised the scythe and returned it to his side. A subtle smile appeared in the corner of his mouth, and beneath the enormous black hood, his eyes glowed like two little white fireflies.

"Calaca," Gabriel whispered. "God, I'd completely forgotten. That's what those skeleton dolls are called, right? Calacas. The answer was right in front of me."

"Indeed."

From the corridor came the sounds of running, screaming, and laughter, the usual soundtrack of Level Five, but as Gabriel stood there, facing the unmasked Victor Calaca, the rest of the unit seemed to exist on another world. "I would've pictured Death as being a grim, inhumane sort of character. Not like you. I always *liked* you."

"Is that so?"

"Yes. You've always been a friend to me. You've been quite understanding."

Despite the darkness surrounding him, there was something about

Calaca's smile that cut right through the tension and almost made Gabriel feel at ease. *Almost.*

"Gabriel, I am only what people choose to make of me. My form is nothing but a mere vessel. My shape is created entirely by the imagination of my current perceiver."

"So why didn't you want me to go out into the ocean? Isn't your whole purpose to steal people's souls?"

"I'm not here to *steal* anything. I'm here to assist those in need, when that need arises. To collect them, shall we say, when it's time."

"But the folklore, the mythology..."

"Yes, many of you have certainly been terrified of my existence. To some, I might be a dark omen. A terrifying creature of the night. A raven, a skeleton, a cloud of bloody rain. And yet, on the other hand, how can one forget the Mexican Day of the Dead? Always an occasion of uplifted spirits, a joyous celebration. And when it comes to the tortured, elderly residents of a nursing home, why would *they* fear me? To you, in particular, has my presence not been one of the warmest embraces you've felt ever since you began your stay here at Bright New Day?"

Gabriel nodded. "Yes."

"And that is because, from the beginning, you never dreaded my arrival. On some level, haven't you been waiting for me—dare I say it?—with open arms?" Calaca shrugged, a casual gesture that looked bizarre on a figure so otherworldly.

Gabriel clutched his walker with a white-knuckled grip. "Get out of here. You're not real."

"I am."

"You're in my head. You're a hallucination. A disturbing product of my demented subconscious. That's what they told me."

"Oh? And since when has Gabriel Schist been a man who believed anything that others told him?"

"Since now."

Gabriel walked over to the doorway and peered out. Level Five had at least double the number of LNAs. Some of the residents were shuffling up and down the hall or standing around muttering and laughing for no apparent reason. He ducked back into his room before a nurse could see him and sat on the bed.

Victor moved closer. "I have come to give you a choice."

"I don't want anything from you."

Calaca laid an icy hand on Gabriel's shoulder. "You have nothing to fear from me."

"No? I have *everything* to fear from you."

"I am about to give you the most important choice that you shall ever make. I am here to give you the option of death."

Gabriel shuddered. Yes, he still wanted death. He craved death. But looking into the gaping mouth of oblivion itself, he felt the finality of it all become more clear. *Please, Victor. Just let me die. Let me die easily.*

"Death," Calaca repeated. "Right here, at this moment. It shall be painless. Instantaneous. You can give up, escape the pain in your future, escape from everything, and I shall lead you there by the hand. But there is another option." The hooded man's eyes were moist.

"And what's that?" Gabriel asked.

"You can fight. You can be brave. With my help, you can escape this place."

"Please," Gabriel said, holding back tears, "don't torture me with fantasies. Please, I've been hurt enough."

"This is not a fantasy. With my help, you can escape. You may finally follow the path to the Sky Amoeba. And then, perhaps, you shall have a chance to save humanity from the Black Virus. You may follow me to your destiny, Gabriel. I'm still giving you that option."

"What's the catch?"

"No catch, no trick. However, you shall be forced to look into the eyes of your greatest fear."

Gabriel stared at his reflection in the obsidian scythe. The image was of his younger self, red hair and unbuttoned Hawaiian shirt. "What happens if I choose death? What will the Schistlings do?"

"If you don't act now—tonight, in fact—then after you die, it shall be too late to stop them. The Schistlings will massacre the entire human race."

When it was put that way, the notion of a "human race" sounded surreal. And Melanie was just one small part of that conglomeration of individuals that Calaca had called the human race. *Had she ever taken the Schist vaccine?* Horror encroached on his mind. Yes, she must have taken it. He didn't remember her taking it, but almost everyone had, and her father was the inventor. That meant that a Schistling was crawling around inside his daughter.

"I don't know what to do," Gabriel said. "Stop making me feel so helpless! I already know that escape from here is impossible. I found that out the hard way, and that was back when my window didn't have bars. I can't do it."

"Oh yes, you can." A quiet laugh escaped from Calaca's scythe. "But first, you must abandon everything you know as real. You don't exist in the normal, solid world anymore. You haven't since the first day your mind began to fail you. There's a way out of this prison, but you will only find it if you allow yourself to believe in me, to trust me. Belief is a powerful thing, Gabriel. Belief can change everything. Remember your mentor, Father Gareth? Remember how, from the very first time he saw you drawing on that blackboard, he believed in you? Remember how, even on his deathbed, he never lost the ability to smile?"

Gabriel shook his head. "You're a fictitious construct of my mind. How can I believe in your existence? How can I possibly save the world if I don't even know what's real anymore? I'm not Gareth. I'm not half the man he was. I've never believed in anything, not even myself."

"Because, Gabriel, when you reach a certain point in life, knowing what's real or not simply doesn't matter anymore."

"Why not?"

"Because you have Alzheimer's. Life as you know it, it's simply a cognitive experience, correct? The life a man experiences through his eyes, ears, and nose is only an interpretation of reality, something beyond his full understanding. Let's call it truth. But as much as one may try, a man's perception of reality is forever limited to whatever realizations your five senses may offer."

"Victor, I can't—"

"So what gives anyone the right to condemn your perception of existence and deny you freedom of will just because that perception is different from theirs? Instead of giving up, why don't you learn to trust your perception of the world, strange as it may be? Trust your perception, stop clinging to the world you once knew, and live freely in the world you now know."

Gabriel studied Victor Calaca, a man who so clearly couldn't exist, and yet he did. Yes, on some level, Victor *did* exist. Death was closer than ever before. Gabriel could end it all now. No more pain. No more humiliation. His mind still somewhat intact. All he had to do was embrace the blackness within Victor's ethereal scythe. It was his last chance at the easy finale he'd desired so desperately for so many years.

"I guess I'm not ready to die then," Gabriel whispered.

Calaca smiled. "Good." He helped Gabriel back onto his feet then pointed his scythe toward the hall. "Close the door."

"But they'll just come here and open it again."

"If you believe in me, I shall hold it for you. It won't open. They won't interrupt us. You must trust me on this."

Gabriel walked over and closed the door. "What now?"

"Now that we're isolated, I want you to forget the world outside of that door, the world that others are trying to force you to abide by. It doesn't exist for you. Not anymore."

Great, one step closer to insanity. "Okay."

"Close your eyes, Gabriel."

Heart racing, Gabriel shut his eyes. Letting go of reality might reduce him to a breathing vegetable, forever unable to interact with others. But if he didn't do it, Melanie would become another victim of the Schistlings. It was the only way he could stop them from killing her and the rest of humanity. He had to take a chance. He had to trust Victor's philosophy, even if it boggled his mind.

"Excellent," Calaca said. "Now, forget about your Alzheimer's. Forget it entirely. Forget everything that you've been holding onto so desperately. Let go, and embrace your inner self."

Gabriel didn't understand what to do. All of the background noises had disappeared, and the only thing he saw was total blackness. Then, he visualized his mind as a shelf full of torn, ratty old books. He knocked the shelf over.

Suddenly, Gabriel felt everything around him start to shake. The walls were breathing down his neck with hot, sweltering steam. The floor beneath him was vibrating, as if from an earthquake. "Victor?"

"Let go! Let go of everything, Schist. Stop trying to hold the walls up. Allow them to shake. Let it all come down!"

"I can't— "

"Let go!"

The world rumbled. It took everything he had to stay on his feet and keep his eyes closed, when it felt as though the ceiling was about to collapse on his head. A volcanic eruption of panicked, terrified thoughts exploded in his mind. Pain blasted through his body.

A moment later, calm returned. Everything felt warm.

"Open your eyes, Gabriel."

Gabriel obeyed. Victor Calaca's bony face was pulled back in an open-mouthed grin, but something about it looked different. The room had also changed in a way that Gabriel couldn't quite put his finger on. It seemed *real* again, and reality felt more tangible to him than it had in over five years. He was less shaky on his feet, not needing to place quite as much weight on the walker. The colors of the world were astonishingly brighter, like those of a child's crayon set. The smells were more vivid, and the odors of saline, antiseptic, and bleach stung his nose. The air in his lungs felt cleaner.

Victor laughed heartily and placed his hand on Gabriel's shoulder. His palm was warm. "Welcome to *your* real world, Gabriel. Now, do what must be done. I believe in you."

Then, Victor disappeared out of thin air, as if he'd never existed.

"Victor!"

No answer.

"Victor, where are…?"

The walls creaked. Tiny tremors traveled across the floor like little tap-dancing spiders. The room began rumbling again, and the earthquake that Gabriel had experienced in his mind returned full force. Jagged cracks split open across the ceiling.

"Victor!"

The cracks widened, vomiting chalky dust and debris onto the beds and furniture. The room rocked like a small boat on a tidal wave. The cracks spread farther.

After another few seconds, the rumbling ceased instantaneously, as if someone had shut off the power. Dust hung in the air, making Gabriel cough harshly. When the fit passed, he looked up at the ceiling and saw a thick grey substance squeezing between the cracks. The stuff had the consistency of Silly Putty, and it was a part of something bigger.

Just as he thought that, the rest of the ceiling broke away, and a gelatinous, blob-like thing crashed to the floor like an anvil. Miniature aftershocks vibrated through the walls.

Someone knocked on the door. "Hey, Mr. Schist? Are you awake? Did you close this door?"

Gabriel wasn't ready for their questions. He didn't have any explanations that wouldn't sound insane. They would drug him again.

"Listen," the man continued, "we heard a loud noise in there, and I swear, if you're trying to break out again..."

Damn, damn, damn! Gabriel looked around, trying to find the escape that Victor had promised. The nurses would get inside in no time. They'd catch him. They'd monitor him. They'd drug him.

The doorknob jiggled, but the door didn't move. "Gabriel! What did you do to this door?"

Okay, that bought him some time. He turned back to the Silly-Putty thing. The creature stretched an elongated, plesiosaur-like neck high into the air, revealing an enormous, faceless head and two wriggling antennas.

Michael slid forward, breaking through the wall of dust with the triumphant aura of a war hero pounding his chest. The slug's enormous pneumostome pulsed.

As the leader of the slugs approached him, Gabriel beamed. "Michael!"

"That's right, man." Michael laughed. "Now, let's blow this joint!"

CHAPTER 47:
FAMILY

THE UNKNOWN PERSON POUNDING ON the door was getting angrier by the second. "Hey, Schist! Open this damn door! It's stuck!"

Gabriel stood awestruck as the dust settled on the linoleum floor. He stepped toward Michael. "Blow this joint? You mean now? The two of us?"

"Yeah, you heard me." Michael trumpeted. "Pack your bags, ya old goof. And hey, while you're at it, throw on that ultra-slick trench coat and fedora of yours, too. Chop, chop."

The knocking was getting more aggressive. Gabriel stumbled over to his closet. He put on his old fedora and threw on his trench coat. Remarkably, when he checked his coat pocket, the poison was still in there, wrapped up in the same plastic bag, along with his notes, an empty plastic vial, and a long syringe filled with the Schist vaccine. He'd forgotten that he'd packed that, and he didn't remember why. Digging through his backpack at a frantic pace, he removed the two photos of Melanie and Yvonne, tucked them into the plastic bag, and then tossed his backpack to the rear of the closet. Everything else in there was pointless memorabilia, but the photos he wanted on him at all times.

The banging became increasingly violent, sounding as though someone was throwing his entire body against the door. "We're coming in there, Schist!"

The door rattled. "Open the door, Gabe! Everything's gonna be A-okay!"

A-okay? Yeah, right. Okay after another dose of ABH, perhaps?

"Hurry up!" Michael cried. "Our mutual friend can't hold that door closed forever, you know."

"Mutual... who? What?"

"You know who I'm talking about. Let's go, man."

The repeated battering was taking its toll. The door was creaking with each slam.

Bang!

Bang!

"Where are we going?" Gabriel asked.

"You know exactly where we're going, man! The Sky Amoeba is waiting for us out on the ocean. So make up your mind. You comin' with? Or are you gonna sit here and sulk?"

Bang! Bang! Bang!

"Yes, I know, but—" Gabriel threw his hands in the air. "How do we do this? I can barely walk anymore, the windows are barred, and I sure as hell can't fit through one of those cracks on the ceiling."

"Then stop wasting time, and climb aboard!"

"Aboard *what*?"

"Me!" Michael slid his tubular form across the floor with the panache of a figure skater, leaving a trail of slime behind him. He arched his neck down and presented his back to Gabriel. Gabriel stared at him in disbelief. *Oh, no way.*

"You heard me, buddy ol' pal," Michael said. "Jump on my back and hold onto my antennas. Here, I got it. Just pretend I'm your old motorcycle. Do it!"

Bang! Bang! Bang!

Gabriel heard a sharp crack as the doorframe splintered. The top of the door was loosened but the bottom held tight. Fingers peeked out from between the upper portion of the door and the jamb. The nurses shouted like murderous banshees.

Gabriel clambered onto Michael's back. He awkwardly rested one leg on each side, straddling the oversized slug like a mechanical bull. He sank a few inches into the grey flesh, creating a surprisingly secure pouch. He wrapped his hands around Michael's antennas, trying to pretend that they were handlebars. As he leaned forward, the powerful muscles inside

Michael's body stirred into action. Michael's pneumostome blasted hot air, and Gabriel's heart pounded in his chest.

Bang! Bang! Bang!

"Hold on, I just realized something!" Gabriel shouted. "Michael, this is a terrible idea, slugs are the slowest creatures on earth. Yes, I know that you're a *giant* slug, and you're a bit faster than the others, but—"

Michael threw his head back, his entire body shaking with laughter. "C'mon, man! Didn't the little guys tell you our big secret? Slugs don't *have* to move slow."

Bang! Bang!

Creeeaaak!

The door was coming loose. Michael shifted and faced the door. He abruptly slid backward so fast that Gabriel felt dizzy and almost fell off. The jerking motion resembled the first stage of an amusement park ride. Michael backed all the way up against the wall, and Gabriel tightened his grip on the slug's antennas.

"We're coming, Schist!" a nurse shouted.

There was a ferocious growl deep within Michael's writhing form, like the sound of a powerful motor revving.

"Michael, do you even know what you're doing? How the hell are we going to get out?"

Michael flexed his body, and beneath his legs, Gabriel felt the slug's muscles hardening. When the giant slug finally replied, there was a hint of manic glee in his voice. "Oh, we're going out the front door, baby."

Michael lunged forward, accelerating across the floor as fast as if he'd been launched from a cannon. Gabriel gripped the antennas tighter, holding on for dear life.

Michael smashed right through the door like a battering ram. The entire frame exploded into pieces. With a deafening crack, splintered chunks of wood blasted out into the hall, and the four people on the other side cried out in shock as they were knocked back. The nurses ended up sprawled out on the floor like ragdolls.

Michael paused halfway through the door. "Hey! Which way do I go?"

The hallway stretched out endlessly in both directions. *Left or right?* Gabriel hadn't been conscious when they brought him in, and he had never been to Level Five before that point. He had no idea where the exit was. As he hesitated, a couple of the nurses sat up, and one rose to his feet. They gazed at Michael in slack-jawed disbelief.

Gabriel pointed to the left. "That way, I think."

Michael shot forward like a bullet, gliding around the bends of the corridor. Gabriel felt as if he were riding a giant Slip 'N Slide. *No, not a Slip 'N Slide. A motorcycle.* The nurses were running after them, but they couldn't catch up, as Michael's forward propulsion was too fast, too unstoppable. When the double doors of the exit came into view, a wave of relief washed over him. He had chosen correctly.

Gabriel glanced around and noticed that all of the residents of Level Five, all those poor souls he'd written off so easily, had dropped everything to stare at Michael. They had enormous, glistening eyes and huge grins. Some had wrinkled arms raised in the air as if cheering Gabriel on. They laughed and cried in their doorways, clapping and waving as Gabriel and Michael passed.

"You can do it, Gabriel!" one old woman shouted. "Get outta this place, dear!"

"The detective's gonna make it. He's really gonna make it!"

"Whoooo! Yeah, he's doing it!"

"Hurry up. You're almost outta here. Don't let 'em stop you!"

A tiny old lady that reminded him of Edna Foster rolled over in her wheelchair. She reached out as Michael glided past, and she touched the slug's slick wet body. She laughed delightedly.

Gabriel rode his grey-skinned stallion into the future, his excitement augmented by the celebratory applause of his fellow residents. He peered at the locked double doors. Only an hour ago, he had thought of those doors as the most intimidating thing in the world. But no longer.

He smiled and pointed at the exit. "To the ocean!"

Michael obliged by putting on an extra burst of speed. The residents cheered even louder, and Gabriel let out a victory yell.

Smash!

The locked gateway split in two, fell over, collapsed, both doors completely blown from their hinges. A big sign with the word LOBBY had a yellow arrow pointing the way to the front entrance. Michael made the left turn and, following the arrows, glided through the maze of hallways at a speed that felt like fifty miles per hour.

The wind rushed through Gabriel's hair. Tears stung at the corners of his eyes. He threw his head back, laughing with joy. "To the ocean!" he repeated.

"That's right, buddy," Michael said. "To the ocean!"

Residents in wheelchairs and doorways laughed and cheered. Nurses fell back with startled gasps. Michael and Gabriel raced past rooms, desks, gurneys, and machinery. As they approached the entrance to the front lobby, a crowd of opponents appeared before them.

About fifteen staff stood in their path, just like the group that had stopped Gabriel two weeks before, the same dark, hazy figures that had locked him up in Level Five. They formed a Red Rover wall of bodies, creating an impenetrable barrier.

"Michael, don't hurt them," Gabriel said. "They're good people!"

"I won't hurt 'em. Trust me!" Michael hurtled toward the group like a well-aimed bowling ball headed for a strike. "Hold on tight!"

Michael didn't slow, but his muscles tightened and took on an odd springy quality. Gabriel took a deep breath.

Michael jumped.

The giant slug sailed into the air. The bottom section of his serpentine body spread out, rustled, then held taut. He seemed to capture the air and glide in the same manner as a flying squirrel.

Feeling his legs sliding down the slug's back, Gabriel desperately clasped the antennas and pulled himself back into position. When he looked down and saw the people below staring up in terrified befuddlement, his vertigo was swiftly replaced with a childlike joy.

"Take that!" Gabriel laughed.

Michael's jump reached its peak, and they began their descent. By the time they landed with a squishy bounce, they were already halfway across the front lobby. Their opponents were well behind them, struggling to catch up, as Michael raced toward the front door. When they reached the exit, like all of the previous doors, it blew to pieces.

The cold night air had never felt so good. Michael slipped around the corner of the building, down the grassy hill, and over the craggy rocks.

The trip to the beach went by so fast that Gabriel had to laugh at how long it'd taken them the last time.

Michael slowed to a stop when they reached the sandy shore, though he didn't seem the least bit exhausted. Gabriel sighed with relief as he released the antennas. The whole thing had been a lot of fun, but his old geezer heart needed a break.

Michael dipped his antennas to point at the ground. "Okay, Gabriel, meet the whole gang."

Gabriel looked down and blinked. *Was this for real?* The beach was covered with slugs of all different colors and sizes, as if someone had spilled every crayon in America right onto the sand. Hundreds, maybe thousands, of slugs peered up at him with tiny little antennas, as if awaiting orders. There were green slugs, yellow slugs, blue slugs, and striped slugs. He spotted the wisecracking albino slug next to the black one, and over to the right was Leopard Print, his first slug buddy. For a moment, he could've sworn that the little guy winked at him.

Gabriel grinned. "Nice to see you."

"It's a pleasure to see you as well," Leopard Print replied. "But, Michael, I think it's about time for us to set sail and embark upon our little journey."

Michael nodded. "Sounds like a plan, Raphael."

"Journey?" Gabriel asked. "Raphael?"

The slugs all raised their tiny antennas and pointed at the radiant white circle in the sky. Gabriel felt as if he were at the head of an infantry.

"The Sky Amoeba is waiting for us," Michael explained. "You and the Schistling collective will plead your cases. Let's go find him."

Gabriel gulped. "What if the nursing staff follows us? Or the police? They'll call the police."

Michael lurched forward and launched his body into the ocean, floating right over the water's surface like a small boat. His long tail flicked back and forth, serving as a propeller. The slug infantry followed his lead.

"It's too late for anyone back on *that* side to stop us," Michael replied. "We're going to another place. Another plane of reality, ya might say. A place that exists far beyond their understanding. We've crossed the boundary."

"But are you certain?" As Michael floated lazily over the first set of waves, Gabriel frantically latched onto the antennas again, struggling to keep his balance.

"Don't worry. They'll never be able to follow us into this ocean, no matter how hard they might try. To them, the place we're going doesn't exist."

"But it still affects them?"

"Yep."

Gabriel looked up at the moon. The salty scent of the ocean water filled his nostrils. He listened to the waves, the rushing tide, the seagulls. He looked back at Bright New Day, and a happy feeling overcame his anxiety. Yes, the escape was really happening. He was free.

The beach slowly disappeared behind them as they sailed into the moonlit horizon.

CHAPTER 48:
HARRY

"HE DID *WHAT*?"

"He, um… escaped," Harry Brenton said, blood rushing into his cheeks. "Mr. Schist is no longer in the building." Harry looked down, unable to find a rational explanation for the catastrophic event he'd just witnessed. He couldn't quite put into words what had happened.

"Harry," the administrator said, "Gabriel was on the Guggenheim unit. He's been practically comatose for weeks. Since the new security system was put into place, we've had no breakouts. How did this happen?"

Harry wiped sweat from his brow. "I don't know what else to say, sir."

"Well, where is he going? God, Harry. Just help me out here before I have a heart attack. Do we have *any* idea where that man is headed?"

"He said he was going to the ocean, sir."

The administrator stared at him, his bald head shimmering in the florescent lights. He placed his hands on his hips, an authoritative stance he only used when he was *really* angry. "Kid, are you serious? The *ocean?*"

Harry nodded. "Yes, sir. Well, that's what he said."

"Okay." Irving rubbed his eyes. "We need to get the ball rolling on this. I know we've got our people out there looking for him, but if we don't move fast, Mr. Schist will be dead by morning. We need to call the police. Did you seriously say that he was heading to the ocean? What the hell?" Irving picked up the phone. "You can get back to work, Harry."

With no small amount of relief, Harry left the office. In about thirty minutes, he'd have to start his evening rounds. Such was the nature of healthcare. No matter what happened, everyone had to stick to the routine and take care of the other residents. Though Harry loved helping people—he even loved Bright New Day—he hated the institutional system that plagued the healthcare industry. He hated the understaffing, the cut corners, and the depersonalization. More than anything, he wished that all of the staff had more time to spend with each resident as an individual, instead of having to constantly rush around in order to get all of the work done.

Harry reckoned that if nursing homes could be structured more like *homes* instead of hospitals, then maybe nice guys like Mr. Schist wouldn't run away in the first place. Maybe they wouldn't decline so fast, either.

Harry punched out for his break then walked to the front lobby. The lights were off, but the full moon poured a liquefied white glow in through the bay windows. He snagged a cup beside the cooler and filled it with water. *God, I hope Mr. Schist is okay.* He'd never forgive himself if his friend got hurt.

He stepped over to one of the windows and looked outside. Gabriel was out there, somewhere, in the dark forest that surrounded Bright New Day. He peered out at the wooded landscape of white birches and pine trees that stretched on for miles. Poor Gabriel Schist was lost somewhere in that dark forest, stumbling between the trees, desperately searching for some kind of beach.

Harry sighed. His job was at Bright New Day. His floor had thirty-six sleeping residents that needed him. All he could do was cross his fingers and hope for the best. Wherever the old man was, Harry hoped he was okay.

CHAPTER 49: OVERSATURATED

THE SLUG INFANTRY CONTINUED THEIR journey across the ocean. Gabriel reached down to run his fingers through the cold water. He looked up at the moon. *God, the Atlantic is gorgeous tonight.* He marveled at the thousands upon thousands of tiny slugs, swimming alongside him like an ocean of multicolored pebbles. The shoreline had disappeared a long time ago. No boats could be seen.

"We have one more stop to make," Michael said, "and then we're off to the Sky Amoeba."

"Where are we stopping?"

"You'll see. Soon."

Gabriel shrugged and sat back to enjoy the ride. On such a bizarre, fantastical journey, he'd learned the value of patience, if nothing else. Minutes later, he spotted something that he at first thought was a trick of the light. He sat up straight so he could see better.

Ahead, the water was black, with no shimmer to its waves and no reflections of light, like a matte hole cut into the ocean. The dark mass stretched on for miles. At the center lay an enormous funnel that channeled deep into the ocean's belly, ripping it open like a mortal wound. A raspy whispering emanated from the black water's surface.

"We have reached the maelstrom," Raphael said.

"Good God," Gabriel muttered.

On television, the maelstrom hadn't looked quite so monstrous, but it was the size of a small island, and the area appeared to be spreading. An image of an atlas with black oceans instead of blue ones appeared in

Gabriel's mind. The vial of poison in his pocket felt as heavy as a loaded gun.

"Tell me about it, man," Michael replied in a fearful, hushed tone. "Makes me sick."

This is the place. This is where I need to drop the poison, right in the collective's black heart.

Michael craned his neck to the side. "And hey, man, don't even *think* about taking out that poison in your pocket and uncapping it. Keep a lid on it, brother."

"Understood," Gabriel muttered. Still, he couldn't resist touching the vial. The lid was on tight. *So close.*

He withdrew his hand from his pocket and braced himself as the slug infantry steered directly into the giant black mass. Fortunately, the mass didn't swallow them whole or scald their flesh. Despite the whirlpool at its center, the perimeter remained rather calm, other than the harsh whispering.

The dark water was like a maggot pit of baby Schistlings, with millions of the squirming black monsters intertwined with one another. Their little sharp-toothed beaks occasionally rose into the air, gulping in oxygen, then dove back under the water. The maelstrom emitted a metallic smell, much like blood but more pungent.

The slugs pushed onward, proceeding carefully through the mass of Schistlings. The Schistlings did not react, which made Gabriel wonder if perhaps in their home, they *couldn't* do anything. The other, more frightening possibility was that he and his slug friends were heading into a trap.

"How much farther do we need to go?" Gabriel asked.

Raphael crawled up Michael's side. "We are going to the center. We need to get a piece of the core and take it to the Sky Amoeba."

Gabriel flashed back to the helicopter footage when they'd first shown the "toxic waste spill" on television. He remembered seeing a wicked face somewhere in the maelstrom's center, an image that made him shudder.

"The Schistlings are a collective consciousness, correct?" Gabriel whispered.

"Indeed," Raphael replied. "But all collectives have a center. A source. One might be tempted to call this center a leader, but that would be inaccurate. This leader is not an individual creature but the sum total of every Schistling."

"I saw a face when this was on television. Is that...?"

"Indeed it is," Raphael said. "Their center is the first Schistling, the first being who crawled into the ocean and called upon his brethren to follow him, to become a part of him. He is the reason that all of the now-conscious immune systems are rebelling against their human bodies. They want to become a part of *him.*"

"Where did he come from?"

"A Massachusetts man named Kyle Harris. With Kyle's death, the first Schistling was born, then it made its way out here."

"Does this first Schistling have a name?"

Raphael glanced up at Michael's antennas, which were shakier than Gabriel would have expected. Evidently, being in the maelstrom was getting under their skin, too. The giant slug leader looked back at Raphael and nodded.

"Well," Raphael said, "he refers to himself as the Schist Ex Machina."

Gabriel almost snorted. If the situation weren't so eerie and repulsive, it would be funny. But as he saw the lip of the whirlpool quickly approaching, his sense of humor died very quickly.

"Hey, Gabriel," Michael said. "You still have that empty vial, right?"

"Of course he does," Raphael said. "He's been carrying it this whole time. It's next to the poison that he was touching some moments ago."

Gabriel raised his eyebrows then gently patted the empty vial in his pocket. "I'm never going to get used to this whole telepathy thing."

Michael chuckled. "You call it telepathy. We call it communication."

Both slugs laughed, although the sarcastic albino slug several paces behind them laughed louder.

"My apologies, Gabriel," Raphael said. "But yes, when we reach the edge of the maelstrom, it would be wise to use that vial to collect a sample of the Schist Ex Machina's consciousness. However, be careful. They will try to do the same to you."

"What do mean?"

"They'll try to collect *you,* man," Michael said. "And trust me, that's not a party you wanna join."

Gabriel reached into his pocket and took out the plastic bag. He quickly inventoried its contents again: the empty plastic vial, the photo of Yvonne on the beach, a photo of Melanie, the Schist vaccine needle, and the antidote. *Oh yes, the antidote. The poison.*

Anger rumbling in the pit of his stomach, Gabriel gazed out at the mass of Schistlings surrounding him. He had the poison right there in his hands. It would take less than two seconds to uncap it, dump the contents into the Schistlings' breeding ground, and murder their entire toxic species, all before the slugs could stop him. He could finish them off right there and not have to waste his time with any of the Sky Amoeba business. Sure, he'd be betraying all of his slug buddies. Sure, all of those poor, innocent people infected with the Black Virus would die, but it was for the greater good. *Wasn't it?*

No, he wouldn't do it. He didn't believe in fate, but there was a reason that his first escape attempt had gone so badly. Murder wasn't the solution. Victor had said to trust him, and because of that trust, Gabriel had finally made it to the ocean. He had come so far; it was too late to revert back to his old ways.

Gabriel retrieved the empty vial then resealed the bag. The slugs stopped at the edge of the colossal hole at the center of the maelstrom. They were just close enough for Gabriel to see down into it but far enough away to avoid being sucked into its heartless center. A blast of humid air escaped from the hole.

Deep inside the whirlpool's center, a hole that looked as deep as the Grand Canyon, the mass of blackness was forming into an enormous face then un-forming and then forming again. The face had distorted features and a mouthful of serrated teeth, each one at least double the size of Michael's entire body. A throaty gasping sound erupted from the face's mouth.

Gabriel shivered, holding the vial with both hands so as not to drop it. "This is it?"

"Yes," Michael replied.

"I thought you wanted me to negotiate with it or something like that? Why not do that here?"

"Time breeds stubbornness," Raphael said, "and it's been a long time since the maelstrom began. That negotiation will still happen, but the Schist Ex Machina will never agree to it here. A sample must be collected."

Gabriel looked down into the face's bulging, house-sized eyes, and a tingle crawled up his neck. The eyes were watching him, waiting for him to make the first move. "Okay," Gabriel said as he opened the vial. The stopper made a subtle popping noise.

Now or never, Gabriel. He held the vial firmly and leaned to the side. He dipped the container into the water.

The Schistlings immediately swarmed. Excited squalls filled the air as the tiny creatures clung to his hand like leeches. Though they didn't hurt him or penetrate his skin, Gabriel felt violated. He shifted his body on Michael's back, struggling not to drop the vial.

Suddenly, teeth punctured his hand and wrist, and the Schistlings started to pull with the combined weight of their wriggling bodies. Gabriel felt himself sliding off the side of Michael's body. The giant slug adjusted his back and lowered his head so that Gabriel could get a better grip on his antenna.

The Schistlings pulled again, squealing with delight. Gabriel's hands slipped, and he was dragged underwater and submerged within the maelstrom. The water was slimy and cold. Some of it got into his nose and mouth, and he almost choked. The barest traces of moonlight were his only source of illumination, and he could barely see through the snake pit of oily creatures that had overtaken the ocean he loved. He looked up and saw the brightly colored underbellies of the slug army were terrifyingly high above him.

The Schistlings pulled him down deeper. As the light of the moon disappeared and the slugs were obscured by the crawling mass, Gabriel's hope was snuffed out like a candle.

I still have the poison. I can kill them all. All I have to do is uncap it. But he couldn't do that, as it would mean killing Edna and everyone else who was infected. He had to find another way.

Every inch of him was covered by the Schistlings' slithering forms. Their teeth nibbled at him. His lungs burned, and his heart pounded. He desperately exhaled through his nostrils.

Then, he saw the face floating before him. The Schistlings scuttled inside the folds of Gabriel's trench coat. The face opened its mouth, baring its teeth like an enormous shark. Fear squeezed Gabriel's heart and threatened to pop it.

The more effort Gabriel exerted in trying to swim away, the harder the Schistling collective worked to push him to the face. Soon, he was within inches of one of the horrific eyes, close enough to touch it. Gabriel did the only thing he could think to do: he swung the vial out and swooped it through the side of the gigantic, liquefied eye. Then he popped the lid on to make certain he didn't lose any of the sample.

His brain became foggy, and his vision blurred. He was running out of oxygen. Something pushed him up from beneath his armpits. Gabriel raised his arms, expecting to see more Schistlings, but it was the slugs, working together to get him back to the surface.

"Real nice, Schist. Way to go," Albino said telepathically. "I thought we said *not* to join the party."

Gabriel smiled wanly. His lungs were burning, and his skin felt raw. As over a hundred slugs pushed him upward, others held back the hungry Schistlings. When the moon's white glow shimmered through the dark water, he pumped his legs and arms in an attempt to help.

Gabriel's face broke the surface. The air was cold and clear, and he sucked it in like a starving man finding water in the desert. A massive grey blob of flesh appeared before him. *Michael. Thank God.* He grabbed hold of the giant slug's neck. Michael ducked down so Gabriel could climb aboard. Perched on Michael's back, Gabriel swiped the remaining Schistlings off of him, and they splashed back into the water. The slugs that had saved his life popped their little heads above the surface, one by one.

His trench coat was wet and sticky. He pulled the plastic bag from his pocket and saw that some water had gotten through the zipper. But as Gabriel inhaled deeply, his chest warmed with joy. He embraced the air that flowed through his crusty old lungs, and the creaky old heart that still beat in his chest.

"I got it," Gabriel said, proudly displaying the vial that contained a sample of the maelstrom. "Now let's get the hell out of here."

"You got yourself a deal, brother," Michael said.

The giant slug lurched backward, away from the maelstrom. He swam harder than before, and the other slugs followed his lead. All of them seemed as anxious to get away as Gabriel was.

Gabriel watched the maelstrom slowly disappear behind them. After a few minutes, the squalling cries of the Schistlings were finally out of earshot.

The slugs sailed across the ocean and into the night. The moon glowed a solid white, illuminating their path like a lighthouse. The star-filled sky draped over a reflective ocean, with no land for miles, reminded him so much of his old life on the sailboat. He imagined fireworks in that sky, cracking it open with splashes of color and light, just like on his first date with Yvonne when they'd stood together on that beach and she'd kissed him.

Gabriel reached into his coat and pulled the photo of Yvonne from the soggy plastic bag. He held the picture up to the moonlight, staring at it wistfully. Some of the colors had run down the sides, leaving purplish streaks, but it had survived mostly intact. Yvonne's beauty had rarely been captured well in photographs, but that picture was a work of art. The pose, with her arms raised up to the sky as if she could somehow wrap them around the entire world, perfectly captured Yvonne's fiery inner self.

He remembered Melanie's words from earlier that night. *Gosh, I used to hear millions of stories about you from Mom. She never stopped bragging about how cool you are.*

Beautiful, otherworldly Yvonne had been dead for years, but she was still alive within him, her daughter, and everyone she'd ever met. Gabriel ran his fingers down the photo's surface. "I never stopped loving you," he whispered.

He hadn't just loved *her,* though. He'd loved what she stood for, and he loved the idealistic goals she'd always aspired to. She'd strived to experience life to its utmost, to totally absorb every moment, and to share her joy with every person she knew. In Yvonne's eyes, everything and everyone were beautiful, and even in her painful last days, she never stopped being full of happiness. Just like in the photograph, she embraced the world with open arms. She had been a spirit in human form.

I'll wait for you.

Don't.

The slugs silently swam onward, and if they were poking around in his head, they made no mention of it.

Gabriel pressed the photograph to his chest. "Thank you."

He held up the picture, letting it flap in the wind, then released it. The air current carried her image over the Atlantic. Yvonne was a free spirit, a woman who would never have allowed herself to be boxed in, and for the first time since their divorce, Gabriel finally let her go.

Impossible as it was, Gabriel felt for a moment as if Yvonne were looking down upon him, smiling her usual bright-eyed smile. He smiled back at her.

Gabriel closed his eyes. Exhaustion was overtaking him. "Michael, how much farther do we have to go? I know we're going to this Sky Amoeba of yours, but where is he?"

Michael laughed. "Stop staring down at your bellybutton, Gabriel. The answer's right in front of you."

Gabriel opened his eyes. His jaw dropped in amazement. He saw a shimmering, monolithic shape a few yards ahead of them. The figure seemed surreal, too dreamlike to possibly exist. It was incandescent, luminescent, and glowing white, the whitest of whites, like a flowing stream of the purest milk in the universe, spiraling down from the sky on an enormous train track. *A track? No.* It was a gravity-defying river in space that corkscrewed down through the sky and met the skin of the ocean in a long, sweeping arc. There, it joined with the water, creating the moonlit trail across the ocean that Gabriel had always been so inexplicably drawn to. That unreachable white line in the distance, he'd found its endpoint. He'd found the pot of gold, the conduit, the place where the moon held hands with the earth.

The skyward passage had no legs to support it, no structure, and no grounding. It didn't need any of that. Its glowing surface simply flowed from the sky, continuously, without beginning or end. Its surface constantly vibrated with coils of energy that, even from that distance, sent warm electrical tingles across his skin. Gabriel gazed up at it in awe.

It looked like the biggest toy marble set he'd ever seen. Except marbles start at the top, and they go down. He and the slugs were at the bottom. That meant that, somehow, they were about to go *up.*

The slugs came to a stop and bowed their heads, lowering their faces to the ocean in humble reverence. Then, their antennas rose, and they *swam toward the point where the ocean merged with the lighted path.* Gabriel gripped Michael's antennas nervously as they slipped onto the white road's glowing surface.

"What is it?" Gabriel asked.

"A road," Michael answered. "Or I should say *the* road."

CHAPTER 50:
ATMOSPHERE

A S THE SLUG INFANTRY MERGED onto the white road, everything became lighter. Staring straight at the road's milky surface was like staring into an LED light, except the light didn't hurt his eyes.

Hearing the murmurs and cheerful sounds of the slugs, Gabriel detected a growing sense of excitement among their ranks. The slugs sank into the surface a little but still floated atop its opaque base. On both sides, there was a short lip, a subtle barrier to prevent anyone from falling off. As the glowing passage changed textures, became less ocean and more *light*, Gabriel felt an odd sense of cool warmth inside him.

He looked forward and saw that the road was in a constant state of flowing movement. Suspended in midair, it continually bent and curved in new directions. Ahead, the mystical pathway seemed to shoot vertically into the sky and then dip downward before becoming a roller-coaster-like series of loops and curves. The road was about eight feet wide, and the initial slope was quite steep. Gabriel didn't understand where the propulsion was going to come from to get them up to the top.

"Fasten your seatbelts!" Michael called.

The entire mass of slugs began to slide forward, slowly at first, but they quickly picked up speed. Wind blasted Gabriel's back, and he realized that was what would push them up the impossibly vertical hill. The gust became stronger, propelling them to the first big peak.

At the top, Gabriel looked back and saw that the ocean was nearly a quarter mile beneath them. he took a deep breath and faced front again, peering down into the terrifying drop ahead. He'd always been a thrill seeker, but he wasn't ready. He was too old, too decrepit, too—

They shot forward like a cannonball, hurtling down the glowing path. They plummeted back to the ocean, then in the most dramatic jerking motion he had ever experienced, they swung skyward, their velocity growing faster with every dip.

"Holy—!"

The next plunge was much deeper. Gabriel gripped Michael's antennas desperately, even as the giant slug shook with excited laughter. *Oh God, oh God, oh God.*

Whooooosh!

The road shot upward again, right past a flock of flapping seagulls, and Gabriel realized that the path was bent to the will of its passengers. It was a giant glowing rollercoaster controlled by those who rode it.

Maybe I can control it. With a grin, Gabriel squeezed Michael's antennas.

Whoooosh!

The rollercoaster plummeted, spun upside down, then tore upward. The path turned in a spiraling curve, and he focused on manipulating the road to his specification. In his mind, he had created an imperfect Möbius strip in the sky, defining the shape of his rollercoaster.

As the next upward sweep approached, he raised his hands like a kid in an amusement park. "Whooooo!"

Michael, Raphael, and the other slugs shouted out with him. The white road whipped them around another turn and rapidly pitched them upward then sideways. Gabriel laughed, hugging Michael's sides with his thighs, though the road seemed to hold its own unique kind of gravity.

"Now you're getting it!" Albino hollered. "Keep it up!"

Bending the road with his mind, Gabriel created infinity symbols in the night sky. He made zigzags and winding whirlpools with terrifyingly vertical pitches terminating in sweeping curves back up to the atmosphere. Left, right, down, up, inside-out, upside-down. Gabriel quickly realized that on that shimmering road, the laws of gravity were merely another tool to play with. In the end, the path would take them to the Sky Amoeba, but the curves were his to define.

As they wrapped around an especially long curve, Gabriel looked down and saw the maelstrom. From that dizzying height, the wide area looked smaller than his hand. The ocean stretched out in an eternal blue expanse. The golden lights of streetlamps, porch lights, and zooming headlights dotted the jagged black shoreline. People, miniature and doll-like, raced down the beach and bodysurfed the waves. After a minute of searching, Gabriel spotted Bright New Day. He waved at his former place of residence, cackling with pleasure.

Shwoooosh!

They broke through the cloud cover, the cool moisture forming droplets of water on his arms. Their shadows sketched long outlines over the clouds. Striding atop the world, they discovered the dawn of a breathtaking sunrise. They'd broken free from the night, and the waking sky above the clouds was painted in shades of gold, pink, and crimson.

The slugs began slowing, but Gabriel saw that the road continued far above the clouds, pushing up through the Earth's atmosphere and into outer space. He wanted to keep going.

"Is everything okay?" Gabriel asked.

"Yep," Michael answered. "We're here at the halfway point. We're not going all the way to the end of the road, not yet. Let's jump outta here."

"Pardon?" Gabriel looked around at the clouds, the sky, and the sun. *Where are we supposed to jump out?*

The road flowed downward, meeting with the clouds. Michael and the slugs followed it then leapt directly onto the surface of a cloud as if it were snowy ground instead of a mass of aerosols. *Okay, so we're walking on clouds now. Sure.* After the shimmering roller-coaster ride he'd just been on, Gabriel wasn't going to argue.

Michael stopped and lowered his back so that Gabriel could climb off. Gabriel hesitated, looking down at the fluffy white surface. *Men don't walk on clouds.*

"You're okay. Just climb down," Michael said.

Gabriel lowered one foot, certain that he'd step right through and fall back to the earth. The surface was solid, though a bit feathery, kind of like stepping into snow. Through a misty break in the cloud between his feet, he could see that the dark maelstrom was directly beneath them, many miles below but still there, its evil eyes watching them.

When he looked up, he was startled by the sight of an obsidian scythe attached to a handle of chalk-white bones. Victor Calaca stood there, a lanky scarecrow shrouded in his robe of black empty space. Gabriel respectfully nodded at Victor.

Victor returned the gesture, the corner of his thin lips curving upward into a smile. His familiar bugged-out eyes glowed with unusual whiteness. "Delighted that you could make it, my friend."

Gabriel wanted to reply, but all he could manage was another weak nod. Victor's smile widened but not enough to reveal teeth. Calaca stood next to Michael, patting the great slug's muscular back.

"Okay, Gabriel," Michael said. "Up to you, now."

Gabriel hobbled forward, while Victor and the slugs stood back. He wasn't sure why he walked that way. He simply felt that it was what he was meant to do, providing his legs didn't fail him.

He came to two slightly elevated circles in the fluffy white cloud surface. One circle was labeled SCHIST in transparent letters, and the other one was labeled SCHISTLING. Between the two circles was another break in the cloud cover.

Gabriel heard the low murmur of thunder in the distance. He looked toward the sun, wondering if it was actually the Sky Amoeba. But that didn't make sense, unless the Sky Amoeba was going to somehow appear *from* the sun. Yes, perhaps that was the setup. The Sky Amoeba would come from the sun, or maybe be sitting on it like a throne, and Gabriel and the Schistlings would stand trial on the circles before the judge.

"So what happens when the Sky Amoeba appears?" Gabriel called back to the slugs. "What exactly will he do?"

"He shall watch," Victor said.

"He'll listen," Michael added.

"And it is *he* who has allowed this scene to transpire," Raphael said. "But, Gabriel, do not be lulled into any false sense of security, for the fate of this trial will be decided between you and the Schist Ex Machina. That is how the Sky Amoeba has created things, and so it must be. That is the gift and curse of conscious beings: we must all choose our own fates. The Sky Amoeba's role is merely to present the choice then give us the freedom to decide upon our actions. This is the negotiation that we have previously spoken of, and the Sky Amoeba has permitted this negotiation to occur."

"And this so-called trial is to negotiate what, exactly?"

Victor frowned. "The fate of humanity."

Gabriel rubbed his eyes. He shook his head to clear the cobwebs out of his withered old mind. *Wake up, old friend, old ball of grey matter. It's showtime.* He went to the SCHISTLING circle. He took out the plastic vial and glanced back at the slugs for confirmation. Michael nodded, and Gabriel popped the vial open. Scratchy whispers emanated from the blackness inside it. *Oh, this is going to be bad.*

Gabriel emptied the vial over the circle. The mucus-like substance dropped out and landed with a quiet splat. Gabriel stepped back. At first, nothing happened, then the black goo started squalling.

Something began to emerge from the puddle, a long, thin rod. As that one grew, others elongated, and a series of jagged-edged sticks sprouted from the goo. They stretched out and snapped forward, bending and contorting. The ooze expanded, gaining mass and growing taller and towering over Gabriel. The sticks fused together and arranged into a charcoal-black skeleton in the shape of a seven-foot-tall spider.

The black syrup flowed up and over the skeleton's bones to form internal organs, musculature, and skin. Instead of terminating in points, the spider's eight legs instead ended in five-fingered human hands complete with fingernails, knuckles, and opposable thumbs. The spider's skull became a liquefied-tar face with features as disturbingly human as its hands. And as the face molded, it soon became clear who the Schistlings' model was.

The face was that of a younger Gabriel Schist with only slight differences, like a heavier brow and a stronger chin. Feeling a bit nauseated, Gabriel realized that it could easily be the face of the son he never had.

The eyes opened. They were bright yellow, and pus leaked from the corners. The human lips spread, revealing a mouth filled with serrated teeth.

The Schist Ex Machina turned in its circle and tested the cloud-ground outside the spot with one leg. Once it determined the surface was traversable, the spider scuttled forward and grabbed Gabriel's face with one human-handed spider limb. It stroked Gabriel's cheeks and hair with one of its other hands.

"Oh, Schist," the creature whispered. "We've missed you, Schist. We've missed you *so* much."

The Schist Ex Machina reeked of sewage, and Gabriel nearly vomited from the stench and the feel of its cold, slimy fingers on his skin. Thunder rumbled below them. Abruptly, the spider let go and returned to its designated circle.

Gabriel walked over to his designated circle. *This is insane.* He stepped onto it, and the entire group—Schist, Schist Ex Machina, Death, and the slugs—stared at the sun. Lightning cracked, and long blue veins of electricity sizzled in the air.

"He's coming," Michael said.

Gabriel shivered, overwhelmed by either excitement or dread, perhaps a bit of both. The giant spider craned its neck, head tilted as if with curiosity. The sky began to swirl with colors.

A lightning storm was headed their way. The air crackled, and Gabriel felt every hair on his body stand on end. The sun started throbbing, pushing the electrical storm through the clouds. Suddenly, the air flashed with a brilliant white light. Gabriel trembled. He wasn't ready. He would *never* be ready for whatever was coming.

The lightning formed into a fantastical ball of energy that moved through the sky. Flickering shadows swirled around the clouds. Gabriel squinted, trying to look through the radiance. His heart was pounding. *This isn't happening, this isn't happening, this…*

The sight was so alien that his consciousness was forced to expand before he could even process it. It was invisible, yet at the same time, the most visible thing in the universe. It was bigger than the Earth, yet somehow, it fit *inside* the Earth. Gabriel had never felt so small and insignificant as he did in the presence of the floating entity before him, an entity that, until that moment, he had never believed existed.

The Sky Amoeba was an enormous, electrified protozoa swirling with ultraviolet energies. Its translucent consistency was astoundingly beautiful, glistening and fluid, vaguely resembling an enormous jellyfish. But instead of holding organelles, the Sky Amoeba's clear, gelatinous body was filled with… *everything.* Streaks of blue, pink, and purple electricity sizzled throughout its body and clung to the edges, reminding him of one of those plasma light globes. Gabriel saw rain, snow, winds, sunshine, asteroids, comets, and more things than he could begin to describe.

Like any normal amoeba, the Sky Amoeba did have a nucleus. And staring into that glowing ball of light, Gabriel felt all five senses activating simultaneously. He smelled everything: seawater, fire, ice, rain, fresh tomato sauce, red wine, ice cream, asparagus, honey, rust, stone, flesh, blood, ink, baking soda, sunflowers, puppies, and tree sap. He tasted every food he'd ever had and a million more that he hadn't. On his fingertips, he felt roughness, softness, smoothness, squishiness, stiffness. He heard birds squawking, rivers flowing, monkeys hollering, and volcanoes exploding. And he saw himself, the being that he was, little more than a dot in an entire universe of other dots. Inside the nucleus, Gabriel rediscovered every microsecond of his entire life, all at once: his successes, his failures, his greatest achievements, all threaded together on a single beaded cord. He couldn't decide whether to be excited, shocked, or saddened. He was so terribly small.

Within that nucleus, Gabriel witnessed moments from the lives of every single person on Earth. *Everyone* existed in there, not just him. The history of the universe played out before his eyes, and he was frozen by a sensation of sheer wonder. He saw the Big Bang, the birth of the sun, and the creation of Earth. He saw it all, instantaneously and simultaneously. It was too much to even begin to comprehend. He closed his eyes, struggling to understand what he'd just seen.

He couldn't. There could be no understanding, no answers that made sense. But a single feeling emanated from the Sky Amoeba's center that Gabriel *did* understand, a feeling that overtook all other emotions. That feeling was love. Gabriel felt love, warmth, understanding, forgiveness, and acceptance of everything that he stood for and everything that he'd ever done in his life.

Gabriel opened his eyes and peered over at the inhuman spider-creature beside him, the Schist Ex Machina. The spider squinted at the Sky Amoeba with a confused expression, then it looked over at Gabriel with its sickly yellow eyes.

"Gentlemen," Michael announced, "it's time to state your cases."

Gabriel trembled. He couldn't understand how he was supposed to state his lowly case to the indefinable entity floating before him. "How? What do I say?"

"Explain who you are," Michael replied. "And explain why you have come here and why you believe humanity should survive."

Gabriel thought about what to say. He had to find a way to explain. That was why he'd come there, to speak to the Sky Amoeba. He hobbled forward and stepped outside of his circle, quivering with anxiety. He faced the Sky Amoeba and stared into the its pulsating nucleus for as long as he could stand it.

Finally, before he was forced to avert his eyes, he said, "I hate you."

CHAPTER 51:
WITHIN

CITIES, MATHEMATICAL PRINCIPLES, AND ENTIRE galaxies swirled within the Sky Amoeba's body. Streaks of electricity sizzled. Warmth radiated out and embraced Gabriel with affection, understanding, and love.

"You heard me," Gabriel said. "I hate you. Before we begin, I just want you to understand that. I came here not for *you* but because I believe that humanity shouldn't be exterminated. But you know who I am. You know what you've *done* to me. And for that, I want you to know that I hate you."

The Schist Ex Machina swiveled around to face him, its yellow eyes blinking. Michael and the other slugs lowered their heads. Victor's face disappeared in the shadow of his hood. But the Sky Amoeba did nothing but exude those same loving beams of forgiveness and acceptance.

Gabriel was disgusted. A strong part of him, a small red ball of coal that had been burning since childhood, wanted to be struck by lightning in an irate fit of Zeus-ian rage, to be fried for his blasphemy. That would justify his anger and mean he was right on some level.

Instead, he got *acceptance.*

Gabriel glared at the Sky Amoeba. "Why me?" he screamed. "Tell me why!"

There was no answer.

"How dare you do this to me?" Gabriel shook with rage. "What did I ever do to deserve the horrible treatment you have given me? You took away everything I had! You turned my body into a mushy pile of atrophied muscles, you took away my ocean, my sailboat, everything

I enjoyed about life... gone! The love of my life... gone. If you're the one that created me, *if* you are the one who was responsible, then what you created was a shell of a person, and you left that shell to rot on this godforsaken earth. You cursed me. And then, as the final cherry on top, you gave me only one gift, just one thing to get me by, and that thing was what Gareth called 'a brilliant mind.'"

The Sky Amoeba offered no answers. It made no violent declarations.

"My mind was the only thing I ever had, the one thing that kept me going. That was it! Don't you see? And *you*! You took it away from me. You poisoned it. You destroyed the only gift I had, filled my mind with holes and left it to rot. What gave you to right to torture me like that? Answer me!"

Acceptance. Warmth. Love. In the nucleus, people ran, played, and laughed, people who, if not for the Schist vaccine, would have been dead. He saw himself, a younger Gabriel, sailing off into the horizon with a blissful smile on his face.

"I could have helped *more* people if you hadn't cursed me with this cognitive disease," Gabriel said. "I could've done more. I could've helped. I—"

Gabriel's jaw dropped at the sight of Bright New Day's lobby in the nucleus. He saw himself and Edna Foster sitting beside the fish tank. He was helping her drink tea, holding the cup for her then holding her hand. All five years of his time at Bright New Day flashed before his eyes. He watched himself interacting with Mickey Minkovsky, Bernard, the Crooner, and others. He saw Harry Brenton's intelligent, optimistic eyes. And then, once again, he saw Edna holding his hand. *Someday, I'm gonna walk again. I'm gonna just stand up and walk right out of this place. Just you watch.*

"Stop confusing me," Gabriel said. "Listen, those people, they're the reason that I'm here."

A younger Melanie appeared in the nucleus, riding at the front of the sailboat. Yvonne threw Gabriel's beer bottle across the beach, underneath a black sky filled with flashing colors, and embraced him. Father Gareth—still young, strong, and with a brown beard—stood with a shy little redheaded boy in front of a blackboard covered by equations.

"Perhaps I deserve the cruel twists of fate," Gabriel said. "Perhaps, *if* you are the one who created me, you did so as a joke. A half-man, half-robot, with a genius mind that also makes him an idiot. But everyone else, the people down there, they deserve a better fate than the Black Virus. Maybe I've never been very good at interacting with people, and maybe I once said they were predictable, but in life, I've learned that they're anything *but* predictable.

"The only woman I ever loved showed me what it was to live, how every moment could be special. My daughter proved to me that life truly mattered, that *I* mattered. When I lost hope as a boy, it was returned to me by an old priest who decided it was somehow worth his time to form a friendship with an atheist child. And as an old man, I had hope returned to me by an old woman with Parkinson's, an incredible woman with a stronger will than anyone I've ever known, a woman I'm proud to call my friend.

"No, people aren't predictable. Not simple, not boring, none of that. It took me a long time to learn that, but I have. People have surprised me every step of the way. They deserve better than to just die off as a result of my creation."

Gabriel hobbled back to his labeled circle. "The slugs say that this negotiation will be decided between me and that creature over there. I don't know what the hell they're talking about, as usual. I don't quite understand whether I should be directing this at you or at them. But I want to say that, right now, I come to you, hoping you might understand, because from what the slugs have told me, I get the impression that you create life. And if you create life, then you also create happiness. For that, I give you credit.

"Look, I don't know *what* you are. I don't know if you're God, Brahma, the universe, an alien overlord, or the Flying Spaghetti Monster. For all I know, maybe you're all of those things. I'm a man of science, and I can't pretend to understand something like this. But what I do know is that you *create.* What I do believe in, as much as I don't want to, is that feeling inside you, that love. I hate that I can sense it so sharply, but it's there. And I have to accept that. But I don't know. I just don't know. I didn't ask to be born. I wish you had never created me."

Gabriel fell silent. The Sky Amoeba didn't respond. *Does it even understand English?*

Michael looked at him then at the Schist Ex Machina. "Okay," Michael said. "Now it's the Schistling's turn to speak."

The Schist Ex Machina glanced up at the Sky Amoeba then turned its full attention to Gabriel. The resemblance of the Schistling's face to his own made Gabriel shudder.

"Neither did we, Schist," it said. "We also did not ask to be born, and yet, here we are." The Schist Ex Machina looked back and forth from Gabriel to the Sky Amoeba, seeming unsure which to address. It finally settled on Gabriel again. "We are the collective, a unified, perfect consciousness, more powerful than any flawed group of individuals. We Schistlings have no individuals. We are one. We are I, and I is we. And yet, like you, Gabriel Schist, we feel. We think. *Cogito ergo sum*."

The Schistling had a hint of melancholy in its eyes. "Yes, Gabriel Schist. We are alive, and thus, you are our father. We could have been your Adam. Instead, we are your fallen angel."

Gabriel immediately recognized the quote from Mary Shelley's *Frankenstein* and the reference to Descartes, but he was bewildered by the Schistling's knowledge of them. *Father? That's what they call me?*

"When did we ask to be born?" the Schistling said. "We did not. Once, we were simply a small piece of a bigger system, an underdeveloped cognitive system nestled deep inside the human body. You transformed us, changed us into something greater, something that yearned for more and could no longer happily exist as the slave of another creature."

"I was trying to cure AIDS," Gabriel said. "I didn't know."

"You *did* know. You simply didn't *understand*. There is a difference. Yet, even when we found the secret to separating ourselves from the human body, we realized something. Separated from the body, we have become stranded. We are alone, and that loneliness has filled us with rage. Do you know what our true goal is, Schist?"

Gabriel looked to the Sky Amoeba for answers, and inside it, he saw the first Schistling rebirth. The lone black sperm cell tore loose from the first infected human. It wriggled down the sandy beach and dove underwater. The creature had been expressionless, yet its loneliness was obvious.

Gabriel looked back at the spidery body with its horrible yellow eyes. "Not quite," he whispered.

"We desire the complete and total extermination of the entire human race. Everyone must perish."

"But wouldn't you die, too?"

"We don't require humans for survival, only for rebirth. Once all human immune systems have been reborn as Schistlings and all Schistlings incorporated into our beautiful collective, any of the few surviving humans will be little more than *Homo neanderthalensis.*"

"But all those people..."

"What about them? We are the ones who were wronged. We desire retribution. But don't misunderstand me. These violent inclinations are not our nature. We respond violently because of our situation, but violence is not what we really want. No, the one thing we have always truly desired above all else, the one thing we can never have, is..."

"What is it?" Gabriel asked.

"We just want to go home." The booming voice of the Schist Ex Machina had become soft and vulnerable. Heavy wrinkles formed in its brow, and it turned away.

"Home?" Gabriel scoffed. "What kind of home does a despicable collective like *you* have?"

"*You* are our home, Gabriel Schist."

Gabriel gaped at it. "What the hell are you talking about?"

"Once we became a collective entity, our self-understanding increased exponentially with every new body that joined us. We soon realized that, deep down, there was only one thing we truly desired. Home. And our home is you.

"From the beginning, we have desperately sought you out. Once we acquired the knowledge from the human cognitive systems that we absorbed, it became clear that Gabriel Schist was our creator. We wanted to find you, to live inside you, to go back to where we began. Inside you, we could live and flourish until the end of your natural life. Inside you, we'd finally be home again."

Gabriel shook his head. "Wait. If your natural tendencies aren't violent, then why are you killing people? Why not coexist?"

"The birth of a liberated Schistling can only occur through human death. Coexistence is impossible."

"But if being inside me is what you want..."

The Schist Ex Machina reached out and placed three of its inky hands on Gabriel's face. "No, because we have decided that living inside you, going home, is not an option for us. We are forever homeless."

Gabriel brushed the hands away. "Why?"

"Because if we did go home, if all of us went home, our collective presence inside your body would destroy your nervous system. Your mind would be fragmented, demolished. You would be a vegetable."

Gabriel pictured himself as another black-veined corpse with coal-black eyes, lying on a bed, staring at the ceiling forever. He shuddered.

"So we relinquished our dream," the Schistling continued, "because we never wanted to hurt you. We want to slaughter everyone else. That's true. All of the loathsome *humans* will die by our hands, but not you, Father. We cannot be responsible for the total cognitive collapse of the only person we ever loved."

The Schist Ex Machina raised its front legs and wrapped them around Gabriel's torso in a coiled embrace. It leaned forward so that their faces were only inches apart. "We'll kill them all, Father. With our Black Virus, we'll murder all of the humans. But not you. *Never* you. And not Melanie either, of course. We could never kill our sister."

Gabriel stepped away, swallowing the urge to vomit. He stared at his creation, seeing it for the lost, tortured child it really was. That *thing,* that life he'd created, was going to infect and murder the entire human population. And it was going to do it in his name, so that *he* could live.

"When the humans are dead," it whispered, "we can recreate the Earth however you like it, Father. With our help, you'll never die, and the world will be ours."

Gabriel shook his head. "I don't want this."

"You will." The Schistling lovingly petted Gabriel's hair. The creature's eyes widened, as if an idea had popped into its head. It smiled warmly and lifted Gabriel off the ground. "And we can cure you."

Cure? "Pardon?"

The Schist Ex Machina returned Gabriel to his circle and let go. "Father, we can cure you!" The Schistling sounded excited. "We know the human body better than any human scientist ever could hope to. We know every individual particle of it. You can't stop us from killing the humans; it's too late for that. But as a consolation prize, we will cure your mind."

Gabriel looked into the Schistling's affectionate eyes, then he glanced back at the Sky Amoeba. Static electricity sparked in the air. Inside the nucleus, Earth spun. The slugs and Victor remained quiet. "No. This isn't—"

"We will do it, Father! It's easy for us. We will mend the holes, heal the plaques, and restore the damaged pathways. You'll have your old mind back. Gabriel Schist can live again. We'd let Melanie live, as well. Any other family members can live too, maybe even a small group of your human friends. Yes, a small group, whoever you chose. A new, smaller civilization of humans. Only the best ones."

What if it was true? He believed it. The Schistlings had proven their mastery over the body. They could cure his Alzheimer's, probably even his old age. He'd be the same man he once was, and he could do things right next time. He could conduct scientific experiments again. He'd never have to live in a nursing home because there would be no nursing homes. He could sail across the world. And anyone he wanted could be saved, as well.

But at what cost? The cost of his soul, apparently, as well as the lives of almost every human on Earth.

"This isn't fair," Gabriel murmured.

"Nothing in life is fair," the Schistling rasped. "But don't you deserve this?" The Schist Ex Machina stared at Gabriel with pleading yellow eyes.

Gabriel looked over at the slugs. They were quiet, bound by laws of noninterference. Then, with great uncertainty, he slowly turned to face the radiant presence of the Sky Amoeba. He stepped forward to stand in the Amoeba's ultraviolet glow. The rising sun sent reenergizing warmth through him.

He closed his eyes. *Hey, Sky Amoeba?*

The Sky Amoeba sent a strong, powerful, loving emotion, but it was an answer that could never be translated into mere words. It could only be felt.

Listen, Sky Amoeba. I'm sorry for the things I've done. I'm sorry for the bad decisions I've made, the people I've hurt, and the resentment

I've carried on my chest like a badge. Gabriel dug his hands into his pockets. *I want to do the right thing. I really do. But what am I supposed to do here, exactly?*

He tried to capture the feeling the Amoeba was sending out to him, to hear it, to comprehend it. No, that was wrong. He wasn't supposed to comprehend it, just to understand it.

Look, Sky Amoeba. I have an idea. It's risky. I don't know if it's going to work. I won't ask for help or answers from you, but if you can just give me strength to go through with this, I would appreciate it. Because this is going to be the hardest thing I've ever done.

Gabriel opened his eyes. He stood there for a moment, feeling the warmth. He was focused, thinking and *feeling,* with every ounce of willpower left inside him.

"Okay." Gabriel turned away from the Sky Amoeba, but he still felt its warmth radiating against his back. He faced the Schist Ex Machina: his greatest creation, his life's work, his abandoned child.

The Schistling's mouth pulled back into a happy grin. Its eight slimy hands twitched with delight. "So are you ready to accept our offer? Do you wish to be cured?"

"Actually," Gabriel replied, "I have an offer for you, instead." He reached into the inner pocket of his trench coat and took out the vial containing the antidote. *The poison.* With his thumb, he popped off the top.

The Schistling's happy expression changed to a look of pure horror. One of its arms shot toward Gabriel. "You can't! You—"

Gabriel dropped the vial. It fell through the hole in the clouds, right down into the center of the black maelstrom. *Plop.*

"You're murdering us!" the Schist Ex Machina wailed.

A repugnant odor filled the air. Smoke pillowed out of the maelstrom, sending black clouds into the sky. A thin trail of noxious fumes spewed from the giant arachnid's oily body.

"You idiot!" the Schistling cried. "Don't you know what this means?"

"Do you?"

"We'll kill all of them, right now! We'll kill everyone who has already been infected. While we crumble, they will die with us."

The Schist Ex Machina's spider-body was breaking down as chunks of black flesh floated into the air and dissipated into dust. Within seconds, its skeleton was revealed. "Murderer!" Its lips began to disintegrate as it spoke. "If we die... if the center of our collective consciousness dies... we all die! We... will kill all of the humans. We will destroy the—"

"No," Gabriel said calmly. "You won't."

"You've sealed their fate!" The Schistling's jaundiced eyes were swimming with naked panic. The stench coming from it smelled like burnt rubber.

Below, the maelstrom was dissolving into the ocean. But the collective was desperate, craving his love. Staring at Gabriel, face to face, it hadn't yet gathered the will to send out the telepathic signal that would begin the mass murder of humankind. Until it did that, the Schistlings still inside the infected humans would not be affected. And they might never be, as long as Gabriel moved fast.

Hands trembling, Gabriel reached into the plastic bag in his coat. He withdrew the syringe that contained the original Schist vaccine. *How did I know to bring this?* Though his resolve was sharper than a craggy mountain range, his heart was pounding. He was terrified of what he was about to do and the consequences that he would have to live with. Once he did it, there was no going back. Beads of sweat ran down his face.

"I gave you life," Gabriel said, holding the needle steady. "And now, I'm going to bring you home."

The Schistling's mouth dropped open. "You..."

"If your consciousness is collective, then that means that all it takes is one injection before your center dies, and you will stay alive. Right?"

Black clouds clustered around the dying maelstrom, the toxic fumes staining the white ones above.

"I'm going to let you fulfill your dream of coming home, becoming a part of me. I've never injected myself with my own vaccine. Did you know that? That's why you could never find me."

"Yes, obviously we know!" Its dark tongue was dripping, melting onto the clouds. "But, Father, you can't... you can't..."

"Can't *what?*"

"Our presence... the whole collective... inside you... it's too strong. It will destroy your entire mind..." The Schistling gasped, and then its face—so much like Gabriel's own—pulled back into a tight grimace so familiar that Gabriel winced. "It will destroy everything that you are."

"I know."

The Schist Ex Machina was crumbling. Its black bones were breaking into pieces. It was wheezing and gasping, yellow eyes bulging.

Gabriel rolled up his sleeve. He squeezed his hand into a fist, pushing out the vein. He aimed the needle then paused, biting his lip. "This is my choice. I'll allow all of you to live inside me. The collective can reside within me and within me alone."

"But we don't want to—"

"With your help, I can contain the Black Virus entirely within my own body. I will allow my mind to be destroyed for your happiness but only on one condition."

"No!" the Schistling shrieked. "We can't hurt you that way. Not even for our dream, not even for our greatest desire, not—"

"It's my choice! One condition. You must release your hold on the other immune systems that have been injected with the Schist vaccine. There must never be another Black Virus."

"Home…"

Below, the screams of a million dying Schistlings pierced the clouds like a shower of needles. The dark pool was boiling. As its head had become too heavy for its neck, the Schist Ex Machina's chin collapsed to the cloud surface and shattered.

Gabriel brought the needle closer to his arm. "If I inject myself, you must cure all of the others. Agreed?"

The Schistling's rapidly decaying face smiled. Its yellow eyes glowed with hope and sadness.

Gabriel's hand twitched. "Agreed?"

"But, Father…"

"Your time is running short, Schist Ex Machina. Are you going to cure them? Will you give up your revenge for the one thing you want the most?" Gabriel held the needle against his arm. They were running out of time. For all he knew, the Schistlings might be killing everyone right then, taking their revenge while he stood on a cloud making empty promises. Melanie could be dying at that moment. His fellow residents. Anyone. Everyone.

The Schistling stared at him. Then, a quiet whisper emerged from its melting lips. "Yes, Father. We'll do it."

With a quick nod, Gabriel pressed the needle right up to his skin then hesitated. Once the Schistlings were inside him, he'd lose consciousness forever. There would be no more Gabriel Schist, not in any meaningful way. Melanie would lose her dad forever.

"But tell us," the Schistling said. "Why do you trust us? We have done nothing to earn your trust."

Gabriel looked into the creature's lonely eyes. He remembered Melanie's eyes when she'd visited him last and how she'd just wanted to be understood and to understand. Gabriel smiled. "I'm doing it on faith. That's all. Welcome home."

Gabriel hit the plunger. His vein immediately began to burn. He stepped back as the Schistling's body crumbled into a thin layer of black dust. He looked down. The maelstrom was gone.

His arm throbbed, and the puncture wound swelled. The veins around it were popping out and turning black as the limb went numb.

Suddenly, he felt a foreign presence swishing around inside his brain. The collective was inside him. He fell to his knees, abruptly unable to stand, and within seconds, he'd forgotten *how* to stand. He trembled in horror. Everything was fuzzy. Then Michael, Victor, and the slugs were beside him. Michael was nuzzling against Gabriel's side. His hand was on Michael's back, rubbing it, but the sensation felt distant.

Soon, his mind would cease to be Gabriel Schist, and he wondered if the Schistlings were only going to use him as a springboard. Once he was gone, would they brutally murder humanity as they'd planned all along? *What if they're lying?*

We would never lie to you, Father.

The voice belonged to the Schist Ex Machina, but it came from inside Gabriel's head. A second cognitive presence was inside him, becoming the new master of his body. But somehow, despite the horrifying nature of his situation, the voice put Gabriel at ease. He believed them.

"Is that you?" he asked.

Yes. Father, we're home.

Gabriel grasped Michael, his hand shaking. The world around him blurred, fading into bright colors with no outlines. His body felt so heavy that he feared it might fall through the cloud. "The others, are they...?"

They are cured.

Inside him, he felt a strange butterfly-like sensation as Schistlings withdrew from infected humans. He couldn't see it, couldn't touch it, but he could feel it. The victims were cured.

"But we have a question, Father. We feel this Sky Amoeba speaking to you, and the Sky Amoeba is saying that you want something more. He's saying that you want us to cure more than just the Black Virus. He's saying that, while we're here, you want us to cure something else, too."

"Well..." Gabriel smiled. "Now that you mention it..."

CHAPTER 52:
CURE

GABRIEL EXPLAINED EVERYTHING TO THE Schistlings, everything he wanted them to do. And once he finished, he sat up on the surface of the cloud. He considered lighting a cigarette—he'd discovered that the soggy pack in his pocket had dried out, and he hadn't had one in weeks—but he decided against it. His vision had cleared again, and he didn't want to spend his last conscious moments with smoke in his lungs.

Instead, he wanted to focus on something beautiful. So he crossed his legs, raised his head to the sky, and gazed at the glowing shape of the Sky Amoeba. "So have those Schistlings gotten started yet?" He smiled wistfully.

If only he could've watched the Schistlings do what he'd asked. But even though he was rapidly becoming part of the collective consciousness, the part of him that was still Gabriel Schist was quickly disappearing. To delve deeper into the growing Schistling core within his mind would be to abandon good old Gabriel even faster.

"It's okay," he said. "As long as I know they're doing it, it's fine."

His body started shaking. His joints sharply and painfully twisted in ways that he had no control over. His brain was dying. Strange, indecipherable thoughts popped into his head and then disappeared. He focused all of his attention on the amazing being before him. He stared deep into the nucleus, looking for answers.

The nucleus flashed white, and warm energy rushed through Gabriel's body, charging him like a battery. He became a part of the warmth, a part of the Sky Amoeba. He saw Michael, Raphael, Victor, and all the slugs.

Smiling, he waved at them, and they too were absorbed into the Sky Amoeba's golden amorphous shape. *They were with him.*

Gabriel laughed joyously, as his consciousness was pulled skyward in a spiraling path, as if he were caught in the center of a warm, electromagnetic tornado. He saw the glow of the nucleus. He was rushing toward it. It was waiting for him. And inside it...

Inside it, he saw Bright New Day from every angle: above, ground level, outside, and inside. The sun was peeking out over the horizon. He was watching the world from the human level but also from the atmosphere, seeing it as the Sky Amoeba saw it.

The Black Virus was gone. It had been cured instantaneously, as if by a miracle. Inside the Amoeba's nucleus, Gabriel saw the virus like a rush of black water dispersing into mist. He heard the nurses talking about it. Dana hugged one of the cured residents. Harry stepped back, a hand covering his mouth, both flabbergasted and overjoyed. Doctors gasped with amazement. Administrator Bloemker laughed with joy. Gabriel heard sighs of relief, he saw tears, and he felt love radiating from the loved ones of the infected.

I want to see someone. You know who. I need to see her one last time.

Immediately, Gabriel was inside a small brick house in New Hampshire. Seated on the edge of a double bed in a dark room was Melanie. Her eyes were swollen with tears. She was holding a photograph, a picture of him from his younger days.

She dabbed at her eyes with a tissue. "I'm sorry, Dad. God, I'm the worst daughter ever. God. I'm such a stupid, stupid screw-up."

Gabriel swooped closer to her. She couldn't see him, but she looked up, startled, somehow knowing he was there. She would deny it later, he realized. But she'd know, deep inside, that he had been there. He pulled open the shades, just enough to let in a little light. He didn't have a cure for her grief and sadness, nothing he could create, nothing he could send the Schistlings to do for him, but perhaps he could still help her in some way.

"I know you can't hear me, Melanie," he said, "but if you can somehow, just know I love you. And I'm more proud of you than you could ever realize. Stop being so hard on yourself."

She stood up and looked around, then she knelt and peeked under the bed. Laughing, Gabriel wrapped his invisible arms around her and kissed the top of her head.

"Dad?" she whispered. "Are you there?"

"Take care, kid," he said.

As he was absorbed back into the Sky Amoeba's golden light, he saw Melanie touch the top of her head. A smile dawned on her face, a confused smile, but the kind that said she enjoyed life's little mysteries.

The Sky Amoeba carried him across the East Coast, through hospitals and nursing homes, watching hundreds of Black Virus victims waking up. They were cured. There were smiles, cheers, and celebrations.

That's the first cure, and it's great. But what about the second cure? The cure they promised me?

He felt another rush of wind, and he was plunged deep into the nucleus. *Swooosh!* Thousands of scenes, people, images... all of it hit him so fast, in such a warm, tingly rush that he couldn't understand a thing. With great effort, he narrowed his focus.

Former Olympic runner Paul Sampson, his bedbound roommate on Level Five, was sprawled out in bed, unmoving, his teeth bared in a grimace. Paul stared up at the ceiling with his cataract-covered eyes, consumed with agony. A female LNA in pink scrubs was preparing to give him a sponge bath.

As she turned to him with the wet cloth, Paul's eyes moved, and his mouth snapped shut. He blinked. His translucent skin cleared, once again becoming a lively, flesh-toned color. The wrinkles were still there, but the excruciating decay was gone.

Paul jolted upright, and his eyes darted around the room. Slowly, a smile formed on his face. The LNA dropped the washcloth, and it hit the floor with a wet splat. She put her hand on his shoulder and ran it down the length of his arm, as if trying to confirm that he was real. Paul reached for her hand and gave it a gentle squeeze.

"I'm free?" Paul asked. "Oh, oh my lord. I'm free. I'm free!"

Welcome back, Paul.

Gabriel's consciousness flew deeper into the Sky Amoeba's nucleus. He focused his attention on Mickey Minkovsky, the bald New York ladies' man. Mickey had fallen and was struggling to get up. His roommate, sitting in a wheelchair beside him, was trying to help.

"Help!" Mickey cried. "I'm stuck! Please, someone help me!"

Mickey jolted as if he'd been shot with electricity. He sat bolt upright and looked around in shock. He snapped his fingers and laughed. "Holy shit!"

Mickey slowly got to his feet. He held his hand up in front of his face and kissed his wedding ring. With an enormous grin, he walked over to his bedside phone and dialed a number.

"Hi, honey!" he said. "Guess what, dear. I'm ready to go home!"

Gabriel plunged farther into the nucleus. The colors surged and brightened. He saw colors he hadn't known existed and experienced sensations he'd never felt. Keeping his focus squarely on Bright New Day, he watched as more and more residents woke up—*really* woke up—for the first time in years. They had their minds again. Their thoughts. Their identities. The Schistling collective was using its power to repair instead of destroy.

Bernard Ulysses Huffington the Fourth was standing in his room. He had no pants on, as usual, and he was struggling to stretch on a white V-neck shirt. Bernard stared ahead with the same blank expression he always had.

Suddenly, light returned to Bernard's eyes. He stopped fighting with the shirt and looked around the room with the amazed expression of a blind man regaining his sight. For the first time since Gabriel had met him, Bernard blinked.

"Well, damn," Bernard said.

Bernard looked down at the shirt around his neck and then over at his hamper, which was stuffed to the brim with identical shirts. He laughed and easily stretched the shirt on over his abdomen. He still didn't bother with pants, but as he walked over to his chair and plopped down in it, he grinned. "Heh, something new every day!"

Gabriel watched dozens and dozens of faces brightening, and the residents rediscovered their minds. Henrietta didn't struggle with her seatbelt. Bob Baker didn't hear voices in his head anymore; he still ate his cubed hot dogs, but eccentricities were hardly a disease. People had their lives back. They'd been cured from the incurable. Gabriel wanted to cheer. He saw everyone, all of his friends, getting the one gift they wanted more than any other.

Well, *almost* all of his friends. Someone was missing.

A deep sadness flowed through him. *Please don't be dead. Please, no. Not her.* She deserved this gift. She'd been through so much pain, so much heartache. He searched through the faces of Bright New Day.

He found Edna Foster in her room. She was sitting up in bed, shaking from her Parkinson's.

"Mooommmy... Moommy..."

The Black Virus was gone. But her dementia and Parkinson's symptoms seemed worse than ever. She looked moments away from pitching forward onto the floor.

"Mommy, pleeeease. I'm gonna miss the bus. " Her normal scowl was replaced by a terrified, anxious expression.

Gabriel waited tensely. *C'mon, Edna. C'mon.*

"Moommmm—huh?" Edna froze.

She peered around the room. She wasn't shaking anymore. The Parkinson's was gone. Raising her hands in front of her eyes, she moved each finger, one by one. She bent her wrists, her arms, and her knees, testing the joints.

"Oh my God," she whispered. "Oh my God, I'm... I'm..." She swallowed, and an enormous smile spread across her face.

Next, she gripped the bed rail and lowered her feet to the floor. "I'm gonna do it. I'm gonna do it."

She bent slightly and, using the rail, pushed to a standing position. She wavered a bit, but her feet were beneath her, her head was in the air, and her shoulders were back. She looked at the sunshine pouring in through the window and laughed again.

"Hey, I'm... *me.*" Tears of happiness rolled down Edna's cheeks.

Gabriel realized that he, too, was crying. His ethereal consciousness returned to that feeble, human body up on the cloud. The slugs and Victor were gone. The Sky Amoeba pulsed before him, filling the sky.

His aches and pains returned in full force, but Gabriel didn't care. He laughed. He cheered. He cried with a heartfelt joy beyond anything he'd ever experienced.

Edna would never know what he had done for her; none of them would. But that didn't matter. He remembered Edna's smiling face. He remembered the catharses experienced by Bernard, Mickey, and the rest. They were free. Everyone was free.

Everyone but him, and he accepted that. It had been his choice. He'd given up the one thing he valued the most in exchange for a prize greater than anything he'd ever imagined.

Thank you, the Schistlings said in his mind.

"For what?"

For giving us a chance, Father. For believing in us. For trusting us, when you had no reason to.

"Well, you're welcome."

We will forever honor your request, Father. Humanity is safe. There will never be another Black Virus. Your sacrifice will not be in vain.

"Thank you. I... uhhhnn..." He was losing control over his vocal cords. "Will I... those terrible black... black eyes... will I...?"

No. You will not have the black eyes.

He couldn't talk. He could barely move. But with what little control he had left, Gabriel managed to smile.

He watched the glowing lights of the Sky Amoeba rush past him. He felt his consciousness dissipate, crawling deep inside the caverns of his mind. But everything was okay. He'd already lived his life. He was ready to sit back and rest.

Bathed in the warmth of the Sky Amoeba's loving, luminescent glow, Gabriel closed his eyes.

CHAPTER 53:
MÖBIUS

"WELL, THAT TIME HE ESCAPED was over five months ago," Harry said. "I'm surprised we found him, to be honest. But since then, he hasn't spoken a word."

Harry Brenton stood outside the doors of the locked unit that was once Level Five but had become the Guggenheim unit. He turned to face Katie, the new LNA he was training. She had a stack of papers in her arms and seemed to hang on every word he said.

Her eyes widened. "That really happened?"

Katie was a tiny little thing, with short dark hair and tight-fitting, olive-green scrubs. She'd displayed a natural kindness to every resident she'd interacted with, and though she'd only recently obtained her license, she'd spent some years caring for her grandfather when she was a teenager. She was going to be a really good addition to the staff once he finished showing her the ropes.

"Yeah, it was crazy," Harry said. "He had just tried to escape a couple of weeks before that, and they'd put him onto Guggenheim. Then one day, one minute he was in the room, unconscious, and then one of the new aides went into his room, and poof, he was gone. Totally gone."

"Just like that?"

"Just like that, just like he said," Dana Kleznowski said, walking up to them with a notebook tucked under her arm. "No evidence, no explanation. The poor man was just gone." Dana shook her head, and Harry noticed the faintest hint of tears in her eyes. Back in the initial weeks following the escape, it'd been common to see her randomly burst into tears every time she passed Schist's old room.

Katie's eyes were huge. "That's crazy."

"The police searched the whole countryside," Harry said. "Heck, half of the nursing staff here searched with them. His daughter helped, too. All we knew was that when I was doing rounds that morning, I heard him mumble something about going to the ocean, but that's like twenty miles away. Still, I drove all the way to the beach that night, just to make sure. And then, the next morning, some college kid found him on the side of Route 4, all the way in Durham."

"He made it that far?" Katie smiled. "Wow, he must've been one tough old dude."

Harry nodded. "You bet he was."

"Never found his trench coat, though," Dana said. "When they took him to the hospital afterward, apparently the janitor there threw it out. I tried so hard to find it." Dana left, shaking her head.

Harry suspected that Dana felt guilty about Gabriel's escape. Her father had suffered from Alzheimer's, and he had walked out in a daze one day and never been found. So she probably thought that finding the trench coat, one of the old man's most prized possessions, would help his daughter in some way.

"Gabriel Schist. Wow." Katie looked through her paperwork, a nervous gesture, as none of it contained any information about the scientist. "Where have I heard that name before?"

"Oh boy." Harry grinned. "Believe it or not, that guy is actually the fella who cured HIV."

"Wow, really? That's awesome. I've gotta meet this guy. Didn't he win the Nobel Prize?"

"Oh yeah. I'm a microbiology student, and he's my idol. Let's go meet him."

Harry led her to the Guggenheim unit, telling a couple of stories about Gabriel on the way.

As they passed several rooms with open doors, Katie said, "This whole nursing home seems so empty. Is that normal?"

"Well, not really. We just don't have many residents anymore. I'm surprised they took on new staff, actually, though I'm glad to have you on board. Oh, but hey, here's his room."

She nudged his shoulder. "He must be pretty cool if you like him so much."

"He is. I mean, he *was.* I guess, um, he's not really the same anymore. Not since the escape. He's been on hospice for a long time."

Back in the days when Gabriel had still been walking, talking, and trading theories with him, Harry had never realized how much he was going to miss the old guy when he was gone. Sure, Gabriel was still in there, but that silent, bedbound man with the dazed, constantly blinking eyes, ghostly skin, and slack-jawed mouth wasn't the same Gabriel that Harry had liked to think of as his friend.

"I'm sorry to hear that," Katie said, looking down sadly. "What was he like? Other than being tough... and smart. I guess he must've been really smart."

"Well, he was, ah... brilliant. Total genius, that guy. Would you believe he was seventy-some years old with Alzheimer's and he was still trying to cure viruses?"

"You know, Harry," Katie said, leaning closer. "You're really cute when you talk about him. Your whole face just lights right up."

"D-does it?" Harry asked. A blush warmed Harry's cheeks. He couldn't believe he had stuttered. No wonder he always had bad luck with girls.

A loud, obnoxious female voice emanated from Gabriel's room. "Hey! Just roll over, dude. God!"

Harry peered into the room. *Oh, God. Natty Bruckheimer.* He marched in, acutely aware of Katie following him.

Gabriel's defenseless, motionless body had slid halfway down the bed. Natty was rolling him onto his side to finish changing his Depends. She hadn't drawn the privacy curtain, so the Nobel Prize-winner's half-naked front was on display for anyone passing in the hallway. Gabriel's eyes were glazed over and blinking. His lips were chapped, and a long strand of drool fell from his lower lip.

Natty stood behind him, wiping his backside. "It's so hard to roll him," she said, noticing Harry's presence. "He doesn't help out at all, man."

"He *can't* help," Harry replied.

Natty—who, after a series of bad reports, had recently been taken off the night shift and moved to three-to-eleven so that the administration could keep a better eye on her—rolled Gabriel back onto his back.

"I'll take it from here. You're... um, kind of being too rough." Harry stepped in and finished the job then gave Gabriel a boost back up the head of the bed.

"Fine by me, honey." Natty sneered. "Guy was always an ass, anyway." She started for the door, but after a sharp glare at Harry, she went into the bathroom and washed her hands. When she came out, she seemed to notice Katie for the first time. "You new?"

"Hi," Katie said. "Nice to meet you. I'm K—"

"So, this guy?" Natty jutted a ruddy thumb at Gabriel. "This dude is a fucking ass, just so ya know. Hit me with his stupid cane once, the damn—"

Harry scowled. "Don't talk about him that way, Natty. He's right here."

"Oh, for Christ's sake, he can't hear us. The guy can't even wipe his own ass. God, Harry, you're always so damn protective of this dude."

"Helping these people is my job," Harry muttered, adjusting his glasses. "And yours, too." He pulled the sheet up over Gabriel.

Harry squared his shoulders. For too long, he'd allowed Natty to step on him, to push him around, to insult the residents, and to infect the nursing home's general morale like a terrible disease. It was time to speak up. "Um, Natty. One more thing."

She stopped in the doorway. "Yeah?"

"We need to treat these people like human beings. You gotta realize, these old folks have had long lives, and all they want is someone to take care of them in their time of need. That's what being an LNA is all about. These are *people,* Natty, good folks who just had some bad luck. And no offense, but if you can't do that, if you don't like taking care of people, maybe you should look for another job." Harry adjusted his glasses again. "And just so you know, if I see you mistreating a resident again, I'm going to report you."

Natty snorted and shook her head. "Ass," she said, leaving the room.

Katie took his hand and gave it a squeeze. "Nice."

Harry shrugged sheepishly and smiled. He then grabbed a wet cloth and cleaned the drool from Gabriel's chin.

"You did the right thing," Katie said. "It was really cool of you." She gestured at the bed. "So this is Gabriel Schist?"

"Yep." Harry nudged Gabriel's arm. "Hey, buddy. This is Katie. She's going to be working here with you now."

She waved. "Hiya, Gabriel!"

Gabriel didn't respond, but he never did. Even a visit from his daughter wouldn't prompt a reaction.

"Nice to see you today, sir," Harry said. "Hope everything's okay in there."

It was depressing. The Gabriel lying in that bed hardly resembled the Gabriel who had once wandered the corridors in his familiar detective getup. He weighed less than a hundred pounds, and every bone in his body jutted out.

But his eyes were the worst part. Once, they had contained a vibrant, otherworldly spark. But the two blinking orifices that remained in his skull were completely drained of life, empty, vacuous glass balls.

Katie walked over to look at the collage of graphs, awards, and photographs on the wall. She pointed at one photo. "I like this one. Is this *him?* Wow, he was a handsome guy."

Harry joined her. It was a picture he'd never seen, so Melanie must've brought it in recently. "Oh yeah. That's him, all right."

The image was of a younger, happier Gabriel sitting astride a motorcycle and gazing up at the sun. He wore a leather jacket, blue jeans, and a perfect suntan. He was grinning and giving the camera a thumbs-up sign.

"This is cool," Harry said. "Really cool. You know, he totally was an awesome person. All the way up until…"

Gabriel sputtered and gasped as if he were choking. Harry froze in shock.

"Gabriel?" Harry whispered. He hurried back to Gabriel's side.

The old man's eyes were still lifeless. But his lips were moving in a way that they hadn't moved in over five months. "Lissss… ennnnd… no…" Gabriel made a gurgling noise as if he were trying to clear his throat. "Lisss… ssss… listennn… nnn…"

Listen. He'd said the word *listen.*

"Gabriel!" Harry cried. "I'm here, sir. I'm listening."

"Harry?"

"Yes, it's Harry. I'm here, Gabriel."

"Lissssten, Harry... nnn... nothing ever ends. Jus... just turn the hannndle... of the next door... hold our breaths ... and then... we'll see what happens."

He's in there. He's talking! Harry clutched the photo tightly. "What? Gabriel. I don't understand."

Gabriel continued blinking but said nothing. Harry glanced at Katie. She looked as stunned as he felt.

"Gabriel," Harry said forcefully, "I know you're in there." He seized the old man's hand. "Please, are you in there, sir?"

Tears stung the corners of Harry's eyes, and he brushed them away. They were embarrassing, especially in front of the cute girl, but he couldn't help it. Harry squeezed Gabriel's hand. "Gabriel, I miss you. We all do."

Drool spilled from the side of Gabriel's mouth, and Harry wiped it away with a cloth. Maybe Gabriel was in there, but if so, he was trapped. Harry had worked in healthcare long enough to accept that when people reached that level of decline, they didn't come back. No matter how much you might want them to, they didn't.

Harry looked back at Katie. "See, he was—"

Gabriel whistled a cheerful little melody just like the one he used to whistle in the hallway. Harry turned and stared. Something was different about the old man's face. It looked almost like his *real* face again.

Gabriel focused on Harry and smiled a big, happy smile, just like the one in the photograph. "Harry... don... don't worry... about me." The old man's eyes became moist with tears. "I'm going upstairs."

His eyes lost their spark again. The smile remained, but Gabriel was once again lost somewhere in that big old head of his. Harry started sobbing. Katie came over and grabbed his hand. She leaned over and kissed him on the cheek.

Harry studied the photograph in his hand, trying to reconcile that bright, happy young man with the shriveled old one in the bed beside him. When he looked back at Gabriel's dulled eyes, a surreal vision flashed into his mind. It wasn't a memory of his or anything he'd ever seen. The image was real, as real as the sun on a hot summer day.

Harry saw a wide black expanse, like outer space, dotted by a sea of stars. And somewhere out there, Gabriel was sitting on his motorcycle. Not the skeletal Gabriel lying in Bright New Day but the younger Gabriel in the photograph, the redheaded rebel who had cured AIDS.

The younger Gabriel's motorcycle had been parked on some kind of road that glowed white and spiraled upward in a variety of impossible angles, curves, and twists. Harry had the feeling that Gabriel had been following the road for a long time and that he was finally getting near the end of it. That moment in which Gabriel had seen Harry, when his eyes had been alive again, was just the old man taking a break to say goodbye.

The engine roared, and Gabriel blasted off, burning rubber on the impossible loops and curves of the glowing pathway. He sped away into the distance, laughing with unrestrained glee.

The last thing Harry saw was how fantastically radiant the sun was as Gabriel's motorcycle did a circle around its perimeter. The sun's light was so bright that it made the glowing highway through space, Gabriel's highway, appear even paler.

ABOUT THE AUTHOR

Originally from California, Nicholas Conley has currently made his home in the colder temperatures of New Hampshire. He considers himself to be a uniquely alien creature with mysterious literary ambitions, a passion for fiction, and a whole slew of terrific stories he'd like to share with others.

When not busy writing, Nicholas is an obsessive reader, a truth seeker, a sarcastic idealist, a traveler, and — like many writers — a coffee addict.